CREATE A LIFE
TO LOVE

What Reviewers Say About Erin Zak's Work

Falling Into Her

"*Falling Into Her* by Erin Zak is an age gap, toaster oven romance that I really enjoyed. The romance has a nice burn that's slow without being too slow. And while I'm glad that lesfic isn't all coming out stories anymore, I enjoyed this particular one because it shows how it can happen in a person's 40s."—*The Lesbian Review*

"I loved everything about this book. …I'm always slightly worried when I try a book by someone who a) I've never heard of before; b) never published anything before (as far as I know). Especially if the book is in a sub-niche market area. But I'm quite glad I found my way to trying this book and reading it. And enjoying it."—*Lexxi is Reading*

"[A] great debut novel from Erin Zak and looking forward to seeing what's to come."—*Les Rêveur*

Breaking Down Her Walls

"If I could describe this book in one word it would be this: annnngggssstt. …If angst is your thing, this a great book for you."
—Colleen Corgel, Librarian, Queens Public Library

"*Breaking Down Her Walls* had me completely spun. One minute I'm thinking that it's such a sweet romance, the next I found it sexy as hell then by the end, I had it as an all-encompassing love story that I just adored."—*Les Rêveur*

"I loved the attraction between the two main characters and the opposites attract part of the story. The setting was amazing. …I look forward to reading more from this author."—Kat Adams, Bookseller (QBD Books, Australia)

Visit us at www.boldstrokesbooks.com

By the Author

Falling into Her

Breaking Down Her Walls

Create a Life to Love

CREATE A LIFE TO LOVE

by

Erin Zak

2019

CREATE A LIFE TO LOVE

ISBN 13: 978-1-63555-425-0

This Trade Paperback Original Is Published By
Bold Strokes Books, Inc.
P.O. Box 249
Valley Falls, NY 12185

First Edition: June 2019

CREDITS
EDITOR: BARBARA ANN WRIGHT
PRODUCTION DESIGN: SUSAN RAMUNDO
COVER DESIGN BY MELODY POND

Acknowledgments

I wanted to write a book that told the story of finding love in the most random of places and I really feel like I did that. It's crazy the things that happen in our lives. One minute we're floating along just fine, and the next we're being pulled in another direction entirely. Life's twists and turns are what keep our individual stories exciting. I've learned that lesson over and over again, especially in the past year.

I want to start off by thanking Rad, Sandy, and the rest of the Bold Strokes team. Without you all I'd still be hoping someone someday would read my work. You are all the very best.

I'd be completely foolish if I didn't thank Barbara Ann Wright right now. She takes my words and helps me sound like an actual writer. Thank you so much for that…and for making me laugh. A lot. You are amazing and I'm so happy you're my editor. And friend.

My family…where would I be without you, Gail and Cadie? Aside from the obvious answers of "living in a van down by the river," I'd also be a complete mess. So, thank you for encouraging me and being there for me always. I especially need to thank Gail. You're my rock. As cliché as that sounds, it's true.

My writer friends…I don't know where to start. I love you all so much. Thank you for the encouragement and the laughs.

Thank you to my readers, my friends, and my beta readers. You are all worth so much more than you even believe.

Dedication

To Gail—Thank you for creating a life to love with me.

CHAPTER ONE

JACKIE

"You're Jackie, right?"

I looked at the teenage girl standing in the doorway of my St. Petersburg beachside condo. It wasn't out of the realm of possibility for a random stranger to find where I lived and want my autograph. It came with the territory of being a rather successful romance author. But it still took me by surprise regardless of the amount of times it has happened. And it happened four times—each time as weird, and slightly scary, as the time before.

This fan had a different look about her, though. She had sea green eyes and a dimple in her chin that made my stomach bottom out. Not a normal bottoming out feeling like the way I was used to when I saw someone who took me by surprise. It was more as if I had met this person before, but I wasn't sure where or how or when. She looked frightened and adrift. Soaked to the bone, her light brown hair was hanging around her face, and her mascara was running down her cheeks. There was something eerily familiar about her, though, and it was making me more and more uneasy as the seconds ticked past. All I could do was continue to stare.

"Jackie Mitchell, right?"

I didn't know what propelled me, but I finally nodded.

"I'm Beth. Well, Elizabeth. Um, Weber. Elizabeth Weber." She was nervous. Clearly. Her voice was shaking, and she hadn't stopped fidgeting. What the hell was wrong with her? "But I go by Beth. I'm, well, look, there's no way, to like, *ease* into this, so I'm going to come out and say it." I saw her take a deep breath. "I'm your daughter."

My mouth went as dry as the Sahara Desert. "I'm sorry, *what?*"

"You gave up a baby sixteen years ago, right?"

I couldn't respond because all I felt was bile rising in the back of my throat.

She reached into her back pocket and pulled out a few pieces of paper folded into a square. She shoved it at me. Her nails were painted green, and they were chipped around the edges, and *what the hell was happening?* She waved the paper square as I stood there gawking at her unkempt nails. "Here. Take it."

I slowly pulled the square of dirty papers from her hand, unfolded them, and studied the words. The papers were damp and hard to read, but they were adoption papers with my signature on the adoption agency's letterhead. After a quick reread, and then another for good measure, I looked up at her, my mouth hanging open.

"I mean, I'm obviously yours. It's not really a question because, like, it's not hard to see that I have your eyes. And well, the papers kinda prove it." She bounced on the toes of her checkerboard Vans slip-ons. "Um, can I like, come in or something? I'm dripping in your hallway."

I was flabbergasted. Completely and utterly, yet I opened the door farther for her to slip past me. She was shorter than me, but everything else aside from her height and her hair color was *me*. Her complexion was mine, and the dimple on her chin that made my stomach bottom out minutes earlier was mine. Even the way she was standing, the lanky teenager stance, was *mine*.

How was any of this possible? It was closed, right? I asked for a *closed* adoption. This kind of thing only happened in Hallmark movies. And my life was anything but movie-worthy.

"So, Jackie." She looked around my apartment, hands shoved into the front pockets of her ripped, wet jeans. Her inquisitive stare was causing my anxiety to skyrocket right off the charts. I was absolutely not okay with surprise visitors, especially if the person claimed to be the kid I gave up years earlier. I was a deeply private person. I worked hard to keep it that way. So, the last ten minutes were making my skin crawl almost right off my body. "Do you have any towels?"

Like a shot, I sprang into action, more because I couldn't stand there cursing my existence anymore. I rushed to the linen closet and fumbled through the towels. My hands were shaking; my breathing was becoming erratic. Was I going to have a panic attack? *Fuck.* I could not lose my shit right now. I tried to focus and pulled deep breaths in through my nose, out through my mouth. I steadied myself on the doorjamb of the linen closet. Once I felt I could walk without collapsing, I pulled out two large beach towels and another smaller one for her hair. I pushed them at her in the living area. "You can use the guest bathroom."

"Thanks."

The instant she was tucked safely behind a closed door, I looked around frantically for help. This whole thing was fucked! And quite possibly the worst experience I ever went through. Except, of course, deciding to give up my baby in the first place; which to this day, the thought still made my chest ache. I turned around and looked at my reflection in the mirror that hung on the wall near the living room. The humid Florida air had caused my natural wave to be more apparent in my blond hair, and all I could see was my kid staring back at me.

"Jackie?"

Her voice pulled me from my thoughts, and I looked over at her. "How did you find me?"

Her face twisted at the question. "I hired a private investigator."

I huffed. "You're not old enough to be able to afford a private investigator."

"I stole my mom's credit card, but *shh.*" She held a finger to her lips. "She doesn't know that yet."

Certainly sounded like something I would have done back in my heyday. I was an idiot when I was growing up. And I had a wild streak that wasn't tamable. It seemed my facial features and the wave in my hair weren't all I passed on to Beth.

Observing her from my vantage point in the open concept condo made it easy to never lose sight of her. She was studying the pictures on my walls, the books on my shelves, the movies piled next to my television stand. I was under investigation. And the more she perused my belongings, the more uncomfortable I felt. "Look, Beth," I said, then waited for her to react, but she kept her eyes glued to my bookshelf.

"So, you're a writer, right? Like of romance novels?"

I sighed. "Beth, seriously, I'm kind of not sure what you want from me."

"Lesbian romance novels, right?"

I looked around the room. Was a cameraman going to jump out and yell that I was being punk'd? This was my worst nightmare. Being questioned by the daughter I gave up for adoption was certainly not on my top ten ways to pass the time. Against my better judgement, I finally gave in and answered. "Yeah."

"And you're, like, pretty good?"

The grammar police officer inside my head was cringing. "One could say that." I folded my arms across my chest. The microscope she was using on me for her research was making me sweat.

"How did I happen then? Or when did you figure out that you're a lesbian or whatever?" She glanced over at me, finally pulling her eyes from my books. "I'm totally okay with it, by the way."

Like I even care...

"Also, Jackie?" Beth turned around, her eyes pleading. "I am probably going to have to stay the night here."

I let out a laugh that had no earthly reason being in the conversation. "I'm sorry, but what?"

"Yeah, I mean, unless you want to drive me back to Savannah. Hitchhiking here is one thing, doing the same thing at night is another entirely."

"You hitchhiked here?" Maybe I was kind of impressed. It was a bold move that was for sure.

"Yeah. I'm sixteen, but I'm not a fan of driving. So, I don't drive by myself yet. Of course, you probably knew I was sixteen already, didn't you?"

She was certainly blunt. Who knew that bluntness and sarcasm could be passed through the womb?

Beth took her backpack off and set it on the floor next to my couch. "So, what's it gonna be?"

"I can drive you home." She looked hurt by that answer, but I was not about to let her stay in my condo after barely knowing her. I felt horrible admitting that to myself, but until a DNA test, how was I going to be one hundred percent positive?

"Yeah, like, that could work, I guess." Beth pushed her damp hair away from her face. I actually had to stifle a gasp. That move was so *me* that it was impossible to think a DNA test would do anything but prove she really was mine.

"Let me get some things together, and we'll go."

"You know it's like a five-hour drive, right?"

I looked at Beth and shrugged. "It's better than trying to get you out of my place tomorrow morning." The twinkle in her eyes made me smile. My comment was supposed to be a jab, but she seemed to agree with me. "I won't take long."

❖

After throwing a couple changes of clothes into a duffle bag and grabbing my toothbrush and other toiletries, I went back into the living room. Beth had made herself comfortable on the ottoman in front of the couch, and she had found a photo album.

"Are any of these your girlfriend?"

"You ever hear of boundaries?"

She shrugged but never looked up from the album. "You ever hear of keeping a baby?"

What the hell?

Beth finally looked up. "Is that tea too hot for you?"

She had a lot of nerve. "Look, kid. I do not deserve…I absolutely have no…" I didn't know what to say or how to say it. I wanted to slap her, and I barely knew her. "You have no idea why I did what I did."

Her eyes locked on to mine, and I planted my foot. She was going to argue with me. "Y'know, you could, like, tell me why you did it then."

I laughed. "You act like I want to talk about this. I don't. Especially with you." My tone was not nice. At all. And her face fell, and tears started to well in her eyes. *Goddammit.*

"I should be the only person you want to talk about it with." A single tear ran down her cheek. Son of a bitch, she even cried like me.

"Beth, look," I said as I made my way over to the ottoman. I squatted down and looked at her. "I will talk to you about it. But not now. Okay?" I was lying. I hoped to God I never saw her again after I dropped her off in Savannah.

She sniffled and wiped the tears from her eyes. "Okay."

"Also," I said and made myself smile, hopefully to lighten the mood. "These are friends. And *only* friends."

"Not even this one?" She held up the album that was open to a page of my best friend Tabitha.

I laughed. "God, no. We are definitely only friends."

"Too butch for you?"

"Oh my God." I stood. "Listen, kid, my love life is off limits. Okay?"

"Fine."

I rolled my eyes for what felt like the hundredth time. "Are you ready?"

"Yeah. Don't you have, like, a cat or something to take care of?"

"Why? Because all lesbians have cats?" I walked to the door and looked back at her.

Beth stood and stared. Was that the hint of a smile I saw tugging at her lips?

"No, I don't have any animals. In fact, I don't like animals. Especially cats."

"We have a dog."

"Especially dogs."

"You *just* said especially cats."

"Especially both." Beth sighed as we boarded the elevator. I could see her in the mirror-covered walls of the elevator car looking at me. "What?"

"You don't like animals at all?"

I shook my head. "Seriously? That's what you were thinking?"

"No," she said softly. "But what I was thinking is off limits."

We made our way out of my apartment building and toward my car. She was dragging her heels, and it was annoying me something fierce. "I don't drive a Jeep Wrangler, either," I threw over my shoulder as we got to my car.

"Shit, this is a nice car. Is this a BMW?"

"It is." I opened the trunk and secured my belongings. "Do you want to put your backpack in here or keep it with you?"

"Keep it with me."

"Get in the car then, kid." As soon as she did as I said and the passenger door slammed closed, I had every second thought a person could have. I did not want to do this, but I did not need Beth in my home, asking questions, trying to get to know me. I didn't want anyone trying to get to know me. Ever. "Keep it together, Mitchell," I mumbled as I made my way to the driver's side door. When I climbed into the car, I glanced over at Beth, who was clearly thinking something by the look on her face. "What now?"

"Nothing."

I didn't argue. I didn't really care what her answer was.

"It's really cool to finally meet you."

Ugh. She had to tell me anyway, didn't she? "Yeah?" I asked, and she beamed. *Ugh again.* "Same here." I lied to her, but I didn't know what to say. And for some reason, the idea of hurting her feelings again was too much for me to handle.

❖

BETH

I swear to God, we hit every ounce of traffic on the way to the Georgia state line. It was annoying. And Jackie was *so* touchy on the brakes. Maybe she was trying to throw me through the windshield or something. I had no room to judge, though. I wasn't a fan of driving, nor was I any good at it. The idea that I was controlling a three-thousand-pound object made me way too nervous. Also, I hated when my mom was in the car with me, backseat driving, correcting every move I made. It was nerve-wracking. I would grind my teeth and eventually get a headache. It was not fun. She had me convinced that I would die in a car crash caused by myself. So, I don't use my learner's permit unless absolutely necessary. And I was definitely going to hold out to get my license for as long as I could.

"It's because everyone in Florida is ninety-five years old," I said as I tried to make Jackie discuss something, *anything* with me. Even if it was the driving conditions, it was better than nothing.

"That could be it."

"It is. And tourists. So many tourists."

"That also makes sense."

It was a riveting conversation, wasn't it? I tried to figure out what to say to her next. I mean, I was trapped in a car with my *biological* mom. Talk about a weird-ass situation. I'll be honest, though. I prepared myself for many different scenarios. But the one thing I didn't prepare myself for was how much I was going to look like her. When she swung open that door and her green eyes looked at me as if I was a lunatic? I kind of thought I was going to pass out. It was so surreal. I grew up with a mom whom I looked nothing at all alike and a dad, well, I looked even less like him. Let's say it was never a *complete* shock that I was adopted.

Seeing Jackie for the first time, though... *That* was a complete shock. She was so pretty. Like, be jealous of if we were in high school together, kind of pretty. I hoped I continued to resemble her as I got older. If I really tried, I could look like a downgraded version of her. My hair was a little darker, and much to my dismay, I didn't have her boobs, but aside from that, we had a lot of the same features. Especially the chin and cheekbones. And the eyes. It was weird, though. I guess there was a part of me that wanted her to be ugly or a horrible drug addict or a drunk or something equally as awful. It would have made it easier to understand why she gave me up.

I glanced over at her. She was gripping the steering wheel like a lifeline, sort of how I would grip it when I drove. "How long have you lived in St. Pete?"

"Long enough."

Seriously? Talking to her was worse than talking to a boy. "Long enough for what?"

"I've lived there long enough to like it."

"Did you not like it when you first got there?" It was like pulling teeth.

"Not really."

"You don't like talking about yourself, do you?" I didn't need to ask that question. It was pretty fucking obvious.

"What gave you that idea?"

I laughed and motioned to her hands. "Every time I ask you a question, you white-knuckle the steering wheel. I know you probably think because I'm young, I'm some sort of idiot. But I'm not. I understand the way things work…especially body language."

"Well. Okay then." Jackie glanced over at me before quickly looking back at the road. "I, in fact, do not like talking about myself."

"Why?"

"Seriously, kid?" Jackie tightened her grip on the wheel again. "Because. I'm a writer. I like to *write*. I don't like to talk. So, probably best to zip it up over there."

"Damn, Jackie, who brought the good-time bear?" She cracked a smile. "Oddly enough, I don't really like to talk about myself, either." I looked out the window and sighed.

"When did you find out that you were adopted?"

I snapped my head to look at her. At my *mother*. *What the hell?* Was she really asking *me* a question now? "Ha! No way. Question for a question."

She sighed. "Fine."

"Last year. My mom told me." I cleared my throat. "I mean, my *adoptive* mom."

"She's your mom, kid."

"I mean, yeah, I know. But I was explaining." Tough crowd. "I kind of had an idea since I don't look a thing like her. Or my dad. She sat me down and asked me a bunch of questions. She explained that I was adopted in this weird voice I never really heard from her before." My mind flashed back to the day she told me. We were sitting on my bed, and I was so upset about a dumb assignment in class that had to do with family trees. And I was crying, and she broke down and told me everything. It was one of my most treasured memories. Not because of the tears but because I knew how much she loved me. And I knew in that moment that it didn't matter what anyone said or did, she would always be my mom.

"And how did you take that?"

"Uh, no. Question for a question." Reminding Jackie of that was so fun.

Jackie groaned.

"Do you have a girlfriend?"

"No." Jackie glanced at me again.

"Is that why you're such a fucking peach?" I asked and again got a small smile.

"You need to figure out how to ask open-ended questions, kid."

She really did think I was an idiot. "I'm still getting the information I want."

"Oh, really?" Jackie changed lanes and flew past a semi. The traffic had cleared, and now she was speeding, zig-zagging around the cars. How was this trip crawling then? "So, tell me about your relationship with your mom."

"Whoa, Jackie, really pulling the big punches, aren't ya?" I rolled my eyes and didn't wait for her reaction. "My relationship with her is really great. She's kind and has a big heart. She's always welcoming to my friends, too. They all call her 'Mom' when they come over. She expects good grades and for me to listen, so I do those things. I love her to death. I was devastated when I found out I wasn't hers."

"Then why try to find me?"

"Um, no. That's two questions. It's my turn." I watched Jackie roll her eyes. "Tell me why you gave me up." It was ballsy to ask when she specifically said she wasn't going to answer it, but I thought I'd try again. I don't know why, but I was dying to know the reason.

"No." Her answer was so final that I couldn't even argue.

"Then I'm not telling you why I wanted to find you."

"Fine."

"*Fine.*" And that was it. We sat in silence for the next two hours, only speaking when she asked me if I had to go to the bathroom at the rest area we stopped at. I didn't respond. Only shook my head. She left the car, though, and took her keys with her. I slipped my iPhone from the outer pocket of my backpack. There were fifteen texts from my mom, all of them her freaking out. I hadn't talked to her since last night before bed, so I knew I needed to say something.

I'm okay, Mom. I promise. I'm on my way home. Please don't ask what happened. You'll find out soon enough.

The response bubble popped up immediately, and I held my breath. I knew she wasn't going to like that answer. But when she responded with, *Okay, honey. I love you. Be careful*, I felt tears start to sting my eyes. Why did she have to be so awesome? Why did I need to find out about someone that didn't want me to begin with?

The truth was that I wanted to find my birth mom because I didn't know who I really was. Where did I come from? Why did I have green eyes and shaggy hair and why, oh why, was it so hard for me to keep weight off? I had so many questions. But when Jackie wanted to know why I wanted to find her, I didn't know what to say. There was a large part of me that was scared to find her. Afraid that she would be exactly how she was turning out. Someone who didn't want me then and didn't want me now. I didn't know why I hoped for different because my mom was amazing. She was wonderful and had a heart of gold. And she loved me so much. Like, we still had the mother/daughter relationship where she kissed me on the cheek, and I never squirmed away from her. Especially after she told me I was adopted. There was no way I was going to push her away for saving me from the one person who should have loved me through everything. When I told my mom that, she cried. She cried so hard. I never saw her cry like that before. And she hugged me and told me she would never give me away. And then *I* cried. It was awful and great all at the same time.

So, telling Jackie that I wanted to make sure I was right? That she really was a giant asshole who never wanted me? I guess it didn't seem like a good way to end this six-hour relationship. Not that I cared. Like, at all.

Jackie climbed back into the car, applied the brake, and the engine came to life when she pushed the ignition button. I tried not to look at her. I really did. But when I finally broke down, I noticed she had been crying.

For some reason, seeing that made a thin crack appear in my resolve to hate this woman. She was human after all.

As Jackie sped down the onramp to the expressway, she flipped on the radio. "Do you like alternative music?" she asked and cleared her throat. Even her voice sounded as if she had been crying.

"Yeah. I mean, look at me. Of course, I do."

A light laugh came out of Jackie, and it made me feel slightly better. "Good," she said softly as she checked her blind spots and floored it onto I-95.

The rest of the drive was filled with the occasional "jackass driver" and "motherfucker, get out of the left-hand lane!" I didn't say much else and let Florence + The Machine and The Head and the Heart take me away. I will admit that I was happy to find out that my taste in music was similar to Jackie's. Not that it mattered, but at least I wasn't being subjected to country. I think I would have rather hitchhiked.

❖

When we made it into Savannah, there was a weight that sort of lifted from my shoulders. It felt really good to not be completely on Jackie's territory any longer. I wasn't going to say I felt reassured by any stretch of the imagination, but I definitely felt lighter, not as confined.

"Turn here?"

"Yes. We're the fourth house on the right-hand side." I watched as my house got closer and closer. When she stopped in front of it, I grabbed my backpack, and reached for the car door.

Jackie breathed out, "Wow." And then said, "This is a great house."

I looked at my childhood home. It *was* a nice house. We lived on Whitaker Street, near Hall, and we bordered historic Forsythe Park, which was definitely the best part of Savannah. I didn't think I really ever appreciated how awesome Savannah was, though. "Yeah. It is." I cleared the emotion that raised into my throat. "You don't have to come in."

"Don't you think I should?"

"No. I don't."

Jackie's brow furrowed. "Beth, let me come up. At least to apologize."

"For what? You did nothing wrong here." I did not want or need my mom to meet Jackie. Like I wanted to make her feel worse? Fuck no. "It's seriously okay."

"I'm not negotiating with you." Jackie turned the car off and looked at me. "Let me do this one thing."

Goddammit. Was that what I looked like when I gave that *please let me* face? No wonder my mom never said no to me. "Okay," I finally relented. As we climbed out of the BMW, the weight that had so casually floated away moments ago had found a new home right on top of my chest. In every dream of finding my birth mom, not once did she meet my actual mom. I had no idea what to expect. I did not prepare myself for this. We got to the front door of the house, and I glanced back at Jackie. "You really don't have to do this."

Her stern look made me roll my eyes. As I reached for the door, it was being pulled open, and there stood my mom.

CHAPTER TWO

SUSAN

"Beth, my God." I could hardly get her into my arms fast enough. "Don't do that again. Do you hear me?" I said into her hair. In between the short seconds of being pissed off and being relieved, I breathed her in as much as I could. She smelled like *Beth* still, which made me so happy. I knew she was sixteen, but she had never disappeared like that before.

"I won't, Mom. I promise."

Her words were muffled by my shoulder, but I could tell she was near tears. "Oh, honey." I pulled her away from me and kissed her on the cheek. "What happened? Where were you? Why weren't you answering my texts?" I finally glanced at the woman standing behind my daughter, and the sight of her with her long blond hair took my breath away.

"Mom, this is—"

"Jackie Mitchell," I whispered, finishing Beth's introduction. "You're Beth's birth mom, aren't you?"

"Um, Mom, what the heck? How did you know that?"

I watched Jackie standing there with her arms hanging at her side, the same striking green eyes as my daughter, the same dimple in her chin, the same awkward look on her face. I couldn't stop staring at her. "You look exactly like her." My words weren't meant to come out in a whisper, but they did. The expression that washed over Jackie's face made my heart ache.

"Yeah, I mean, my genes must be really strong," Jackie said. She shrugged and smiled at me. She was nervous. That much was obvious.

"Yes, they really are." I didn't know what else to say. I pulled my gaze from Jackie and focused back on Beth. "Honey, why don't you go wash up for dinner?"

"You guys didn't eat yet?"

"Well, your father is still at work. And when I finally heard from you..." I paused and looked at Beth. She scrunched her face apologetically. "I wanted to wait for you." Beth smiled at me and bounced gently on the balls of her feet before she bounded off up the stairs to her bedroom and bathroom. I looked back at Jackie. She seemed uncomfortable standing there in her skinny jeans, light blue oxford, and flipflops. I had no idea what she was thinking. "Would you like to come in for some iced tea or..." My voice trailed off as I stepped out of the way and motioned for her to come inside.

"Got anything stronger?"

I laughed. "Car rides with Beth do that to me, too." She was watching my every move when she came through the entryway and stood in front of me. Her gaze was unsettling. I moved my hands up to my hair and pushed the dark locks away from my face. "I have bourbon."

"That'll do," Jackie said. Her voice was smooth but had an edge to it. It made me wonder.

As I closed the screen door after Jackie entered, our cocker spaniel Myrtle came flying around the corner barking like a wild woman. "Oh, my goodness, Myrtle, it's okay! You're about ten minutes late!" I could barely grab on to her collar as she lunged at Jackie. "Please say 'hello' to her. She is perfectly nice, but she needs you to say 'hello.'" I watched Jackie's eyes. She was obviously not a dog person. "I promise she won't bite."

Jackie bent down and let Myrtle sniff her hand, and then the dog was all over her, sniffing her legs, jumping up to be petted, wagging her little nub of a tail. "Hi, Myrtle." Jackie laughed as the dog kept weaving in and out of her legs.

"I'm sorry. She's a handful."

"Is she a puppy?"

"Uh, no, she's ten."

Jackie laughed when Myrtle got on her hind legs and danced around in a circle. "She's so talented."

"She's a ham." Jackie followed me to the study with Myrtle not far behind. I invited Jackie in and offered her the armchair to sit, but she continued to stand as I stood in front of the liquor cabinet and tried to breathe. The decanter clinked against the tumbler as I poured the bourbon. I was nervous. I handed her the tumbler with a two-finger pour of my best bourbon and watched as she took the glass with a shaking hand. She noticed me noticing, and I locked eyes with her for a brief second before she raised the glass to her lips and took a swallow.

I sat on the leather couch in the study, and Myrtle quickly jumped up on the seat next to the big bay window and curled into a ball in the sunlight. The natural light was perfect in the study at this time of day, and it made everything in the room glow, including Jackie's blond hair. Even though the color was so different from Beth's, the way Jackie's hair fell in loose waves was similar. She kept it much tidier than Beth did, though, and it was about three or four inches shorter, landing right below her breasts. When she sat across from me in the wingback chair, her eyes began to wander over the bookshelves surrounding the room. It was strange how we kept watching each other, and I wasn't sure if I should be creeped out or something else entirely.

"You have a lot of books. Do you read a lot?"

"I do," I answered, following her gaze to the shelves to the right of me. "I love reading."

"Me, too." She cleared her throat before she drank again.

"So, Jackie," I started and waited for her to look at me. "What have you done with your life?" The look that passed over Jackie's features was so intense. I wasn't sure if I offended her, but I certainly offended myself with my judgmental tone. "I didn't mean that how it came out," I said quickly. "I mean, you know—"

"What do I do for a living?"

I nodded. I felt so stupid.

"I'm a writer." Jackie paused. "Romance novelist, actually."

"Oh, wow!" I don't know why I was so shocked. Women that gave up their babies didn't automatically turn into horrible people with no drive or desires in life. I was being an asshole. "That's really great. I'm sure you are very successful." I tried to cover up my faux pas.

Jackie smiled at me. "Yes, I am."

Well, she certainly didn't lack confidence. "How many books have you published?"

"Twenty-two."

"Holy cow! That's a lot!"

Jackie nodded. "It is."

"All in the romance genre?"

"Yes," Jackie answered, her tumbler only an inch from her lips. "*Lesbian* romance." She dropped those words before she took a drink. Her eyes stayed glued to me while she drank. It caused a shiver to roll through my body.

"Oh." Nothing really stunned me these days. I was a substance abuse psychologist, so believe me, I'd heard it all. But seeing her sitting on my couch, holding that glass, looking at me like that? Yeah, that *stunned* me.

"Is that a problem?"

"Hmm?" I looked down at my own glass and quickly brought it to my lips to take a drink. The dark liquor burned on the way down, but it felt satisfying. "A problem?"

"That I'm a lesbian?" Her voice raised slightly at the end of *lesbian*, and it made her much more endearing than I think she planned or I expected.

"Of course not." My tone was matter-of-fact because it wasn't a problem. At all. Why would it be? I held myself back from psychoanalyzing her, but I wanted to, because what the hell must have happened in her life that her first thought was that being gay would be a problem. It made me sad. Really, really sad. I looked at her sitting there, staring down at her drink. "Jackie?" When she looked up at me, her eyes were just as sad as I felt. "Are you okay?"

She nodded, but I could tell she was barely holding it together. I couldn't blame her, honestly. Look what she'd gone through. Getting pregnant. Having a daughter. Giving that daughter up for adoption. And now she was sitting in the adoptive mom's study...drinking bourbon. "I'm good."

I didn't believe her. At all. "Are you sure?" She looked at me again. God, her eyes were so green.

"I'm sure," she answered.

I heard Beth flying down the stairs. I glanced at the door to the study as she entered. She looked at me and then at Jackie. "What's going on?"

"Nothing," I answered quickly. "Just talking."

"Yeah, kid, just talking," Jackie echoed. "I should probably be going, though."

"Why don't you stay for dinner?" Beth and Jackie both looked at me, surprise written all over their faces. Clearly, I wasn't the only person shocked by my invitation.

"Look, Ms. Weber—"

"Susan. Please. Call me Susan." I reached out and gently touched her arm. She looked down at my hand, then back up at me, and I wished I could say it was because she was taken aback by my kindness, but it wasn't. There was something there. I felt it. She felt it. And I cannot describe it. It was a spark but not electricity, and it was intense in a way I didn't know if I'd ever experienced. Surely it was because of our connection with Beth. *Surely.*

"Mom," Beth said, snapping me back to reality. I pulled my hand away from Jackie's arm and looked at Beth. "She has a long drive home."

"Beth is right."

I saw the look the two exchanged. "You can stay in the spare room tonight and take off in the morning." What the hell was wrong with me? Why was I inviting her to stay in our house? Explaining a random stranger in our spare bedroom was not going to be a good conversation when Steven finally got home. I didn't need a crystal ball to see my future, which included an irate expression, a lot of choice words, and me keeping the kitchen island between him and me the entire conversation. It was sad that I was used to his erratic moods and horrible behavior. I disgusted myself. I swore I would never wind up in a relationship where I lived in constant fear. The first time he got angry with me, though I learned quickly that the back of his hand left a bruise the length and width of an eight-ounce New York strip. Needless to say, I walked a pretty straight path that kept me out of harm's way. I wasn't an idiot. I knew when to push a subject matter and when to keep my mouth shut. But for some reason, explaining Jackie's presence was a fight worth fighting. And the look on Jackie's face made me feel good about my offer. "Then it's settled. You'll stay. Beth, did you get washed up?"

"Mom, can I talk to you in the kitchen?"

"Of course, honey." I could tell by Beth's clenched jaw that she was going to question the hell out of me. I followed her into the kitchen, shouting that Jackie could wash up in the downstairs powder room.

"Mother, what the hell are you doing?" Beth whispered as she spun around when we got into the kitchen. "Dad is going to flip if he comes home to my freaking birth mom in the guest room."

It broke my heart that Beth knew how temperamental her father was. I thought I hid it so well. And after we adopted Beth, he did a great job of making sure the bruises weren't visible. *God, what a fucked-up life.* "It'll be fine. And besides, I figured we could both get to know her. It's cruel to send her on her way without feeding her. And it's late. *And* she drove you home. You, who ran away and made it all the way to wherever. Actually, where *does* she live?"

Beth's shoulders relaxed, and she stopped leaning forward in attack position. "Not here."

"Beth."

"St. Pete."

"*Florida*? How the hell did you get there?" It still blew me away how much I sounded like my own mother sometimes.

"I hitchhiked. Mom, please, it's over and done with." Beth clasped her hands together and begged. "She does not want to be a part of my life. So, I want her to leave."

"She will leave in the morning. I promise." I placed my hands on Beth's cheeks and kissed her forehead. "Maybe she needs to get to know you and see how incredible you are."

"Mom," Beth whispered. "She seems like she hates me."

My heart broke. "She could never hate you," I said softly as I dried a tear from Beth's cheek. "You scared her. You're her past standing in her present. It'd freak anyone out."

"Fine," Beth said and pulled away from me. She took a few steps out of the kitchen and mumbled, "I guess you're right."

"I'm sorry, what was that?" I asked while smiling.

"You heard me!"

I laughed. "Dinner is ready, girls." I said it loud enough that Jackie popped her head out of the powder room and smiled at me through the entryway. I smiled back and waved for her to come into the kitchen.

❖

JACKIE

To say that I felt like an intruder was a little too harsh. Susan had been so gracious and accepting. And Beth, even though she was not happy with me, was no longer shooting daggers at me. But I was definitely not fully welcomed at the dinner table, and it was apparent.

Meeting Susan had been almost too much for me to handle. She seemed so...normal? Sincere? *Perfect?* And she treated Beth so well. And wow, was she breathtaking. I could not stop looking at her. She had these dimples in her cheeks when she smiled, and her hair fell right above her shoulders in curls that framed her face wonderfully. She had it parted on the side, and every now and then a stray curl would fall into her face when she looked down at her meal. When she would tuck it behind her ear, I found myself wanting to do it for her so I could feel how soft her hair was.

"So, what do you do, Susan?" I watched her chewing her food. "I saw you had quite a few psychology books in your study."

Susan swallowed. "Yes, I, uh, I worked with troubled teens that were addicted to drugs and alcohol or had mental health issues."

"Worked? Past tense?"

"I'm taking a break. It gets…" Susan paused and picked at her green beans. "It gets pretty depressing."

"She was really good at her job," Beth said. She reached over and placed her hand on Susan's arm. The gesture made my heart hurt.

"I'm sure she was," I said. "I can see how it'd be rough, though."

Susan looked up at me. It was almost as if no one had ever believed her before. "Thank you," she said, her voice barely above a whisper.

I nodded and kept eating. Susan had made roast beef and mashed potatoes with green beans. A home cooked meal that *I* didn't have to home cook? It was freaking delicious. I could barely stop myself from inhaling it. I was already on my second helping of mashed potatoes, and if no one was looking, I was going to get a third.

"Mom, did Jackie tell you that she writes books?"

Susan was in the middle of drinking, so she raised her eyebrows and I heard a soft "Mm-hmm," come from her.

"Yeah, she's like super famous or whatever."

I laughed. "I wouldn't say that, Beth."

"Oh, no, you are. I did my research," Beth said around a mouthful of mashed potatoes. "You have so many reviews on Amazon. Your last book was like number three on the bestseller list."

I rolled my eyes. "The lesbian romance bestseller list. There's a big difference. It's not the New York Times Bestseller List."

"Don't sell yourself short," Beth said. "People obviously buy your books."

I smiled. That was actually really nice of her to say.

"I'll have to give one a whirl."

Beth let out a loud laugh. "Mom! They're *lesbian* romances! You aren't going to like them."

"I read all things, Beth. I do not discriminate."

"Oh, Mom, you're going to be so uncomfortable." Beth immediately looked at me. "No offense."

"None taken." I raised my glass of iced tea to my lips. "Of course," I said from behind the glass, "a lot of straight women read my books and like them."

"See, Beth? I will be fine."

"Yeah, but like, how straight *are* they? Am I right?"

I couldn't help but laugh at Beth. "Yeah, I mean, you're right. Sorry, Susan."

Susan's perfectly sculpted eyebrows raised slightly. I had to take a breath because dammit, she was sexy. "I am going to prove to you that I can read one of your books and not be gay by the end of it."

It sounded like a challenge. One that, in my younger years, I probably would have jumped at the opportunity to participate in *and win*. But now, as I looked at the mom of the kid I gave up for adoption, all it did was make my stomach twist. "Good luck," I finally said with a smile.

A silence fell between us. I continued to eat, making sure to not stare too much at Susan, even though all I wanted to do was give her one of my books and watch her read it. Watch those thin fingers turn each page, watch her dark eyes bore holes into the paper, watch her clutch her chest during the heart-warming scenes, and watch her squirm with her legs crossed during the sex scenes. I had to put the brakes on this fantasy immediately. There was no way it could happen! At all!

But wow, wouldn't it be fun to see her unfold?

When dinner was finished, I helped carry the dishes to the sink. Beth started rinsing the dishes without being asked, so I fell in line and started to load the dishwasher. It felt as if we had done this a hundred times before. Beth must have felt the same way because she kept looking at me and smiling. "What?" I asked as she handed over the last dish.

"I don't typically get help with dishes. Mom cooks; I clean up."

"What does your dad do?"

"When he's home? He eats. And then watches TV. Whatever Georgia sport is on at the time." Beth sighed and scrunched her face up. "Can we not talk about him?"

I didn't know how to feel about neither of them wanting to talk about this guy…what the hell kind of person was he? "Yeah, kid, of course." I smiled and put my hand on her shoulder. She looked at it and then back at me. I moved it quickly. "Sorry."

"No," Beth said with a chuckle. "It's okay. I kinda thought…"

"Thought what?" I asked. Beth started wiping the kitchen counter, and I could tell this was one of those moments she didn't want to talk. "You tell me when you're ready."

She stopped wiping and looked at me over her shoulder. "Okay," she said softly and then went back to wiping. I made my way out of the kitchen and saw the front door was open. I walked over to it and pushed the screen door open. Susan was sitting on the porch swing, a cup of coffee in hand, her left leg pulled up under her.

"Come. Have a seat." Susan patted the open seat next to her.

I walked out and sat on the swing. I looked around at how peaceful everything was. The air was heavy, but it wasn't too hot, which was nice.

Susan offered me her coffee cup. "Would you like some coffee?"

I smiled as I took the cup and brought it up to my nose to breathe it in. "Is there Bailey's in here?"

She looked at me and smiled.

God… That smile, with the crinkle at the corners of her eyes and those sexy as hell dimples, it was going to be the death of me. "My kind of coffee," I said before I took a sip. It tasted delicious and was perfect for this night. "So, is your husband going to wonder why your daughter's birth mom is camped out in the spare room?"

Susan shrugged. "If he comes home, you mean. I don't really care either way."

Man, was that a loaded statement or what? "I would love to ask what that means, but I fear I'm not the right person to confide in."

"It means what you think it means, Jackie," Susan said and followed it with a deep sigh.

"Is everything okay, Susan? I mean, I know I barely know you or Beth, but is…" I couldn't find the words to ask her if Steven was abusive, but I was seriously getting that impression. It made my stomach roll when I thought about something bad happening to either of them.

"He has never hurt Beth," Susan whispered as her gaze landed on something across the street. "Don't worry, okay?"

"Are you sure?"

"Yes." Susan looked at me, and she seemed to be begging me to drop it. Whatever "it" was.

I nodded. She broke our eye contact and I took a swallow of the coffee. It wasn't nearly strong enough for this conversation.

"I took time off because it was rough on our marriage. Me being gone all the time, him being gone all the time. It was rough."

"Has it helped?"

"Is he home?"

"Oh."

"Yeah." Susan leaned her head against the chain of the swing. I found myself holding back from touching her arm. It would be crossing a line for sure. But the connection I felt to this woman was so strange and intense. Was it Beth that connected us? Was it something else? I had no idea. All I knew was that when Susan touched my arm in the study, the feeling reminded me of falling or flying or maybe both.

"Susan?"

"Hmm?" She didn't move but continued to swing us ever so gently.

"You've done an amazing job with Beth."

She stopped the swing and looked over at me. "Yeah? You think so?"

"Yes." I took a deep breath and let it out slowly. "I don't know her well, obviously, but from what I do know, she's seems really great. Levelheaded, well put together, a good head on her shoulders. Catching rides from strangers aside."

"You should tell her that." Susan moved her gaze and looked out across the street to the park. "She thinks you hate her."

What? Did she... Was that... What?

"She's a fragile soul. Her spirit is bright, but she wears her heart on her sleeve…"

"Susan, I don't *hate* her. How could I?"

She laughed. It was small and delicate, but she laughed. "Oh, Jackie, I know," she said as she looked over at me. "She's not a mom. She doesn't get it."

"I'm not a mom, either."

"Yes, you are." Susan smiled. "If you weren't, you would have let her hitchhike home."

"God," I said softly. I looked down at my lap and tried to not cry. "I need to talk to her."

"She's probably in her room. Upstairs. Third door on the right." I stood and handed the coffee cup back to Susan. She waved it away. "You're going to need it," she said and winked. I almost dropped the cup.

I turned and headed back in through the screen door. It was such an awesome house. The entryway was gorgeous, and the hardwood floors were so well done. Even the staircase was grand. I wondered if Beth ever slid down the railing as a rebellious youth? There was no way I could ever live in a house that beautiful. It'd make me feel small and insignificant.

When I climbed the stairs, I noticed the pictures that lined the walls. They were of Beth and Susan, Susan and a man, who I assumed was Beth's dad. There were a couple of them together and some of other people, probably family members. I couldn't help but look at the picture of Susan and Beth. Even though their physical features were not similar, their smiles were.

As I stood outside of Beth's door, there was a moment that I wanted to turn and flee. Yesterday, I was fine. I was writing my next book, I was happy, I had friends and things to do, deadlines to meet. I did not need this. At all.

Then I remembered Beth's face when she first saw me. The light in her eyes and the way she bounced on the balls of her feet. It was so adorable. The way I acted, though. God, no wonder she thought I hated her.

I raised my hand to knock on the door, and before I even got the full knock out, she was saying, "Come in." I turned the knob and pushed the door open. Her room was immaculate. It was as big as my first apartment, kitchen and bathroom included. There were paintings all over the walls. Some were on paper, others on canvases of multiples sizes. She was sitting in a papasan chair over by the window, a giant pad open on her lap and a pencil in her hand.

"Hi," I said softly. "Am I interrupting?"

She repositioned herself and crossed her legs up under her in the chair. "Not at all." She motioned toward a window seat. "You can sit if you want."

As I made my way to the window seat, I stopped and looked at a canvas next to her desk. It stood from the floor almost to the ceiling, and on it was a painting of a giant oak tree with a girl swinging on a rope swing. "This is amazing," I said softly.

"Thanks."

I looked over my shoulder at her and then back to the painting. The girl was small, young in age, with her hair in braids, but she had on jeans and a hoodie and checkerboard Vans. Just like someone else I knew. "This is you, isn't it?"

"Mm-hmm."

I looked over my shoulder at her. She was biting her bottom lip, also staring at the painting.

"It's supposed to represent how I feel all the time."

"Which is?"

"Small? Alone?" She paused, and I could see she had focused the biting attention on the inside of her cheek. She stopped abruptly, though, and shrugged only one shoulder. "Scared." She let out a breathy sigh, and it sounded as if she was fighting back some serious emotion. Truth be told, so was I. My *daughter* just told me she felt small, alone, and scared. How the fuck was I supposed to handle that? "I won first place with it at my school's art competition. I got third at the state finals."

"Are the rest of these yours then?" I was happy for the subject change, so I went with it and motioned to the various drawings and paintings. They were all awesome. I was never much of an art buff, but this kid obviously had the talent and the emotion to back it up. A lot of both, it seemed.

"Yeah. Art's kind of my thing."

"You're good at it." I took the remaining steps to the window seat and sat. My heart was beating so hard. I knew she couldn't hear it, but the strangest sensation came over me. Almost as if I could *feel* her heart beating just as hard as mine. It was a biological connection I had no idea could exist. "So, I wanted to tell you," I said as I looked at her. "That I am actually kind of glad that you decided to find me."

Her eyes lit up, and that small, alone, and scared kid vanished, and in her place sat this beautiful teenager with so much sparkle. "Really?"

"Yes. But only kind of," I said with a smile. She smiled back, so I knew my humor was received.

"Because you didn't seem like it."

"Honestly?" I looked down at my hands and then up at her ceiling. It had glow-in-the-dark stars all over it. "You freaked me out."

"Ya don't say."

I laughed at her sarcasm. "I'm sorry. I really am."

"I forgive you."

I needed a subject change. And fast. "What are you working on there?"

Beth looked at the pad of paper and then back up at me. "Don't make fun of me."

"I promise, I won't." She handed it over, and my breath caught in my throat as I took in the artwork. It was a charcoal drawing of me in the car. She captured everything. The natural wave of my hair, the slight bump on the bridge of my nose, the scar on my neck that a cat gave me when I was ten years old. She even caught the blur of the scenery in the background. "Beth," I whispered. "This is beautiful."

"Thanks."

"You did this from memory?"

She shrugged. "I mean, yeah. I would never be able to forget how you look." She smiled. "I mean, since we look so much alike and all."

"It's weird how accurate that statement is." I chuckled.

"I would never forget anyway, though." Her voice was so soft when she said it.

I reached forward and placed my hand on her cheek. My eyes filled with tears, and before I knew it, I was crying like a baby. "God, I'm so sorry." I frantically wiped at my tears. "I'm gonna go lie down. You, um, you be good." I rolled my eyes at myself as I rushed over to the bedroom door. I fumbled with the doorknob before I got it open. "Good night," I said quickly and left the room. I couldn't handle the feelings that all of this was causing. I did not want to be a mom, goddammit. I did not want any of this. Ever.

So, why didn't I want to let it go?

CHAPTER THREE

BETH

When I woke up in the morning, I was positive that Jackie would have snuck away in the middle of the night. That was what I would have done. It wasn't that I ran away a lot or anything. It was that I hated the feeling of being trapped. Even as a little kid, I would freak out when my legs would get wrapped up in the blankets or if someone held me down to tickle me. So, being here in the house with people she wasn't super excited about? I would have bolted.

So, when I walked downstairs and saw Jackie sitting at the kitchen island having coffee with my mom, I was absolutely shocked.

"Good morning, sleepyhead," my mom said as she walked over and kissed me on the forehead. Everyone was taller than me. Mom and now even Jackie was taller than me. I wondered who I got the height from—or lack thereof—because obviously, I drew the short end of the stick. Pun intentional. I didn't think now was the time to start asking questions about my biological father. Would I ever know anything about him?

"Morning, Mom." I smiled at Jackie. "Morning, Jackie. How'd you sleep?"

I didn't miss the look she gave my mom before she answered. "I slept well. You?"

"Like a baby." The whole conversation was surreal. It was even more surreal that my mom was making pancakes. This wasn't some big family reunion breakfast, so what the hell was she doing? "You're making breakfast?" She nodded and smiled when she looked over her shoulder at me. "Is there bacon?" She pointed to the plate covered with paper towels. "Yesss."

Jackie laughed. "You're a trip."

No, this entire fucking morning was a trip so far. "Did Dad make it home last night, or did he have to pull an all-nighter?"

Mom nodded. "A full thirty-six-hour shift. The hospital never sleeps."

"Doctor?"

"Yes, in the ER. He's been there forever." I really disliked talking about my dad. When I was growing up, he was great. But ever since I turned ten, he changed. I didn't know what happened or why, but he started staying later at work, never saying no to on-call shifts at the hospital, and Mom and him would fight a lot. It scared me, actually, because I didn't understand what was going on. Why were they fighting? Why did Dad constantly tell Mom things weren't okay? That she wasn't okay? That none of this was working? I would hear it at night, and it would make my stomach roll.

"Sounds pretty important."

"Oh, he is," I said. Mom must have sensed my sarcasm because she gave me a look. "What?"

"Not at the breakfast table."

"I'm at the island."

"You know what I mean."

I rolled my eyes. When I looked over at Jackie, she was watching my mom like a hawk. I knew my mom was pretty. I used to hate that I didn't look exactly like her because she had this way about her, this natural beauty that I would have killed for. She never wore a lot of makeup, maybe mascara and blush. She barely had to do her hair. Let it air dry, and the curl was so perfect. And she always dressed nice and trendy, even for an older lady. Even when she didn't need to.

And then there was me. I literally had to try every single day. Even when I didn't try, I had to *look* as if I wasn't trying. I mean, I wasn't ugly, but I wasn't breathtaking. And I wanted to be so badly. It was absolutely infuriating. But seeing Jackie looking at Mom...I didn't know how to describe it, but I guess the term "territorial" sprang to mind because all I could think was, "Take a picture, it'll last longer."

Jackie looked over at me, her eyes wide, and I realized I had actually said it out loud. "Oh, I was playin'," I said, quickly covering my tracks. "You looked so deep in thought."

She didn't buy it. She knew she'd been made because she immediately stopped looking. I almost felt bad for calling her out. *Almost.*

As breakfast moved from the kitchen island to the table, I started watching Jackie and Mom's interactions. They seemed awfully comfortable with each other, especially considering their connection. I found it odd because I kind of figured they'd hate each other. I mean, why wouldn't they? I'd seen way too many stupid after-school specials where the biological mom tried to steal her kid back. Or TV shows where the adoptive mom turned into a raging bitch because the child would rather be with the biological parent. I'd seen some crazy stuff before, and what was unfolding before my eyes was crazy but in an entirely different way.

"Would you like to check out Forsythe Park before you get on the road, Jackie?"

Jackie and I exchanged looks after my mom asked the question. "Yeah, Jackie, would you?" I chimed in. Why was I being like that? Why was I being such a little shit?

Jackie read my facial expression and my tone like an expert. "No, actually, I should get going. It's a long drive back to St. Pete."

"Oh."

My glare immediately switched from Jackie to my mom. What was *that* tone about? "Mom?"

"No, it is a long drive," Mom said as she stood and grabbed our plates. "Are you finished?" She looked at me and gave me a smile I haven't seen from her in ages. It was the same smile she used to give me when she would patch up my skinned knees after falling off my bike or when she would console me if I came home crying because kids were being mean to me on the playground. It was all lips and nothing else, and it made my throat ache.

"Mom," I said after her as she walked away with our empty plates. I stood and followed her, not really sure what I was going to say, but I felt compelled to talk to her in that moment. "Are you okay?"

"Yes, dear," she answered. Oh, man, how well did I know *that* tone?

"C'mon, Mom," I urged. "What's going on?"

"Nothing, Beth. I promise. Let's help Jackie get her things together and say good-bye."

I watched her rinse each plate and place it in the dishwasher. "Jackie?" I shouted from the kitchen. I heard her scoot her chair across the floor and then emerge from the dining room. I looked over at her. "Let's do the walk. I think you'll really like the park. You can see a little of where I grew up."

It might have been mother/daughter telepathy, but Jackie understood what I was trying to say. She nodded and smiled. "Okay. That sounds like a nice idea."

"Mom, let's go."

❖

SUSAN

Beth had this uncanny knack of seeing right through me. I guess it was years and years of being alone together, even though I was married and was supposed to be raising Beth with Steven. At the end of the day, I raised her by myself. I did it all: I cooked, I cleaned, I patched up her scrapes and cuts, I took her to school and picked her up.

And yesterday? I had to deal by myself with not being able to find Beth, as well. I called and called and texted and texted, and Steven never responded. It was maddening, but the stark reality that I was actually a single mom was becoming more and more obvious as the years went on.

When Beth was around eight or nine, Steven started working later and later. Not a couple days a week, but four or five days a week.

Now, I realized he was a doctor in the emergency room, and that meant being on-call and dropping whatever he was doing on a dime when asked, but I was not an idiot. I'd been around the block a time or two. I might not be a Rhodes Scholar, but I knew the difference between a medical emergency and a booty call, as well as the difference between a lipstick stain and a bloodstain.

I wish I could say that I was a strong, confident woman and confronted him about his transgressions, but I'd be lying. I kept my mouth shut. Like the idiot I claimed I wasn't. But it wasn't for me. It was for Beth. Everything I did, I did for Beth. I refused to raise her in a broken home. It was my worst nightmare. Maybe because I came from a broken home myself with a horrible father and a mom that was in her grave before Beth was even in my life. Or maybe I feared it would ultimately lead to her having a breakdown, especially once she found out she wasn't *mine*. Either way, I made my choice. And I stood by it. But as the years passed by, the broken home I refused to raise her in was happening all around us.

I loved Steven. Even when he wasn't the person I fell in love with, I still loved him. I loved him with the part of my heart I hadn't given Beth. I felt as an adoptive mother, I had to make a conscious choice: how much of my heart did I give to my significant other and how much did I give to my new child? I didn't get to keep any for myself. That was fine with me, though. I didn't need it. All I ever wanted was a child, so giving my heart to Beth was easy. Giving some to Steven became more and more difficult.

"Mom?"

I looked over at Beth, who was walking next to Jackie on our way back to the house. Beth looked a lot more at ease than she did earlier in the day. "Yes, honey?"

"Are you okay?"

There was that sixth sense she had about me. "Oh, yes. I'm fine. Enjoying the spring day." Beth shook her head. Only I saw it, but I knew what it meant. It meant she didn't believe me. I smiled at her. "You know spring in Savannah is my favorite."

"I can see why," Jackie said. "It really is beautiful."

"Mm-hmm." I pulled my gaze away from Jackie's profile and looked straight ahead. I could see our house. The front was so picturesque with it's gorgeous wrap-around porch and elegant, stained-glass windows. I loved everything about it. But for some reason, the thought of walking back was unsettling.

I looked over at Beth and Jackie. They were walking a couple steps ahead of me now. I heard Beth say Jackie's name.

"Do you think, y'know, you and I could keep in touch?"

I heard Jackie's smile more than saw it. "Of course," she said. "I'd actually really like that."

"You would?" Beth's voice was so surprised, so genuine. It broke my heart that she was so unsure of herself.

"Oh, Beth, of course." Jackie draped her arm over Beth's shoulders and pulled her close. "I'm sorry I ever gave you the idea that I wouldn't want to."

"It's okay. I mean, I'm sure it wasn't how you expected to spend your weekend."

Jackie's laugh was so lovely. It was deep, wonderful, and layered with hope. "You're absolutely right about that." She squeezed Beth a little tighter. "Now you can text me when you want to hitchhike over."

"Jackie!" I said.

They both laughed. "I was kidding." Jackie looked back at me. Her eyes were sparkling. "She can fly. Flights aren't horribly expensive. Or take the bus. Either way."

"You researched it?" I didn't know why, but the thought of her on her phone in the darkness of the spare bedroom, researching different modes of transportation from Savannah to St. Petersburg made my hands ache. It was so not what I expected out of her.

"Yeah, Jackie, you did?" Beth's eyes were filled with love. Boy, how her mood had changed from this morning. She'd acted as if she was ready to get rid of Jackie, and now she was two seconds from asking if she could go spend spring break with her.

Jackie laughed. "It's not like it was hard. Google maps, people."

We finished the walk mostly in silence. The birds were chirping, and the air was so crisp. It wasn't normal. Even the Spanish moss in the southern live oaks hung less limply. The break in humidity was welcomed by all, it appeared.

As soon as we got in front of the house, I could feel a heaviness return to the air. It settled right under my throat and made it hard to swallow. I slid my hands into the front pockets of my khaki, cropped chinos and tried to fight the suffocating feeling. "So, you'll text Beth when you make it home?" My voice sounded strained and not at all like mine.

"Yes, I'll text you both now that I have your numbers."

"I gave her yours, Mom." Beth smiled at me and nudged me softly with her shoulder.

"Okay, then, I guess this is good-bye?"

Jackie's smile didn't quite reach her eyes. "I guess so." She turned to Beth and held out her arms. "C'mere, kid." Beth left my side and wrapped her arms around Jackie's waist. Jackie's arms wrapped easily around Beth's shoulders, and she kissed her light brown hair and then her forehead. "Don't be a stranger," she said into Beth's hair. Her voice was muffled, but I could hear the emotion behind it.

"I won't be." Beth pulled away and looked at Jackie. "You, either, 'kay?"

Jackie smiled and hugged her again, but this time, she looked right at me. I couldn't explain why, but the look made my stomach clench and my throat tighten. I tried to smile, but I couldn't. All I could feel were the tears stinging my eyes.

"Okay, I'm getting out of here." She held Beth's hand quickly, then turned to leave. "I'll text you."

"Drive safe," Beth shouted as Jackie climbed into her car and started it. I felt Beth put her arm around my waist and lean her head into my shoulder, but I couldn't reciprocate. I had no idea what was happening to me, but the sight of watching Jackie drive into the afternoon sun was too much for me to handle.

"Let's go inside," I finally said when we could no longer see the black BMW on Whitaker.

"Is Dad home?" Beth asked, and as she finished her question, I heard the door into the kitchen from the garage open. My heart sank when she ran over to him. I was half expecting her to throw her arms around him, but she didn't. And it thrilled me. I hated myself for being happy that she was finally having reservations about him. She didn't have as many as I did, and I hoped she never would. It made me such a horrible person that a small part of me wanted her to know about his anger and his indiscretions so I'd have someone on my side.

Steven pulled on Beth's arms and then looked at her. "What's going on? Where were you?"

"Hi to you, too." Beth huffed as she shrugged his hands from her shoulders. "Dad, I'm fine. I'm actually really great." Beth was fighting a smile. I could see it in her cheeks. I found myself fighting my own happiness, as well.

"What happened?" Steven looked at me from in front of the refrigerator before he pulled out a can of Yuengling beer and snapped it open. "Are you okay?"

I nodded. I wasn't okay, but I didn't want to talk about it in front of Beth. I honestly didn't know if I would talk about it at all. It wasn't worth it, was it?

"Where were you yesterday? You gave your mom quite the scare," Steven said after he drank from his beer.

Beth looked at me and then at him. "I met my birth mom."

Steven looked absolutely horrified. "What?"

"Yeah, I found her. I mean, it was easy."

"Elizabeth, why would you go and do something like that?" His voice was booming. *Shit.* The sound made the hairs on the back of my neck stand up. I'd heard that voice before.

"Dad, I needed to do this." Beth stood her ground, which made me proud, but also worried. "You wouldn't understand because you aren't adopted. I *needed* to meet her."

"That isn't for you to decide. Not until you're old enough. How the hell did you find her?"

Beth blinked, once, twice, three times before she finally said with her shoulders pulled back and her head held high, "I hired a private investigator." Her answer was so firm and matter-of-fact.

"What the fuck did you say?"

"You heard me, Dad." Beth folded her arms across her chest and took a step back. I wanted to rush over and stand in front of her like a mama bear would protect her cubs, but fear had frozen me in place.

"Beth, Jesus *Christ*." He pointed his free index finger at me. "This is your fault."

I couldn't hold back my shocked laughter. "I'm sorry, what?"

"This. This whole thing is your fault." He slammed his beer on the granite countertop, and it splashed all over his hand. He shook it off, and the sound he let out was enough to cause me to back down. "If you hadn't told her she was adopted, this never would have happened. What if something bad had happened to her?"

"Like that would have fazed you!" Beth shouted and then turned from him and started toward me. "You didn't even call Mom yesterday, did you?"

"I was busy, Beth. Making money. For this family."

"Bullshit!"

She was not afraid of him at all. I made a move, sidestepping her so I was in front. I wrapped my hand around her wrist and squeezed. "Beth," I whispered as I looked over my shoulder at her. "Honey. It's not the time. Go upstairs."

"Mom, no," she said, but I cut her off with a look, and she did as I asked.

When she was out of earshot, which I knew she really wasn't— she was standing at the top of the stairs listening, I was sure of it—I looked at Steven. "You are out of your fucking mind."

He took a couple steps toward me, dragging his beer on the countertop. "She did not need to meet her biological mother," he said, his voice low and gravelly. His ears were so red, and his face had broken out in a sweat. "Ever."

"That really isn't for you to decide." I clenched my hands into fists. "She was nice."

"How would you know she was nice?"

"Because she drove Beth home. So she didn't have to find a way back."

"A complete fucking stranger drove our kid home, and all you can say is, 'she was nice'?"

"Really, Steven? She is her *mother.* She gave birth to her. She is the *reason* we have Beth. So, don't you stand there and act like you are so perfect. Because you aren't. And we both know it." I didn't know what had gotten into me, but whatever it was coursed through my veins like a highspeed freight train. "I'm sure the only person that thinks you're perfect anymore is that goddamn whore nurse you've been fucking."

It happened so fast. He let go of his beer, and he backhanded me right across the face. I couldn't feel anything, and yet I could feel everything all at once. I tasted blood as I raised my hand to where he struck me. I slowly turned my head and looked at him. There was no remorse in his eyes. No sign of hope. Nothing.

"Don't you ever speak to me like that again," he said between breaths.

"You son of a bitch," I said in a whisper. "Get out of my house." I don't know what had gotten into me, but for the first time ever, there was something inside of me that didn't want to roll over and give up.

"This is *my* house."

"Get out of my house before I call the cops, Steven." He stood there. "Get out!" I screamed. "Get out!"

He turned on the heels of the Gucci shoes I'd bought for him for Father's Day and left the kitchen through the garage. I heard the door open, the engine of his Porsche roar to life, and then the tires squeal as he sped away.

When I knew he was definitely gone, I collapsed onto the cold tile floor of the kitchen.

CHAPTER FOUR

JACKIE

The drive home was uneventful. I was in no mood to deal with traffic jams or horrible drivers, so it thrilled me that I made it back to St. Pete in reasonable time. I tried to keep my mind occupied while I drove, so I didn't think about Susan's eyes as I climbed into the car or Beth's sweet smile as I pulled away. I shook my head as I stepped off the elevator to my second-floor condo. What had happened to me in the last couple of days?

After I let myself in and dropped my bag on the floor. I walked to my couch and dove onto it, face first, so I could groan into a turquoise throw pillow. How was I supposed to go back to the life I was leading before Beth knocked on my door? Did she know when she first climbed into a stranger's car on its way to St. Pete that she would change my life forever?

She had to know, right? Her life had to be changed now, too. How could a person go from not knowing to knowing and not be completely different? It was impossible. Everything people did changed them somehow. It was silly of me to think my life could go back to normal. There was no way I could pick up my laptop and start typing madly away at my latest manuscript after all of this. Too much was different. Including my heart.

I flipped onto my back and sighed. "Forty thousand words down the drain," I said to the emptiness in my apartment. The afternoon sun was streaming in the sliding glass door. I made myself get up from my sprawled-out position and walk over to the door. When I slid it open, the warm gulf breeze met me. I stepped out and breathed the air in. There was something about the way the air smelled on the gulf. It was salty yet sweet, and if sunshine had a smell, it would smell like that.

I leaned against the railing and watched as the sun sank lower and lower in the sky. This condo was everything to me. I picked it out during an emotional break-up and ever since, it was the only space that felt like home. It was a great size. Three bedrooms, three bathrooms, and an awesome kitchen with a view that I literally could not buy right now if I wanted to. I got in right before the real estate market started to climb. Lucky me. Otherwise, I would have had to pay four hundred thousand dollars instead of the two hundred and fifty thousand I paid ten years ago.

The view was why I bought it. It wasn't updated at all, but I figured it'd be perfect for writing. Turns out, I was one hundred percent right. The morning light came in the back bedroom where my desk was, and the afternoon sun came in the sliding glass door. And the sunsets. My God, the sunsets. They were amazing. Especially in October. I wasn't really sure why, but I had always heard it was because the humidity finally subsided, and the air was dryer. Whatever the cause, I loved my condo even more during the fall.

I looked out over the water and could see a pod of dolphins right off the beach. It was so calming to watch the water, the way the dolphins cut through it so effortlessly. I loved this time of day.

Except today, I couldn't get my mind to sit still. I wanted to relax, breathe, let the events of the past hours fade away. But it wasn't happening. If I wasn't thinking about the weather, my condo, or the dolphins, my mind found its way back to Susan.

It had been a long time since I'd been taken by anyone. I prided myself on that fact, actually, because as a writer, I felt it was difficult to really guard my heart. So far, I'd been successful, which was great. At least that was what I kept telling myself.

Don't get hurt. Don't obsess. Don't give myself something or someone to write about. I should have been getting my ideas and my material from my imagination; not thinking about full, pink lips and curvaceous hips and chocolate dark hair that had a lovely natural curl that I wanted so badly to run my fingers through.

Dammit…my usual protect-heart-and-brain-at-all-costs façade had faded significantly since Beth knocked on my door.

I heard my cell phone beep from my back pocket. I pulled it out and smiled when I saw *Tabitha Harling* on the screen. I opened my texts and hers said, *You home? I'm coming over.*

Yes, I'm home. ETA?

2.2 seconds.

And then there was a knock at my door before it opened, and Tabitha was standing there. "Yo, yo, yo, Jacks, what is going on?" she shouted.

"I'm on the balcony, you fool."

She burst through the door and grabbed me from behind, hugging me like a maniac. "I haven't seen you in forever. What the fuck?"

I started to laugh as I squirmed away from her. "I've been writing. You know I can't be bothered when I'm writing."

"That is so lame." She ran her fingers through her short blond hair. It was so wild, yet she never did anything with it. It was always all over the place. "So, what's up? How's the next bestseller going?"

"It's good," I answered with a smile. She was going to know something was up if I didn't start getting my act together. I sat on one of the chairs on the balcony and propped my feet up on the ottoman.

Tabitha followed suit and sat opposite me. "You're never going to believe what the group wants to do."

"Oh, Jesus, I can't even imagine."

"Strip club. Next Friday. Are you in?"

"Fuck no!" I laughed. "There is no way I'm going into a strip club."

"Dude, we're going to Tampa. Let's go. It'll be so fun."

"Absolutely not."

"Ugh. You're such a drag these days." She was still wearing her football attire, and she had grass stains all over her shins.

"Did you have a game?"

"Practice." She flexed her bicep. "What do you think? I've lost some weight and gained muscle."

Honestly, I couldn't tell that she lost any weight. She always bulked up for football season. "Sure. Looks great."

"What the fuck?" Tabitha stood as she pouted and went inside. I heard her open the fridge, and then she promptly returned with a six pack of Cigar City Brewing Invasion Ale. She thrust a can at me and opened one for herself. "Drink with me, at least?"

"Are you okay? You don't normally drink during the week," I said as I popped the seal on my can and took a big swig. It tasted incredible.

"Janice is being a dick. She wants to see other people, which whatever, I knew it was going to happen, but then she's all, 'I still want to have sex!' And what the fuck am I supposed to think?"

"Janice is young. She's going to be a little crazy for a while until she settles down."

"Fuck that."

"Who does she want to see now?"

"*Dawn.*"

"Dawn?" I asked with a laugh. "Are you fucking kidding me?"

"Would I kid you?" Tabitha looked at me, an eyebrow arched.

I nodded. No, she would not kid me. She had been in love with Janice since the young thing started hanging out with us. It was a strange phenomenon how groups of lesbians sort of acquired newbies. We always had to have a certain number at all times, and when one fell away, another got picked up. It never failed.

"So, what's going on with you?"

I kept my eyes on my beer. Tabitha knew that I hated talking about myself. I usually never engaged and when I did, it was bad. I was an introvert, and I was slightly selfish with who I let know me. But Tabitha had been my person for as long as I could remember. So, without even really thinking about the repercussions, I said, "I met the kid I gave up for adoption." Luckily, Tabitha had been in my life when it all happened, so I could spring the information on her, and it wouldn't need an hour-long explanation first.

She leaned forward, still clutching her beer, and shook her head. "Are you kidding me?"

I raised my eyebrows. "Would I kid you?"

"Touché, my friend." She looked down at her flipflops and then back up at me. "What the hell happened? I thought it was a closed adoption?"

"The kid hired a private investigator."

"Wow."

"Yeah."

"So, details, please?"

I leaned forward and propped my elbows on my knees. I tasted something other than beer on my tongue, and it was slightly nauseating. "Her name is Beth, and she hitchhiked here." Tabitha's eyes went wide as I told her. She listened intently when I laid out the course of events and how it all unfolded. I told her how I felt bad letting her get back in the car with strangers, so I drove her home to Savannah. "So, I dropped her off, and that was pretty much it."

"Wait. That's it? Did you meet her parents? Are they good people? Are they assholes like you always feared?" Tabitha tried to get me to look at her by moving so she was in my line of sight. "Jacks, tell me. Come on."

I finally looked at her. "She was actually really perfect," I said, and my voice snagged in my throat from the emotion. My mind flashed back to Beth's brown hair and green eyes. "She was wearing Vans and a hoodie and ripped jeans, and she was beautiful. And I was a complete fucking dickhead to her. And her mom…" My voice trailed off as I brought my fingers to my lips and pinched the top one. I wasn't going to let myself cry, even though the tears were on the verge of making an appearance. "Yeah, they're perfect."

Tabitha was silent for what felt like forever until she finally said, "So, her mom?"

"Yeah?" My eyes found Tabitha's. "What about her?"

"Mm-hmm."

"Stop."

"Stop what?"

"Tab, don't."

"Mm-hmm."

"I'm serious."

"Are you?" Tabitha tilted her head and then stared at me. "What about her mom then?"

"Her name is Susan. And she's a good mom." I shrugged. "She's a really good mom. That's all."

She squinted her eyes at me. "Okay."

"I swear."

"Okay, I believe you."

She didn't believe me. I could tell. "I hope so," I said softly. "I'll never see her again anyway."

"Why would it matter if you saw her again or not?" Tabitha asked with a tone that meant *I fucking told you so.*

"Tabitha, please stop. I have had the craziest day and a half that I have ever experienced."

Her face softened, and she reached out and put her hand on my knee. "I'm sorry, Jacks. I really am. I know you never thought you'd have to go through this."

"It's okay, though. At least she's good."

"Yeah, she's good. And she's in a good spot, and you're good, too, so we're all good, right?"

I smiled at Tabitha. "Yes, we're all good. Even you. Who is clearly trying to butter me up."

"Let's go out. Let's go get fucked up."

There was a part of me that wanted to tell her to fuck off because I was too tired and too emotional. But there was a larger part of me that was absolutely game. "Okay. Let me go get cleaned up."

"Yes!" Tabitha shouted as she pumped her fists in the air. She spilled beer all over herself and started laughing. "Perfect! I look so classy now!"

I couldn't help but laugh at her as I rushed inside and into the bathroom to clean up. Maybe a fucking one-night stand would clear this Susan bullshit right up. Fuck 'em and forget 'em. Of course, I had a really bad feeling I was never going to forget Susan, regardless of how hard I tried.

❖

BETH

I knocked on Mom's door around nine, hoping she was still awake. I heard her muffled, "Come in," so I pushed open the door. The room was dark except for the light coming from her cell phone which she quickly put down. She had gone to bed so fast after my dad left that I barely got a chance to even make sure she was okay. I tiptoed into the room, Myrtle hot on my trail. She jumped up on the bed, promptly snuggled up to Mom, and laid her head down.

"Are you okay?" I whispered. I could barely see her in the dim lighting from the nightlight in the hallway that was across from her bedroom door.

"Yes," she answered. "Can't sleep." Her voice sounded strained and shaky.

I crawled onto the bed, and she pulled down the covers so I could lay next to her. I heard her breathing and knew she was waiting for me to speak. "I'm sorry. I'm sorry for everything. For finding my... for finding Jackie. For running away to do it. For stealing your credit card."

"You stole my credit card?"

"Yes," I said sheepishly. "I'm so sorry."

"What the hell did you buy with it?"

"It's how I got the private investigator."

"Jesus, Beth," she whispered. "You sure were determined, weren't you?"

I nodded even though she probably couldn't see me.

"Why'd you need to know so bad?"

I shrugged. "Because? I don't know. I had this burning need to find out. Like, why did she want to give me up? Why wasn't I enough to keep? I wanted to see if she had more kids, or if I was the unlucky one." I heard the way her breath caught after I said that, and it was enough to make me want to throw up. "Wait, no, Mom, I didn't mean it like that. I love my life. I am so happy. I'm like, the most well-adjusted kid I know."

She put her hand on mine. "I understand what you mean. I get wanting to know. I wish you would have come to me."

"I know," I sighed. "I thought I could handle it all myself."

Mom turned, clicked the light on the bedside table on, then rolled so she could look at me. "So, you know your father and I aren't happy."

"What the hell, Mom? Did he do that to you?" She didn't need to answer me. I knew he had. I heard the entire fight. But seeing the aftermath on her face was a completely different story.

"I don't want you to think this has anything to do with you. You are why we have tried to make it work."

"Has this happened before?" I watched her expression as I waited. "He's hit you before, hasn't he?" She blinked and winced from the pain even blinking caused. "Mom, how could he do this?" I was so angry in that moment that I was having a hard time breathing. "How could he?"

"Beth, baby, I'll be okay."

"No."

"What do you mean, 'no'?"

"This is complete bullshit." I heard her sigh after my curse word usage, but I didn't care anymore. "You've raised me to be such a strong young woman. You preached and preached at me for years. 'Don't let men walk all over you. Don't let anyone walk all over you.'"

"I still feel that way."

"But you can't do that for yourself?" I tried to get up and leave, but she reached out and grabbed onto my forearm. "*What*?"

"Don't," she said softly. "Beth, please don't. I know I'm a hypocrite."

"We need to leave. You know that, right?"

She sighed. "Where would we go?"

I was at a loss. I had no idea where we would go, but we needed to leave. "I don't know. Let's go on a trip. Spring break is next week. Let's leave early. We can go to Tybee Island, or we could go use the condo in Gulf Shores or hell, we could fly to Chicago and see Aunt Melissa. Anywhere but here."

"He's not coming back."

"I don't care, Mom. I don't want him anywhere near you again."

"Beth," she said with a calm voice. "I'll figure out what we're going to do, but I'm not making any decisions tonight. We were both upset, and he overreacted."

The idea that she was going to even consider forgiving him made me sit upright. I was outraged. "What are you talking about? You're leaving, Mom. *Period*. Maybe we don't know where we're going to hide out while you get your shit together with a lawyer, but we are *not* staying here."

"I realize you're sixteen, but you should probably cool it on the curse words around me," she said softly. I could barely look at her. Her eye was black and blue, and the bruise stretched down into her cheek. "I'm going to make the right decision. I promise you."

"Mom—"

"No, honey, I am *promising* you."

I sighed. She was being sincere, but I still didn't trust her words. I looked down at my hands. I was clenching them so tight that I drew blood where my nails dug into my palms. "Okay."

She repositioned herself and patted the spot next to her. "Lie down." I did as she said and snuggled into her and Myrtle. "Tell me," she said, her voice barely above a whisper. "How do you feel now that you've found your birth mom?"

I looked at her. She was looking at the ceiling, and I couldn't see the bruise on the other side of her face any longer. "I guess good?"

"You guess?"

"Yeah, I mean, we didn't get to talk a whole lot. She was so standoffish at her apartment and in the car. I guess I assumed she would drop me off, and that would be the end of it." I closed my eyes. "I really liked her, though. I think…" I paused. "I think maybe it'd be cool if she was in my life more. I mean, if you're okay with that." I watched for her reaction. I didn't know exactly how to take the small smile that appeared on her lips.

"I'm okay with that," she answered. She glanced at me. "She seemed genuine."

"Are you at all concerned that she's gay?"

A huff came out of her mouth, followed by a chuckle. "No? I haven't really given it much thought." That sounded like a lie. A poorly rehearsed lie. "Are you okay knowing that about her?"

I shook my head and said, "Yeah, of course. But I meant, like, do you think I could be gay?"

She finally looked at me. "Why? Do you think you might be?"

I shrugged. I didn't really think I could be, but I guess I'd heard that it could be hereditary. Biology and all, right? So, wouldn't it be able to be passed on? I mean, I'd never really had a relationship with a guy. I'd liked some of them, sure. This boy Dan was super cute, and he talked to me a lot, but I felt like one of the guys a lot of the time. We'd skateboard at the park, and I could do the half pipe as well as they could, so I fit in. And the girls I had in my life were super pretty and feminine, and yeah, maybe I might have been attracted to a couple of them over the years. Especially Tamara. But we weren't even friends anymore. "No? But I haven't really ever had a boyfriend, so…"

Mom smiled. It was the first time the smile felt real since before Jackie left. "I would love you the same no matter what," she said as she moved my hair away from my face and pushed it behind my ear. "Wherever your life's journey takes you, I hope you'll always feel proud because I'll be proud of you."

"Thanks, Mom," I whispered. She rolled over and turned the light off and then turned back toward me.

"Get some sleep."

We lay there in silence for a few beats before I found the courage to ask, "Did you *like* Jackie?" Mom didn't answer right away. Was she already asleep?

I finally heard her take a breath, and she said, "I thought she was completely unexpected."

"Because you weren't expecting to meet her?"

I heard her breathe out through her nostrils. "No," she said. "Because she was…not what I expected."

"In a good or bad way?"

"Beth, honey, you need to go to sleep. You have school tomorrow."

Why wouldn't she answer the question? I felt her reach over and put her hand on mine again.

"I love you," she whispered.

"I love you, too, Mom." I closed my eyes and tried to fall asleep, but it was pointless. All I could think about was when we were going to escape. I wanted to get up and text my Aunt Melissa or check to see if our condo in Alabama was empty for the next however many weeks. Everything about our conversation made me want to spring into action. My dad was an asshole and apparently an abusive prick, my mom was frightened more than she was willing to admit, and my biological mom was *unexpected.*

What was I supposed to do? How was I supposed to help? Where did I turn? They were all questions I was dying to get answers to, but as my mom gripped my hand as she drifted off to sleep, I knew I would have to wait until the morning. But I would definitely figure the answers out. No doubt about that.

CHAPTER FIVE

SUSAN

I heard Beth come home around three the next day. She shouted, "Mom!" from the bottom of the stairs, and when I answered that I was in my bedroom, she came flying up the steps.

"Goodness, honey, what's going on?" I asked when she burst into the room panting.

"The condo is booked. So, Gulf Shores is out." She threw her arms outward and looked around frantically. "And you're not going to fucking believe this."

I rolled my eyes. She had grown up so much in the past four or five years, but the cursing was something I had a hard time dealing with. "Is there even any use in reminding you that I'm your mother, and the f-word is off limits?"

"Um, probably not. Dad has already gotten to Aunt Melissa. I texted her, and she called me and said that he sent her texts and threatening phone calls about how if we come up there, *he's* going to come up there, which is ridiculous, but whatever." Beth plopped down on the bed and sighed. "She said she didn't care and that we could still come. But she wanted us to know. He has *no* right to do that."

"He has every right. We're his family."

"Mom!" Beth shouted. "Are you high?"

I tilted my head and raised my eyebrows at her.

"Ugh, sorry, I didn't mean it like that. I mean, Mom, come on. We cannot stay here!"

"I talked to your father today. He's going to come home tonight, and we're going to have a conversation. An *adult* conversation. I know you are not necessarily keen—"

"Keen? Are you kidding me? I cannot believe you are going to let him come back into this house after he hit you!"

I stood from the chair where I was sitting by the window and moved to where Beth was on the bed. "You have got to calm down," I said softly. I put a hand on her leg, and she instantly started crying. "I promised you that I would make the right decision."

"Make the right decision for *you*, though, Mom. Not me. And not Dad. You hear me?"

I laughed as I knelt down in front of her. "So, you're the parent now?"

"I will be if I need to be!"

"I promised you," I said as I reached up and dried the tears on her face with my right hand. "Please, stop crying."

Beth breathed in deep and then let out a ragged breath. "I'll never be okay with him being here again. I hope you know that." She stood and moved past me, leaving my room completely. I heard her door slam.

"Great." If she only knew the *number* of times he'd been violent with me…

I sighed and looked around my bedroom. When I was a child, all I ever wanted was a large bedroom with a huge, fluffy bed and a great window to sit next to so I could read and read and read. After years of scraping by in college and the first few years of my practice not taking off and Steven's inability to not spend like an idiot, I finally had it. The whole house was what I always wanted. So, the idea of leaving and running away from the house and my life didn't seem like an option. We'd gone through so much together. Especially in the beginning with the countless attempts at conceiving and the in vitro fertility treatments… I didn't know why I thought that because he kept his anger to bruises around my biceps or on my wrists, I could survive it. As long as he wasn't hurting Beth, I could stay. I could put up with it. I could even put up with him cheating on me. But the second his hand hit my face and the proof of his hostility reached the light of day, I knew it was time.

In the end, it wasn't admitting that after twenty years of marriage we failed. Because I knew we had failed the first time he got angry at me, the first time he raised his voice at me, the first time he raised *his hand* at me, and the first time he actually followed through with the threat of violence. I knew it would never be the marriage I dreamt it would be. It was a sham. It was a façade for his fancy doctor friends, his stupid "keeping up with the Joneses" act that I fucking hated.

The last nail was finally in the coffin. Now all I needed to do was bury the damn thing. Unfortunately, divorce was never as easy as people made it sound. Especially when it involved separating from a man who didn't love me; he only *needed* me. And that obsessive need was so much scarier than I ever imagined.

Beth was right. We would need to escape. We would need to run away and hope to God he wouldn't find us. He wouldn't let us leave quietly, and he would never stop trying to get me to change my mind if we stayed.

I heard the floor creak behind me, and I spun around. "Steven." He looked horrible. He was in the same clothes from yesterday. His shirt was wrinkled, he had sweat stains under the armpits, and only one side was clumsily tucked into his navy-blue dress slacks. He was wearing his shoes, which pissed me off because he knew that I didn't allow shoes on the floors upstairs.

"I said hello. You didn't answer." Steven took another step into the bedroom. "Thank you for agreeing to talk to me."

I stood, and within a second, he had bridged the distance between us and was hugging me. For the first time in a really long time, his touch did nothing to me. In the past, my anger would melt instantly the second his begging commenced. But now? All I could do was see Beth's scared reaction after seeing the bruise. For some reason, her reaction made me want to stand up for myself and for her. I pushed away from him, my hands on his strong shoulders, and looked down. "I can't, Steven."

"Okay," he whispered.

"I don't want—"

"I know," he said.

I looked up at him. "You called my sister and *threatened* her?"

"I'm not giving up."

"Steven, no." I took a step back from him because if I stayed that close, with that look in his eyes, I probably would have given in. Not because I still loved him or that I wanted to be with him, but because at the end of the day, I was weak and stupid and small.

"So, you're going to end our relationship because I messed up once?"

I almost laughed. *Almost.* "What do you mean *once*?"

"Hitting you," he said as he reached up to touch my face. I jerked away from him, and the flash of anger in his eyes was unmistakable. "Susan?"

"You don't get to touch me." I took a deep breath. "Ever again."

Steven's jaw clenched. "You're going to flush our entire marriage down the drain?"

"*You* flushed this entire marriage down the drain the first time you raised your hand to me." I crossed my arms. "I am not doing this again, Steven. I'm not. I'm not going to let you come crawling back this time. Beth saw this!" I motioned toward the bruise, and his face twisted as if he knew it had to be killing me, as if he had a goddamn heart that even fucking cared. "I don't care what you do to me, but you will not drag my daughter through this. Not anymore."

"Our daughter."

That time, I did laugh. "Get out."

Steven didn't respond. He stood there expressionless.

"What is her name?"

That did it. There was the expression I was half hoping for, half scared of. If steam could come out of a person's ears, it would be pouring from his.

"Whose?"

"You know damn well who I mean."

He clenched his jaw again. This time the vein in his neck was sticking out. "You are unbelievable. I'm begging you to take me back. I'm promising I'll be better. And you're bringing up Natasha? This isn't about her."

"How is it not about her? You're the one who has not only been abusive but also has been having an affair for the past however many years."

He smirked. *The mother fucker smirked!*

I'd had enough. I didn't want to listen to him or look at him any longer. I was sad it took me so long to finally reach my breaking point, but God, it felt really good. "Leave. Now."

"*No.*"

"Steven. Leave, *now.*" I stood defiantly, my arms folded across my chest.

Steven continued to stand there. He was swaying now, his hands clenched at his sides.

"I am no longer putting up with you and how you treat me. Are you hearing me?" I saw his jaw clench, so I took a step back. *There it was.* I took another step back. *The look.* I knew that look *and* that stance better than anything in my life. I'd seen it countless times. It all depended on me what would happen next. If I stood there, he'd strike. If I tried to dodge him, he'd grab me. If I ran, he'd find a way to pick me up by the biceps and slam me against a wall until I relented. How fucking fucked up that he practically followed a playbook for domestic abuse.

"Don't you dare do it," I heard Beth say from behind Steven. He turned and looked at her. "Get away from her." She was holding a baseball bat. It was horrifying that years of softball had prepared her for this moment. "I will swing, and you know I can get a homerun on a mean slider, so don't even test me."

Steven turned back to me. "You haven't seen the last of me." He turned and went to leave the room, but Beth was still in the doorway. "Elizabeth Weber, don't make me move you."

Beth glared at him. "I cannot believe you hit Mom."

"Elizabeth," he said through clenched teeth.

"Beth, move."

"You are an awful person," she said softly. "Not only did you cheat on her, but you also hit her? How could you do that to her? To our family?"

Steven went to raise his hand, and I lunged at him. I grabbed his hand, and he almost picked me up off the ground. Beth moved out of the way as fast as possible. Her eyes were huge. "Dad?" she asked, her voice layered with pain; she was in tears instantly. My heart was breaking watching it all happen.

"Leave. Now!" I screamed the last word as I let go of him. He didn't say anything as he brought his hand back down to his side and rushed past her, down the stairs, and out of the house.

"Come here," I said softly, and Beth ran into my arms, dropping the bat as she did. The clang of the metal on the wood floor was deafening. She was crying so hard. I tried to hold my tears back, but I couldn't. I sobbed right along with her. "We're going to be okay. I promise."

When Beth finally calmed down, she pulled away from me and looked into my eyes. "What are we going to do?"

"We're leaving." I walked over to my cell phone and picked it up. I quickly found my best friend's phone number. She finally picked up on the third ring. "Veronica?"

"Susan. I haven't heard from you in—"

"I'm leaving Steven." I sat on the edge of the bed and felt the walls start to collapse around me.

"Did he hit you again?" Veronica's voice was frantic. "Susan, tell me right now—"

"Yes. And he almost hit Beth."

"Jesus *Christ*," she said. Her voice was seething. "Are you okay? I can draw up divorce papers. Please tell me that's what you're finally doing."

"Yes. I can't do this anymore."

"Suzie, honey, how have you done this for so long anyway?" Veronica asked. She didn't need an answer, but I could almost see her sitting at her kitchen table, forehead in her hand, shaking her head slowly. "Why now? What happened?"

"Well, I met Jackie Mitchell," I started with a sigh, then launched into the story of Beth running away, Jackie bringing her home, and Steven's affair that I knew about but didn't care about because at least it meant he wasn't touching me. Veronica knew the details about the abuse. She knew he hit me, she knew I hid it, and she knew it was only a matter of time before I either found the courage to leave or... "I've needed to leave for years."

"Roni!" Beth shouted as she yanked the phone from my hand. "How long has he been hitting her? Has this been a thing? What the frick?" Beth was shouting into the phone and looked crazier than I thought she was capable. She was always such a calm person. She held herself together. I'd like to think she got it from me, but these days, I wasn't so sure.

"Beth," I whispered. I held my hand out and waited for her to put the phone back in my hand.

"Sorry," she said softly and slapped the iPhone back into my hand. "But you aren't going to tell me."

"Yes. I am. Can you please give me a minute?" I waited until she stood and started toward the bedroom door. "Close the door, please."

Beth looked back at me. "I'll be right out here if you need me."

"I'm the adult here," I said quietly. "Please, let me handle this." Her shoulders fell as she did what I asked. I put the phone back to my ear. "I'm sorry."

"Suze, he could have killed you. You know that, right?"

"God." My voice was strained. My head was killing me. And my stomach was in a knot so large that I wasn't sure it'd ever relax.

"Do we need to meet? Do you need to come here? You know you can."

"I think," I said, then felt emotion rising up my esophagus until it voiced itself as a sob. "How did I let this get so bad?"

Veronica sighed. "You are stopping it. Finally. That's all that matters. Okay? You can't go back. You cannot live in the past."

She was right. She was always right. "We're going to leave. We need to leave. Don't you think?"

"Yes." And she knew Steven almost as well as I did. Years of being my best friend, of helping me pick up the pieces, of buying me that eight-ounce New York strip to put on my bruise, made her an expert in Dr. Steven Weber. "Do you want me to buy you a plane ticket to Colorado? My best friend has a ranch. You guys can stay there."

I chuckled. It felt good. "No. I'm not going to hide out on a ranch."

Veronica laughed with me. "I mean, horses and shit. I don't know. I've heard they're therapeutic."

"I don't know where we're going to go," I said softly. "He already threatened Melissa."

"He's a fucking lunatic," she shouted, and I heard her wife Mary say that she needed to get us to come there. "Did you hear her?"

"He'll know, though. You'll be the first person he'll harass here." I rubbed my forehead with my free hand. Hearing Veronica's voice was making everything feel more real. "God, Veronica, Beth had a baseball bat and I...I don't want to even imagine how bad this would be if he hit her. Or if she hit him? *Christ.*"

"Honey, you need to get your shit together and leave. I can draw up the papers, file it with the courts, and get your signature remotely. Do not hesitate." I heard Veronica take a deep breath on the other end of the phone. There were a couple beats of silence before she asked, "Where did he hit you this time?"

"He backhanded me," I answered softly. "Across my face. My right eye is..." My voice trailed off as the tears started to form. I was so strong up until that exact moment.

"Leave. Get your things together. Start driving and don't stop."

"Roni..."

"Listen to me. You know how crazy he gets. You've seen that look in his eyes before and have barely dodged his fist." I flashed back to the last time this happened, to the drunken stupor I found him in, to the way he lunged at me, and hit the wall behind me. That hole in the wall stayed there for weeks until I finally paid a contractor to fix it. My stomach churned. "Get Beth out of there before he does something else insane."

She was right. She was absolutely right. When I first found Steven in college, he was so sweet and kind. But as the years progressed, as he slipped further and further away from our family, he became more and more volatile. I knew how to deal with him ninety percent of the time. It was the other ten percent, the moments when his nostrils flared, his fists clenched, and his vein popped on the side of his neck that scared me to death. "Okay."

"I'll get the papers together, and you tell me where you've landed when you get there. Do you need money? I have a lot saved for the stupid addition to the house that Mary won't let us start."

"No, I'm okay. I have an account he doesn't know about."

"Suze, have you been planning this for a while?"

I sighed. "No? Yes. I don't know. I guess so? I knew it wasn't going to last much longer. I never thought it would come to this."

"We never do." Veronica's deep intake of air was loud and clear from the other end of the phone. "I'll take care of everything here. I'll handle the judge. You'll be able to take Beth wherever you need to, I can promise you. Temporary protection orders, whatever it takes. Okay?"

"Thank you, Roni."

"Susan?"

"Yes?"

"Take care of yourself. I've got you covered here."

"I'll call you," I said. "I love you."

"Love you, too, Suze. You're going to be okay."

We hung up, and I felt my hands shaking. I hoped she was right. I hoped we were going to be okay. At that point, with nowhere to go and no idea what my next move really was, I wasn't super sure.

❖

JACKIE

It had been forever since I went to dinner with the girls. Tabitha insisted on going even though I told her a hundred times that I was working against a deadline, and I could not miss it.

"Six thousand words is nothing! You can bang that out in two hours. Come on."

"Two hours?" I shouted at her from my bedroom. "You must be out of your fucking mind."

"I'm not," she shouted back. "Hurry up. We are meeting them at Fresco's in a half hour."

I ran my fingers through my hair and hoped my curls wouldn't fall out the instant we walked outside. The humidity wasn't as bad as it normally was in March, but it was still rough. I quickly applied eyeliner and mascara, sprayed myself with perfume, and then stepped back to check myself out in the mirror. I really did clean up well. And when I was nervous or working against a deadline, I rarely ate. So, the weight that was dropping off me was turning out to be a good thing. The long black skirt I threw on hadn't fit two months ago, and now it looked great. I straightened the loose-fitting red tank top I paired with it and then grabbed my jean jacket. If we were eating near the water, the wind always cooled things off. I knew I was becoming more and more like a true Floridian when "cool" was eighty degrees.

"Okay, okay, let's go," I said as I breezed into the living room where Tabitha was lying on the couch. I heard her whistle low and slow. I started to laugh at her. "Stop, please."

"You look great. What the hell? I look like a damn scrub."

"That's how it's supposed to be."

"You dick," she said as she opened the door and let me leave first. "If you pick someone up tonight, I'm gonna be real mad at you."

I looked at her over my shoulder. "I will not pick anyone up tonight. I promise."

She guffawed as our Lyft driver pulled up to my condominium. We climbed in, and he was off toward Fresco's.

"So, have you heard anything from your…daughter? I mean, are we calling her your daughter?"

"God, no. I call her Beth. And no." I reached for my purse and checked the pockets. "Speaking of, I forgot my fucking phone."

"Don't worry. I got mine." Tabitha held up her phone and winked at me. "You won't be able to pick up anyone without a phone."

"You severely underestimate me."

"Hardly!" Tabitha shot back, and we sank into an easy conversation about her job at the elementary school as a librarian. It was weird to see her in that setting, but man, she loved it. She would go on and on about the kids and getting them hooked on different books and helping them find what they're passionate about. It was fun hearing her be excited. She'd taken forever to get through college, which was where we met. I graduated with a degree in English, and she was still figuring out her major. Three years later, she finally graduated with library sciences. It was the strangest thing to imagine her reading a book, let alone being the keeper of the books. But she kept telling me that the librarian at University of Tampa really helped her see the beauty in reading and unleashing her imagination. Later, she confessed that her and said librarian used to fuck in the stacks. I always suspected it, but she would deny it up and down. No worries. I teased her thoroughly once she came clean. Either way, she still loved what she did. I guess that was all that mattered at the end of the day.

We pulled up to the restaurant, Tabitha finished up her conversation with the Lyft driver, promised to tip on the app, and then we headed into Fresco's. Our group was already there, nestled in a corner on the patio. Everyone shouted at us, and I was thankful that Fresco's was our normal haunt; otherwise, we would have been thrown out for being rowdy.

When we got to the table, Barbara tackle-hugged me. A friend for ages, she started out as a girlfriend. It wasn't until she finally found a significant other that we were able to actually *be* friends. We tried, of course, but nine times out of ten, we ended up in bed together. I was always the one breaking her heart, though, so when she told me about Jenny, I thanked every single higher power I could think of.

"Jacks, you look awesome. How can you look this awesome and never leave your condo?" She asked as she squeezed me to death. "I have missed you so much!"

I squeezed her back, then released the hug. "Barbie, you look good!"

"I have been doing that stupid P90X bullshit that Jenny is doing. It's ridiculous." Barbara was always thin, and her legs looked like toothpicks. There was no way this woman was lifting any weights. Ever.

I glanced over at Jenny, who was involved in a conversation with Tabitha. "She looks ripped. Is she taking steroids?"

Barbara slapped me on the arm. "She does look good, though, doesn't she?"

Jenny looked a little too muscular for my likes, but I nodded and smiled big. Dana and Ryan were seated next to Jenny, and they both flipped me off from their seats. "What the hell?" I asked with a laugh as I made my way over to them.

"You never fucking text me back. You never come over. All you ever do is hole up in your condo," Dana said as she stood so she could hug me.

"Dana, you know I'm writing my next book, right? And that writing is my job. Kinda like you have a job?" I was lying. I was a big fucking liar. I didn't text Dana back because I knew what she wanted. And I couldn't give and give and give to her when at the end of the day, what she wanted was not at all what I wanted.

"Um, yeah, but what the fuck? Text me back. Tell me how it's going. Lament to me that you actually miss human interaction. So I don't think you've been eaten by an alligator."

Ryan stood to hug me, ran his fingers through his intentionally messy hair, then nodded. "I mean, she has a point. I haven't heard from you since God was a boy."

"I texted *you* last week!" I smacked him on the ass when we finally hugged.

"Oh my God, she texts *you* but not me?" Dana's irritation was probably meant to come across as sarcasm, but I knew better. She was a little clingy with me sometimes. And stupid me, I started to take complete advantage of her clinginess when I needed her so-called "human interaction," which, of course, was a code word for sex. I was working on distancing myself as much as possible lately because I knew I was a horrible person. I did give in from time to time. I *was* human after all. But damn. She was like a dog with a bone. "I swear. Who do I have to fuck to get a text back?"

I raised my eyebrows at her. "Um, me?" I was awful. Why did I flirt so shamelessly with her?

"Ryan didn't fuck you!"

"He would if he liked vagina."

"This is true. Jacks is hot as fuck." Ryan smiled at me, and I blew him a kiss. He was such an adorable asshole that I could never not tease him. I was proud of him, though. He had built up quite the following in the gay community from his drag show appearances. Stackey-N-the-Backey was his show name, and he really was incredible.

Dana laughed and sat on my lap once I found a seat next to Tabitha. Regardless of Dana's inability to keep me at arm's length and my inability to do the same, she was probably the only friend I could see myself giving in and settling down with. Like, if the world ended, and we wound up surviving a zombie apocalypse together, and the thrill of outrunning attack after attack led to screaming hot sex. That sounded really horrible, I know, but I did not want to settle down with anyone. Especially someone as clingy as Dana. Even though she was beautiful and really good in bed... One day, I was sure I would make an exception. She had a massive amount of curly, jet black hair that fell somewhere past the middle of her back. She typically wore it down, and it never looked frizzy. I swear it was a wig. It was too perfect. Especially in the Florida humidity. Every now and then, she'd tie it up into a bun, which made her look far younger than she really was. She always smelled like Aveda products, too. The rosemary and lavender mingled with brown sugar and vanilla because she owned a bakery. Her smile was ridiculous, too. The first time I met her, she wouldn't stop smiling at me, and I was thankful she was in my life because regardless of my incapacity to commit, or to fall in love, sometimes that smile was all I needed to remind myself that my life really wasn't that bad.

I looped my finger through the belt loop of her skinny jeans and pulled. "What's been going on?" I asked, and when she looked down at me, I couldn't help but smile back at her.

"Well, since you never text," she said, then reached forward so she could push a lock of my hair behind my ear. "I've been really good. I've missed you." There was a sharp inhale of breath, and I knew she was mad at herself for saying that. We'd had the talk numerous times about her clinginess. God, my relationship with her made me sound like such a giant asshole. And maybe I was. Dana gathered her thoughts and continued. "The bakery is doing really well. I had to hire a couple more people to help in the kitchen, so that's good."

"I'm really sorry I've been awful about texting." I figured it'd be a good idea to at least appear human. I scrunched my face.

"Didn't need my distraction?"

"Yeah," I said softly. She was one hell of a distraction, too. Falling into bed with her while working on a book never did anything good for me. And in the long run, it wasn't that great for her. The more I slept with her, the more I fucked her up.

"When you're finished, maybe we could, y'know, distract each other?" She stood and leaned down to place a kiss on my lips. Her hair fell over her shoulder, and the scent made me want to rip her clothes off right there. It had been way too long for me. And to be brutally honest, maybe that human interaction with Dana would distract from my constant thoughts about Susan.

"Maybe that can be arranged," I said as she started to walk back toward her seat next to Ryan.

"Yeah, so she met her fucking daughter!"

My head snapped toward Tabitha. Was she kidding me? "What the hell, Tab?"

"What? You didn't say I couldn't tell anyone! They all know your background!" Tabitha's hands flew in the air to indicate she thought she did nothing wrong. I should have known better than to tell her.

Instead of taking her seat next to Ryan, Dana pulled out the chair next to me. She sat and made sure to lock her eyes on mine. "You met the baby you gave up for adoption?" she asked with a quiet voice, but the rest of the table seemed to hear because they all quieted down.

I let myself look at each person at the table and then stopped when I got to Tabitha, who gave me a tiny smile that for some reason gave me strength, even though I could have killed her for not keeping her mouth shut. "She found me. She's sixteen. Her name is Beth. And I don't know if I thought I'd ever survive such a fucked-up couple of days."

Ryan put his elbows on the table, his hands now under his face as he listened inquisitively. "My God, this is crazy."

"I know. Believe me."

"Well, how did it go? Was it weird? Was she nice? Did she look like…" Dana's voice trailed off, and I looked at her. I knew she wanted to ask if Beth looked like her father. I refused to ever talk about him, so I was thrilled she didn't finish her sentence.

"It was okay. She was nice. A good kid," I said. "Look, you guys, I don't really want to rehash this. I'm sorry." I pointed at Tabitha. "And you will be buying all my drinks *and* my food. Pony up, ya dick."

"I'm sorry," Tabitha said when she leaned into my space.

Deep down, she knew she shouldn't have blabbed. It was absolutely the biggest secret in my entire life, but thankfully, everyone at the table knew about the skeleton in my closet, so I wasn't as mad as I probably should have been. I was trying really hard to stop obsessing about things in my past, especially that time period. I started writing right after it happened, and I hadn't stopped. I had obsessed on paper and didn't talk unless absolutely necessary, and now I had no burning desire to rehash anything. Especially the only people I'd been able to think about since I pulled away from Savannah. I needed to stop.

I glanced around the table. Everyone else got the hint and started to have their own conversations. I took a deep breath and calmed down. "It's okay. I promise," I finally said. I leaned forward and looked at Tabitha. "I…"

"Susan."

"Yes."

"I know." Tabitha put her hand on my leg. "I can read you like a book."

I rolled my eyes. "Your librarian jokes are not that funny."

She laughed at me as she put her arm around my shoulders and pulled me into a side hug. "Yes, they are," she said while laughing. "And you love me."

"I know. I do."

The rest of the dinner was fairly uneventful. Jenny and Barbara told us they were going on a cruise. Ryan reminded us of his next appearance at Hamburger Mary's (the local drag show bar). And Dana, from her seat next to Ryan, kept looking at me with her big brown eyes and her stupid pretty face. I was not in the mood to keep talking about anything to do with me. Especially Beth. And the last thing I wanted to do was fall into bed with someone who, as time passed, was having a harder time separating her feelings from reality.

When Tabitha and I peeled ourselves away from the group, completely inebriated and also slightly high from the vape marijuana pen Ryan made us hit, we fell into a Lyft and headed toward my condo. Tabitha and I joked and laughed and knew we were probably scaring the Lyft driver with our drunk and high shenanigans. He laughed with us, though, and thankfully seemed not at all annoyed. I gave him my address, and he made a pitstop to drop me off. I threw a twenty-dollar bill at him for his trouble, and he thanked me four times before I said my good-byes to Tabitha and slammed the door.

The ding of the elevator was loud as I waited to get to my floor. I closed my eyes and thought how happy I was that I'd fought Dana off successfully. She was two seconds from inviting herself to come home with me, but I pumped the brakes like a taxi driver in rush hour and told her I couldn't. It was ridiculous. Completely and totally. Was I stupid for not taking her home and fucking her brains out? Probably. But I knew what it meant, and I could not turn my brain off.

The elevator doors opened, and I stepped out onto the floor of my condo.

"Jackie?"

I lifted my head, my heart jumped into my throat, and my mouth fell open. "Beth? *Susan*? What are you guys doing here?" I saw Beth holding a leash attached to their cocker spaniel. "And why do you have Myrtle with you?"

❖

BETH

Her face. Ugh. She was not expecting us. I'd made the wrong decision. *Fuck*. "Hi," I said. "I take it you didn't get my nineteen text messages."

"What is going on? What happened?" Jackie smelled like beer and…what the hell? Was that *weed*? Was Jackie *high*?

"Jackie, we're sorry. I don't know why I let Beth talk me into this." Mom was embarrassed. I could tell by the way she was rubbing her hands together. She still had her sunglasses on, so I nudged her, and she put her left hand up to silence me.

"No, we're not sorry. Jackie, we need your help. You're literally our last resort." I took Mom's hand and held it. "I promise we would have never done this if this wasn't an emergency." Jackie's face was an equal mixture of shocked and confused. "Can we please come in and explain?"

Jackie shook her head almost as if she was snapping out of a daze. A weed-induced daze. "Yes. Come in." She fumbled with her keys, dropped them on the ground, bent down to pick them up, and looked dizzy as she stood. She put her hand on the door frame and steadied herself.

"Let me help you." I took the keys from her shaking hand, and she held her breath. "How'd you get home? I hope you didn't drive."

"I took a Lyft. Also, I'm an adult," she mumbled as I opened her door, let her in, then my mom.

"You wouldn't have to tell me you're an adult if you act like one," I offered. My sarcasm was spot on. It was one of my greatest strengths. I saw Jackie roll her eyes, look at my mom, then Myrtle, and then back at my mom.

"Is she always like this?" Mom's shrug and nod were small gestures, but Jackie's spine stiffened.

"Okay, so." I took a breath and sat next to Mom on the couch. Myrtle quickly jumped up next to me, and I tried to push her down. I was sure Jackie didn't want an animal on her couch since she said she wasn't a dog person. Myrtle wouldn't budge, though. "I don't even know where to start."

"Jackie," Mom started. "I left Steven." She slid her sunglasses from her face, and the gasp that Jackie let out made her being drunk and stoned insignificant.

"Are you okay?" she asked, and the tone of her voice was the same one she used on me when she promised she wouldn't make fun of my drawing. "Have you iced that? It looks awful."

Mom was staring down as Jackie kneeled in front of her. Mom's eyes filled with tears, and she said, "Yes," so quietly that I barely heard her. "I didn't want to come here."

"I can't imagine why not. Your daughter's biological lesbian mom? I'm a perfect and obvious option." Jackie smiled, and the smile that echoed on my mom's lips was breathtaking. It was the first time she'd smiled since we left Savannah.

"We won't stay long."

"You'll stay as long as you need to," Jackie offered. "I have two spare rooms. Both have beds." She stood with determination. Apparently, the past five minutes sobered her up. "I'll get you some ice."

I handed Myrtle's leash to Mom and followed Jackie into the kitchen. "Jackie?" She didn't answer, but when she turned around, she pulled me into a giant hug. The familiarity took my breath away. I didn't expect that from her, and I was not at all prepared. "We won't be any trouble. It's my spring break next week. I took a couple extra days off. I emailed my teachers from Mom's email account," I explained as Jackie continued to hug me.

"Don't worry," she whispered. "You guys will be okay here."

It was the first time since all of it happened that I really *wanted* to cry. Not that I had to or was made to, but that I actually wanted to. I held back my tears, though.

She pulled away and looked at me, her hands on my shoulders, and she squeezed. "Are you okay?"

I nodded because yeah, I was going to start crying for sure if I answered her.

"Did he hurt you?"

I shook my head.

"Is she okay? Is that all he did?" Jackie's jaw clenched.

"I don't know," I said softly. "I don't know if she's okay."

Jackie pulled me back into a hug, and she smoothed a hand over my head. "It's going to be all right. I promise."

"You can't promise that."

"Yes, I can." When she let me go, her face was hard, and when she said she did promise, her tone was firm. I was so shocked by everything that was happening that I couldn't really say much else at the moment. I watched her, though, as she took out an icepack from the freezer and wrapped a kitchen towel around it. She poured two glasses of white wine and then looked back at me. "Do you need a drink?"

"Like, an alcoholic one?"

She tilted her head and smiled at me. "I know twenty minutes ago I was pretty lit, but unfortunately, my buzz has waved buh-bye. I'm talking about a glass of water or a pop."

"A pop? What the hell is a pop?"

"A pop. A Coke, a Sprite, whatever."

"Oh, you mean a soda." Jackie rolled her eyes while holding the two glasses of wine by the stems in one hand and the icepack in the other. For the first time since we arrived, I actually laughed. "What? Who the hell calls it pop?"

"Oh my God, I am not having this debate with you." She left the kitchen and made her way back to my mom, who was sitting on the couch, her eyes closed and her head leaned back. When Mom picked her head up and saw the wine, her eyes lit up.

"You read my mind," she said, her voice so soft and hard to hear. She took the glass of wine in one hand and the icepack in the other. She took a long drink before she applied the icepack to her face, but when she did, she breathed in through clenched teeth. "Aren't bruises supposed to get better as the days pass?"

Jackie sat on a comfy-looking chair across from the couch. She was gripping her wine with two hands, the same white knuckles as apparent as when she drove me to Savannah. Was her kindness from the kitchen fading away? Was she having second thoughts about opening her home to us? I couldn't tell, but her facial expression was causing my teenage anxiety to skyrocket.

"So," Jackie started and then took a drink. When she lowered her glass, she looked directly at me. "Do you want to tell me, or is your mom going to?"

I looked at Mom. She looked relaxed. Way more relaxed than she had been in months. "He flipped out," I said, deciding to answer and take the pressure off Mom. "He flipped out because I hired a private investigator. He snapped."

"Sadly, that's not the only reason he snapped." Mom slipped her shoes off and propped her bare feet on the ottoman. She smoothed her hand over Myrtle's head. She had promptly dozed off the second she snuggled next to Mom. "It was a lot of little things that added up over the past couple of years."

"Seriously?" I asked. "The past couple of *years*?" I was floored.

Mom moved the icepack, looked at me, then closed her eyes. "Yes, honey, the past couple of years."

"Wow."

"Has he always been dangerous?" Jackie's voice was so smooth and soothing. I was jealous of what seemed to be an uncanny ability to remain calm, at least in *this* stressful situation. I was so quick to beat the fuck out of my dad, a man I loved and cared for, and here Jackie was, a pillar of strength. Well, at least a pillar of weed-induced serenity. Either way, I was so glad she wasn't freaking out. Because I was. And my mom was. And that wasn't going to change any time soon.

Mom was looking right at Jackie. She didn't answer, and I knew it meant the answer was *yes*, which caused my stomach to bottom out. I was going to vomit. I stood and ran to the bathroom where I had first dried off, where I looked into the mirror and psyched myself up, where I told myself I could do this; I could be strong and meet my biological mom. This time was much different as I dove at the toilet and narrowly got the lid up in time to retch into the bowl.

I collapsed against the wall when I was finished. I was crying and coughing, and what the *fuck*? *My dad was dangerous?* What rock was I living under that I didn't know this? Why was this such a surprise? Did I really never notice before? I thought back to the times when he would get angry at me or Mom. His face would get so red and his ears…God, his ears would always look as if he was going to blow smoke right out of them. But I never remembered him hitting me or Mom. I certainly never heard him getting physical with her behind closed doors, either.

That thought nauseated me again. I took some deep breaths; in through the nose, out through the mouth. Like Mom used to tell me when I'd hyperventilate because of the stupid bullies in middle school.

"Beth?" A gentle knock followed, and the door opened slightly. Jackie poked her head in. "Are you okay?"

I leaned my head against the bathroom wall and sighed.

"Get ready for bed. I'll take your stuff to the bedroom." She left and closed the door behind her, but she turned the handle so it didn't make that awful loud clicking sound as it latched. For some reason, that made me like her even more.

After I washed my face, rinsed my mouth, and pulled my hair into a French braid, I emerged from the bathroom. The living room was dark except for the moonlight spilling in the open sliding glass door to the balcony. I walked past Mom on the couch, a blanket over her, sound asleep. Myrtle was of course curled into a ball right behind Mom's legs. Jackie was standing on the balcony, and when I stepped out, she glanced over her shoulder at me. I walked up next to her and leaned against the railing with her. The gulf breeze felt really good and smelled like salt. I could see the waves as they crashed onto the beach, one after the other. The sound was so calming, especially after the past couple of days.

"I take it you didn't know about your dad?"

I took a deep breath, shook my head, and mumbled a simple, "Nope."

"Your mom is stronger than you realize," Jackie said as she leaned into my shoulder.

"How would you even know that?"

"I can tell."

I didn't respond, but I wanted to tell her she was crazy. Mom was clearly not strong if she let a man continue to bully and beat her up for years and only now gained the courage to leave. What kind of person does that?

"You should probably cut her some slack."

I looked over at Jackie, at her hair blowing in the wind, at the remnants of makeup around her eyes that I could still make out in the moonlight. "I'm trying."

"Are you?" Jackie took a breath and closed her eyes. "Try to remember one thing in this lifetime, Beth. It takes a strong woman to leave. It takes an even stronger woman to stay."

It sounded like such bullshit. "I don't know about that."

"One day, you'll get it."

"Oh, yeah, when I'm older, I'm sure."

Jackie let out a small chuckle. "You'll get it sooner rather than later. I guarantee it." She turned to go inside. "I'm going to bed. You ready?"

I looked back out at the gulf and sighed. "Yeah, I'm ready." I only hoped that sleep would take me quickly, but I was pretty sure I was going to fight it all night long.

CHAPTER SIX

SUSAN

I woke up sometime around eight in the morning with a pounding headache. When I tried to sit up, I quickly remembered I had fallen asleep on the couch. My body was throbbing from being in the same position all night long. I needed water and ibuprofen, and I needed it STAT. I fumbled around the dark condo and finally found my way to the kitchen. After opening six of the nine cabinets, I discovered the ibuprofen next to the juice glasses. I grabbed a glass along with four pills and filled the glass from the refrigerator dispenser. The coolness of the water tasted amazing. I navigated back through the dark toward the bedrooms Jackie mentioned the night before. I opened the first door on the right and saw that it was Beth's, so I crept to the bed and slid under the blankets next to her. Myrtle must have found her way into the room at some point because she was snoring at the foot. Beth turned and opened her eyes. "Hi, Mom," she whispered.

"Go back to sleep." I put my hand on her arm and lay there until I dozed back off.

❖

When I woke up the second time, it was to the smell of bacon. Beth and Myrtle were no longer with me, so I sat up and looked around the room. It was still pitch black because of the world's best room-darkening curtains. I climbed out of bed and caught a glimpse of myself in the mirror on the dresser. "Jesus," I whispered as I peered at my reflection. I looked like absolute shit. And the bruise was not doing anything but getting darker and angrier.

I opened the bedroom door and slipped into the bathroom. Thankfully, Beth had unpacked our toiletries, so my toothbrush was ready for me. I washed my face, too, which felt incredible. I was ashamed to admit that I hadn't taken a shower in a good forty-eight hours, but the idea of showering, washing everything away, was too much to handle.

After I freshened up, I found Beth and Jackie in the kitchen. Beth was flipping pancakes on an electric griddle, and Jackie was checking on bacon in the oven. Myrtle was, of course, begging for scraps. I cleared my throat, and both turned toward me, their similar smiles glowing. Each had her hair pulled back in a braid, too, which made my heart clench.

"Good morning, sleepyhead," Jackie said, her voice still holding the happiness from her smile.

"Yeah, Mom, did you sleep?"

"I did," I answered when I sat on one of the barstools along the island. I was greeted with a cup of coffee from Jackie in a mug that had a unicorn with a rainbow mane and tail that read, *My other ride is a unicorn.* I couldn't help but smile. "Thank you."

"How do you take it?"

"Black."

"Well, that's easy," she said as she spun around and leaned against the counter across from where I was perched. "I heard you rummaging around for medicine. Did you find what you were looking for?" She eyed me over the top of her coffee mug. I couldn't tell if her mug said anything, but the handle was shaped like a fox's tail.

"Yes." I looked down. I couldn't explain it, but the level of embarrassment I was fighting was absolutely horrifying. I could barely look at Jackie without wanting to crawl under a rock. The idea that this woman, this complete stranger, the fucking biological mom to my daughter, knew all about me and my failed marriage and now about my abusive husband, was causing me to stress out like crazy. *No one* knew about him. Not even Veronica knew *all* the details. She'd seen bruises on my arms and had asked, but I always had an excuse for why they were there. I'd blamed myself, of course, because it was my fault. I knew how I needed to behave at all times. So, stepping out of line meant…well, it meant I'd get taught a lesson.

I took a deep breath as I pushed that memory from my brain.

My stomach was rolling. My palms were sweating. I was on the verge of a full-blown panic attack.

I was going to vomit if I kept thinking about it.

About *him*.

About his stupid hands and his inability to be a gentle human being.

God, I was so stupid! So very stupid to put up with Steven for as long as I did. I would never go back to that. For as long as I lived. The thought of him finding me, finding *us*, continued to creep into my brain. My insides would tremble, my heart would race, and my hands would turn instantly clammy. He had no real idea about Jackie, though. He would never be able to find her; he never knew her name. He didn't want to know. So, when Beth suggested it, I said fine and only protested it a small amount. Because at least we would be safe. Beth would be safe. Even if it meant that Jackie would know without a shadow of a doubt that I kept her child in a volatile environment because I was scared.

I hated myself.

Letting Jackie into my fucked-up existence was freaking me out. My insides were filled with anxiety and fear. *And now I have to face her!* At least until it was safe to go back to Savannah, even though there wasn't really anything to return to. I had to keep reminding myself that Beth did, though. She had school and friends. Pulling her away for a week was fine, but forever? That would be a different story entirely.

We ate breakfast on the balcony. Well, they ate. I picked and moved around the pancakes and hoped neither of them said a word about it. I was not in the mood for food. At all. The only thing I was enjoying was the weather. It felt wonderful to be outside with the gulf breeze and the warm Florida air. The last time I was in Florida, I was twenty-two, and it was for a spring break trip in college with all my girlfriends. We barely made it home alive. Sadly, I didn't remember much from the trip because I was intoxicated for all of it, but I do remember the way Florida smelled. The air had a sweetness to it that Savannah didn't. In fact, Savannah kind of stunk. So, being able to breathe deep and pull the sweet-smelling oxygen into my lungs was helping my mood. Not much, but a little.

"I think I'm going to go explore," Beth said, interrupting my thoughts. She finished the last piece of bacon on her plate before she said, "Do you want to go with, Mom?"

"Why don't you and Jackie go?" I did not feel like getting ready and leaving the small bit of safety I had acquired in the past twelve hours.

Jackie seemed to understand me without question. "Yeah, kid, I can show you some sights."

Beth's face twisted, and she looked at Jackie. "Would you be okay if I went solo?"

A laugh bubbled from Jackie's throat. As was with everything about her, the laugh was unexpected and really quite lovely, especially considering the morning I was having. "You hitchhiked to me the first time. I'm sure you can handle the streets of St. Pete by yourself. We're not too far from the touristy part of the beach, so I'm sure you'll be fine. You can take my bike if you want. There's a lock on it, and the key is hanging by the door." Jackie looked at me. "I mean, if you're okay with that. I need to write…working against a deadline."

I was sad that I wouldn't get to be alone with my sorrow, but I understood since we were literally imposing on Jackie's life, so I smiled. "Of course. You be careful."

Beth tilted her head. "I'll be fine, Mom." She slid away from the table, took a step toward me, and leaned down to kiss me on the cheek. "I love you," she said when she hugged me.

I was fighting back tears when I said I loved her, too. I watched her walk into the condo in her short khaki shorts and long legs with the same pair of Vans she wore every day. Her hair was still in a braid, and she looked so much more at ease than she had in months.

Jackie stood and reached for Beth's plate, then mine. "Are you finished?"

The sound of her voice pulled me from my thoughts, and I glanced up to her face. She was hovering over me, and the color of her eyes in the natural light made my breath catch. I blinked once, then twice, before I finally nodded. She smiled, which saddened me because I wanted to smile back, but I couldn't. I was so sad, so mad, so *depressed*. I wanted to get to know her, to laugh with her, but I couldn't fathom it right then. All I wanted to do was to be left alone. It was so unlike me, too. And that frustrated me to no end. Deciding to leave was not supposed to break me. It was supposed to repair me.

My gaze followed Jackie as she made her way to the kitchen. She was wearing yoga pants and a white tank top. She moved so freely in her home, so much differently than she moved in Savannah, when she was clearly censoring herself. She seemed so nervous and scared, which, *of course,* that was how she felt. But here? She was free, and it showed in her movements. Even her facial expressions weren't reserved. She was at peace.

She looked across the living room at me from the sink and caught me staring. I looked away and cursed at myself. *Way to be a giant creep.* I glanced back at the water and waves as they crashed onto the beach. There wasn't a cloud in the sky and hardly any humidity. Maybe I should have gone with Beth.

"Hey, Susan?"

Jackie's voice once again broke me from my thoughts. She was leaning against the door jamb, and her braid had fallen over her shoulder.

"Hmm?"

"I was thinking…" She bit her bottom lip before she finished with, "What about tracking your cell phones?" She reached up and pulled on the end of her braid, fidgeting with the rubber band.

"Thankfully, he's not super smart when it comes to technology. But we both changed our passwords on our iCloud accounts, so no way he could get in there and track us." I shrugged. "And we both blocked his number. I also told Beth no social media."

"And no one knows you're here?"

"My sister knows." I saw the worry on Jackie's face. "Let me worry about him, okay?" Jackie took a deep breath and nodded. A silence fell between us, and I looked down at my hands before I pulled a deep breath into my lungs and looked out at the gulf.

"Susan?"

"Yeah?"

"There's a pretty nice tub in my bathroom if you want to take a bath. I have some awesome lavender Epsom salt, too, if you'd like." After I looked at her, my eyebrows raised, she quickly added, "Not that you smell or need to bathe; I thought it would be nice, if you wanted to relax."

Her voice, the way it rose at the end of her sentence, was so considerate. If I was forced to explain how it affected me, I wouldn't be able to conjure a sentence that would do my feelings justice. All I could say was that I noticed. My body noticed, which caused my heart rate to elevate. I pressed my lips together, then licked them before I finally answered. "Actually, that sounds like a really nice idea."

The smile she flashed me was gorgeous. "I'll go lay everything out." She held my gaze a second longer before she bowed her head, turned around, and headed toward her bathroom. Again, I stared as she walked away, the gentle sway of her hips, the way those yoga pants hugged her curves; it was kind of...*hypnotic*. I shook my head and chuckled at myself. I was clearly sleep deprived.

I heard Jackie call my name from her side of the condo, so I stood and followed the sound. Her bedroom was gigantic. And her bed was a king, which she obviously made after getting up. I turned a corner into her bathroom. It was twice the size of the guest bathroom. I couldn't help but look around, stunned. She had two sinks, but only one of them had any products around it. The other was unused. When my eyes finally landed on Jackie, she was kneeling next to a large clawfoot tub with the water running. She was scooping one, two, three scoops of Epsom salt from a large glass jar into the tub. She stirred her hand around the water and then stood.

"It's all yours." She motioned toward the towels and said, "Those are for you. One's a hair towel if you get your hair wet. The other is a bath sheet, so you can wrap it around you." She grabbed a robe from the back of the door. "And this is mine, but it's clean. I just washed it, so if you want to put it on afterward, feel free." She bounced on the balls of her feet before she started to walk away. The move was so very *Beth* that it warmed my soul.

"Jackie?"

She stopped and looked at me in the mirror. "Yes?"

"Thanks," I whispered, my voice catching from the emotion I was doing a horrible job of hiding.

Jackie turned to look directly at me. "Anytime," she answered, and the sincerity in her voice was so genuine. My eyes followed her as she left and closed the door. I looked at the tub and then at myself in the mirror. Seeing the bruise again in the well-lit bathroom made me cringe. I leaned forward to inspect it. I could not believe this is where my life led me. In college, I used to volunteer at the crisis center for women. I was the girl who told other girls they didn't deserve men who hit them. I surrounded myself with other strong women and attended women's liberation rallies, and wore the word "feminist" with pride.

Now look at me. Barren, bruised, battered, and scared for my life. Because of a man I fell in love with.

Life had a funny way of saying, "Hey, this is not what you wanted for yourself, is it?"

As I slipped my clothes off and climbed into the tub, I couldn't help but feel strange that I was taking a bath in Beth's birth mom's bathroom. But when I immersed myself in the lavender scented water, I felt some of the stress float away, and I welcomed the relaxation that started to take over.

❖

JACKIE

The cursor on the page blinked at me. I only needed six thousand words. That wasn't a lot of words. I could bang that out so fast, like Tabitha said the night before. But these six thousand words had to be great. It was a turning point in the novel, and if it fell flat, the entire book would fall flat, and I could not do that. Especially after my last book was such a hit. I couldn't follow it up with a stinking pile of poo.

I stretched out my legs on the couch and tried to get comfortable. I was out of my element. Normally, I would write in the bedroom Susan was staying in. But I felt so rude marching in there and taking over my space. I pushed my laptop to the side and leaned my head against the cushions. As I closed my eyes, I felt a nudge and then a weight come jumping onto my lap. My eyes flew open, and Myrtle was standing there looking at me. Her floppy ears perked, and her nubby tail was wagging. "What?" I said, and the dog whined. I tentatively reached forward and ran my hand over her head. She nuzzled my hand with her snout and started to turn in circles before she lay down on my lap and promptly started snoring. "How the hell am I supposed to write with you on my lap?" She didn't move. At all. She was dead weight. "Jesus."

I never wanted an animal. Never. Not even when I was a kid. But this dog…

"She's warming up to you, I see."

I looked up at Susan standing in my white, terry-cloth robe, the sash pulled tight, with a towel wrapped around her head. I had never seen anything so heartbreaking in my entire life. She was so gorgeous yet *broken*, and it made my stomach bottom out. "Yeah," I said. "I think she wanted some attention."

"She is definitely a brat when it comes to that."

I could not stop looking at her. And I was trying to pull my eyes from her and focus on something else, the dog, my computer, the bare wall, *anything but her.* But I was transfixed by how serene she looked, even with that bruise across the soft skin of her cheek. I didn't think I'd ever be able to smell lavender again without thinking about her, naked, in my tub. I knew my constant stare was more than likely creeping her out; she kept changing her stance. "How was the bath?" I finally managed to ask. I felt like an asshole. Not only was she super fragile right now, but she was so not interested in me. And there I was, staring like a horny teenager. I was disgusting.

She gathered the robe with her left hand and sat on the arm of the chair. "It was exactly what the doctor ordered."

Myrtle picked her head up, realized her mom was back in the room, and jumped down to go sit by her. I stood and walked over to Susan; her eyes were glued to me as I approached. "May I?"

I motioned to her bruise, and she whispered, "Yes."

I bent down, studied the purple area, and reached out with an unsteady hand to touch the edge along her cheek. I had to stop myself from sliding my hand to the back of her neck and making her forget all about the heartache she was going through. *Wrong time, wrong place, Jackie.* But dammit, she was breathtaking. How had I lived my entire life and never experienced this kind of beauty? "I have this comfrey salve that I bought at an herbal remedy store in downtown St. Pete. It might help if you want to try it. I put it on my volleyball bruises."

Susan's face was only inches from mine, so when she smiled at me, the sight made my breath catch. "You play volleyball?"

I composed myself by clearing my throat. "Yeah. Beach volleyball."

"When do you play?"

"Sundays. In Gulfport, this little town about fifteen minutes from here."

It was Susan's turn to stare, apparently, because I could feel her gaze raking over me as I stood. "We'll have to come watch you play," she said, and even though she wasn't smiling, I swear I could hear it in her voice.

"Yeah. That'd be cool." *Cool?* Could I really not think of a better word than *cool?* I started to walk away from her when all of a sudden, I felt her hand latch on to mine. She pulled gently until I turned and looked back at her. I could barely feel my hand, though, and only knew she was still holding on because it was all I could look at.

"You have no idea how much this means to me, Jackie."

When I finally raised my gaze, her eyes were so, so dark. I found myself getting lost in them but knew I had to stay grounded. Especially right now. "It's really not a problem."

"You keep," she started and, *Jesus, she is still holding my hand,* "saying that, but…" She paused again, and my knees were weak as I looked into her eyes. "But I don't think I could do this alone."

I felt myself reaching toward her face again. I traced her jawline lightly, and dammit, during any other moment, it would have been so fucking *smooth* of me. But right then and there, I knew I charged over every boundary that could ever exist. I didn't care, though. I couldn't stop myself. And she didn't flinch or move away. (Maybe she even leaned into my touch.) "You're so much stronger than you realize," I said as my fingers lingered half a second longer under her chin.

"You barely know me," Susan whispered, but she gripped my hand a little tighter.

"You're right." *I barely know her.* How many days had it been since I first laid eyes on her? Three? Five? A week? I couldn't remember the exact amount of time, but I felt as if I had known her for years. "I know for sure that you raised the only person in my life that I ever regretted leaving. And you did it with so much love and kindness that it shows in every single movement Beth makes, in every word she speaks, and in every single line that she draws. And that?" I took a breath, studied how her full lips came together so perfectly. "That is enough for me to know you."

The look on her face was unmistakable as she loosened her grip and let go. I had said way too much, way too soon. And fear and confusion were written all over her face. If I had a dollar for every time I'd said too much to a woman that wasn't ready for it, I'd be a wealthy woman.

I smiled, shrugged, then turned and walked into my bedroom where I shut the door behind me and collapsed against it. *Fuck fuck fuck.* Why did I always put my big fat foot into my mouth when it came to women I actually liked? Especially this one! She was straight! And going through a messy split with an abusive husband. Why would I cross that line? Why would I even *consider* ever crossing that line? If I could've punched myself in the nose, I would have.

There were so many things I needed to learn. Not about being a lesbian because that part was pretty self-explanatory for me. More about being a human being. I often stepped on toes, said things I shouldn't have, and generally didn't care what people thought or expected from me. This entire situation was testing me. And I was failing. Horribly.

❖

After I calmed down, which took what felt like forever, I decided to show my face again. I cracked open the door and smelled something coming from the kitchen. I crept through the hallway and poked my head around the corner. Beth was standing next to Susan at the stove. There were a couple cans of tomato sauce on the counter next to a bag of tortellini and a box of spaghetti. I smiled at Myrtle when she picked her head up from the tile floor and looked at me. Her cute face was really starting to grow on me, as well as her shaggy ears. She stood as soon as she saw me smile and pranced over, her entire body wagging with her butt.

"Well, someone sure warmed up to the dog," Beth said as I reached down and mussed the fur on Myrtle's head.

I glanced up at Beth. "Only because she's cute."

"I feel like you say that about a lot of girls," Beth joked. Susan's mouth was hanging open as she gaped at Beth, who did a double take at her mom. "What?"

"It's fine," I said, and Susan kept her eyes averted. I wasn't going to lie and say it didn't sting when she wouldn't make eye contact because God, it really hurt. But I understood. I needed to watch myself. I had been an out lesbian for a long time, and I knew who I could cross lines with and who I couldn't and shouldn't. Susan obviously was not okay with it, so it was time to put that wall up and not let my façade break again.

"You're sure?" Susan asked.

"Yes. I can take a joke. As long as I can joke about how bad her feet smell from being in those Vans without socks."

Beth let out a gasp. "Are you serious? My feet do not stink!"

"Um," I started as I held my nose. "You might want to reevaluate that." I heard Susan's low chuckle. It was odd how the sound of her being happy made the event from earlier all but disappear. "So, whose idea was this?"

"I know it's weird, but I found this awesome food kiosk. The older lady running it said she made all the pasta from scratch. I sampled a couple different things and bought a bag of the tortellini. I thought I'd make dinner, and Mom wanted to help." Beth looked at me. Her face held so much hope and happiness.

"Well, I'm super excited for dinner then," I said. I hoped Susan would turn and look at me, but she still hadn't dared to look my way. What was I going to do? How were we going to stay in the same living space for however long without even glancing at each other? I was getting angrier and angrier with myself for letting the stupid, hopeless-romantic asshole part of me get in the way. I really needed to remember that life was not a romance novel, and rarely did it ever play out like one.

I studied the two of them as they moved in the kitchen. They clearly cooked together many times because Susan never asked for the spices as Beth handed them to her. It was really wonderful to watch. It was also really strange at the same time. I never thought I'd be in this spot, watching this unfold in front of me, but there I was.

Beth was growing on me, too. I was starting to love all of my observations of her, how she acted with Susan, how she held herself, how she seemed so sure of herself. Throughout the years, there was not a single bone in my body that didn't question my decision to give her up. But knowing she was in good hands the entire time made me feel almost okay about it. I could finally take a breath I had been holding for sixteen years.

Not to mention the fact that her relationship with Susan was adorable to watch.

Adorable?

Shit. I was already in way over my head. I needed to get my act together and quick. There was no way that I could pine after my biological daughter's mom. That could not happen. At all. What the hell was wrong with me, and why did I always put myself in these stupid, unwinnable situations? This was not an opportunity to tell a story, to write a best-selling book, to get more fans. My skin crawled at the thought of it. Even if something were to happen, I did not want to hurt Susan any more than she already was.

At this rate, I was going to be the one getting hurt.

"Jackie?"

My head jerked toward the sound of my name. "Huh?"

"Geez, where were you?" Beth asked with a smile that could only mean she thought she had an idea, but there was no way she was even in the vicinity.

"How was sightseeing?" I was trying to deter her. Hopefully, it worked.

"It was great. I think we should go to dinner down there one night." Beth shrugged. "It'd be nice for us all to get out of the house."

I saw Susan's spine straighten and her shoulders tense. Beth didn't notice because she was draining the spaghetti into a colander in the sink. "Yeah, I think that'd be good for you and your mom to do that. I can hang back. Watch the dog."

Beth glanced at me. "I meant you, too."

"That's super nice of you, Beth. Seriously. But I think it'd be cool for you and your mom to go."

Beth was glaring at me now. "Are you avoiding us?"

"No!" I lied. "Not at all!"

"Beth," Susan finally interjected. "It'd be nice to spend some time together. You and me."

And there was the confirmation I needed. I'd really freaked her out. *Fuck.*

"But Mom, I want Jackie to go—"

"I'll be fine. I live here. I can go whenever." I watched as Beth's shoulders slumped, then Susan's eyes flitted from the spaghetti sauce to Beth and then to my eyes for one second, two seconds, before she was looking back at the sauce.

"Fine. Then you and I will go one night without Mom."

"That's fine with me," I said softly. I was so mad at myself for being so dumb that now everything we did would be done separately. Oh, well. It was going to be fine. I needed to spend time with Beth solo anyway. Regardless of Susan's newfound contempt for me, I still wanted to be part of Beth's life. I was going to make the most of it, no matter what.

CHAPTER SEVEN

SUSAN

Steven and I used to say maybe six words to each other every day, and they were always in front of Beth. I was adamant that she never knew that we were unhappy. And according to her reaction to finding everything out, my plan had worked. I wasn't necessarily proud of myself for hiding my unhappiness. Especially since every word I said to Beth always stemmed from encouraging her to find happiness, her true north. To not ever let other people bring her down a notch, to stand firm, laugh, and above all else, love herself.

I was such a fucking hypocrite.

I raised a pretty amazing daughter. Ninety percent of the time, she had her head on straight. She was a great student, loved art and drawing, and had a knack for memorizing movie quotes. She loved binge watching televisions shows on Netflix and listening to her music way too loud on school nights while Steven and I were trying to sleep. Beth was a typical high school student.

Except that she wasn't. At all. She was adopted at two days old and was everything I ever wanted. She was an answered prayer, a blessing, an angel sent from Heaven. Every cliché I could think of, Beth was it. And the moment she was handed over to me and I cradled her in my arms, I was in love with her. Her so soft skin, her baby-gray eyes, the little birthmark on her thigh. Literally everything about her I loved. I even loved the month-long bout with colic, the discovery of her inability to drink regular milk, and her allergic reaction to eating a strawberry for the first time.

All of those reasons and signs and answered prayers were the only reason I agreed to let Beth drive us to St. Pete on her learner's permit. She had me gripping the door handle more than once, and she asked me to please be quiet at least six times, but we survived. She did say when we got out of the car outside of Jackie's complex that she would never drive with me again, but I knew she was being dramatic.

We accomplished running away from Steven together, and I wanted us to not ever be in that kind of situation again. It was horrifying that the two people in her life who were supposed to protect her didn't speak or get along. So, being in the same predicament with Jackie was infuriating. I was furious with myself, with Jackie, and with the entire situation.

Why did Jackie have to be so goddamn nice to me? I didn't want or need that right now. In fact, I wanted someone to tell me I was overreacting, that Steven was fine, that I deserved everything that happened to me because I did not want to live a life of solitude. I wanted Beth to have a father, a male figure in her life who cared and loved her.

I adjusted my sunglasses as my sneakers hit the sidewalk. I needed to get out of the condo and get some air. Beth was still asleep, so I pulled on a pair of shorts, slipped on my shoes, and took off. I needed to get away from Jackie and her stupid face. I was so mad at her for making me feel uncomfortable. Why did she have to go and ruin the nice and easy comradery we were establishing? Why did she have to go and be so…so…*wonderful*?

The gulf breeze blew through my hair, and I regretted not bringing a ponytail holder to pull it back. It was getting long enough that I could get it out of my face if I needed to, but it didn't look ridiculous. Now it was going to look like a giant puffball because of the wind and humidity.

The humidity. Another reason we should have never left Savannah. I should have stayed with Veronica and found a way to get Steven out of the house without being afraid of him.

A shudder ran through my body when I thought about him and saw his hand in slow motion coming toward my face.

What am I thinking? Leaving was the right decision. Protecting myself, protecting Beth, was the right decision. Staying with Jackie was the right decision. Wasn't it? It had to be because I couldn't put Beth through leaving, taking off to some other place to hide out. Running was never something I advocated, so this was a big step for me. It was going to be real difficult staying with Jackie, though if she continued to be...*attracted* to me. If that was even what it was. I had no idea. I was pretty naïve when it came to understanding matters of the heart. Hell, I'd spent the last however many years of my life making sure nothing intimate ever happened with Steven. So, I could have been completely wrong about Jackie. She was just a nice person. Her touching my chin and jaw with her delicate fingers, and looking at me with her beautiful eyes, and smiling at me with that breathtaking smile did not necessarily mean she was attracted to me.

But what if it did mean that?

Not to brag, ever, but I was not ugly. I had nice skin, and deep-set eyes, and my lips were full, and I had a decent body, even if it was a little soft after eating my way through the last few years of depression. I kept myself together, though, and I held myself well. So, someone who was attracted to women could possibly be attracted to me. It wasn't out of the realm of possibilities. Even with the remnants of the humiliating bruise.

Of course, running away from Steven was not supposed to include any of this. I didn't have the mental or emotional stability to deal with all of these feelings, on her end or mine. I didn't sign up for that. And I certainly didn't sign up for the way it made me feel when I did catch her studying me. Or the way it made me feel when I grabbed her hand, and she looked at me with that amazing eye contact she had. Or the way I felt when I closed my eyes in her bathtub and thought about her in there with other another woman, washing her back, her hair, her breasts...

My breasts.

Jesus. Christ.

Another shudder ran through me, but it felt entirely different than the first one. What the hell was she doing to me? She had me thinking and questioning, and I did not want to do any of those things. Not now. Not ever.

I breathed in deep and peered into the distance. There were a couple people out exercising but not as many as I expected at this early hour. I found a spot to sit on the beach, right off the sidewalk. The sun was getting higher and higher. The moon was still up, too, which was always such a strange phenomenon to me. Even in the brightest of times, darkness was always there, lurking…

When I propped myself up and soaked in the morning sun, I heard someone approaching in the sand. The person was running, so I opened my eyes to make sure he or she wasn't going to run into me. My stomach sank when I saw blond hair in a ponytail swaying back and forth. *Jackie.* And of course, she had tiny spandex shorts on and only a sports bra with no shirt. Her body was ridiculous. *Of fucking course it is.*

She slowed when she approached and took her earbuds out of her ears. She nodded at me, and I closed my eyes, ignoring her completely. I heard her let out a huff as she continued past. The coast was not clear, though, as I opened my eyes and saw her in my peripheral vision.

"Is this how it's going to be now?"

I didn't answer.

"Seriously? You're not going to answer me?"

"What do you want me to say, Jackie?"

"At least acknowledge my presence. This has all been hard on *me*, too."

"How? How in the world could this be hard on *you*?"

Jackie let out a laugh that caused my heart to shoot into my throat. "You're joking, right?"

She was still out of breath, and it was driving me crazy in a way I wasn't prepared for, but I really didn't want to talk to her about this. Not now. Not ever. And especially not when she wasn't wearing a shirt.

"I know this is insanely difficult for you, Susan. Believe me. And even though I don't know you that well, it's really hard to see you like this."

"It's not like you've ever seen me any other way." My voice was low. I could barely hear myself above the sound of the waves.

"So? That's supposed to make your sadness okay?" She was using her hands to talk. I hadn't noticed until now that she had a thick silver ring on her middle finger. Why was I noticing that? "I know I overstepped some boundaries. I know I did. But I have boundaries, too, and you and Beth sort of flew right past those without permission and without any fucking remorse."

"Are you serious right now?" I was pissed. "You think I wanted to come *here*? For you to see me like this? For you to see that the woman that has your kid is a fucking mess?"

Jackie took a breath and held it. Her abs flexed. I couldn't look at anything else. I hated myself in that moment. I was staring at her as if I wanted to rip her clothes off. "Susan," she said softly. She took a step toward me, and for reasons that had everything to do with my past and Steven and nothing to do with her and her wonderfulness, it made me flinch. She stopped immediately, and her face softened, and if we were closer emotionally, I would have apologized. I bit my lip, stared at her, and hoped maybe telepathically she heard my apology, because I couldn't find the words to actually say I was sorry. She held her hands up in surrender. "You're stronger than you realize," she said and pulled her shoulders back so she was standing tall. "And I know that all of this with Steven has really thrown you."

"You know *nothing*." Those words hurt her. Maybe even more than my inability to control a flinch when backed into a corner. I could see it in her eyes and the way her sweat-covered face fell.

"Why are you so mad at me? I literally asked for none of this!" She threw her hands in the air and looked around. "I never asked to meet Beth. I never asked to meet *you*! And I certainly never asked to share my simple life and home with either of you." She pointed at me. "You think you're the only one that's going through a lot of shit right now? Well, you aren't. You don't get to have the monopoly on feelings."

"The *monopoly* on feelings?" She was out of her mind! I stood quickly, probably too fast because I felt a little lightheaded. I spun around and followed her as she walked away from me. "You have some nerve. You act like *I* wanted this. Do you think I wanted to be in an abusive relationship? Or that I wanted to come here? Of all places? I never wanted to meet you! Or find out how much you fucking look like *my* daughter. I never wanted *her* to meet *you*! I never wanted to worry that you're better than me or cooler than me or goddammit, prettier than me. So, fuck you!"

Jackie stopped in her tracks, hands on her hips, and turned around to face me. We were only inches away from each other. "Prettier than you? Are you kidding me right now?"

I folded my arms across my chest and squared my jaw and shoulders so she knew I meant business.

"You are serious, aren't you?"

I still didn't respond, but yes, I was serious. I was very serious. And it sickened me to know that when faced with all of this, deep down, the real reason for my inability to handle whatever was happening with Jackie was vanity. I was a psychologist, for Christ's sake. I should have known myself better than that.

"Susan," she said quietly, and her voice cracked. "Do you even realize that the first time I saw you, it took my breath away?" She tilted her head as she continued to look at me. Her eyes were lovely even when sad.

My heart was in my throat, and I could barely feel my legs. Was I still lightheaded from getting up too quick?

"Do you even understand how much I want to tell you that you deserve someone who would never hurt you or hit you, someone who would take care of you and Beth forever?" Jackie breathed in, and I could see the muscles in her neck tighten as she held the breath for one beat, two, before she slowly let it out. "I don't *want* to freak you out. I want you to feel safe. So, I'm sorry that you feel all that you're feeling because I never meant for any of this to happen." I wanted to reach out and touch her hand and tell her that I was so sorry and so stupid and an awful human being, but I couldn't. Every muscle in my body was paralyzed. I watched her eyes, how they roamed my facial features before she turned and headed in the direction of the condo. My heart was beating so hard. I reached up to my face and realized that I was actually crying. What the hell was going on with me?

And why was I still watching her walk away? Why did I even care if she was hurt or sad or crying?

I turned and looked out at the water, at the waves crashing onto the shore, at the blue sky. I could feel the warmth from the sun as it crept higher. This was one of the most calming spots on Earth, and here I was wound tight as a snare drum.

I glanced back in the direction that Jackie walked and saw that she had started running and was way past the condo.

God, I really messed up.

❖

BETH

Four days.

Four *whole* days.

I had been in St. Pete for four days now, and I wasn't supposed to text my friends. I wasn't allowed to call them. I was supposed to stay *hidden.*

Well, I was going freaking crazy!

Not because I was bored or didn't like it in St. Pete. I was enjoying the salt, sand, and sun. But there were only so many things I could draw and paint, so many books I could read, so much music I could listen to, before I wanted to post something on Facebook or FaceTime my friends. And to top it off, I was sunburned from falling asleep on the beach yesterday. I was so mad at myself. I even put sunscreen on. *SPF 50, my ass.*

There was this tension in the condo, too, that I couldn't put my finger on. Mom and Jackie both denied it, but I felt it in the air. I didn't know why they both acted as if I was a child. It was obvious Jackie was not used to sharing her space, but she was being really patient. At least as patient as a person could be who wasn't used to having to be patient. I only heard her get super frustrated once, and it was because

Myrtle had an accident in the hallway, and Jackie, unfortunately but hilariously, found it with her bare feet. I heard a "Oh, for fuck's sake" and a "Myrtle, you're lucky you're so fucking cute!" and a lot of groans and gags. It was only pee, but Jackie acted as if it was the most disgusting thing she'd ever cleaned up. And I rushed to help her, of course, because Myrtle, according to Mom, was my responsibility.

Walking her became my job. Mom didn't take any interest whatsoever in going with or helping, which wasn't like her at all. But twice in the morning hours and four to five times throughout the day, I'd grab my longboard and head down to the sidewalk that connected the condo buildings along the beach. I didn't mind it so much because it got me out of the enclosed space. And Myrtle was getting so good at pulling me while I was on my longboard that it really was a lot of fun.

I sat on a bench lining the sidewalk, and Myrtle jumped up next to me. She was getting antsy, so I knew I needed to head back soon, but being trapped in the condo was not something I could handle right now.

There were people all up and down the sidewalk. Runners, walkers, roller-bladers, you name it, they were there. *I should take up roller-blading.* It looked like something I could handle. I needed to do something to stay in decent shape, too. Sitting around eating Starbursts and Oreos was doing nothing good for my love handles.

As that thought passed through my head, a flock of seagulls flew past. Myrtle's ears perked, and before I knew it, she took off after them, her leash dragging behind her.

"Myrtle!" I shouted, but she was not listening. "Myrtle!" Still nothing as I ran to catch up with her. Dammit, she was fast!

I saw her approaching a group of people, and one of them saw me chasing Myrtle. A girl stepped out and said, "Here, puppy!" and thank God, she actually listened!

I ran up to them, panting, covered in sand, and smiled. "Thank you so much," I said as the girl handed over Myrtle's leash. She was going crazy still, even though that particular flock was long gone.

The girl laughed. "No problem at all. I heard you yelling and figured you needed a hand."

"Um, yeah, she doesn't listen when she catches a scent. Must be the hunting dog in her or something." I pushed the loose hairs that had fallen out of my ponytail away from my face and looked at the girl. She was tall and slender with this super dark red hair. She had a purple streak toward the front of the part down the middle. And she had a small piercing in the right side of her nose. She looked like the epitome of *cool*.

"I'm Peggy," she said as she reached out her hand. "Well, Margaret, but everyone calls me Peggy."

I took her hand. "I'm Beth. It's nice to meet you."

She winked when we shook hands. "You're not from around here, are you?"

"No." I looked out at the water, then back at her. The group of people she was with were getting curious. "I'm from Savannah."

"Well, welcome to St. Pete."

"Thanks."

"Pegs, who is that?" The boy who asked came walking over. He didn't have a shirt on, and maybe for the first time ever, I couldn't take my eyes off his muscles. "And who is this?" He asked as he bent down and started petting Myrtle.

"This is Beth," Peggy answered. "I think I heard her yelling for 'Myrtle.' Is that correct?"

I smiled and nodded. "Yes, that's right."

The boy looked up at me; his brown hair was long, but it was pulled back into a messy bun. He had a closely trimmed beard, and I was absolutely sure that they both were at least twenty-five. "Hello there, Beth," he said, and when he smiled, I felt it in my knees.

"Hey," I replied. I felt like such an idiot.

"I'm Brock." He motioned behind him. "These are the rest of the guys. They're not important."

I giggled. I honest to God *giggled*. What the hell was wrong with me?

Peggy rolled her eyes. "He's the charmer of the group. Don't worry. I won't let him get to you on your first day." She nudged him with her hip while he was bent down, and he lost his balance and fell to the sand. She laughed as he gasped, and I couldn't help but join in. "How old are you, Beth? You look like pretty young."

"I guess that's a compliment?" I shrugged. "I'm sixteen. I'll be seventeen in about three months."

"Oh, wow, that's how old I am. Well, seventeen. I'll be eighteen in a few weeks. Brock here is eternally fifteen. No age identification required."

"Fuck off, Pegs," Brock said with a deep voice when he finally stopped brushing the sand from his muscles. "I'll be eighteen at the end of May."

"End of June for me."

"How long are you going to be in town?" Brock asked. He grinned at me, and my entire body flushed with heat.

I looked at Peggy first, and she was still smiling, so I hoped this wasn't her boyfriend or something that I would eventually find out about and be disappointed. "I'm not really sure," I answered. "At least through the end of this week."

"Great!" Peggy smiled. "You can come see us perform at the Rusty Nail tomorrow night."

"She probably has plans already, Pegs. It's Saturday night." Brock smiled. *God. His smile...* "I mean, do you?"

"I do not have plans." Did I? *Shit.* I would cancel whatever Mom or Jackie thought I had to do with them. That was for sure.

"Then you can come!" Peggy put her hand on my shoulder and squeezed. "I can come get you if you want? Or you can bring whomever you want. It's an all-ages show. Whatever you want to do." She reached out. She had a tattoo of a cardinal on the underside of her forearm. "Give me your cell, and I'll put my number in it."

"Put my number in it, too," Brock whispered as he leaned into Peggy's space.

She rolled her eyes again but was still smiling. The more Peggy spoke, the more I realized how pretty she was. Her purple streak was growing on me, too. "Okay. We're both in there." She handed my phone back and then added, "I texted myself from there, so I have your number, too."

"That's cool." I smiled. "It was really great running into you guys. I was going kind of stir crazy."

"Oh, geez, I've been there." Peggy laughed. Her voice and laugh were so smooth. Like beach glass would sound. "Where are you staying?"

I pointed to Jackie's complex. Her eyes went wide. "That's a sweet complex. Must have some money."

"Oh, no, it's my—" I stopped. What was she? She wasn't my mom. "It's my, um," I paused again. "Jackie."

"Your Jackie?"

I shook my head. "It's a long story."

"Maybe you'll tell me one day," Peggy said softly. The lift of her voice at the end of her sentence was so hopeful that it made my stomach flip. I couldn't help but nod. The smile she gave me was beautiful.

"C'mon, Pegs, we gotta go," Brock said as he nudged her. "Beth, we'll see you tomorrow, right?"

"Yes, absolutely," I replied. I watched as Brock threw his arm over Peggy's shoulders as they walked away. I literally had no idea what to make of them. Were they a couple or not? I hoped not.

When I got back to the condo, Jackie was on the balcony, and Mom was nowhere to be found. Myrtle sprinted over to Jackie and jumped into her lap. I watched and chuckled to myself when Jackie finally started petting her, and she promptly curled into a ball on her lap. I knew Jackie would eventually warm up to her.

I found Mom in her bedroom reading a book. She put it down when I leaned against the door frame. "How was the walk?" she asked. Her voice sounded different. Not worse but different.

"It was really good. I actually met some people on the beach. They're my age. They want me to go to a show tomorrow night. I think a couple of them are in a band."

The grin that stretched across my mom's lips was incredible. "That is so great, honey. I am so happy for you."

"Yeah, I'm super excited." I pushed off the door frame. "I'm going to go get a snack. Do you need anything?" I watched as she contemplated it, then shook her head. After grabbing a banana and

LaCroix from the fridge, I walked out onto the balcony and Jackie looked at me, one eyebrow raised.

"According to what you see here, it would appear that I like dogs." She had her hand on Myrtle's body, and she smoothed it across her fur a couple times. "You would be wrong to believe that."

I started to laugh. "Oh, really?"

"Yes, really," she replied. The twinkle in her eyes said otherwise.

When I sat next to her on the outdoor couch and propped my feet on the ottoman, I noticed we both had our legs crossed left over right. Little things that we did the same made me feel good, validated, as if she really was supposed to be in my life and I in hers. Of course, then I noticed the Band-Aid on her knee. "What the hell happened?" I pointed to it.

"I fell on my run this morning."

"You fell? How old are you? Six?"

"Shut up," Jackie said with a laugh. "I'm a klutz, okay? Don't judge me."

I laughed. "That's so weird."

"Why? People are klutzes all the time!"

"Oh, I know. I mean because I am, too. Why do you think I don't play sports?"

"But you ride that damn longboard."

"Do you know how many times I've fallen off?" I bent my leg and showed off the numerous scars. "Oh, and the pièce de résistance," I said with a smile when I leaned forward and hiked up my tank top. "Do you see that scar?" Jackie's fingers landed on my skin. It was the first motherly touch I had felt from her, and it gave me chills.

"What the hell happened, Beth? It's six inches long." Her voice sounded truly concerned.

I leaned back onto the couch cushions and shrugged. "A half pipe trick that went horribly wrong. I had a concussion, sixty-five stitches, and a mom who wouldn't let me ride my skateboard for three months."

"I'd have been the same way. That's dangerous."

"So, should I ban you from running then?" I smiled at her when I leaned my head back on the cushion. She glanced at me and did a double take. Then she looked back out at the gulf. Her profile was so perfect. Like, come on. How did someone so beautiful have a kid that was so not?

Jackie laughed. "I should ban myself. Or not run when I'm upset."

"Why are you upset? What happened?"

I listened to her take a deep breath and say, "Sigh."

I laughed. "Sigh, eh?"

"Yes. Sigh."

"Not gonna tell me what happened?"

"No."

I reached over and rubbed Myrtle's head. She opened her eyes briefly before promptly dozing off again. "Little Myrtle loves you."

"Yeah, well, whatever. She's okay, I guess. For a dog." Jackie smiled after her words, so I knew she was joking.

"So," I said, knowing there was a need for a subject change. "What do you know about the Rusty Nail?"

"It's a gay bar downtown. I haven't been in ages. But they have open mic nights and all-ages shows. At least they used to. Why?"

A gay bar? *What*? "Oh, okay."

"Hello? Why?"

"I met a couple people on the beach. They were my age, and they're doing a show tomorrow night there. They invited me to go."

"Hey, that's awesome! It's a really cool spot." Jackie must have sensed the confusion on my face. "Which one of them did you think was cute?"

"The guy." I didn't even bother beating around the bush. "I mean, the girl was pretty, too, but…"

Jackie reached over and put her hand on my shoulder. "Rule number one: just because they're playing at a gay bar does not mean they're gay."

"Okay."

"It *could* mean that, though."

"*Great*."

"You'll be able to tell."

"Um. How?"

Jackie laughed. "Do you need me to go with you?"

I kind of wanted her to go. Was that weird? "Kind of?"

"I'll go with you." Jackie looked away from me. "Are you inviting your mom?"

I sighed. Did I have to? "I guess. Will she even want to go?"

"She might. It'd get her out of the house. Her bruise can be covered up with makeup now." Her eyes looked so sad, though.

"What happened between the two of you?" I asked, and the way Jackie's head snapped toward me and the look displayed on her face made me think that something really big happened.

"Nothing. Why?"

"You're a horrible liar."

Jackie reached up and pushed her hair out of her face. She didn't have it pulled back at all, but even wild and wavy it looked good. "Nothing happened." She paused and glanced at me. "I think I overstepped my boundaries, though."

"Oh, God, Jackie, what'd you do?"

"I didn't *do* anything. I told her that I think she's stronger than she realizes."

"Well, that's not bad at all." I was confused. "I thought you were going to say you tried to kiss her or something, and I was going to be like, 'um, Jackie, she's straight.'" The forced laughter that came out of Jackie's mouth was unmistakable. I raised an eyebrow. "Jackie?"

"I don't like your mom like that, kiddo," she reassured me. Or was she trying to convince herself of that? I had no idea.

"Okay."

"I don't. I promise."

"I wouldn't be mad at you if you did, you know?"

Jackie froze. I think I stunned her into silence.

"I wouldn't. She's beautiful, and she's kind, and she still has a pretty awesome body. I mean, I don't check out my mom, but I'd kill for boobs as big as hers." Jackie chuckled at me. "Well? I would! But I don't think she swings that way. It'd be dumb to even try."

"For sure," Jackie replied with a voice that sounded way weaker than I think she meant. She looked away from me and cleared her throat. "So, the Rusty Nail?" I could hear the smile in her voice. "I've had some good times there."

"Oh, *really*?" I asked as I leaned forward and looked back at her. She was grinning like an idiot. "Do tell!"

"Absolutely not!"

We both laughed, and I sat back and leaned into her. "So, this guy's name is Brock."

"Brock?"

"Yes. It sounds gay, doesn't it?"

Jackie raised a bottle of beer I didn't know she was drinking, and her eyebrows lifted before she drank.

"That was enough of an answer."

"Hey," she said, and she pointed her beer bottle toward the gulf. "A lot of people have thought I was straight. And I'm not. Don't judge a book by its cover."

"True. You look very straight."

"Exactly. I guess?"

I laughed when Jackie furrowed her brow and then shrugged. "Actually, I think him and this Peggy girl are together."

"Ooo, Peggy?" Jackie smiled at me. "My main character in my next book is named Margaret."

"That might be a sign! Maybe she's the gay one!"

Another laugh spilled from Jackie's mouth. "That could definitely be it."

I laid my head on Jackie's shoulder and breathed in deep. "Thank you so much, Jackie."

"Stop thanking me," she whispered, and then I felt her kiss the top of my head. It felt so good. It brought tears to my eyes. I didn't think Myrtle was the only one Jackie was warming up to.

❖

JACKIE

Everything about that day totally sucked. Every single thing. From me not being able to catch my breath on my run to the way

Susan talked to me to the way I stumbled, tripped, fell, and scraped my fucking knee on the way back to my condo. It all sucked.

Even the shower I took sucked. My knee was *killing* me. The scrape wasn't really that bad, but I thought I actually sprained it, which pissed me off because I'd have to take some time off from running and playing volleyball: my two biggest stress relievers. Well, masturbating, but I was not going to touch myself with them only a few hundred feet away from my bedroom. No way!

I wiped the condensation from the mirror and peered at my reflection. I looked horrible. The last remnants of my tan had finally faded earlier in the month, so all I had now were the leftover freckles along my shoulders and the bridge of my nose. I hated those stupid freckles. I did have a slight tan line from my sports bra, but that was it. I needed some sun, and I needed it fast.

But that wasn't going to happen while they were here.

God.

They.

Dammit.

What was I going to do? I could not handle these feelings for Susan any longer. I clearly needed to fuck them away with someone else. *Maybe I should call Dana?* While she wasn't necessarily the perfect option, she was most definitely a sure thing and one hell of a distraction. I could go to her apartment, and I could push her up against a wall and get my fingers inside her, and she could bury her face into my wetness, and it would be *perfect*. There was nothing better than making Susan come.

Dana! Not Susan! Fuck!

My brain was already replacing fantasies with a picture of Susan's face. That was not good. Not good at all.

I pulled the towel from my hair and let the wet locks fall to my shoulders. I ran my fingers through them and found some product to hopefully keep the frizz at bay. Of course, it was Aveda.

Which made me think of Dana. And then, of course, Susan. Kissing Susan. Making her forget everythi—

I rolled my eyes at myself in the mirror. Yep, I needed to get laid.

I quickly dried off, threw on a pair of khaki shorts and a tank top. No bra. I didn't have time for a bra. I sprayed myself with perfume and didn't even put makeup on. My hair would dry in the car with the wind.

❖

The drive to Dana's was much faster than normal. No traffic and yeah, I sped. So what? I didn't get pulled over, and I didn't even see a cop. Good thing, though, because my breasts were out of control in the tank top I had pulled on. Why was I so driven in that moment?

After I climbed the stairs to her apartment, I raised my hand to knock on her door, and I froze. It suddenly occurred to me that she might have someone else over. My stomach started to twist. How was I going to explain myself in my current, haphazardly dressed state? She was going to know. Or at least have some sort of idea.

"Fuck it," I mumbled as I knocked. It took her a little bit longer than normal, but then again, she had no idea I was coming over.

The door swung open, and there she stood in short shorts and a baggy T-shirt. Her hair was an absolute mess. I smiled and shrugged, and she returned the gesture. "Did you finish your book?"

"Um, no."

"But you're clearly wanting a distraction," she said as she motioned to my clothes. "Are you not?"

I didn't know what came over me, aside from the need to get Susan out of my system, but I clenched my fists and lunged at her. I somehow managed to get the door closed behind me, but as I pushed her back into the wall by the door, I heard her moan into my mouth, and I felt the way it reverberated against my tongue and *holy fucking shit*, it was so hot.

Her hands were up under my tank top and on my bare breasts before I even realized what she was doing. She pulled away from me and looked into my eyes. "What's wrong?"

"What are you talking about?" I asked.

"You're kissing me weird."

"No, I'm not. Everything's fine."

"Okay," she said softly, and she leaned forward to kiss me again. And that was when I knew what she meant. Because the second her lips hit mine again, all I saw was Susan. Her lips, her tongue, her hands on my breasts, her voice in my ear saying my name. I tried to push the vision out of my head, but I couldn't get her to leave.

I pulled away from Dana and took a step back. "I'm sorry," I whispered.

"What is going on, Jacks? Am I doing something wrong?"

Her question broke my heart. "Oh God, Dana, no. You're absolutely amazing. As always."

Dana reached out and ran her fingertips down my arm to my hand. "What's going on then? You're stressed beyond belief." She pulled on my hand, and I followed her to the couch in the living room. She sat and patted the spot next to her. "Let's destress you."

"This isn't the kind of destressing I had in mind."

"It's obviously what you need, though, because those were not our normal, searing hot kisses."

I leaned my head back against the couch cushion and sighed. "Beth and her mom are at my condo right now."

"Excuse me?"

"Yeah. And you know how much I like sharing my space with people."

"I'm shocked you didn't put them in a hotel."

"I know, right? I'm on edge and have literally no way of releasing the stress." I rolled my eyes and sighed.

"Not fair," Dana said. She smiled at me. "I'd relieve that stress for you, but you're the one that's kissing all weird. Not me."

"Whatever."

"So, why are they here?"

How did I even begin? "It's a long story. A long and *bizarre* story. Especially with Susan."

"And that's Beth's mom?"

"Yes." When I swallowed, I noticed a lump in my throat.

"So, are you really *only* stressed about them being there?"

I kept my eyes closed, nodded, and hoped she couldn't see right through me. As a writer, you'd think I'd know how to tell a decent lie, but damn, I was horrible at it.

"I don't believe that at all," Dana said as she nudged me with her knee. See? Horrible liar.

"Her mom." I sighed after I admitted that there was more.

"You like her, don't you?"

I didn't need to answer because Dana would know the answer by my body language. Years of being casual lovers meant she knew me like the back of her hand.

She touched my jaw muscle that was flexed from my clenching. "Oh, honey. That's not gonna turn out the way you want it to, you know that, right?"

"I know."

"Jackie, baby, she's *straight*. You have got to stop doing that to yourself. Straight women are not going to make a lifestyle change to be with you like they do in your books. Haven't you learned that yet?"

"I have. I've learned it."

"Have you, though?" Dana's lips pursed, and she reached forward and pushed my hair away from my face. "You're too amazing to keep doing this to yourself."

"You're only saying that because you want to fuck right now."

She laughed that sexy laugh that always got under my skin. "You're damn right I do. But..." She stopped, leaned forward, and kissed me. It was deep, but it was missing that passion we always had. When she pulled away, she looked at me, a small smile on her lips. "But not until that kiss is fixed."

"Oh, come on. You're not going to help me out here?" I was whining, but I didn't care. I would beg if I needed to.

"Look. I love our little arrangement. Okay? It's basically stress-free." She stopped talking and sighed. I knew "basically stress-free" meant that she wanted more. and I didn't. "But the other thing I love is that I do not have to fight for your attention when we are together. Ever. You focus when you fuck me. And I love that."

I could hear in her voice that it wasn't going to happen. Even if I did beg. I should have been happy that she was being strong. I had been trying so hard to distance myself from her, to let her find love with someone who could give it to her, and now she was doing exactly what I wanted her to do. I needed to be fine. "Okay," I said quietly.

"You caught me on a bad day, anyway."

"Why? Period?"

"No, I haven't shaved in like a week and a half."

I faked a gasp. "My God!"

"I know!" We laughed together as she leaned next to me on the couch. She pulled me closer and started to play with my hair when I put my head in her lap. "You're going to get your heart broken by this woman. You know that, right?"

I closed my eyes. "I know. I already really freaked her out," I said as I started the story from earlier. She listened, offered some advice, and didn't sound like a judgmental bitch, even though I'm sure it was hard for her.

When Dana walked me to the door, we stopped and she kissed me once more. "Go home and get those in a bra," she said as she pointed to my breasts.

I started to laugh when I pulled her into a hug. "I love you, Dana."

"I love you, too, Jacks. Now get out of here."

I felt her watching as I left, but I didn't look back. On the drive home, I made a promise to myself that I was going to work on not feeling anything about Susan. Her and Beth were surely going to leave soon and head back to Savannah. I didn't need any of this. I didn't need the heartache or the distraction from my current book. I was feeling really good about the talk I had with Dana. I knew what I needed to do and how I needed to do it. So, when I walked into the condo and neither Beth nor Susan were in the living room, I thanked God. Being faced with immediately putting my plan into action was a different story.

❖

When I entered the kitchen and walked over to the fridge, I heard a throat clear behind me. *Please be Beth.*

"Can we talk?"

Fuck. It's Susan. I took a deep breath as I grabbed a beer and popped it open before turning around. She looked absolutely stunning. The bruise was fading nicely, and the light blue button-down she had on with her tight, dark jeans was, for some reason, sexy as hell. Maybe it was that she hadn't buttoned the first couple of buttons, and the skin exposed looked so soft.

Whelp, my plan was already failing. I was so turned on from earlier that seeing her like that in front of me was doing things to my body I couldn't control. My nipples were hard, and if her eyes traveled a little lower, she would notice.

"What do you want to talk about?" I asked after I drank from the beer. *Stay cool, Jackie. Stay cool.*

"Earlier."

"There's really no need." It hurt so bad to say that because this was what I wanted. I wanted to talk about it. I wanted her to apologize and rush into my arms, and I'd carry her to the bedroom and we'd—

Do nothing because she was straight! I really needed to start remembering that.

"Jackie—"

"No, you said what you needed to say. It's fine." I pushed away from the counter and breezed past her into my bedroom. "We're good." I turned and shut the door in her face. The pain in my chest could only mean one thing: I was not enjoying any of this at all. I still had my hand on the doorknob when I felt it turn and her push it open. I stumbled from the force and stared. "W…wh…what are you doing? You can't burst into my room."

"I'm sorry," she said quickly.

Her chest under the blue shirt was rising and falling with every breath she took. My eyes locked on to hers, and I got so lost in the dark brown that I almost dropped the beer onto the cold, tile floor. She licked her lips and broke our gaze when she looked down at her hands. My eyes landed back on her breasts, which, from this vantage point, I could see her cleavage.

"I don't know why I said all of that. I didn't mean it." Her voice was so soft, so serene. It made my palms start to sweat. "You have done nothing wrong, and you don't deserve to be treated like that. You were right, too. You didn't ask for any of this. We showed up here. We interrupted your life. So, I'm sorry. I really am."

I eyed her as she spoke. Was there a catch? I wasn't sure. "Susan," I started, but when she looked up at me, I lost my thought. "Do you have makeup on?"

"I want you to go out with me."

This time, I felt the bottle slip right out of my hands and gasped when I heard it crash against the tile. The alcohol spewed everywhere, but miraculously, the bottle didn't break. "Oh, fuck!" I started laughing, and then she started laughing, and then I couldn't stop. "I need a towel!" I ran into the bathroom and grabbed one. When I turned around, Susan was in the doorway, beer-soaked and smiling. I walked up to her and dabbed at the beer on her face and neck. Her shirt had splatters all over it, too. "I'm so sorry. I don't know what came over me."

"It's okay," she said and when she pushed a breath out, I could hear the shakiness behind it.

"Are you okay?"

She nodded. My eyes locked on hers when she said softly, "Your eyes are so green."

"Susan..." I barely said her name. My entire body was aching. What was I supposed to do now? I had a plan, dammit. And now that plan was being derailed by quite possibly the most amazing woman I had ever been around and her stupid apology that was so heartfelt. And she was looking at me like *that*, with those eyes and that hair and *sweet Jesus* those full, pink lips. If she didn't move soon, I was going to kiss her. That was going to be a disaster.

I mean...*wasn't it?*

"Let's get this cleaned up. And go out. You and me."

I cleared my throat. "You're not going to kill me and leave me for dead, are you?" I was a dramatic person. I knew this. I knew I embellished things a lot. I was a writer! I was supposed to embellish. But I swore on everything good and holy that when she raised her perfectly sculpted eyebrows at me, my stomach literally did a somersault.

She let out a small laugh, followed by a *pfft.* "That's not the idea I had, no."

When Susan turned, I took a chance and grabbed her wrist like she had done to me only days earlier. "What did you have in mind then?" I asked after she looked down at my hand and then back up into my eyes. I could not handle how adorable our height difference was. She was a good three inches shorter than me. The only thing I could think about was how easily I could pick her up and fuck her up against the wall. My entire mind was in the gutter along with my body.

"I'll tell you. One day." She motioned toward the mess in my bedroom and said, "C'mon."

And I did exactly as she said. Because I was stupid and smitten. Or was I stupid and horny? Maybe I was all of those things? Who knew? I knew that if she kept this charade up, I was unequivocally going to crack. And it was either going to be the best decision ever... Or the worst.

CHAPTER EIGHT

SUSAN

I didn't know what had gotten into me. I thought it was seeing Jackie running full speed away from me that made me hate myself for being so stupid around her. I also thought it was because I didn't know how to handle whatever I had been feeling about her. I was not an idiot. At least I liked to think I wasn't. Clearly, she was attracted to me. I was not trying to toot my own horn by saying that. I mean it was pretty obvious. The worst part about it all was that I knew she was attracted to me the second we met, and it didn't bother me at all. I had been stared at before. I'd been undressed by someone else's gaze. Normally, I was completely okay with it, too, because who the hell didn't like to be looked at and admired? It was getting to know her, understanding who she was, where she came from, how much she resembled my daughter and how similar they were that really started to wear on me. Maybe wrapping my brain around the entire situation was what freaked me out. It wasn't that she was a woman or Beth's biological mother. It was that I really started to like her. I started to realize why my breath would catch, why my hands ached, why my stomach flipped when she looked at me. It wasn't nerves or my sadness and depression playing tricks on me. It was my heart coming back to life after lying dormant for such a long time.

I'd never considered that I could possibly be bisexual. It'd never been a thought that crept into my mind, even though Veronica was a lesbian. I'd met all of her friends, been invited to their gatherings, and never once did I feel a twinge of anything toward any of those women. But Jackie... I didn't know how to really describe what went on in my body when she would look at me. My heart had never clenched in my chest before like it did around her. My knees and thighs trembled, my mouth went dry, and my palms would turn clammy, all from the thought of her eyes or her hands or her lips. All of those feelings were new for me. It was as if I was a teenager realizing things about my body for the first time.

It worried me slightly because my body never responded to Steven like that. Ever. There was only one way my body responded to him, and that was with fear. Even the sight of his name in a text message from Veronica made my skin crawl. He had finally given up the hunt to magically find Beth and me holed up in her house. She wondered if maybe he had a screw loose but said after the fifth interrogation, he got the picture. I prayed he didn't move on to my other friends but knew that was a pipe dream. Hopefully he wouldn't be too ridiculous... I wanted to warn them all, but how did I do that without telling them where I was?

My life was slowly becoming a made-for-TV-movie on Lifetime, and there was nothing I could do to stop it.

Not only did I have a crazy, abusive husband who I was finally finding the courage to leave, but I was also feeling things for my adopted daughter's biological mom. Hell, would anyone even watch if it were made into a movie? I thought not. Too much drama.

None of it made sense, and I was trying my hardest to answer questions about why it happened, why me, why, why, why? But the only answer that seemed suitable was maybe this was where my life was supposed to go. Everything happened for a reason, and all of this was in my future. Including the intense connection to Jackie I had, which could only be because of Beth.

Unless I really was bisexual, which really wasn't that big of a deal. I was open and honest and never judged other people in my life. Most of the things I saw throughout my career conditioned me to have an open mind. But for some reason, I couldn't really wrap my mind around me possibly liking the same sex in more than a friendly way.

Maybe because I spent so much of my life with men that the idea of being attracted, sexually, to a woman, made me think I really didn't know anything about myself. It was dramatic to go to that extreme, but how could I have not known this when I usually felt so sure about who I was as a person, as a psychologist, and especially as a woman. Every feeling I ever felt never confused me as much as my feelings about Jackie were confusing me.

At the end of the day, it didn't matter why I was feeling my feelings, even though I was obsessing about them like crazy. I wanted to put this awkwardness to bed.

Well, not directly to bed.

That saying sounded way more appropriate in my head.

Either way, I knew I had two options: continue to be a raging bitch, which wasn't nearly as easy as one would think; or throw caution to the wind and figure myself out. Maybe flirt a little. See where things went.

And when I finally could say to myself that yes, I wanted to make mad, passionate love to Jackie, I would put *that* to bed.

When I saw her breeze out of her room while I was waiting nervously on the couch, I thought my realization was closer than I anticipated. Her makeup was simple, a little mascara, some eyeshadow, and maybe blush. But damn. The sight of her made it hard to breathe. What did that mean? Why was that happening to me?

I hoped I looked okay standing next to her. I decided to change my beer-soaked shirt and swapped it out with a white button-down. I didn't bring all that many clothes with me. At least not enough to get all dressed up. I also threw on a pair of skinny black pants. Barely eating anything since everything went down made the pants fit a little looser than normal, but they were still tight enough that they showed off the curve of my backside. And I had to admit that my butt was pretty nice. Everything else was slightly out of control. Being depressed for years and eating my feelings definitely hadn't helped matters. Of course, not eating while being depressed wasn't the healthiest option, either.

Jackie was wearing a black wrap-dress that had large colorful flowers all over it. Her blond hair was pulled up and away from her face into a messy bun. She looked like the epitome of a Floridian. A tan in March, a floral dress, and sandals. I was so taken by the sight that I literally had to remind myself to breathe. Especially because seeing her in a dress was so not what I expected.

I couldn't even get started on how good she smelled. Like honeysuckle. And fabric softener. The entire elevator car smelled like her. My brain was short circuiting. We barely said anything to each other as we waited. I was sure it was due to nerves. I knew it was on my part, but why was Jackie so nervous? She was so perfect. So. *Very.* Perfect. I was so enamored as I glanced over at her when we finally got into her car. I noticed for the first time that she had the cartilage at the top of her ear pierced.

"Do you like tapas?" Her voice was smooth and so much softer than earlier.

"Yes," I said. "I do."

"Good." She put the car into drive, and we took off.

I kept my eyes glued to the passenger window, watching the palms pass by and the cute, beach-town shops. I was starting to see why people fell in love with St. Petersburg. The charm, the gulf, the breeze, sun, and sand. It was all really wonderful. I completely understood why she lived there.

Neither of us really said much, and that worried me a little. The radio was on, though, and it helped fill the silence. Her music reminded me of Beth, which made me smile. A lot of things about her made me smile. Like the way she drove, both hands on the wheel, her thumb tapping out the beat of the alternative rock song on the radio. She must have seen my amusement because she asked what I was smiling about.

"Your music. Beth listens to this." Jackie smiled back but didn't say anything.

Jackie pulled up to the restaurant and found a spot in the parking lot. The place was called Jones' Wine and Tapas, and it looked really cute from the outside. "My best friend's parents own this place." She glanced back at me as we walked up to the entrance. "So, be prepared for questions."

"Couldn't take me somewhere no one would know you, eh?"

Jackie laughed. "Oh, Susan, everyone knows me here. Famous author. Remember?"

The way her eyes sparkled when she said that made my knees almost buckle. When she opened the door and motioned for me to go in first, I smiled at her. "You think you're pretty funny, don't you?"

Another silky laugh spilled from her mouth when I walked past her into the restaurant. "You have no idea," she said softly from behind me.

The smell of garlic and wood and wine crashed into me. I instantly fell in love with the ambiance. The walls were covered with beautiful paintings. The bar was packed with people. They had a lot of beers on tap, which I loved seeing, even though I wasn't really a beer girl.

"Jacquelyn!" A large, round man shouted from the host stand. "Aren't you a sight for sore eyes!" He rushed around the stand and pulled Jackie into a hug, breathing heavy the entire time. "And who is this?" he asked when he released Jackie.

She smiled at him as she put her hand on my arm. "This is Susan."

"Well, she's beautiful." He held his hand out, and I took it. "I'm Jones. It's lovely to meet you."

"Jones, so nice to meet you, as well."

"This is your first time in St. Pete?"

"Actually, yes," I answered as he walked us to a table. The entire place was full, but Jackie clearly had pull. We had a great table with no wait, and we were facing the gulf. I was impressed.

Jones patted his belly before he said, "It's a beautiful city. You're going to love it here."

"You're right," I said with a smile. My eyes caught Jackie's before I looked back at him and finished with, "I already do love it."

"Well, good. Jacquelyn, you have a good dinner. Your server will be Michael tonight."

"Thank you so much, Jones. Tell Marie I said hello."

"She's bartending tonight, but if she has time, I'll tell her to come say hi!" he shouted as he waddled away.

I looked at Jackie and smiled. "You walk in and get sat with no wait?"

"That's how I roll," Jackie replied with a wink. "It's not like that everywhere I go, but certain places, yes. Especially here. Jones and Marie have been in my life for years. Tabitha is my best friend and their daughter. I went to college with her. So, I mean, I've known them for..." Her voice trailed off as she did the math in her head. "A long time," she finished and giggled. "I'm so *old*."

"Oh, please."

The server approached and immediately squealed with delight that Jackie was his guest. I watched her as she spoke to him, a skinny, young man named Michael. He was cute, flamboyant, and seemed to be good friends with Jackie. Was everyone here going to know her? She introduced me, and I shook his hand while he commented on how pretty I was. I didn't want to sound ungrateful, but was I really that pretty? Or were people here that nice?

I listened to her order for us, which I liked because I had absolutely no idea what to get. She asked me if I wanted red or white wine. I wanted white, so she picked a bottle of sauvignon blanc for us to share. Not having the pressure of trying to figure out what to eat and drink made it so relaxing. I was so calm. It was maybe the first time in months that my inner peace was present and accounted for. Listening to and watching Jackie was calming in a way I did not expect, especially because, up until now, she'd made me so nervous and unsure of myself that the word "calm" wasn't in my vocabulary.

"So, Jackie, tell me about the book that you're working on." I lifted my glass to my nose and breathed in deep. The smell was wonderful, floral and peach notes with a hint of grapefruit. I loved Marlborough Sauvignon Blanc, so I was thrilled. The sip I took was delightful, too. It was so smooth and delicious.

Jackie set her glass on the table, and her fingers slid down the length of the stem. Why did the thought of them sliding down my neck instantly make me wet? She shrugged and said, "It's not my best work. Another lesbian romance. I feel like I've told the story before, you know? Sometimes, I wonder if I should branch out."

"I'm sure there are a million different ways to tell the tale of two women falling in love. Right?" I asked before I took another drink. The way she looked at me from across the table… I couldn't stop myself from giving in the slightest to what I was feeling. How caring her eyes were, how beautiful her makeup was, how adorable her hair looked in that messy bun. Her arms were toned as she stretched one out over the back of the booth, and as my eyes traveled the length of her arm, I noticed she had a tattoo on the underside of her bicep. It was of a feather, plain black and skin-toned, but God, was it sexy. *Is the temperature in the restaurant a hundred degrees, or what?*

"I guess you're right," she finally replied. "The book is about these two women who find each other after a traumatic car crash involving one of the women's significant other. There's a heart transplant and a cute dog and a lot of things I know nothing about. I've had to research a lot of different topics."

"Sounds like you're getting some good research in now about cute dogs with Myrtle always near you."

Jackie laughed. "She really is a cute dog."

"Oh, trust me. I know."

"I'll make sure to include her in my acknowledgements."

"Oh, I'm sure she'll love that," I said as I leaned forward and propped an elbow on the table. "The book sounds really good, though."

"I hope it turns out okay. My deadline is in two weeks."

"Wow! Us being here is probably really screwing you up, isn't it?"

Jackie smiled. Her teeth were so straight and white. I knew she never had braces without having to ask because Beth's smile was the exact same. I was always slightly jealous but also grateful. Braces were expensive! "Not at all," she said before she looked down at her wineglass.

I let my eyes wander over her features, her nose, her cheeks, her perfect lips. "So, Jacquelyn, hmm? That's a pretty name." The deep red that filled her cheeks was so cute. Getting her to blush made me feel so good about myself.

"Yes, Jacquelyn." The look on her face was so intense.

"And your middle name?"

"Why? So, you can middle name me when you get mad at me?"

I started to laugh because I always middle-named Beth. "How would you even know that I do that?"

"I can tell."

"I promise I won't pull out your middle name if I'm ever mad at you."

Jackie's left eyebrow arched, and she said softly, "Mardine."

"Jacquelyn Mardine?" She nodded after I asked. "That's gorgeous. And so different."

"It was my grandmother's middle name."

"When did you start going by Jackie?"

"First grade." Jackie chuckled when she leaned forward and mimicked my posture. "My teacher Mrs. Nabhan called me Jackie all the time. It stuck. My mom always called me Jacquelyn, though."

The image of a young, towheaded Jackie running around made my heart so happy. "I'm sure you were adorable."

"What about you, Susan?"

The way Jackie said my name made chills erupt all over my arms and legs. "What about me?" I asked as I tried to hide any shred of evidence that she was having an immense effect on me. I sipped my wine and hoped my nervousness wasn't obvious.

"Do you have a middle name?"

"Isabel," I breathed. "Um, my middle name is Isabel." I quickly downed the last of my wine, and Michael was Johnny-on-the-spot filling my glass again. Whatever was happening to my body had seriously never happened before. I was on fire. My palms were sweating. My armpits were even sweating! I was a mess. "Y'know, Jackie, is it hot in here?"

The smile that stretched across her lips did not fucking help, either. "No," she said quietly. "It's not hot in here."

"Are you sure?" I asked as I picked up a menu and started to fan myself.

"I'm pretty sure."

I watched as she glanced around the restaurant. The line of her neck was incredible. She was literally the prettiest person I had ever been around in my entire life. I wasn't used to being around people like her, people who were so put together and *striking*. This was such a change of pace for me. That had to be it, right? It wasn't that I was having an issue with the slope of her bare shoulders or the delicate bones of her wrists or how soft her skin looked along her jawline. "I'm going to go use the restroom," I said as I slid my chair out a little too forcefully and stood. "I'll be right back." I took off toward where I hoped the bathrooms were. When I finally found the door that said "Gals" on it, I pushed through the door and into a stall. When I got it closed behind me, I rested my head against the cold, steel door. What the hell was going on with me? Was this...oh, God...was I falling for *Jackie*?

That couldn't be it.

No way.

No how.

I was not a lesbian! I couldn't be. I'd spent my entire life with men. And I loved being with a man! I loved sex with a man! So, why did I seem to be attracted to her?

Could I really be bisexual?

That was the only explanation, which still didn't help matters because why was I discovering this about myself now? So late in life? I wasn't sure if I wanted to have this revelation at this age.

Especially about Jackie *fucking* Mitchell.

Even though she was really gorgeous.

And she had such a wonderful heart.

And her eyes...

Fuck.

I opened the stall door and walked over to the sinks. I ran the cold water and cursed when only lukewarm poured out. I looked at my reflection in the mirror. My bruise was fading, but I could still see a small outline on my cheek peeking through my makeup. I leaned forward, looked at my eyes, at the wrinkles at the corners, at the appearance of the tiniest bit of gray hair that framed my face. Even if I was falling for Jackie, there was no possible way the feelings would ever be completely mutual. I was at least ten years older than her, if not more.

She was a nice person who was being wonderful to me. I had to keep reminding myself of that. Jackie didn't want to be with me. So, this falling for her bullshit? Or whatever the hell was going on with me? It was a passing phase. It had to be. Period.

After my mental pep talk and after I washed and dried my hands, I headed back to the table. Jackie was sitting there, her hands folded in her lap and a concerned expression on her face. "Are you okay?" she asked.

I waved her off. "Oh, yes. I'm so sorry. I think it was a hot flash." Oh, Jesus. *A hot flash*? My wrinkles and gray hairs weren't bad enough, now I was having *hot flashes*? Why didn't I put a sign on my forehead that read *I'm FIFTY.*

Jackie put her hands on the table and went to stand. "We can leave if you'd like."

"No way! I'm having an amazing time. I am totally fine. I promise."

She eyed me from her half-standing position. "You're sure?"

"I swear," I said softly when I finally sat. I took a deep breath and then took two large gulps of wine. I probably looked like a total lush, but I had to do something to calm myself down. The second I set my glass on the table, Michael swooped in to refill it. He winked at me before he switched and poured more wine into Jackie's glass. He certainly saw me getting blitzed. I hoped he wasn't doing it on purpose. Oh well if he was. At least I was feeling slightly calmer. I knew I needed to talk about something that would distract me, so I settled on, "Tell me about your friend Tabitha?"

I think she realized what I was doing by the look on her face and in her eyes, but she complied without hesitation. She launched into a story about knowing Tabitha for years and years, and how she was the only person in St. Pete who was there for her through everything. Tabitha sounded like a really great friend. I felt better for some reason knowing that Jackie had someone to count on.

The rest of our time together at the restaurant was much better. We focused on easy, back and forth banter with little to no emotion whatsoever while we shared a variety of tapas. I was much more comfortable with the small talk, and it seemed Jackie was, too. I think it was becoming more and more obvious that we were both struggling with something around each other. I'm sure she was only struggling with the fact that I was the one who adopted her daughter. It seemed logical that would possibly be hard to deal with. So, I understood completely. Of course, I really didn't know for sure if that was what was going on in Jackie's mind or not. It was clear that she was not the type of person to open up and talk. She did have really intense eye contact when she was looking at me… Could that mean what I thought it meant?

After our second bottle of wine and she paid the bill, which I fought her for, we decided to leave the restaurant. I think I drank most of the wine, and that worried me slightly, but what the hell? It felt really nice to relax, and my inhibitions were melting away.

Jackie said she was fine to drive, so I didn't argue. She seemed completely okay, and I was sure she was not nearly as drunk as I was starting to feel. I was nearing that *tipsy enough to not have an argumentative bone in my body* feeling.

Apparently, I was also tipsy enough that I needed a little assistance getting into Jackie's BMW. She helped me into the passenger seat without any audible judgment. Her hand was on my arm and her other was in my hand. I couldn't stop myself from noticing how soft her hands were. And she still smelled like that damned honeysuckle. I was impressed by the longevity of whatever perfume she wore. Mine never seemed to last more than a couple hours. When she reached over to help me buckle my seat belt, I noticed she had a small scar above her lip, right under her nose. I wondered how she got that. Was it a volleyball injury? Did she have an abusive person in her life like I did? The thought of someone hitting her made me queasy. How could anyone hit her? She was so amazing. And so pretty. "So very pretty." Oh, *shit.* I heard the words come out of my mouth before I even had a second to hit myself for thinking them, let alone saying them.

"Susan," Jackie breathed as she clicked the seat belt into place. She looked at me, and our faces were so close. "You had a lot to drink."

"That's Michael's fault." My words were slurring together. *Great.*

"I will let him take the blame."

"Were you going to take me anywhere else?"

"Not in this condition."

I laughed. "I'll be okay. I promise." Why didn't I let her take me back to the condo?

"Are you sure there, Ms. Slurry?"

I laughed, and it felt really good to actually mean it.

"Where would you like to go then?" Jackie squatted down beside the car and looked at me. Her hands were on my legs, her left hand on my thigh, right on my kneecap, and I could feel the heat radiating from them.

"The beach."

She looked directly into my eyes, into my soul, and my mind took off with itself. Would I ever recover from the way she was staring at me? Was I having an out-of-body experience? Unless it was the copious amounts of wine. She squeezed my leg lightly before she finally stood and closed my door. The four or five seconds that I was in the car by myself, I tried to breathe deep and snap out of my drunken stupor. Then her door opened, and she climbed in, followed by her scent, and I couldn't help but look over at her.

❖

JACKIE

Susan was borderline freaking out. I could tell. Or she was completely wasted. Either way, something weird was happening. But whatever it was, it was completely different than what had happened earlier in the week. This freak out was her figuring something out. I wasn't sure what she was figuring out, but I was about ninety percent sure she didn't know what to do with her feelings about me. I couldn't be one hundred percent because she kept taking two steps forward and then one back, but she was getting there. At least I wanted to think that was what was happening. Of course, I was a hopeless romantic.

I had no idea how *I* really felt about everything that was going on with Susan, though. Dana was right when she told me I deserved someone who wanted me from the get-go. Not someone I had to encourage to want me, like me, *love me*. So, I should have continued with my so-called plan to stay strong and not get mixed up with this woman who clearly had no idea what she was doing. Getting involved with a straight woman was like riding a downward spiral all the way to the bottom: no brakes, no exits, adrenaline and speed and a heart to break the fall. Why would I ever want to do that again?

When I pulled into a parking spot at my favorite beach and turned my car off, Susan let out a deep breath. I had no idea how long she had been holding it, but when I looked over at her, she looked absolutely terrified.

"You said the beach," I said calmly. "Would you rather go home?" She shook her head and reached for the door handle. I grabbed her other hand, and she finally looked at me. "Susan. We can go home."

"No," she whispered. "I want this."

I let out a huff. *Want what?* is what I wanted to ask, but I kept my mouth shut and exited my car. I walked around to the trunk and popped it open with the remote. I grabbed a blanket to spread on the sand and another in case we got cold. It was still spring, after all, and I knew it could get chilly with the breeze. I shut the trunk and walked over to where she was standing. "Ready?"

"Yes," she said firmly, so we started walking toward the beach. My feet were cold, but I didn't care. The desire to sit by her, wrapped in a blanket, was spurring me on. I knew it was so stupid, but I didn't care. I'd never understand why lesbians always got hooked on straight women. Was it because they were unattainable? Or that they seemed slightly interested at the time? Or was it their curiosity, and it really did kill the cat? Except this time, I was the cat.

We found a spot on the beach that was uninhabited. Typically, the beach closed at a certain time, but as long as we weren't acting like fools at the private beach where I took her, we could sit and not get in trouble. I laid the blanket on the ground and patted the spot next to me. Susan sat, and I saw a shiver shoot through her body. "Here," I said as I offered her the other blanket. I wrapped it around her shoulders, and she leaned gently into me.

"Thank you."

"Of course."

"You really know how to take good care of me," she commented, and I could tell she was smiling.

I kept my eyes glued to the water, the waves, the way the moon was sneaking through the clouds. I didn't respond because I didn't know what to say. I was being way nicer than normal for me, yes. In the beginning, it was all for Beth because I saw how sad and scared she was. But now? It wasn't only for Beth. It was for Susan, too, and I couldn't stop myself. She was so easy to take care of, to like, to want more from. It was frightening. I mean, what would happen when she and Beth left? What would happen to the start of my relationship with Beth, to whatever was happening between Susan and myself, to this weird little family unit we were creating? I'd be heartbroken, and they'd go back to Savannah. Maybe Susan would go back to Steven. Maybe not. But she wouldn't be sleeping in my bed next to me. That was for sure.

"Jackie?" I heard her say with a voice that sounded like silk. She was so close to me that I could feel her body heat through the blanket. I could feel her gentle intake and outtake of air. And when I looked at her, all I could see was how gorgeous she was. I wanted to touch her hair and bring her closer to me, press my lips into her full, dark red ones. I was not able to focus on anything but the curve of those lips and the way her tongue parted them and licked them lightly before she said, "I have had such an amazing night with you."

Her words had my heart clenching in my chest. "I'm really glad."

"When I first met you," she started, and I could smell the wine on her breath still. Why did that turn me on so much? "You were so… not what I had anticipated."

I let out a tiny chuckle. "You mean because you had no idea Beth had come to meet me?"

"Well, yeah, that but also…" She paused again and looked away from me. "Y'know, Beth asked me about you. Like, how I felt about you. And the only word I could come up with was that you were so unexpected. And even now, I feel the same way."

I shrugged. "I guess that's good. It'd be a real drag to be exactly how you pictured me."

"You are nothing at all how I pictured you." Her voice was so low and seductive. It sounded like sex and felt like honey, and I could barely handle it. How was I supposed to *not* kiss this woman?

"Is that good or bad?"

"It's scary," Susan responded after she looked at me in the moonlight. Her eyes were searching mine as if she was looking for answers, a lifeline, something, anything… But I didn't know what to say because I was also hoping for some sort of lifeline. "What is happening to me?" She asked, and her voice—her dear sweet, beautiful, sexy voice—cracked at the end, and it made my entire body shiver.

I couldn't respond. My voice was caught in my throat behind all of the emotion I was feeling, all the joy and happiness and fear. I waited one second, two, three, before I finally asked, "What do you mean?"

"I can't stop thinking about you," she said with more conviction than I imagined she'd have right now. "Ever since you said you knew me…and you touched me." She reached up to her face and ran her fingers along her jawline where I touched her only days earlier. "You ran your fingers right here. But," she stopped and turned more toward me, "but you touched me here." Her hand rested now on her heart and *goddammit*, I was crying. I could feel the tears sliding down my cheeks. I was so fucked.

"Susan," I whispered. "You don't have to do this. I am really okay with us only being Beth's moms."

"*I'm* not okay with us *only* being Beth's moms, though."

"You've had quite a bit to drink," I said. "You're tipsy and probably get super emotional when you drink. I mean, who doesn't, right?"

She smiled at me before she placed her hand on my cheek. She turned my face toward her. "I've never done this before." Her voice was so quiet I barely heard her.

"Never done what?" Even though I knew what her answer would be.

"Cheated on my husband?" she replied.

Maybe I didn't know the answer. "Susan, we haven't done anything wrong."

Susan smiled at me as she moved her hand from my face. When she reached down and took my hand in hers, I allowed her to pull it until she placed it on her heart. "Can you feel that?"

And I could. Her heart was beating so hard.

"You do that to me. Every time you look at me, talk to me, get near me…"

I could barely breathe. Was what I wanted really going to happen?

As I thought that, Susan's cell phone started to ring. She let out a breath as she let go of my hand and growled. "What the hell?" she said as she patted the pockets of her light jacket and pulled out her phone. "It's Beth."

"You need to answer it."

"Jackie—"

"We have time," I said softly as I picked her free hand up and brushed my lips against her knuckles. The look on her face made my stomach bottom out.

"Hello?" she said after she slid her finger across the screen and put it up to her ear. "Honey, we went to grab dinner. I left you a note." Susan was looking at me the entire time. "You were sleeping. I didn't want to wake you." I reached forward and moved her hair behind her ear, and she leaned her head into my touch. "No, what? I'm sorry. You broke up." I smiled at her and then turned her hand over and kissed her palm. "I know. We're okay, though. I promise…. I know." Her breath hitched in her throat when I pushed the sleeve of her jacket up slightly and kissed the soft underside of her wrist. "But we talked…. I guess you could say that we made out." I smiled against the palm of her hand and heard her breathe out a chuckle. "No, no, no! Made up! Not out. I said made up!" I glanced up at her, and she rolled her eyes while she held in her laughter. I bent my head back down and kissed her palm again. "Yeah, Jackie is a wonderful person." She moved her hand to my chin and tilted my head so I was looking at her. She smiled at me, and all I could think was that smile was going to be the death of me. "Yes, honey. We'll be home soon. No, we'll leave now and come home… Okay, I love you, too." When she hung up, she groaned. "I'm so sorry."

I chuckled at her exasperated voice. "That's what it's like having a kid, eh?"

She nodded while continuing to smile at me. "Can we press pause on this conversation?"

I rearranged myself on the blanket and knelt in front of her, leaned into her space, and kissed her on the forehead. "Of course." I felt her hand on my side, and even that gentle touch made chills shoot through me. "Let's go home." I stood, helped her up, and we both grabbed a blanket as we started toward the car. After we took about ten steps, I felt her get closer and then her hand as she intertwined it with mine. When I looked over at her as we trudged through the sand, her eyes locked with mine for the briefest of seconds. No words were exchanged, but for some reason, it was the most intimate moment that we'd had.

❖

BETH

So, my moms were out to dinner together. Like, in the world of really strange and fucked up things, that was near the top of the list. And it made absolutely no sense. Why would they be out together? There was really no need for them to be all chummy. I mean, them both being in my life now didn't mean they had to actually be in each other's lives. Or did it? I guess it kind of did mean that, didn't it? I was the one that thrust them both into this whole thing.

It seemed really crazy that they were out to dinner. I mean, like, six hours ago Jackie basically said she crossed a line and freaked my mom out, and now they were sharing a meal together? Like two actual adult human beings?

Something smelled really fishy.

Maybe they were fighting? Or maybe we were going to go back to Savannah? If Jackie really did freak my mom out, then maybe that was what was going on. I could totally see Mom being completely over all of this and throwing in the towel. Even though I would be so upset with her for giving in and giving up.

Man, I hoped none of that was the case. Aside from the fact that Mom should not go crawling back to Dad after everything he put her through, most of which I was still finding out about, I was actually enjoying it in St. Pete. Of course, I wasn't in school right now, and I had a couple new friend prospects on the horizon, so it wasn't a complete drag anymore. But still…I wasn't ready to leave whatever it was Jackie, Mom, and I were figuring out.

And I was really starting to like getting to know Jackie. We hadn't shared enough of our deepest and darkest secrets yet, but the conversations we did share were kind of meaningful in a weird, oddly sentimental way. The idea of having to stop all of that and hightail it back to smelly ol' Savannah was not appealing at all to me. I especially didn't want to see my dad anytime soon. That was for sure.

As I waited for Mom and Jackie to come home, I felt my cell phone vibrate. I picked it up and saw *Peggy* on the screen. I tapped the screen until I got to the message.

Hey… It was nice meeting you today.

I smiled at the message. And then another popped up—*It's Peggy, btw.*

I typed out, *I know who it is, you dork. You put your name in my phone, remember?*

Within seconds, she had sent back a smiley face emoji, and the rolling eyes one was next.

Brock liked meeting you, too. He hasn't shut up about it.

Oh, really? Well, you can tell him I thought he was cute.

Um. No. You can do that on your own. I am not passing messages.

I laughed. Wasn't that exactly what she was doing? *Okay, okay. I guess I'll text him.*

Peggy sent the rolling eyes emoji again, and again I laughed.

I'm looking forward to your show tomorrow, I said and waited while the response bubble flashed at me.

You are going to be impressed. At least, I hope you will be.

I will be.

The door to the condo opened, and Mom was the first person to come in, followed by Jackie. Myrtle went berserk and ran up to both of them, wagging her entire body the whole time. Mom looked amazing. She was in tight pants and a cute shirt, and Jackie was in a dress straight out of a magazine about Floridian lifestyles.

"So," I said, and they both jerked their heads up at the same exact time. "What is going on?" I motioned to both of them and their outfits. "You both look great."

"We went to dinner. That's all," Mom said hastily. I was not born yesterday. There was something behind that fast answer.

Jackie scooted behind my mom to get past her, and I saw the hand she placed on Mom's hip as she did so. "We were both hungry, and you were passed out, so we thought, what the hell?"

"Mm-hmm... Did you go to like, a nice place, or what? You're both really dressed up."

"This old thing?" Jackie looked down at her dress.

Mom laughed. "Beth, honey, if you think this is dressed up, I think I need to teach you a thing or two."

I couldn't see myself, but I was pretty sure the look I had on my face said I didn't believe a damn thing either of them was saying to me. "Where'd you go then?"

"A wine bar," Jackie shouted from the kitchen. She glided back with a glass of white wine for herself and a glass of water for my mom, who took it and smiled at her as if she handed her a million dollars.

"Thank you," Mom said, never taking her eyes off Jackie.

"What happened to you guys? You seem...*happy*." I glanced from Jackie to my mom and then back to Jackie. "Do you no longer hate each other?"

My mom gasped. "Beth! I never hated Jackie."

"And I never hated Susan," Jackie commented as she sat on the arm of the couch. "We did have a good conversation, though, if that's what you mean."

"Uh-huh." I looked at Mom, who was still looking at Jackie. They really must have been crazy if they thought I didn't realize something was going on. I had no idea what it could be.

"You should probably get to bed, Beth." Mom looked at her watch and then at me. "It's pretty late."

"It's eleven." I looked at her and saw her raise her left eyebrow at me. That was the *I mean business* eyebrow. "Fine," I said softly as I stood. "I let Myrtle out already." I watched her run toward Jackie and plop down next to where she was perched on the arm of the couch. "I guess she'll stay out here with you guys."

They both chuckled at the dog, who was now on her back letting Jackie rub her belly. So much for not liking dogs!

Mom was right behind me when I got to my room after cleaning up in the bathroom. Something was definitely up because she was all giddy and breathless. "What has gotten into you?" I asked as I got into bed and pulled the covers up. She smiled at me and shrugged. "Are you drunk?"

A small laugh that I hadn't heard in forever slipped from her mouth. "A little."

"Mom!" I laughed with her as she sat on the edge of the bed.

"Are you disappointed in me?"

"Oh my God, no. I am so happy you're not still sad."

"Well," she said as she smoothed her hand over the comforter. "I wouldn't say I'm not sad anymore… But I'm at least feeling a little better."

"Did something happen?" The look on her face was undeniable. Something happened, but what I couldn't tell.

"No, honey."

She was lying. I knew her lying face, and that was it. The way her mouth was slightly pouty, and she wouldn't look at me. I didn't meet her yesterday. "Well, I don't believe you." She gasped, but before she could verbally protest, I smiled and said, "I honestly like that you're smiling. And not thinking about Dad."

Mom finally looked at me, and *that* look? That was the look I trusted. And when she leaned down and kissed me on the cheek, I thought maybe we were going to make it. It was the first time that thought crossed my mind since we drove out of Savannah.

"Good night," Mom said when she stood and walked over to the door. "I love you, Beth."

"I love you, too, Mom."

When she closed the door and I knew she was far enough away that she wouldn't pop back in and scold me, I checked my phone. I tapped the screen until I got to the message from Peggy. I typed out *Hey* and waited to see if she would respond. I didn't get a response, but my phone did light up with a random number.

It's Brock.

My heart leapt into my throat. What the heck? How did he get my number? I thought the ball was in my court?

Pegs gave me your number. Finally. I made her.

I reached up to my mouth and realized I was smiling. What did I say? Did I answer? I didn't want to seem too eager. Maybe I should ignore him?

You must be sleeping.

I quickly typed out, *No. I'm awake,* and hit send.

Hey there. Are you excited for the show?

I was grinning like an idiot. *Yes. I am.*

You're going to love it. We rock. Hard.

I'm excited to hear.

Good. Get some sleep.

I put my phone down and stared at the ceiling. I couldn't believe it. Brock texted me. He actually went out of his way to get my number and text me. Holy fucking shit. Tomorrow night was going to be such a fun night.

❖

SUSAN

When I went to find Jackie, she was on the balcony with Myrtle. Clearly, Beth and I weren't the only ones enamored with Jackie Mitchell. "According to Beth, you aren't a fan of animals," I said as I walked into the fresh air. It was significantly warmer on her balcony than it was on the beach, and it felt nice. I sat next to her on the outdoor couch and welcomed Myrtle as she curled up in between us. She breathed out deep when I started to pet her.

"Well, Myrtle *is* kind of cute. So, I'm making an exception."

"She certainly likes you." I looked over at Jackie. "Can't say that I blame her." I felt accomplished once again when I noticed the pink in her cheeks. Was that twice in one night that I got her to blush?

"So…"

My heart was racing for some reason. It had to be the wine, or maybe it was the way she was looking at me from her position on the couch. She was still in her dress, but she had taken her hair out of the bun, and waves upon waves were cascading over her shoulder. "Yes?"

"I had a great time with you tonight." She wasn't smiling, but I could hear a hint of happiness in her voice. It was really nice, because Steven hadn't seemed happy about spending alone time with me in years.

Our eyes locked. It was hard to breathe around her sometimes. The way she looked at me was so intense, as if she was searching for answers to questions neither of us had even asked yet. I couldn't figure out how to handle it or how to handle these feelings that seemed to form at an alarming rate.

"Are you sure you're okay?"

She was being so perfect and so kind. I needed to put a lid on my dopey grin, or she would think I was a complete idiot. I was enjoying everything with her entirely too much, especially for a married woman who spent her entire life as a straight person. "Yes, I am." I shook my head and looked out toward the gulf. "It's been a long time since I let myself have fun."

"Oh, so you *did* have a good time with me? Me whom you apparently hate?"

I gasped and smacked her on the leg. She laughed when Myrtle picked her head up and looked at me and then her. "Sorry, Myrtle," I said softly. "I didn't mean to hit the woman you're falling in love with."

Jackie reached over and took my hand. "You realize that I'll be whatever you need me to be, right?"

Was I supposed to say *thanks* to something so wonderful? I looked at our hands, then over at her, and in that moment, I was completely speechless. I didn't want to say a thing and ruin this moment. The only thing I wanted was to kiss her. And that was not what I anticipated. Ever.

"I know you're hurting and scared and this," she said and motioned to herself and then me, "is not a priority. And it never will be if you aren't okay with whatever could happen."

I swallowed the lump in my throat. My mouth was so dry. "And what could happen?" My voice didn't even sound like mine. It was low and throaty, and did I sound *aroused*? How was that even me still?

"Susan, what do you want to happen?"

I bit the inside of my cheek.

"Do you even know?" she asked, still holding my hand, still tracing the life line on my palm, running her fingers along the tips of my short, manicured nails. It was so erotic. I could barely stand it.

"No," I said. "Yes? Maybe? I don't know."

"That's kind of what I figured."

"Jackie?"

"Hmm?"

"This is new for me. You know that, don't you?" I asked. She let go of my hand, leaned forward, and grabbed her wineglass. She took a sip, then swirled the remainder in the glass. I watched the way she held the stem. The need to feel those fingers on my skin again was becoming a desire I couldn't control.

"I know," she finally answered. "I don't know why I'm even entertaining this idea."

"Because you think I'm beautiful and sexy, and you want to show me what it's like to be taken care of?" I didn't know what had gotten into me. *Beautiful and sexy?* I was never this sure of myself. It must have been the wine. Or maybe it was Jackie's entire aura. Everything about her was as intoxicating as the wine, if not more so.

I saw her raise her eyebrows, then the corners of her perfect lips pulled upward. "Beautiful and sexy, eh?" She locked her eyes on mine. "I can't really argue with that."

"It's been a really long time since I've felt like this."

"Susan," she said, then sighed. "This morning you were—"

"A different person. I know."

"But you—"

"Didn't know how to handle whatever is going on inside me."

"Then what…" She sighed again. I was beginning to love those heavy breaths of air. "I don't even know."

"Happened?" I asked, and she scrunched her face and nodded. "Is it going to upset you if I say I honestly don't have an explanation?"

"Look," Jackie said. She turned more toward me. "I do not need this in my life. I don't need to be your experiment or your rebound. You are literally getting a divorce. From a man. Fuck." She leaned her head back and groaned at the ceiling of the balcony. "What the fuck am I doing?"

"Hey," I said softly, and she looked at me. Her eyes in the candlelight looked bluer in that moment, and I could tell she was near tears. "Do you want to do this?"

She nodded.

"You want to kiss me?"

She nodded again.

"Do you want to do more with me?"

"Um, yeah," she said and chuckled. "I want to do everything with you."

"I want that, too."

She reached forward and lightly traced my jawline like she had days before, and it did the same thing to me that it did then. I was seconds away from combustion. "You want to jump into bed with me?"

"Yes, actually, which is crazy to me. All of this is crazy to me. I wouldn't even know what to do."

"What do you like?"

"What do you mean?" I shrugged. "Like sexually?"

Jackie laughed. "Yes. Like, *sexually*," she said and leaned back against the armrest of the couch. She never took her eyes off me, though, which was such a turn on.

I didn't think anyone had ever asked me that question before. There had been men in my life before Steven. Quite a few actually. I wasn't exactly tame when I first stepped foot on the University of Georgia's campus. I grew up in Savannah, where everyone knew my name and my business, so college was brand new territory. And I made sure to sow my wild oats. I had no inhibitions and barely any responsibilities. I figured out that I liked everything, as long as I knew the person for more than one date. I was never a first date kind of girl. I tore my gaze away from Jackie and took a deep breath. *Should I tell her what I like? What I want in bed with her?* My heart was beating so hard and fast. "I love being undressed."

She rolled her eyes. "*After* that?"

"Honestly?"

She nodded.

I took a deep breath. *Tell her.* My eyes drifted over her face to her neck, to that soft hollow that I never realized I found so insanely attractive and to the rise and fall of her chest and the swell of her breasts. How could only looking at her fill me with such lust? "I want to be taken control of…conquered. I want…" I paused and took another deep breath. "I want to have an orgasm that I am not giving myself." I locked eyes with Jackie again as she licked her lips and adjusted her position.

"Never had them with Steven?"

"A couple times but nothing to write home about."

"Would you have really written home about that anyway?" Jackie asked, and we both descended into laughter.

"Good point."

"I think you're still drunk."

"I'm pretty sober now."

"I think wine does things to you, though. It's your kryptonite or something."

"I think *you* might be my kryptonite," I said, and the smile that spread across her lips looked delicious. All I wanted her to do was reach over, grab my face, and kiss me like I'd never been kissed before. I wanted her to take control of this entire evening and dominate me. I wanted her to be what I was so done being, which was *in control.*

"I'm your weakness then?" Her voice was breathy, and it made my entire body erupt in chills.

I nodded. "How weird is that?"

Jackie smiled, and it didn't quite reach her eyes. "We are not supposed to be feeling like this. You know this, right?"

"You mean in general or to protect Beth?"

"Both?" Jackie took a deep breath, and I felt my eyes drift to her cleavage without any coaxing from my brain. I bit my lip and tried to control myself.

"So, what do we do?"

"We need to figure that out." Jackie reached forward and put her fingers under my chin. "My eyes are up here."

It was absolutely my turn to blush. "My God, I'm a teenage boy."

"Yeah, you're still drunk."

"You're right." I sighed and pulled my eyes from her. "Let's take a breath."

Jackie took my hand in hers again and squeezed. "I have the patience of a saint."

Yeah, well, I didn't.

CHAPTER NINE

JACKIE

Beth was a hot mess and moody as hell. I wasn't sure if it was because of last night when we went to dinner without her or if it was because she was nervous about going to the the Rusty Nail. Either way, my first taste of hormonal teenage rage was not pretty.

"Y'know, you would never understand what I'm going through right now!"

I stopped in my tracks in the hallway and looked at Beth in the guest bathroom. "What the hell are you talking about? I go to get you a hairbrush and come back to you yelling at me?"

Beth held her hands up. Her hair was a mess, and she still wasn't completely dressed. We were supposed to leave in forty minutes. "Well, you're the one that's so fucking pretty. You probably don't even have to try!"

"Whoa there, missy." I walked toward her and put the brush down. "What is going on?"

"I..." Tears started to appear in her eyes, and I was frozen in place. What the hell was I supposed to do? "I feel so ugly. And Brock is so cute. And Peggy! Don't even get me started on how hot she is. I don't know what to wear. I can't get my hair to behave with this stupid humidity. I'm such a mess."

"First of all," I said and folded my arms across my chest. "Brock will think you're even more beautiful this time than he did the last time. He's not going to see all these things that you think are imperfections. You realize that, right?"

Beth shrugged.

"Well, I can guarantee that he'll see what I see."

"Which is what? A dumb teenager?"

I laughed. "No, although the case could be made for that. I mean that he'll see a beautiful young woman. Coming into her own. Figuring herself out. And seriously, come on. If nothing else, he'll be so excited that you actually showed up that it won't matter if you're wearing a burlap sack."

I saw a smile starting to form on Beth's lips.

"And another thing, why does it matter if this Peggy chick is hot? Is she interested in Brock?"

Beth's eyes found mine. Her eyes that were so *mine* that it was kind of hard to look at her sometimes. In that moment, it was like seeing myself as a teenager, and I did not want to relive those days. "I'm pretty sure she doesn't like him."

"Then?"

She shrugged.

Oh… "Do you like her, too?"

She shrugged again.

"Okay," I said and paused. I tried to gather all of the sage wisdom that I could. All the years of knowledge from trying to figure myself out. "Not knowing isn't necessarily a bad thing."

"It's not?"

"Heck no. Let's say you go to a restaurant, and you like two things on the menu. Wouldn't you want to order and try both? Who's to say you can't do that in this situation, too?"

"It's not that simple, Jackie," Beth mumbled with her head down.

I reached over and gently lifted her face with two fingers until she was looking at me. "It's only as complicated as you make it, my dear."

"Do you think it's weird that I might like her?"

"You're kidding me, right?"

Beth started to giggle.

"I mean, seriously? Do you honestly think *I*, a *lesbian,* would think it's weird that you might like a woman?"

She was still giggling.

"Come on!" We were both laughing now, and it felt *really* good. "Now, if you do happen to like her, or hell, if you end up liking them both, you need to remember to be yourself. Don't change who you are for anyone. Okay?"

"Okay."

"Now," I started as I put my hands on her arms and rubbed them lightly. "You have got to settle down. Let me help you with your hair. If it's anything like mine, I know exactly how to handle it."

Beth's mouth turned up into a small smile.

"And your clothes? It's not a fancy place. You need to chill out. Jeans, tank top, your Vans. That's the best part about it being at a gay bar. No one gives a fuck."

She nodded and wiped at her face.

"As for your makeup, I can help with that, too."

"Jackie?"

"What?"

"I'm sorry I yelled at you."

"You better be," I said, followed by a wink, and she snorted. "Now sit down and let me curl your hair."

Beth sat still as I put large curls in her hair with my curling iron. She told me about her past guy friends and how none of them ever worked out on a romantic level. I noticed how nervous she got when she said she absolutely knew she had a crush on her English teacher, Mrs. Samuels. I never wanted to be a mom, to have these conversations with my child, to see her struggle *or* flourish, but talking with Beth? Finding out about her eccentricities? Learning about the things that made her tick? It was incredible. She was flawless. And I could tell if I kept thinking about how wonderful it all felt, I would start crying.

Thankfully, Susan came home from walking Myrtle around the time we were almost done with the hair. She walked toward the bathroom and without missing a beat said, "Beth, you look absolutely beautiful!" She smiled and folded her arms across her chest as she leaned against the door frame. "I love it."

"It looks okay?"

Susan looked at me and smiled. "It looks so good. I'm impressed."

"Stand up and look." I finished loosening the curls, and she did as I instructed. When she looked in the mirror, she let out a gasp.

Beth turned her head from side to side, pushed a lock of hair behind her ear, and smiled at herself in the mirror. "Holy cow. I look really pretty!"

Susan and I both laughed with her. "Of course you do. I know what I'm doing! And I had good stuff to work with."

Beth turned toward me. "Thank you so much."

"Makeup!" I shouted, and she sat back down on the toilet and let me put blush and mascara on her. She looked fresh and clean, and I was proud of myself. And of her for letting me do it. "Go change. Hurry! We are leaving in ten minutes."

She sprinted out of the bathroom past her mom and into her room where she slammed the door. I glanced at Susan who was looking at me with a grin plastered on her face. She looked so carefree and relaxed in her skinny jeans and black shirt with three-quarter-length sleeves. "You are amazing," she said, her voice smooth. It made chill bumps appear on my arms.

"Nah. She was freaking out."

Susan reached out and lightly grabbed my wrist. "Take the compliment."

"Fine." I shrugged. "I'm amazing."

"There you go," she said as she pulled me into a hug. It was the most intimate contact we shared since the night before, and it made my knees weak.

When Beth's door flew open, Susan jerked away from me, and the abrupt interruption definitely got rid of my weak knees. It actually really hurt my feelings. I hated that I let it.

"Are you ready?" Susan asked, breathless. I wanted to roll my eyes at her, but it was hard to be upset when I understood.

"Yes. I'm ready. Are you sure you guys don't mind coming with?"

"Of course not," I answered as we walked to the door.

As we were leaving, Susan said, "If you decide to hang out afterward, we will get out of your hair." I glanced at her and wondered if she knew that us alone would mean something was going to happen.

"You'd let me hang out afterward?"

Susan looked at me and then at Beth. "Is that not okay?"

"Um, yeah, Mom, but I thought for sure you'd be like, 'It's a new town with new people that I don't trust.'"

I laughed, and Susan gasped. "What?" I asked after we got into the car. "It was a perfect imitation!"

"You two ganging up on me is not okay," Susan said as she looked at me and then back at Beth in the back seat. She giggled, and Susan shook her head. "You both think this is real funny, don't you?"

"Absolutely," Beth and I said in unison. It was so weird laughing and having a good time with my daughter. I always thought if I ever met her, it would hit me like a freight train. But I was wrong. It was hitting me gradually, like a summer rain shower that started slow and ended in a thunderstorm. I was afraid of how it would affect me as I got closer to Beth. Would I cry when they decided they were going to leave? Would I beg them to stay? Would I be okay if they didn't listen? I glanced at Susan in the passenger seat. She was softly singing along to The Lumineers on the radio, tapping out the beat with her fingers of the left hand on her jean-covered thigh. I knew right then and there that I wouldn't be okay. But how did this all happen to me? How did I go from *never gonna settle* to *please don't leave me*?

When we pulled up to the Rusty Nail, I glanced at Beth in the rearview mirror. She looked terrified. "Hey," I said, and she glanced up. Our eyes locked in the mirror. "You okay?"

She nodded.

Susan turned and looked back at her. "Is this boy really *that* cute?"

Beth shrugged but not before looking at my reflection again. "He's pretty cute."

"Let's go." I quickly changed the subject. "We're going to have trouble finding a seat. This place is packed." After we walked in, I scanned the seating area. There was one table open, and it was in the back. Beth shrugged when I motioned at it, and then I heard my name being shouted from near the stage. I peered across the crowd to see who it was until someone tackle-hugged me from behind. I was assaulted by a familiar scent. *Aveda.* Dammit. "Dana!" I shouted when I turned to face her, and she hugged me again.

"We're all over here! I didn't think you were coming tonight," she said over the music. She looked adorable. Her curly mass of hair was pulled away from her face for the first time in forever. Her eyes finally glanced over my shoulder and landed on Beth and Susan. "Oh."

"Yeah, um, I'm with them tonight."

"Hi," Beth said as she seemed to lose her nervousness and came to life. She held her hand out and stood between Dana and me. "And you are?"

"Beth, honey, don't be rude," Susan said with a raised voice. She smiled as she stepped forward and stood next to me. "Hi, I'm Susan. This rude millennial is Beth."

Dana looked at me, an eyebrow arched to her hairline, then she looked at Susan. "I'm Dana. I'm one of Jackie's friends. I didn't mean to interrupt."

"No, we would actually love to sit with you guys if you have room," Beth said. Her smile was huge. "I'm here to see a couple people that play in the band, and you all have great seats."

"I think we have room." Dana jerked her head toward their seats. "C'mon, let's go." I could tell that Dana was irritated and full of questions. I was praying she wouldn't turn into the territorial jealous lover I'd seen from her numerous times before.

When we approached the table, Tabitha jumped up and pumped her fists in the air. "You're here! This is awesome!" She awkwardly made her way around the table and lunged at me, pulling me into a giant bear hug. "My God, is that Susan? She's gorgeous," she whispered against my ear, and I couldn't help my smile.

"Yes," I answered, and she lifted me off the ground. When she set me down, she playfully pushed me out of the way and extended a hand to Beth. "So, you're the daughter?"

I knew Beth was opening up more and more. She was settling down around me, and she seemed to really enjoy the relationship we were building. But the smile that came to her lips when Tabitha knew who she was made my heart burst. I was so happy to see that she was actually proud that I shared that part of myself with someone. She took Tabitha's hand and shook it. "Yes, I'm Beth. You must be Tabitha?"

Tabitha winked at me as she held Beth's hand. "You talked about me? I'm so excited!"

"No, she snooped through my pictures," I said.

"Guilty," Beth said. She shrugged. "I mean, she leaves them out. Like, what am I supposed to do? *Not* look?"

"Exactly, you gotta look!"

I rolled my eyes at the two of them. "Whatever. You both suck."

Tabitha moved her line of sight to Susan and cleared her throat. "And you are Beth's younger friend?"

Susan tilted her head, shook it, and then smiled that megawatt smile that made my knees weak and my head woozy. "You are a charmer, aren't you?"

"I learn it all from Jacks," Tabitha said as she pulled Susan's outstretched hand and wrapped her arms around Susan's body. If I didn't know Tabitha so well, I would have been jealous. But she was turning on her charm to impress the newcomers.

"She uses my best material," I said over the house music that was bumping in the bar. Susan shook her head again and laughed. "What?"

Susan leaned into my space. Her breasts were pressed against me, and her body heat was radiating through her layer of clothing as well as the thin cotton tank top I was wearing. I watched as her eyes flitted from my eyes to my chest then back to my eyes again. "I feel like I haven't seen your best material yet." She raised an eyebrow, and the corner of her mouth turned upward. "Am I right?"

My mouth was dry, and my hands were trembling. How was she able to do that to me so easily? I was normally so cool, calm, and collected, but with her? She unnerved me. And I was liking it more and more as time went on.

"Hey, you two?"

"Yes?" I answered Tabitha while keeping my eyes glued to Susan's.

"Wanna sit down? Or do you two need to get a room?"

Susan's spine stiffened, and her demeanor changed drastically when the realization dawned on her that she was being so brazen with people only a few feet away from us. Her gaze broke from mine, and she glanced at Beth. Thankfully, she wasn't looking, but I saw the fear in Susan's eyes.

"Hey," I said softly when we finally sat. "Are you okay?"

Susan pursed her lips. "This is...too much."

"What is?"

"Us," she said, but she leaned into me, and it made my stomach clench. Her tone was far from freaked out.

"We don't have to do this. I can back off. I can be whatever you need me to be." She looked at the stage after I said that, and I looked at her profile, at her slender nose and her long eyelashes. Everything about Susan was so lovely. And all I wanted to do was let myself fall for her, heart, body, and soul. I was most of the way there already, but I was not about to let myself completely go until I knew I was what she wanted.

Or at least until I knew she wanted it so much that she couldn't say no.

I knew she was close... But not close enough.

❖

SUSAN

It seemed like the place for me to compose myself when it came to Jackie was always going to be in the bathroom wherever we were. Our visit to the Rusty Nail was no different. When I walked into the super-confined bathroom, I thanked God. The temperature was at least fifteen degrees cooler than the bar. I stared at myself in the mirror. There was hardly any purple visible through my makeup, but it was definitely still there. Steven's angry eyes flashed in my head, and I couldn't bear to look at myself any longer.

One of the two stall doors opened, and Jackie's friend Dana walked out. She smiled at me in my reflection as she turned on the faucet. She retrieved three pumps of soap and started to wash her hands. I didn't know if it was my brain's tendency to believe stereotypes, but I was so shocked by how pretty Jackie's friends were, especially Dana. Her hair was gorgeous, jet-black, long, and so curly. It made my hair look horrible in comparison. The second I met her, I started comparing myself to her. How stupid was that? Why was I jealous? I literally knew nothing about her. Except the daggers she shot at me from across the table as I sat next to Jackie and tried to keep my composure.

"Are you enjoying yourself?"

I looked at her again in the mirror. "Yeah, I am. Thank you."

"I don't mean tonight at the bar," Dana said. She faced me fully and leaned her hip against the sink. Her right leg crossed over her left, her arms folded across her chest, and everything about her stance was confrontational.

I couldn't back down from whatever was happening even though I knew I shouldn't engage. "Why don't you enlighten me then?"

"Don't play dumb with me. You know exactly what you're doing." She had a southern twang to her voice that I hadn't heard until that moment. Maybe it was the alcohol that brought it out or her anger. I didn't know. Either way, it made me dislike her even more because it sort of made her even cuter. "You're getting awfully cozy with Jacks."

Something came over me. I laughed. I actually *laughed*.

"What are you laughing at?"

"I'm sorry." I tried to purse my lips together to stop laughing, but I couldn't control it. I glanced around the bathroom and then back at Dana. I took a deep breath and still smiling said, "You have nothing to worry about."

"I'm not worried for my sake."

"Well, whoever's sake you're worrying for, you don't need to."

"Jackie's sake." Her face softened, and the way she was glaring at me changed. "I'm worried about Jackie."

I knew in that instant that my fear of Dana and my jealousy was warranted because that look? That was something other than friendship.

"She's fragile. Way more fragile than she seems."

"Why do you think I'm going to hurt her?"

"Because I know women like you. I know your whole 'broken' routine, and I know how a hopeless romantic like Jackie falls for it. Every. Single. Time." Dana cleared her throat when a guy walked into the bathroom. I did a double take. For half a second, I forgot I was in a unisex bathroom. Dana leaned forward slightly, almost into my personal space. Her skin was flawless. She wasn't wearing makeup, yet she still looked beautiful. I was starting to hate her. "Remember that when you decide this isn't want you want, you'll be hurting two people: Jackie *and* your daughter. Because I can tell by looking at Beth that she thinks Jacks is the best thing since sliced bread."

"So, what are you saying? Hmm? You act like I can control this. Like I'm asking for it."

Dana shrugged as she pushed off the sink and looked into the mirror. She smoothed her hands over her thin waist and then fixed her breasts in her bra. She was wearing tiny jean shorts and a white tank. Her body was perfect. "I'm saying you hurt her, and I'll kill you."

I swallowed.

"And don't think I can't. I went to culinary school. I know how to slice and dice with the best of them."

The door to the bathroom swung open, and Tabitha was standing in the doorway. Her short blond hair was so frizzy. She had been standing in the humidity for far too long. "Jesus, are you two coming or what?"

Dana walked out of the bathroom and left me standing at the sinks. Tabitha took a couple steps toward me. "You okay? You look like you've seen a ghost."

"Yes, I'm okay."

"Is Dana being a dick to you?"

"No, of course not."

Tabitha huffed and came closer. "Hey, whatever she said, don't listen to her. She's been in love with Jackie for years. And Jackie doesn't want a relationship with her."

So, I was right. "I had *no* idea."

Tabitha pulled her head back and narrowed her brown eyes. "Is that sarcasm? I think that's sarcasm."

I laughed and so did Tabitha. "It might be."

"Good," she said. She threw her arm over my shoulders and led me out of the bathroom. "There are three things you need to know about Jackie. One, she comes across as selfish, but that is an act. She cares and gives, even when she probably shouldn't. Two, she's an introvert. Always has been, even in college. Look at her. She's struggling so hardcore right now. All she wants is to go home and read or write." We stood by the bar where we had a perfect view of the table. Jackie's arms were crossed, and even though she was talking and laughing, she was sitting bolt upright, and her legs were crossed tight. "I've only seen her comfortable twice in the entire time I've known her." Tabitha turned and grabbed two shots that were delivered to her from the bartender. She handed one over to me. "Drink."

"What the hell is this?"

She grinned at me and raised her eyebrows. "It's a Wet Pussy."

"You're kidding me."

"I would never kid about wet pussies." We clinked the shot glasses together, and I threw my head back to take the shot. "Good, right?"

I shook my head, still smiling at her and said, "Actually, yeah. It's really good."

"Ah-ha! I knew you'd like a good wet pussy!" she shouted and clapped her hands together.

I leaned against the bar and looked back at Jackie. She was looking over at me, and that sight alone made my knees weak. "So, what's the third thing?"

"She is the epitome of a hopeless romantic."

I sighed. "Yeah, Dana said the same thing."

Tabitha grabbed two more shots from the bartender and handed one over to me. We clinked the glasses together and threw them back in unison. "It's not a bad thing," she said loudly. "It's a good thing. She'll shower you with affection, love you hard, probably fuck you harder—"

I gasped. "Tabitha!"

"Well? I'm being honest with you. Don't you want to be prepared for this? Because if you start this with her, she's not going to be fifty percent in. She'll be all the way in. All the time. She doesn't know how to half ass anything."

"Why are you all so sure something is going to happen?"

"My God," Tabitha said as she turned toward the bar and raised her hand for two more shots. "You act like I don't know everything about Jacks. Or about women. Look," she said and paused before she received the shots and handed me another one. I looked at it. I was getting inebriated quickly. This was not going to be good. "Jackie is far from a sure thing. But I'm telling you right now, I have only seen her look at one other person that way."

"And what way is that?"

"Like you could be her entire world," she said as she clinked her glass against mine. "*Salud*!"

Tabitha's confession made my heart clench. What was happening? This wasn't good… There was no way that I could go through with this. Could I? I was in no place emotionally to give myself entirely over to anyone else. Especially Jackie. Beth's biological mother. *What the hell?* How did this whole thing get so out of hand so fast? One minute I was firmly against everything to do with Jackie. I was against her hair, and her eyes, and the way she touched me and looked at me, and even the way she breathed. And then, a switch was flipped, and my heart was ready to plunge into her body and soul and not look back.

I set the empty shot glass on the bar top with shaky hands and took a deep breath. When I finally made myself look over at Jackie, I saw her toss her loose hair over her shoulder. She was leaning forward, engaged in conversation with some of her other friends that arrived.

Beth was conversing with Jackie's friends now, too: Janice, Jenny, Barbara, and a girl with red hair I didn't recognize. She looked too young to be part of Jackie's crew, so I assumed it was one of the people we were here to see play. Beth noticed me watching her and picked her hand up to wave. I waved back, so she instantly stood and grabbed the red-haired girl by the wrist.

"Mom." Beth's smile was huge. "This is Peggy."

Up close, the redhead was adorable. "Peggy? Wow, it's wonderful to meet you." I reached my hand out, and the girl leapt forward and hugged me. "Whoa there!"

Peggy pulled away while she chuckled. "I'm so sorry. You looked super huggable." She smoothed her hands down my arms and squeezed my forearms. "This is awesome. You're, like, amazing for bringing Beth here for such a long vacation. Like, totes a super cool mom."

Totes? A vacation? I looked at Beth and made sure my eyebrow was arched as high as it'd go. She knew that look like the back of her hand. I smiled when I turned my attention back to Peggy. She was still smiling a perfect smile. Very charming. "Well, thank you so much. I'm so glad you invited us tonight."

"Oh, Ms. Weber, you're going to love it. We have a great playlist. Eighties and nineties. Even some seventies. And I write all the originals."

Beth's mouth dropped open before she asked, "You do?"

"Yeah, for sure. I didn't tell you that?"

Beth shook her head. Her eyes hadn't left Peggy's profile since they came over to me. I kind of had a feeling what was going on in Beth's head since I was literally going through the same thing. It was confusing to be enamored with someone new, someone who wasn't her normal type, someone who was a goddamn woman. That was for sure. "I'm definitely looking forward to it. And I know Beth is."

"Yeah, and holy shit, Jackie Mitchell? That's who y'all are staying with?" Peggy turned and looked at Beth, who shrugged. "She's like my favorite author. I can't even believe this."

Beth smiled and bounced on the balls of her feet. That was definitely her signature move when she was nervous, scared, excited, happy, etcetera. "She was super happy to meet a fan, I'm sure."

"She looked annoyed."

"You should have seen how annoyed she was when I showed up on her doorstep."

"Wait, what?" Peggy smiled at Beth, and I swore to God I saw Beth's heart leap into her throat. And here I thought she wanted to come to the show to see the boy she'd been talking about. I wondered if Beth was even aware of how she was acting?

"Why don't you two talk about that another time?" I said as I leaned closer to Beth. "It's not really the right place, shouting over the music and all."

Beth looked at me, our faces only an inch or two apart, and she grinned. "Mom, are you drunk?"

I pulled back, put my hand on my heart, and fake gasped. "Of course not."

"Maybe tipsy?"

I smiled. "Not at all."

Peggy put her hand on my arm, and I looked at it, then her. "I think you might be a little *tips*, Ms. Weber."

"Maybe a little."

"Yeah, that's what I thought." Beth raised her chin, the smile still on her lips, and said, "You should probably go back and sit with Jackie."

"Okay, why don't you go and mingle with people your own age?" I shooed them away. They both rolled their eyes and walked toward a couple tables near the stage. I stood and watched the crowd, the variety of people. I hated to admit it, but this was the first time I had been in a gay bar. It made me sort of sad. I had been missing out on all of this for so long. These people were so comfortable and okay with themselves. How often had that happened in my life? Probably never.

"You going to come back and join me?"

Chills shot up my spine at the sound of Jackie's voice behind me. She sounded like velvet felt. "I was thinking about it," I said, tossing the words playfully over my shoulder. I had no idea what got into me around her, but instantly I turned into a twenty-one-year-old flirt.

Jackie laughed, and her breath breezed past the bare skin on the back of my neck. She took a step closer to me, so I could feel her breasts against my back. "So, this band doesn't go on until ten."

I tried to respond, to say something, *anything*, but I couldn't. All I could do was feel the swell of her breasts gently grazing my shoulder blades.

"Think you'd want to go home?"

My breath caught, and I swallowed once, then twice, before I slowly turned to look at her. She reached up and pushed her fingers into the hair at her forehead. The curls she had put in her hair earlier were still hanging in there even though it was pretty humid in the bar. Her eyes locked on to mine, and she shrugged.

"I mean, only if you want to get out of here."

She was nervous. I could hear it in her voice. Jackie Mitchell was standing in front of me, and she was nervous. It made my heart swell. "I would love to." The corner of her mouth tugged upward, and she ran her fingers down my forearm to my hand. My heart momentarily stopped when I thought she was going to hold my hand, but all she did was squeeze my fingers.

"Let's go then."

❖

BETH

Peggy was amazing. And Brock! Oh, my God. He was so cute playing the guitar, and he even switched with the drummer at one point. I was so impressed with his music skills.

But Peggy...

They sang songs that I actually knew, which was super cool. I was shocked out of my mind when they covered songs like "Warrior" by Patty Smyth and Rick Springfield's "Jesse's Girl". The crowd went wild during all the P!NK covers, as well. I was having the absolute best time.

Even though my mom and Jackie had left, I didn't care. I let loose. For the first time in forever. I was so relaxed, even around all these new people. I let myself fit in. All of Peggy and Brock's friends were so welcoming and nice. It was kind of strange, actually, because back home, I never really fit in. I had friends, and it was all fine, I guess. But at the end of the day, I never truly felt comfortable in my own skin. Always trying to belong but never really succeeding.

After the band had their break, the second set started, and like, I'd never seen so many people start crowding closer to the stage. The entire bar was full. Even Jackie's friends had moved from their table and were getting closer to the stage. Tabitha kept yelling at me and telling me to behave. As annoying as it would have been in Savannah, it was pretty damn cool here in St. Pete. Maybe it was my chill attitude these days? Who knew?

"Hey again, Rusty Nailers!" Peggy shouted into the microphone.

The crowd erupted. And so did my entire body with goose bumps.

"Thank you, guys for coming out tonight. I know it's like, a week night or whatever, but y'all sticking it out with us is super fucking cool."

Again, everyone in the crowd cheered. They were waving rainbow flags, bisexual flags, transgender flags, and asexual flags. I could not get over how diverse the group was. Was it my small-town mentality getting to me? I didn't know.

"This is an original song I wrote last night. We've only practiced a couple times, so please, be kind."

"Fuck yeah, we love you, Peggy!" someone shouted from way behind me.

"I love you, too, random man!" Peggy held up her hand in the rock devil sign and stuck her tongue out. She gripped the microphone and took it out of the stand. "It's called 'Wake Up'." She looked back at the band, and Brock started the song off with the guitar. The tune was lovely, slower than they'd been singing, but I started to fall in love with the chords. It reminded me of a Florence + The Machine song. All it was missing was the harp. And Peggy's eyes were closed, her red hair over her shoulder. She looked incredible, and her hair so soft, so beautiful. I couldn't stop looking at her as she started to sing.

> *You think this is your last try,*
> *that this will be the end of life*
> *You said you were tired of running,*
> *that you wanted to hold on to something,*
> *but you can't stand there and do nothing*
> *If you want to hold me,*
> *if I could try to find a way around your walls*
> *Your eyes are so sad, so beautiful, so true*

She opened her eyes and looked directly at me. Or at least it seemed that way. Out of all these people, she was looking at me. The entire moment was so surreal. I couldn't feel my legs.

I learned a lot from your scars,
from the way you smile when you're sad
I've tried, I've tried, I've tried to embrace your pain
Your pain is what makes you real, real, real
It's been a long time for you
But I need you to wake up
Wake up, wake up, wake up

My heart was in my throat...

I don't know how to stop these feelings.
They aren't okay
I see your green eyes,
the way you look at me with those eyes,
the way you handle me with those eyes
I want you to know I would never tell you lies, never tell you lies,
*   never tell you lies*
I want you to wake up, wake up, wake up
I need you to wake up, wake up, wake up
Let me love you
Let me hold you
Let me be the person in your life that helps you wake up, wake
*   up, wake up*

My mouth was so dry as the crowd started to cheer when Peggy finished. "Thank you! Thank you so much!" she shouted into the microphone. I finally tore my eyes off her and made eye contact with Brock. He was smiling at me. *Ugh.*

As the set continued, I found myself completely lost in my thoughts. The music was amazing, of course, and watching Peggy up there serenading the audience and dancing to the upbeat tunes was equally so, but there was something happening inside me, and I legit had no idea what to do with it.

I glanced over at Jackie's friends. They were all dancing and having a great time. Tabitha waved at me from where she was dancing, then motioned for me to come to them. I squeezed my way through the crowd, dodging elbows and sliding against a lot of half-dressed women and men. When I finally got over to Tabitha, she pulled me into their circle. "Are you okay there, youngin'? I can take you home if you need me to."

"No, no, I'm totally fine," I shouted over the music. "I'm seriously having such a good time!"

"So, you're friends with the lead singer?"

"I mean, I guess? And the guitar player? We like, ran into each other on the beach yesterday."

Tabitha raised her beer at the stage. "The guitar player is cute. You into him?"

I felt my cheeks start to burn from the blush that was creeping into them. "I guess?"

"You guess? You're fifteen shades of red right now." Tabitha laughed and had a long drink of her beer. "You sound as bad as your mom!"

I furrowed my brow and looked at Tabitha. "Like, Jackie? Or like, my *mom* mom?"

Tabitha's eyes went wide, and she looked around at the group of friends. Everyone was looking away, acting as if they heard nothing. "Uh," Tabitha said and then took another drink from her beer. She wiped her mouth with the back of her hand and then pointed at the stage. "So, like, they're really good, though, right? Woo!"

"Tabitha," I said loudly. And she finally looked at me. "Who did you mean?"

"Definitely Jackie."

"You're lying!"

She rolled her eyes. "Don't worry about it, kid. Hey," she said, and she motioned toward the stage again with her bottle. "You're being summoned. I think they're done."

"Wait a second—"

"No, kid, don't worry about it. Go be with your friends! It's all good!" Tabitha laughed as she pulled me in with her free hand and gave me a half hug. She quickly turned and ushered her friends out of there as fast as humanly possible.

"Georgia! Come on!" I heard Peggy shout at me from the stage as the crowd started to clear out. I was totally digging her nickname for me, which was odd, because I normally loathed nicknames. *My mom named me Beth for a reason, so like, call me it.* But this one? Georgia? I was all for it. I turned and pushed myself through the people back to the stage. I glanced up and saw Brock as he jumped down from the stage. He turned to me and pulled me into a hug. I was so shocked by it that I didn't even know how to reciprocate. I probably looked like a rag doll as he twirled me.

"Holy cow!" I said with a laugh. "Brock!"

"Beth, thank you so much for coming," he said when he put me down. "You have no idea how much that means to me." He ran his fingers through his long brown hair. How did his hair look healthier than mine? I didn't know, but he was so freaking cute. He smiled at me. "Are you going to come hang out? We're going to this spot where we park and drink."

Drink? I didn't drink. I was sixteen! I'd never had alcohol before. Oh God, how did I say no without seeming like a complete dweeb? "Yeah, so, probably not? I guess I can get a Lyft home or something."

"No way," he said, and he flashed his perfect smile at me again. "You can come. If you don't want to drink, you don't have to. I won't drink, either, and I can drive you home afterward."

He wasn't going to drink? For me? Did I hear that right? "Oh, okay... I suppose I could go for a bit."

"A bit? Hell no, Georgia. You're coming for the entire night," Peggy said as she slapped her hand onto my shoulder. I glanced at her fingers as they gripped me. Why did looking at her fingers and the dark, cherry-painted nails make me feel so crazy? My skin was on fire and at the same time, I had chills.

"The whole night?" I asked, and Peggy grinned at me.

"Yes, the whole night." Brock laughed. "Peggy's the boss. And it's her car, so..."

I felt Peggy lean into me slightly, and when I finally found the courage to look over at her, she was only about three inches from my face. "Let loose a little, Beth," she said softly. Her breath smelled sweet and minty. Fuck. Why was I smelling her breath?

"Fine." I groaned, and Peggy and Brock both cheered then high-fived each other. I rolled my eyes.

❖

Peggy's car was perfect for her. An old VW Beetle where she had to slam her foot into the clutch to get it to change gears. I laughed quite a few times when she cussed about what a piece of shit it was.

"It's a classic, Pegs. You know this."

"Classic piece of shit," she said. I watched her in the rearview mirror from the safety of the back seat. Her makeup was so well done. Even after being on stage all hot and sweaty, she still looked flawless. I was impressed.

"Did you enjoy the show?" Brock asked when he looked back at me from the passenger seat. "I mean, I'm sure you enjoyed me playing guitar. Who doesn't love that?"

"Jesus, Brock," Peggy said, and I watched her roll her eyes. "By the way, girls don't like when you say shit like that."

I smiled and shook my head. "The show was really awesome, actually. And yes, your guitar playing skills were top notch."

When the car slowed to a stop and I pulled myself out of the back seat, I looked around. We were at an airport. "Is this what you guys do? Watch planes?"

"And drink."

"And smoke weed," Peggy said as she passed a joint to Brock. He immediately lit it up and took a hit, then passed it to me.

"Nah, I'll pass."

Peggy smiled at me. "You're a straight edge, aren't you?"

I shrugged.

"It's okay if you are."

"Yeah, I mean, you're still hot as fuck," Brock said.

I was slightly offended. "Well, thank God, I guess?" As I was regretting my decision to come with them, Brock took off toward a car that was pulling up. "Look, Peggy, I don't really think I should be out here with you guys."

"Are you okay?"

"Yeah," I said and paused. I looked at her beautiful blue eyes. "I wanna go home."

"I can take you home," she said softly. She reached out and tucked my hair behind my ear. "Or you can come with me, and we can get out of here."

I looked over her shoulder at Brock. He was leaning against the other car that arrived, and he was slamming a can of Natural Light. *So much for not drinking...* "I would like that," I said when I looked back at Peggy.

"Let's go."

I slid into the passenger side of the Beetle, and she revved the engine before we took off, dirt flying behind us. Peggy laughed when I squealed, and it was perfect. Except for the part where she was a girl. And I wasn't sure if that was what I wanted.

We drove around for a while. She played me songs from her iPhone with the auxiliary cord hooked up to the car radio that was obviously newer than the car itself. I listened intently when she talked about why she loved each artist that she played, like Leon Bridges and Grace Potter and Dave Matthews. Except she didn't go on and on about the album version of "41" by Dave, but the "Live from Wrigley Field" version, which was like, my absolute favorite version ever. And then she talked about Sarah McLachlan and how when she was thirteen, her cousin Jessica played her *Fumbling Towards Ecstasy,* and it was like an awakening. She had a love for Tori Amos and The Indigo Girls. When she played a song called "Magnolia Street" by Catie Curtis, I almost cried. The lyrics made my stomach ache.

I couldn't stop listening to Peggy. She had so much to say, and her voice was so beautiful to listen to. Not her singing voice, although that was wonderful, but her speaking voice. She laughed, too, a lot, which I loved. She was witty and cute, and when she told me how she still loved Celine Dion, I almost jumped across the tiny space in the Beetle and kissed her.

I almost kissed her.

What the fuck was I thinking? I couldn't kiss her! She was totally not into me. And I was, like, this stupid girl from Savannah, Georgia who wasn't in town for long. I was going to be leaving soon, right? I was going to go home and recover from the divorce with my mom and Myrtle, and we'd leave Jackie. We'd say good-bye, and I'd have to say good-bye to Peggy.

I looked over at her as she sang along to "Shake It Out" by Florence + The Machine. My heart was beating so fast and so loud. I thanked God for the volume of the music because I was pretty sure Peggy would be able to hear it otherwise.

We pulled into a parking spot outside of Jackie's building, and Peggy looked over at me as she turned her car off. "We're here."

"Do you want to come in?"

"No."

"Oh, okay."

She reached over and grabbed my hand. She ran her fingers over the dark smudges on my index finger and thumb. "Why are you all black here?"

"Oh," I said with a laugh. "I'm kind of an artist, I guess. It's from the charcoal I use to sketch."

"You're an artist?"

"I mean, I'm trying? I don't know if I'm any good."

"Maybe you'll show me sometime?"

I felt my stomach bottom out. "Of course."

"So…"

My eyes wandered over the dashboard, to the radio, to the steering wheel, until they finally landed on Peggy's eyes. "Yeah, so, Jackie is my mom."

"Whoa." Peggy turned toward me and leaned against the door. "What?"

I shrugged. "She's my birth mom. Susan adopted me, so like, Susan is my *mom*, but Jackie is my birth mom."

I saw Peggy's chest contract and fall with the deep breath she took. "That's heavy, Georgia. Are you okay?"

I nodded, then I unloaded on her. I word-vomited all over. I told her the whole story, the private investigator, stealing my mom's credit card, my dad hitting my mom, Jackie meeting my mom, everything. I talked non-stop. Peggy listened the entire time. She smiled when I said something funny, she put her hand on my arm when I cried, and she moved my hair from my face when I got embarrassed about my inability to shut up. "I'm so sorry," I said quietly when I dried the rest of the tears on my face. "I guess I wasn't okay."

Peggy's hand was on mine. "Look, Georgia, I'm so honored that you told me. Like, I want to stay the whole night with you and listen to you ramble and laugh. You're incredible."

"Seriously?"

She smiled at me. "You have no idea how adorable you are, do you?"

I was instantly self-conscious until all of a sudden, Peggy leaned across the tiny space in the Beetle into me. I couldn't breathe.

All I could see were her lips and oh, *holy shit*, was she going to kiss me?

Her soft, full lips landed on mine, and she was kissing me. What was I supposed to do? The only thing my brain said to do was pull away. I couldn't be interested in her. I was interested in Brock. *Right?* Well, my heart was saying something completely different. So, I did what I never do, which was listen to my heart, and I kissed her back.

CHAPTER TEN

SUSAN

I was so ashamed of myself.

I passed out last night.

And not *when* we got home. No. Oh, no. In the *car ride* home. *Sigh.* I didn't even know what happened.

"I think the six shots you did with Tabitha probably had something to do with it," Jackie said after she helped me into my bed. I was *so* embarrassed.

But my embarrassment didn't stop me from passing out *again*. I actually think I was mid-sentence the second time. *Real classy, Susan.*

When I opened my eyes and found the clock on the bedside table, I saw that it was only three in the morning. And I was wide awake. Shockingly, I didn't have a headache. That was a miracle, actually. I thought for sure I'd be hurting. I heard Myrtle's collar jingle, and I put my hand on her to calm her down. She promptly fell back asleep. I was so jealous.

I stared at the ceiling; of course, my mind wandered to Jackie, to her hands, lips, face. She was so kind as she helped me to bed. The way she moved my hair from my face and made sure I had water... I couldn't get over it. How did I live my whole life and never feel this way about someone? Or did I, and I couldn't remember because it was eons ago? I was quite a bit older than Jackie. Maybe that was why I was feeling all of this trepidation. I wanted so badly to let go, shed this stupidity that was holding me back. My issues had to stem from something other than age or inexperience. There was a part inside me (a very small part, but a part nonetheless) that was struggling with knowing that I raised Beth, and Jackie got to live her life and do what she needed and wanted without the responsibility of a child.

Guilt crept into my mind and heart for thinking that about her. Jackie was being so incredible. She did not need to let us stay with her. In fact, she could have told us to leave immediately. There was nothing that made her take us in, aside from what I was finding out was a wonderful soul and a huge heart that wanted to take care of people.

She created this illusion that she was closed off, not willing to find love, only available when she wanted to be, not when someone needed her. But she was the exact opposite of that. How had she not found someone to love and care for?

The way Tabitha said that Jackie only looked at one other person like that in her life... I wonder what that meant? Had her heart been broken by someone before? Was that why she appeared closed off and forever okay to live a single life? Or was she the heartbreaker? And she'd sworn off having to hurt someone again?

My mind couldn't get to the spot where Jackie was a horrible person with no love or kindness. It was impossible for me to believe that she broke hearts. But maybe I was wrong?

When I couldn't stay in bed any longer, I slid out from under the covers and crept over to the door. Myrtle was sleeping so soundly that she didn't hear me. I thanked God because if she woke up now, she'd need to go outside.

Beth's door was cracked open so I peeked inside. She was sound asleep, her phone on her chest, her body half uncovered. I smiled and shook my head. That whole "no phones after ten" rule didn't really last long. Not that I minded that she was actually having fun here. Seeing her smile and laugh at the Rusty Nail with people her age was encouraging. I knew the entire fight between Steven and me was not easy to deal with for her. Especially since I wasn't really handling it all that well.

Or at least, I hadn't been handling it well...until now...

I made my way to the living room. There was a Himalayan salt lamp on the end table next to the couch which lit the entire room. The bookshelf next to the couch was calling my name, so I tiptoed over to it. Jackie's books were all lined up. All twenty-two of them. I pulled out one toward the end of the row. *Recreating Mary*. I smiled because it was *such* a romance book title. The cover was tasteful, though, which surprised me. I grew up seeing my mom buying old copies of Harlequins from garage sales and reading them while on road trips. I never understood until I was much older and actually read one why she seemed to always have her nose buried in one during those stressful family situations. It made sense once I figured it all out.

The cover on Jackie's book was far from Fabio on horseback. There was a woman with her back to the camera, and she stood looking over a cliff with a mountain range spread before her. The colors were beautiful: golds and reds from the changing leaves on the trees, deep blue sky, and white snowcapped mountains. I flipped it over and skimmed the blurb. Two women finding love after being hurt was the gist of it. *Shocking*. I went to put it back, but for some reason, I held it a second longer. There was something extremely calming about holding a book. I was always that way, ever since I was a small child, and I received a copy of *The Velveteen Rabbit* for my third birthday.

Beth's words from earlier about how Jackie's books wouldn't be something I'd enjoy echoed in my head. After everything that was happening, maybe it actually would be something I needed to read. For research. And if nothing else, maybe I could learn a little bit more about Jackie. How she used her words to make people feel things. After all, she'd been using her words to make *me* feel things since the moment she first opened her mouth.

I switched on the small table lamp next to the couch and curled up. I heard Myrtle jump from the bed in the spare room and click-clack her way out to me. She jumped up on the couch and curled up, promptly dozing off by my feet. Her sweet face was propped on my leg, and I took a minute to stare at her cuteness.

After opening the book and reading the acknowledgements and then "Praise for other works by Jackie Mitchell," the strangest phenomenon occurred. My stomach was in a knot, and my center was tingling. How was it possible that simply holding one of Jackie's books was turning me on? As with everything else that was happening, I wanted to understand how and why something so simple as flipping a page, seeing the words "Chapter One," and reading "Mary Russell walked like a goddess in those heels," affected me like that.

Time seemed to fly by as I fell deeper and deeper into the world Jackie created for her main character, Mary. She'd been broken and damaged by people throughout her entire life. She survived, though, and had an amazing mom and a great stepfather, and at the age of forty was starting to actually figure things out. Even though life was hard and she struggled, she always had her mom. And as I got to chapter three, her mom fell ill. Cancer… And that was it. I was a hot sobbing mess. What the hell? It was chapter *three*, for Christ's sake.

When I made it to the burial and the niece of the mom's best friend, Nikki, appeared, with her mass of red hair and fierce blue eyes, I knew instantly that she was who Mary would be falling for. But the story unfolded in a way I didn't expect… And secrets from Mary's past came back to haunt her. I learned that Nikki was far from wild. Mary learned that Nikki wasn't a bandage she sorely needed for her damaged heart, but she was the actual cure…

"Chapter Eight…" Their first kiss was smoldering. I dabbed at my forehead to dry the perspiration beading along my hairline.

"Chapter Fifteen…" I could smell the sex that was about to happen.

I placed the book on my chest and took a deep breath. I was flying through this book, speed reading in a way I hadn't known I was capable of. Where was this skill when I was in college?

"What the hell are you doing up?"

I jerked my head toward the sound of Jackie's voice and immediately felt as if I had been caught with my hand in the, *uh*, the cookie jar… Yeah, that was it!

"Hi," I said as I fumbled with the book so Jackie couldn't see what I was reading.

"How long have you been awake?" She rubbed her eyes and pushed some stray hairs behind her ears. My eyes traveled over her tight tank top and tiny boy shorts. She sat on the ottoman in front of where I was sitting and propped her elbows on her knees. Her legs were so long that she looked kind of comical sitting there. Well, comical *and* beautiful.

"What time is it?"

She blinked once, twice, before she smiled. Even just after waking up, she was breathtaking. "It's like, seven in the morning."

"Seriously?"

"Yeah, why do you think I'm awake?"

"I honestly have no idea why you're awake." I chuckled when she shook her head and finally broke eye contact. "You look adorable."

She lifted her head and looked at me again. "You like this, eh?" She motioned to her ensemble.

"Yeah, I really do," I said softly. "I really, really do."

"Y'know, you could have had all of this last night." She placed her palm under her chin with her elbow still on her knee.

Chills covered my body from head to toe. "Oh, yeah?"

"Mm-hmm. But you passed out like a twenty-one-year-old."

"I was clearly fed shots. Too many of them."

"I shouldn't have let Tabitha near you. She can drink a grown man under the table."

"Probably should have at least warned me about that," I said softly. I reached out and took her free hand in mine. My fingers intertwined with hers, and I kept my eyes on hers. I found myself wanting to recreate the scene from Jackie's book, pushing her up against a wall and having my way with her.

"Whatcha reading?"

Her voice broke through my thoughts, and I smiled sheepishly. *"Reader's Digest."*

"Oh, really?" She laughed. "How are you enjoying it?"

"It's a little boring."

"You could always read something of mine." Her eyes were twinkling as she teased me. They looked so green in the early morning light. It was hard to focus on anything but those eyes and the feel of her fingers mingling with mine. "Of course, I feel like you might be reading something of mine already."

My cheeks were on fire. I picked up the book and flashed her the cover.

"*Recreating Mary*. Really? That's not the one I would have started you on."

I laughed. "Why? Is there an order I should read them in? Like Beth always tells me about *Star Wars* movies?"

"No," Jackie said and shrugged. "That one is emotional. And has quite a bit more sex in it than some of the others."

I widened my eyes. "You mean there's a lot more sex after the first time?"

She nodded.

"*Okay.*"

"Why? Have you made it to the first time?"

"Um..." I could feel myself blushing. "You caught me in the act, so to speak."

"How long *have* you been up?

"I think three?"

Jackie chuckled and squeezed my hand. "I'm glad you're enjoying it."

"I'm loving it," I said, my voice quiet but with enough emotion that I hoped she realized I was being serious. I watched as she pulled her hand from mine and went to stand up but instead stopped and smiled.

"Well, look what the cat dragged in."

Beth came stumbling out of her room, her hair a complete disaster and her eye makeup smeared. She looked like a twenty-seven-year-old waking up from a night of partying. Not sixteen waking up from a night of who knew what. "Why? What time did you stroll in?" I asked and saw Beth look at Jackie, her eyebrows raised, and she shrugged.

Jackie titled her head and smiled. "You really don't remember?"

"Wait a second, were you *drunk?*"

"No!" Beth shouted, and Myrtle picked her head up and released a muffled bark. "No, Mom, I promise. I didn't drink a drop."

"Was there alcohol where you ended up?"

"Uh..."

"Where *did* you end up anyway?" I narrowed my eyes.

"We sat on the beach."

"*Who's* 'we'? Is there a mouse in your pocket?" I looked from Beth to Jackie as they exchanged a look. "Brock?"

"Negative," Beth said and pulled air sharply into her mouth. "Peggy."

"Why not Brock?"

"Well, he was drinking. And I didn't want to be around that because I'm a damn good kid." Beth leaned against the couch, shrugged, and smiled. "It was nothing big."

Nothing big, my ass. "Sure," I said, nodding. "Nothing big."

Jackie laughed as she stood and rubbed her hands together. "Who wants to go out for breakfast?"

Beth's hand shot into the air, and all I could do was chuckle. This was absolutely the happiest I had seen Beth in ages.

❖

BETH

Breakfast was amazing. During the school year, I would rarely eat in the morning. I'd get to school and buy a yogurt from the cafeteria that I'd never actually eat. It was hard to eat when I was always so worried about what people were saying about me. I surrounded myself with really good friends, but damn, there were some real bitches back in Savannah.

I knew it wasn't going to be rainbows and unicorns all the time here in St. Pete, but even the amount of people I'd become acquainted with were way more than the amount of people I talked to back at home. Not that I thought we were going to stay here forever.

Which kind of made me sad. I was really starting to like it here. The light in my bedroom was amazing. I managed to find a great spot for my easel and paints, right near the window where I could look out at the gulf when I needed inspiration. Shockingly, I wasn't struggling for material to paint or draw. I'd filled up one sketchbook already and was quickly filling up another.

I sat on the edge of the stool next to the easel and studied my latest painting. I wasn't sure if Mom or Jackie would be offended, but they were the focus of almost every single piece I had completed. I didn't set out to chronicle their relationship or anything like that. I was ten paintings in before I realized that with each work, while the same people were present, the entire mood was changing. From stand-offish to skittish to unhappy to tentative to whatever was going on. I wasn't sure, but there was a strange electricity in the air, a crackle I noticed after their dinner date, and that crackle absolutely carried over to the night after. The space between them went from red to blue, angry and sad to calm and confused. I did not understand it, but I was having the best time capturing it.

The painting I was working on was of Jackie with Myrtle. I wanted her to have something from me when we left.

Ugh.

The inevitability of us leaving was becoming more and more obvious, and it was nauseating me.

My phone started to vibrate, and I rushed to answer it. My heart lodged into my throat when I saw that it was Peggy. Shit. *What do I do? Do I answer it? Do we talk about what happened? Do we even worry about it?*

"Hello?" I felt breathless. Was I? *Fuck…*

"Hey, Georgia, how are you?"

Her smooth voice coupled with that stupid simple question made my stomach tie into a knot, killing me. I mean, seriously? *I'm not doing anything, Peggy; thinking about you and how I can't quite understand what the fuck I'm doing.* "Um, I'm okay. Working on my paintings."

"I really need to see your work one day."

I could hear her smiling on the other end, the sound of her lips moving around the words *work* and *one day*. "I would love that, you know."

"Maybe we should set it up?"

My heart squeezed itself. "Yeah, I don't know when we're leaving."

"Oh, yeah," Peggy said. Her voice was softer, and it trailed off. Did she sound let down? Or was that me? I couldn't bear to hear her like that.

"Tonight? I mean, if you're not busy. I know you, like, have a life or whatever."

She laughed, and it made my hands feel numb. "I would really like that. Can I take you to dinner?"

It was my turn to smile. "Of course."

"I'll pick you up; you can show me your art. Is seven okay?"

"It's perfect."

"Okay, I'll see you then, Georgia."

I laughed. "Bye, Peggy." When I hung up the phone, I was smiling. Like, *really* smiling. My cheeks were hurting. That was how bad I was smiling.

There was a knock on my door that shook me from my thoughts. "Come in," I said over The Beatles singing "Hey Jude".

The door opened, and Jackie stuck her head in. "We should probably discuss last night."

"Ugh."

Jackie laughed as she moved inside, closed the door, then walked over toward me. "Are you okay?"

"Ugh," I said again. "That's a loaded question."

"You two…" Jackie crossed her arms and cleared her throat. She was *so* uncomfortable. It was kind of comical. Especially since this wasn't my first relationship talk. But it was *her* first relationship talk with me, and she looked as if she wanted to jump out the window.

"Jackie, you don't have to do this, y'know?" I smiled. "I mean, Mom had this talk with me a while ago."

Her shoulders relaxed, and she uncrossed her arms and slid her hands into the front pockets of her jean shorts. "Well, yeah, but you know this is different, right?" Jackie's voice trailed off, and she laughed. "Clearly you know there's not a penis, but that doesn't mean you shouldn't be safe…or whatever."

"Jackie! Jesus!" My mouth was hanging open. "I'm not going to have sex with Peggy."

Her eyebrows raised, and she tilted her head.

"I'm not!"

"Okay, okay." She shrugged, her hands still in her pockets. "You know I don't care who you like, right?"

"No shit," I said with a laugh.

She laughed and then bounced on the balls of her feet. Was it possible that I got that move from her? Were things like that hereditary? "So, what's going on with you and Peggy then? If you aren't…y'know…canoodling."

"Canoodling? You're kidding me, right? Are you eighty-five?"

"I'm being serious," Jackie said with another chuckle before she sat on the floor and crossed her legs. "I feel strongly about straight girls like yourself breaking young lesbian hearts."

"Okay, first of all, I don't even know if she's a lesbian."

"True. Bisexual, then. Or pansexual."

"Does it even have to have a label? Like, why? I don't want to label anything right now." I sighed.

"Look, that's cool. I know you millennials like to be easy breezy or whatever."

"I mean, but honestly, why does it have to be labeled? Does it?"

Jackie shrugged. "No, it doesn't. You're right."

"Cool," I said softly. "But like, yeah, maybe she's bisexual."

Jackie's laugh was hilarious. She sounded so much like me. "You make me get all worried that I offended you and then you say that?"

I laughed right along with her. "I'm sorry, I don't know!"

"That's completely allowed. I promise."

"Good."

"So?"

"Whatever the case may be, label or not, I'm not going to break her heart." I bit the inside of my cheek so hard that I almost drew blood. I tried to give myself a mental pep-talk. *Tell her that you don't even know if you're straight. Say the words, Beth. Come out and tell her now. I. Might. Be. Bisexual. Fuck.*

"I hope you don't. It's not easy breaking hearts. You know that, right?"

I smiled. "You sound like you're speaking from experience."

Jackie leaned back and propped herself up with her hands. "Unfortunately, I've broken quite a few hearts."

"Oh, really?"

"It's what happens when you're an introverted asshole who doesn't like people," she said. But she wouldn't look at me. Even though I really wanted her to. "Breaker or breakee, it all sucks. So, take my advice, and be careful."

"I will be."

"Good." Jackie got up from the floor and adjusted her shorts. "Can I see what you're working on?"

I shook my head.

"What? Why not? You know I love your work."

"I know," I said and put my hands up in protest. "This is a work in progress, though. So, it's off limits." I adjusted the easel and made sure it was completely facing away from her.

Jackie looked around the room. The floor space was becoming limited as the canvases and papers started to pile up. "Can I look at any of these?"

"No." I stood and made sure she didn't make a move for the canvases. "These are all works in progress, actually."

"That is not fair," Jackie said with a huff. She looked so much more at ease than she did almost two weeks ago when I first knocked on her door. Her braid was messy, her jean shorts were ripped and covered with splatters of paint, and she had on a white, V-neck T-shirt that had some wear and tear. I wouldn't say I was impressed with her slight transformation, but I was definitely happy about it. Seeing her like this made her more human. Maybe she really could be a mother figure to me one day. "What are you looking at?" Jackie narrowed her eyes. "Stop being sentimental."

I laughed. "How the hell did you know that?"

"You're my kid. I feel like you can't escape the 'Mitchell Lack of a Poker Face' syndrome." Jackie smiled, then turned to leave.

"Your kid, eh?" I said before she left the room. Her hand was on the doorknob, and she stopped mid-stride.

She glanced at me over her shoulder and smiled before she left the room and closed the door behind her.

❖

JACKIE

My kid.

Shit. I was really settling into this, wasn't I?

I didn't know what else to call it aside from *settling*... Maybe accepting? Or enjoying? Because I actually was enjoying it. The more Susan and Beth let the condo be their home, the more I found myself dreading the day they finally broke it to me that they were going back to Savannah. They weren't making any moves to leave, though. Maybe they weren't going to leave? Honestly, I needed to have a conversation with Susan, but the thought that she'd think I was pushing her to leave made my stomach roll.

If I stated the facts first when I approached her, it might work. I could tell her that there was no rush, that I didn't care when they left. I could ask them to stay. Forever.

How did this happen? How did I go from my peaceful introverted life to wanting to spend time with people I barely knew? And one of them was my daughter! If someone would have told me this was going to happen to me, I would have laughed in the person's face.

The last two weeks had been a crazy fucking ride. That was for sure.

I found Susan in the kitchen looking at her phone. She quickly cleared the texting app from her screen when she saw me and turned her phone off. "What's going on?" I asked.

"Nothing."

"You're lying to me." I pointed at her phone. "What do you have there?"

"A phone."

"Susan, what's going on?"

"So, I haven't really been using my phone much because, well..." She paused, looked down at the iPhone and shrugged. "It's not like I need to update anyone. And honestly? Seeing my inbox pile up with frantic text messages and voice mails from worried friends as Steven continues to look for us is not really helping matters."

"That's understandable—"

"My sister Melissa is on her way here."

Susan blurted the words out so fast and over the top of mine that I barely understood what she said. "Excuse me?"

"My sister. Melissa. She's on her way here. To St. Pete. To your condo."

"I'm sorry. *What?*"

"Yeah, I think she's freaking out."

I was beside myself. "About what? Doesn't she live in Chicago? She jumped on a plane and invited herself here? Who does something like that?"

Susan turned her phone on and tapped on the screen until she had the texting app pulled back up. She slid it over to me. "See for yourself."

I looked down at Susan's phone and started to read text after text:

Okay. So, I had to call the cops on your crazy husband. He came to Chicago looking for you. What the fuck, Susan? What is going on? Why is he acting like this? What happened?

You need to answer me, please.

Susan. What the fuck?

Okay. You're going to make me do something drastic if you don't respond to me.

You know what? Fine!

I landed in Tampa. You better be at this fucking address Beth gave me, or I'm going to kill you.

I looked up at Susan. "Why didn't you respond to her?"

"I don't know." Susan shrugged. "I guess I didn't want to talk to her...tell her anything... I was too worried. And if I start telling her about you, then what? I don't even know what's going on with you. She knew I was fine. And then the last two days I haven't really been on my phone. I figured she'd at least talk to Beth."

"Does Beth know that she's coming?"

Another shrug from Susan.

"So, is she staying here?" My heart rate sped up. I didn't really have room for more people! Or the desire to take in yet another person!

"I literally have no idea, Jackie," Susan said softly. "I am so sorry." Her voice was so sincere, and her eyes filled with tears.

"Oh my God." My heart broke. "Do not worry about it. If she is staying here? Great. If she's not? Even better." I smiled, and Susan chuckled. I reached across the granite counter and lightly touched her right hand. "We'll figure it out."

As those words came out of my mouth, a knock at the door startled both of us. Susan covered her mouth with her hand and mumbled, "I'm so sorry."

I let my head hang as I laughed. What else could I do? I left Susan in the kitchen and walked over to the door. When I opened it, I saw a woman that looked a lot like Susan standing there with a roller bag. "Hi. Melissa?"

"Jesus. Are *you* Jackie?"

"Yes." What the hell was that supposed to mean?

"You're gorgeous."

"Well, okay then. I guess I can get over you inviting yourself down now that you said I'm gorgeous."

Melissa raised her free hand in the air. "I am so sorry about doing this, by the way. I wasn't going to, but when I didn't hear from Susan, I honestly freaked out."

Her Chicago accent was thick. I wondered how long she and Susan had been separated by all those miles. "Ya don't say?"

Susan poked her head over my shoulder. "Hi," she said softly, and Melissa's face instantly changed from worried to melancholy, and she started crying.

"Oh, Suzie, I'm so sorry. I freaked out, and Steven was being so mean, I didn't know what to do. Patrick told me to get on a plane. I listened. I didn't know what else to do." Melissa stopped talking when Susan pushed around me and hugged her sister. They were similar in almost every way, but Susan was about four inches shorter, and Melissa had longer hair. It fell below her shoulders, but it was the same dark brown with natural curls. I stood there and watched them hugging, Melissa still crying and Susan telling her it was okay.

"Do you two want to bring this inside?"

Melissa instantly started giggling as she pulled away from Susan. She wiped at her tears and sniffled before she pulled her suitcase into the condo. "Oh, Lord, you brought Myrtle? This is big," Melissa said as she knelt down to pet the dog.

Susan moved past me, but as she did so, she slid her hand down my arm, wrapped her fingers around my wrist, and squeezed. "Let's get you settled before we get into it." Susan followed Melissa to the living room and then motioned for her to follow to the spare room. "You can sleep in my room, Mel. I'll sleep on the couch," Susan said. I wanted to tell her that she could share my bed, but I thought that'd throw Susan right over the edge.

After I closed the door, I headed for the balcony. Myrtle was right behind me and was in the chair before I could even sit down. She snuggled up next to me and let out a deep dog sigh. This cute little dog was really growing on me. I could guarantee that I never thought that would happen. When I was younger, I'd always wanted a dog, but my parents said no every time, so I got to the point where I buried the desire and turned it into disdain. Every person didn't need to love animals. But I was finding out that maybe I hadn't buried it deep enough because I was really enjoying the click-clack of Myrtle's nails on the tile floors.

I could hear Susan and Melissa shuffling around in the bedroom, an occasional laugh, and then I heard Beth squeal, signaling that she knew Melissa was here. Melissa said how tan they both looked, to which Susan said, "Florida sun is being good to us." Melissa gushed about how much she missed them both, and I heard another couple of squeals. It must have been nice having family that stayed close. After my mom passed away, it was pretty strange to actually hang out with or see family.

"Care if we join you?" Susan said as she walked onto the balcony with Melissa trailing behind her. They both sat in unison on the couch, and I stared at them. The resemblance was really striking, but they had a lot of unique features. Susan's eyes were brown, first of all, and Melissa's were blue. And second, their noses were different. Where Susan's was slender, Melissa's was slightly wider. And Melissa had barely any lips while Susan's were full and luscious. At least, I assumed they were luscious. I wondered if I would get to taste them soon. Or would I not be able to at all now that Melissa was here?

God, was I the most selfish person on the planet or what?

"So, are you going to tell me what happened? And no offense, Jackie," Melissa said as she put her hand toward me, "but why the hell did you impose on her when you could have come to me?"

"Well, this really wasn't my idea." Susan smiled. "And it's not like *you* aren't imposing…"

Melissa let out a groan. "I know, I know. I shouldn't have jumped on a plane like that. But I was worried sick. Jackie, in case you were wondering, I have horrible anxiety. It's ridiculous."

Susan looked at me. "What she's trying to say is that once she had it in her head, there was no way she couldn't do it."

I knew that feeling all too well. "You might not believe this, but I completely understand."

"But Mel, I promise, everything is fine down here. Beth is doing really well away from Savannah. I don't know what we'll do when it's time to leave."

"Shouldn't you be heading home soon? I feel like it's been quite some time now."

Susan looked down at her lap and then at me. "Probably."

My heart clenched, and I tried to put a lid on my emotions. It was not my time to be the center of attention.

"I have to tell you," Melissa said. She bit her thin bottom lip and looked out toward the gulf. "Calling the cops on Steven was quite entertaining."

"Well, what did you tell him?"

"Considering that he was irate, I told him nothing. But dammit, Suzie, you really put me in a bind. And Patrick, too. He was so thrown off."

Susan sighed. I knew she was embarrassed. I could tell by the way she adjusted her position. "I'm sorry, Mel. I really am. I had no idea he'd fly off the handle like that."

"Uh, yeah, you did. He's been doing that for years. Since you fucking met him." Melissa put her hand on Susan's leg and squeezed. "You should have left him ages ago."

Susan nodded, and her eyes briefly found mine.

"He hit you?" Melissa asked, and she turned to look fully at Susan. "If we owned a gun, I might have shot the son of a bitch." Her accent was out of control.

Susan laughed and leaned into her sister. "I kind of wish you had a gun now."

"Me, too," Melissa said while chuckling. It was her turn to look at me and hold my gaze for a few beats. I knew she was silently asking me if Susan was okay, so I nodded, and Melissa smiled. She had a beautiful smile, like her sister's. I smiled back and tried not to think about Susan's "probably" when asked if they should be leaving soon. I could not stop, though, and I could tell it was going to drive me nuts.

After Melissa and Susan had their time on the couch, I moved inside and let them be alone. They were laughing a couple times, and it made me feel slightly better about everything. I wasn't sure why, though. Maybe because Susan wasn't a hot mess any longer. Or maybe because I loved hearing Susan's laugh.

❖

Beth came bounding into the kitchen. "Do you need anything?" she asked and looked around the kitchen at the few items out of the refrigerator. "Even though I'm not going to be here for dinner I can help you if you need help."

"Actually, yes, I could use the assist. Can you chop these veggies for a salad? A rough chop." I watched Beth pull a medium-sized knife from the knife block and begin slicing the cucumbers and tomatoes. She knew how to handle the knife, which surprised me. "Do you cook at home?"

She nodded before she started speaking. "Mom taught me. Y'know, she's Italian, so like, she loves to cook. And when my grandma Joy would visit, she'd take over the kitchen. The whole house would smell like garlic and pasta sauce. She made the best meatballs. I swear."

"I do love a good meatball."

"I mean, right?" Beth chuckled. "I miss her. She was a cool old lady."

"When did she pass?"

"Like, two years ago. Mom was a hot mess." Beth slid the chopped veggies into a bowl, tossed them a few times, and then said, "Do you have seasoned salt? I have this cool concoction I like to do with veggies for salad."

I smiled, raised an eyebrow, and pointed to the spice cabinet. The little things amused me about her, like her ability to throw me off guard by enjoying cooking or how she seemed to be becoming a woman right before my eyes. I didn't have the right to see this progression from a small, insecure kid to a self-aware young adult. I didn't have any rights. But I was enjoying the show, regardless.

"I feel like maybe we should stay."

Beth's words broke my train of thought, and I stared at her, my mouth hanging open.

She looked at me and then back at the vegetable mixture. "I mean, like, y'know, I don't want to go back."

My mouth was still agape.

"It's weird…" she said with a shrug. "I don't know how to deal with this new person I've found within myself. I don't know if she'll survive the suffocation of Savannah."

"Beth, honey," I said. She turned, looked at me straight on, and I stopped. Her eyes were pleading. And my heart broke.

"The idea of going back there after everything is too much. And I don't think either Mom or myself can go back. I know she's trying to be strong. Acting like she can handle going back, when I know deep down…" Beth paused, and I saw her take a deep breath. "She is going through some shit."

I was speechless. What the hell was Beth trying to say?

"I don't want to leave you, either," Beth whispered. She looked at the countertop, and I could tell that she was trying to hold herself together. Her chin was quivering, which was the same thing mine would do, and the dimple I passed on from my grandfather was so apparent.

"Look, Beth, listen to me," I said as I placed my hands on her shoulders and turned her to face me. Her eyes found mine, tears filled to the brim. "You both can stay as long as you want and need. But,"

I paused and wiped a tear as it slid down her cheek. "You're going to have to start at a school. You can't *not* go to school."

Beth smiled and released a small giggle. "You really would let us stay?"

"Yes," I said with a nod. "Of course I would." Was she crazy? I was thrilled that was even an option! Of course, Susan might not be too hip on the idea. I wasn't sure. "So, who's going to break it to your mom?"

"Why do you think Aunt Melissa is here?" Beth smiled, looked at her watch, and then said, "Well, I gotta go. Peggy will be here any minute."

"Whoa there, missy! No way." I grabbed her arm as she walked away and gently pulled her back to me. "What the fuck do you mean why do I think your aunt is here? Don't you lie to me. I can tell when people are lying."

Beth shrugged. She had that same smile she had on when she first met me. It was wide, and her teeth were straight like mine, and I shook my head at her.

"You're a little shit."

"I know."

Beth started to walk away again, and I said after her, "If you think you're going to go out without Peggy coming up here to say hello, you are sorely mistaken."

Beth turned, her mouth hanging open. "Jesus, when did you decide to become a mom? That was really good!"

I rolled my eyes. "I'm serious, Beth."

"Oh, I know, Jackie," she said with a laugh. "I'll make sure she comes up to get me." Beth turned and walked away, laughing the entire time.

CHAPTER ELEVEN

BETH

Peggy was so perfect with Mom and Jackie. And she even wowed Aunt Mel, which wasn't normal. She was difficult and hard to please. But Peggy had her laughing, and I honestly had a hard time dragging her away. I didn't want to stay with adults and talk about what's new on TV (I loved the reboot of *Will & Grace*, so I would have totally talked about that), or what series did they recently binge on Netflix (*Stranger Things*, both seasons, in a day and a half, no fucking judgment please), or something lame like that. When I pulled on the sleeve of Peggy's Beastie Boys T-shirt to signal to her that I was ready to get the hell out of there, she reached over and put her hand on my jean-covered knee and squeezed. I almost passed out.

And I saw my mom notice. And she glanced at Jackie, then at Aunt Mel, and then back at Peggy. She never made eye contact with me, which was probably good because I was ready to combust.

When we were safely inside Peggy's Beetle, she turned and looked at me. "You're so nervous, aren't you?"

I let out a groan. "Yes. I am. I'm sorry. I get so freaking nervous around you."

"Why is that?" She placed her hand on my forearm and squeezed. "I'll never hurt you. You know that, right?"

I couldn't stop looking at her hand. She had a silver band on her middle finger and a tattoo of a heart right above it. Why was that so fucking sexy? Why, oh why, did I find everything about her so goddamn sexy? Literally every. Single. Thing. And I wanted so badly to tell her everything going on in my head, but come on, no one wanted to be word vomited on like that again.

"Georgia, look at me," she said softly. Her voice was so perfect. It reminded me of a summer night: nine at night in a Dairy Queen drive-thru when I finally got to the first bite of the vanilla ice cream cone dipped in cherry. And that fucking nickname? I couldn't handle it.

I pulled my gaze up to her blue eyes. Her makeup was flawless, her black eyeliner had wings, and her eyeshadow was glittery, and I couldn't help myself as I leaned forward and captured her lips with mine. It was so everything I ever wanted in a kiss. It was a million times better than the night before. It was better than any other kiss I'd ever experienced before. She was literally changing everything about who I thought I was, and I didn't give a flying fuck.

I bit her bottom lip and heard her moan softly. My panties were so damp. Was that normal? Was I supposed to be feeling like this from only a stupid kiss?

But God, it wasn't stupid, was it? It was incredible. And I was starting to accept that whatever was happening to me was going to leave me breathless in its wake.

"We should go," Peggy said against my lips and into our kiss. "Or I'm going to do something you might not be ready for."

My entire body was set on fire. I pulled away from her slowly. "Peggy," I whispered.

"C'mon, Georgia, let's get out of here. I want to take you to my favorite spot." She ran her fingertips down my cheek and along my jawline to where it met my ear. I had goose bumps everywhere. And I loved it. She placed one more tiny kiss on my lips before she turned toward the steering wheel and turned the car on. The engine sputtered to life, and she laughed. "I gotta get a new car."

"No," I said when I reached over and put my hand on her leg. "Don't. This car is so you."

"A hot mess that barely starts?"

"A classic with a beautiful soul." *Damn*, that was a good line! I wanted to high five myself. I didn't have to, though, because Peggy looked at me, her mouth hanging open, and laughed.

"Look at you! What a pick-up line that was!"

I started to laugh and smacked her on the arm. "Drive." She smiled at me one last time before she pulled away from the condo.

Watching her drive was really enjoyable. Hearing her curse when the car wouldn't shift properly at a stoplight was even better. She tried to tell me something about how she needed to get it looked at and the timing and some other mumbo jumbo, but I literally was not listening to a word she was saying. I couldn't stop looking at her mouth as she spoke. Her lips were so perfect, full and pink, and I wanted them on me.

What the fuck was happening to me?

Jesus.

We drove through a small town on the gulf coast that she said was called Dunedin. It was a really cute town with this cool little downtown area. We both decided we didn't want dinner, so she took me to get praline pecan ice cream in a waffle cone. Our arms kept brushing together as we made the short walk to the pier. She talked a lot about her friends but didn't mention parents or family at all. I wanted to ask but knew we had tons of time to get to know each other. She mentioned the word bisexual twice. I guess that meant she was bi? It was followed with a comment about hating labels, which made me feel guilty for trying to label her, even when I hated labels myself.

"I love *love*," she said when we found a bench along the water and waited for the sunset. It was cloudy, but Peggy assured me it would be great.

"I understand that." I took a bite of ice cream and kept my eyes on the horizon. The gentle sounds of waves lapping at the wood stilts of the pier was calming, thank God. Otherwise, I would have been a wreck. "Of course, I've never been in love before."

"Never?"

"I'm only sixteen."

"I fell in love for the first time at eleven," she said with a smile. She shrugged and looked over at me. "My science teacher, Mrs.

Lansing. She was so beautiful. Long, curly, dark hair, and she had these gray streaks through it. God, she was gorgeous."

Her eyes were closed as she described how she felt about the older woman from her past. I was so taken by how pretty Peggy was. Her skin was perfect, and I would have killed for cheekbones like hers. The more I was around her, the more I couldn't believe that someone so beautiful wanted to spend time with me, be near me, kiss me… It was blowing my mind.

"Do you remember your first crush?"

Would it be strange for me to say that it was her?

Probably.

So, I wracked my brain thinking of the first time I felt that feeling in the pit of my stomach, the nerves, the fear, the happiness. All of a sudden, the memory crashed into me like a wave in the gulf. "I think maybe our neighbor back in Savannah."

"Girl or boy?"

"Woman."

Peggy nudged me. "You go, Georgia! Tell me about her."

"Well, she had dark hair, dark eyes, kind of like your teacher. I was only seven or eight, though. And she was newly married and moved in with her husband. My friend Kim and I would go and hang out over there all the time. And she was so kind, so caring. I remember scraping my knee once and instead of going to my mom, I went to her. I was crying so hard, and she held me close and gave me a popsicle, and I remember feeling so calm and happy. That whole 'I never want to not feel this' feeling, which is so weird because she was being motherly. So, like, what was wrong with me?"

"Nothing is wrong with you." Peggy placed her hand on my knee like she did back at the condo, and electricity and heat coursed through my entire body. "What was her name?"

"Margaret." I tore my eyes from Peggy's hand and looked straight into her eyes.

"No shit?"

"Guess I should have known when I met you that maybe this was another chance at feeling safe."

"I make you feel safe?" The side of Peggy's mouth was pulling up.

There was no other way to answer her than to lean into her and place my lips on hers.

"You're kissing me in public," she whispered against my kiss, and all I could do was kiss her harder.

❖

SUSAN

"So, tell me what the fuck is going on here?"

I cocked an eyebrow at Melissa as we walked next to the gulf, kicking broken pieces of shells and splashing lightly through the water. "What do you mean?" I knew what she meant, but I needed to hear her say it. I had no idea why, other than to make myself believe that I was actually falling for a woman.

"With you and this Jackie woman."

There it is.

"You both seem surprisingly comfortable with this arrangement." Melissa padded next to me with her feet in the water. The water was cool, but the air was a perfect temperature of seventy-five. The break in the oppressive humidity was welcome. There were only a few people on the beach, too. The sun was going to set in about a half hour, so I knew it wouldn't be long before people started to meander down to the water.

"I guess we do. I haven't really thought about it."

"*Bullshit.*"

Of freaking *course* she was able to read me like a book. It'd been that way for years and years. Probably since high school, when I would beg her to make sure mom and dad didn't know I was staying out past curfew, and she would know immediately it was because of a stupid boy. I stopped to pick up a shell that washed up as the tide was starting to come back in. "I don't really know what's going on." I tossed the broken shell back into the water and looked out at the sun as it crept closer and closer to the horizon.

"You're kidding me, right?" Melissa walked a couple feet to the dry sand and plopped down on her backside. She stretched her legs out. "I feel like you're not telling me something. I know in the past you'd eventually tell me, but now? Now you're being all coy. And it's not a good look on you."

"You're a brat," I said with a smile as I sat next to her.

"I'm not the one that's holding out."

"Look, Mel, I have no idea where to even begin."

"The beginning. You start these things at the beginning."

We both laughed when I smacked her on her bare leg. She nudged me and leaned her head against my shoulder before I stared back out at the sunset. "It's complicated," I said softly. It took me forever to even say that much because in all honesty, I really didn't know how to begin.

"I can tell," she whispered. The sound of the waves crashing almost drowned her voice out, but when she sat upright and took a deep breath, I knew she wanted me to unequivocally hear whatever she was about to say. "Suze?"

"What?"

"She's gay. And you're straight, so there's no way that you want to do anything with her." She cleared her throat. "I mean, right?"

I kept my eyes on the water. I wished it would come and wash me away. I was not prepared for this conversation. I didn't know if I would have ever been prepared for it. And here I was, having it, with absolutely no idea how to handle coming out of the closet when I never even realized it might be somewhere I was. I smiled and glanced over at her. "Right," I answered finally, lying to her. Lying to my own sister!

"She is really pretty, though." Melissa laughed. "I mean, for a dyke."

"Don't call her that," I said. My voice was soft, but she heard me even though I didn't look at her.

"Excuse me?"

"Don't." I leaned back on my hands, dug my fingers into the sand, and looked over at Melissa. "She's a lesbian and happy with who she is." Melissa didn't say a word. She sat there, stone faced, watching me. I could see it, her inability to fully comprehend what I was saying. "She's a really good person," I said when our eyes locked. "You like her."

"What?" I tried to sound shocked. I'm pretty sure it didn't work.

"*You*. You *like* her." Melissa looked away from me and shook her head. "What the hell, Suzie?"

I sighed and mimicked how she was sitting. "I don't like her," I said and wanted to kick myself for trying to backpedal. "At least, not in the way you're thinking."

"I'm thinking in the gay way, sweetie. And you're lying to me. So…"

"Mel, no." Did I really think protesting was a good idea?

Melissa let out a solitary huff. "You're ridiculous."

"Shut up. No, I'm not."

"Admit it," she said, starting the argument that I really didn't want to have but knew was inevitable. "Admit that you like her."

Was it worth fighting? Was it? Because at this point, it was obvious to almost everyone that I liked her. I really, *really* liked her. Even though I was struggling with all of it because I wasn't supposed to like the woman that was my daughter's birth mom. But God, how did I stop these feelings when everything she did was mesmerizing? She was beautiful and flawed yet perfect, and I wanted to know everything about her. I wanted to hold her and look at her and kiss her… How was I supposed to "get the girl" in this situation when I literally didn't know I wanted a girl until two weeks ago? The whole scenario was entirely too screwed up.

"Look, Suze," Melissa said when she leaned forward and started to write something in the sand. "I'm not going to flip out on you. This is your life. You do what you want to. But…" She scribbled an "X" on the tic-tac-toe board she drew. I followed suit and drew an "O" in the upper left corner. She scoffed. "Whatever. You won't win." We quickly got through the game, her winning, of course, and then she finished her earlier thought with, "Steven's not going to be happy."

"I know. God, I know. Maybe…" I paused, took a deep breath and let it out.

"Maybe what?"

"Maybe I should go back."

"*Go back?*"

"Yes. Go back."

"To what? To *Steven?* Why the fuck would you want to go back?"

I didn't even know what to say to answer her question. I didn't want to go back, but… "It would be so much easier, wouldn't it?" I heard Melissa sigh. I wasn't looking at her because the shame was too much.

"If you really think that going back and getting the shit beat out of you is 'easier,' then you really aren't the strong older sister I thought you were."

"Wow."

"No," Melissa said loudly. I heard the seagulls start to caw over the top of the sound, though and wondered if she would stop talking or continue. She continued. "If you go home, I'll never forgive you for doing that to Beth. And I guarantee Jackie won't either."

"Melissa—"

"Stop." Melissa turned so she was looking at me. "Were you happy?"

"No."

"Then stop. Don't go back. Jesus *Christ*, don't go back if the only fucking reason would be because it'd be *easier*."

"He's going to be furious when he gets the papers."

"Who gives a fuck?"

"I do!" I shouted. "He's a runaway train, and I don't think this is going to stop him." I'd spent a lot of years of my life unhappy because of Steven, because of my inability to have courage and leave. Why should I care now if he was happy? I used to starch his fucking boxer shorts, for Christ's sake. I was so done caring.

I watched Melissa visibly swallow. "He was really crazy when he came to the house. I thought he was going to kill one of us."

"Mel, I'm so sorry—"

"No, it was fine. But still. He's crazy."

"God, what did Patrick say?"

"He said you're a goddamn saint for putting up with him for so long," Melissa said with a laugh. "And he's right."

I sighed.

"Hey." Melissa leaned into me. "I'm going to support you no matter what."

"Mel, you're such a good sister."

"Did you ever think you'd say that?"

"Nope. Never," I answered with a laugh. "You proved me wrong."

Melissa was laughing along with me as the sun dipped into the Gulf. Watching the sunset always made me feel insignificant and small in a weird way, as if nothing I did mattered in this world. But now, it made me feel at peace. I'd never felt at peace before. And the reality of that awareness made me pull a breath deep into my lungs as my eyes filled with tears. I blinked rapidly to make sure the tears didn't betray me. They didn't listen, but honestly, I didn't care at that moment. And Melissa didn't notice.

Thank God.

CHAPTER TWELVE

SUSAN

Melissa didn't stay long. She was on her way the next day, and even though it was great to see her, I was so happy when she left. Being under her constant scrutiny, especially when it came to my relationship with Jackie, became infuriating quickly. And so frustrating because I didn't want to be honest with her. I wasn't ready. I barely understood what was going on inside my heart and mind. How was I supposed to explain it to someone else? Someone who wouldn't believe it or want to understand it? I couldn't.

I was a little ashamed of myself. Here Jackie was, living her best life, out and proud, and in waltzed me (and *our* kid), who was utterly confused and scared and broken.

God.

Broken.

I was so broken. And as honest as I was with Jackie, I still didn't want to tell her everything. Because telling her everything meant telling her why I no longer had a job, why I no longer fought when Steven raised his hand, and why I was relieved when Beth actually found Jackie. I didn't know if I would ever be ready to be *that* honest.

So, Melissa breezing in and leaving as quickly as she arrived was a good thing. Except now, all I could think about was Jackie and how I never completely came clean about my relationship with her. I got a text when Melissa landed in Chicago on Wednesday afternoon saying she understood, and she loved me no matter what. I guess I did come out? I had no idea.

Who didn't remember if they actually came out or not?

I was such a mess.

As I watched Melissa drive away in the back seat of the Lyft, Jackie asked me if I would go to the beach with her. "It'll help you take your mind off things," she said softly with her hand on my shoulder. I wanted to, but I was so apprehensive about her seeing me in a bathing suit. The last time I gave a shit about something so superficial, I was eighteen and in college. I didn't know if I liked the feeling of caring about my body image.

But alas, I said I would go. So, I stripped down and pulled on my suit: black bottoms that had a stupid skirt which hid my thighs and a hot pink tankini top. Beth told me the color looked great on my tan skin. I listened, even though I felt like a blob of cotton candy.

When I emerged from the bedroom, Jackie was ready in a white cover-up and brown leather flip-flops. I was kind of disappointed that I wouldn't get to see her in her bathing suit first in the apartment. It was probably a good thing, though, because I was so ready to rip her clothes off that I had a feeling we wouldn't get to the beach.

What was I thinking? We hadn't even kissed yet! *God.* I was acting like a horny teenager.

"You ready?" Jackie's face lit up. She was carrying two chairs, one as a backpack and the other had a strap so she could carry it on her shoulder. She pointed toward a cooler. "I packed us some beers. Is that okay?"

"It's five o'clock somewhere, right?"

"It sure is. Would you mind carrying it?"

I bent down and picked up the cooler. It also had a strap, so I was able to throw it over my head and carry it like a cross-body bag. It wasn't light, so I wondered how many beers she packed. Were we going to get wasted on the beach? Great! The last thing I wanted was to drink too much around Jackie again. I was still kicking myself for the night after the Rusty Nail. I couldn't believe I screwed that up!

Jackie looked back at Myrtle and waved. "See you later, Myrt."

It warmed my heart that she said good-bye to my dog even though I knew she didn't like animals. I couldn't stop smiling. "Myrt, eh?"

"Yes, she loves that nickname. I asked."

"Oh, good. So, you asked first?"

"Of course! I mean, she's adorable. If she was a cat, though…"

We boarded the elevator, and I watched the numbers descend until we hit the lobby. The air in the confined space felt heavier than normal, which could only mean one thing: I was so nervous that I was close to passing out. If I passed out right now in my bathing suit, I would be so embarrassed. I calmed myself down by thinking about the water, the waves, the gentle breeze. I was going to be okay. I just needed to not focus on Jackie in a bathing suit. And sex.

Amazing hot sex that I wanted to have with Jackie so badly I could taste it.

My God, I was a hormonal mess.

I rolled my eyes at myself as I followed Jackie across the sand. We traipsed down the board walkway and to a place near the water. She set the chairs up and put a towel over each chair before looking at me. "This is okay, right?"

"This is perfect." After I sat on one of the beach chairs, I dug my toes into the soft sand. The sound of the waves crashing onto the beach was exactly what I needed. I closed my eyes and pulled the gulf air into my lungs. I couldn't remember the last time I was so at peace yet so nervous and excited. "I am so in love with this beach."

"It does look good on you."

I watched her from behind my sunglasses as she pulled her cover up over her head and threw it onto the back of the chair. Her bathing suit was black, a two piece, and it looked so good on her. Her skin was tan, tight, and I couldn't stop staring. She did have a few stretch marks, which made me slightly happy because it meant she was human. Even though everything about her seemed to be perfect. She had toned abs, and on the side that was facing me, she had another tattoo. This one was of a watercolor sunflower. I let my eyes wander over her thighs, the definition of her quadriceps, and the small scar on her knee. I watched as she sat on the chair next to me, both of us facing the water. She was all legs in the chair, and her stomach had the cutest creases in it from the way she was sitting. I wanted to touch her. I wanted to reach out, run my fingertips along her legs, up to the leg seam of her bathing suit bottom.

The old me would have never made the first move...*never.* But this new me I was becoming? She clearly understood how to make some moves. I gingerly reached out and ran a fingertip over the top of Jackie's smooth thigh. She moved her sunglasses to the top of her head, looked at me, an eyebrow arched, and licked her lips.

"Hi," she said softly.

"Hi."

"What're you thinking about?"

"A sunflower?" I heard myself ask.

"My favorite flower."

"Any particular reason?"

"They always look so happy. It'd be nice to always be that happy."

Her answer made my heart ache. Was it because I wanted to be the one to make her look happy? Or was it because she was the one making me look happy?

"What else are you thinking about over there?" She slid her glasses back and set them on her nose. "I can tell you have something else going on in that head of yours."

I smiled and gathered my courage. "I'm thinking about you."

"What about me?" Her voice was low, smooth, and even though the Florida sun was warm, my body erupted in chills.

"That you have saved me, and I don't know if you really meant to, but you did."

Jackie moved her hand and tugged on my finger that was still dancing around the skin on her thigh. She pulled gently before she said, "I want to take care of you. Always."

"Why, though? You barely know me." I didn't know why it was so hard for me to believe that someone would want to take care of me. Had Steven really screwed me up that badly? She stopped looking at me and stared off across the water. Her profile was so flawless: her nose, her eyelashes, even the creases around her eyes from squinting into the sun. I wanted to grab her face and smash my lips against hers.

"I can tell you, with one hundred percent certainty, that part of the reason is because of Beth." Jackie shrugged. "And the other reason? Is because…" She paused and looked back at me. "I'm fairly positive that I'm falling in love with you." I went to open my mouth to respond, and she raised her hand to stop me. "Please, don't say anything. I don't want that to freak you out. It's the truth."

"Jackie." I took her hand in mine before lowering it to the arm of her beach chair. "That doesn't freak me out. At all."

"But I mean, it might—"

"No," I interrupted. "It doesn't."

"Why doesn't it? It freaks me out," she said and laughed. "Like you said, I barely know you! And this is so unexpected. I didn't ask for any of this. And it scares me so much."

"Why? Why does it scare you?"

Jackie broke our eye contact and looked down at her lap. "Because it's stupid and reckless. And we've only known each other a few weeks. It's absurd."

I smiled and squeezed her hand. "You are so adorable."

She brought her eyes up to mine. "Susan," she breathed. "I won't be able to forget about you when you leave."

"Jackie—"

"No," she said quickly. "You don't get it. I don't share well. I don't like new people, I hate having people stay with me, and I am filled with anxiety when I entertain. But these last couple of weeks? It's been… I got attached to you both." Her eyes snapped up to mine, and she held my gaze for a second longer than necessary. "I don't want you to leave me."

That was the moment that did it for me. I was holding it together up until those words left her mouth. My heart felt as if it was being squeezed by a vise, and all I could do was slide out of the chair and lunge toward her.

When my lips smashed into hers, our teeth knocked together, and I pulled back quickly. My hand shot to my mouth. "I'm so sorry!"

I was so embarrassed. Had it really been that long that I had forgotten how to kiss someone?

She laughed and reached for me. "Are you okay?"

My embarrassment faded because of the look on her face. She was so concerned: her smile, her eyes, the way her hand reached for my face. I didn't answer. Instead, I threw myself at her again. I was more careful this time, made sure my lips cushioned the impact. Her tongue ran against my lips, past them, and dipped into my mouth. Was this how kissing should have been my entire life? I felt alive, every single nerve ending on fire. Everything about her was so luxurious. She tasted like summer, like sunscreen and beer, and I wanted to drink every last drop of her into my soul. And she felt like spring, refreshing and clean, the end to a horrible winter that held nothing but depression and heartache. Her hands moved from the arms of the chair to my hips. I felt her fingernails dig into my skin above the waistband of my bathing suit bottoms. I was kneeling on the cool sand, but the height difference made this kiss feel spectacular, as if I was a kid again experiencing everything for the first time.

Jackie pulled back when we both heard a throat clearing. Her eyes found the owner of the sound, a man walking by with his wife, arm around her, all possessive. My stomach bottomed out. What the hell had gotten into me, kissing her in broad daylight, in front of God and everyone? I went to stand up, and Jackie put her hands on my shoulders. "Don't," she said softly. "I don't care."

"I know, but Jackie," I said, and my voice caught in my throat.

"Look at me."

I looked into her eyes.

"Is this what you want?"

"What?"

"This." She motioned at herself, and all I could do was nod and smile. "Then? Don't stop because an old, straight, white guy doesn't know how to deal with people that aren't exactly like him."

I laughed. "You're right."

"I know I am."

"Then kiss me again."

She reached up and ran her fingertips along my jaw line before she placed her lips on mine. When she deepened this kiss, all I could do was get lost in the feel of her full lips, her tongue, her teeth biting down lightly on my bottom lip. She wasn't just a great kisser. She was an exceptional kisser. I was floored by her ability to not only make my heart speed up but also by the way my toes were curling with every dip of her tongue into my mouth. I could barely handle how good it all felt. I wondered if it would be like this all the time. Would she be able to unravel me with every kiss? I secretly hoped so because feeling like this was incredible. I never wanted her to stop.

"Let's go," she whispered against my lips. "Go back with me."

"Jackie…"

"Please." She latched on to my neck with her lips and bit down lightly before she said, "I need to taste you," against the pulse point on my neck.

Holy shit. "Let's go."

❖

JACKIE

Susan Weber was nothing at all like I imagined the adoptive mom of my daughter to be. I figured she'd be uptight, slightly mean, very strict, and obviously as straight as an arrow.

And when I stripped her bathing suit top off and tossed it over my shoulder before pushing her backward onto my bed, I thanked God that she was, in fact, completely the opposite.

I crawled up her legs, slid my knee between her thighs, and pressed against her center, which was still covered by her bathing suit bottoms. She moaned softly, and I captured the sound in my mouth as I kissed her again. I honestly didn't want to stop kissing her. Ever. Our lips crashed into each other's the instant the door closed behind us in the condo, and I continued to kiss her as we made our way through the living room, kitchen, and finally into my bedroom. She closed the door so hard behind us that it slammed, and we heard Myrtle start barking. She laughed between my kisses, the sound reverberating into my mouth and against my lips. I loved how it felt, the vibrations of her happiness. God, how I loved knowing I was the cause of that happiness.

"Jackie," she said after she broke our kiss. "I have to tell you something."

I looked at her, smiled, and said softly, "Hmm?"

"I've never been with a woman before."

The whole conversation sounded insanely clichéd. And I knew that she was so nervous saying it out loud. If I was writing the romantic sex scene transpiring between us, I'd have edited it three or four times before I was happy with it. Because *of course* she'd never been with another woman. I knew that. She was straight. She didn't need to tell me that. She didn't need to tell me that I would have to be gentle, that I would need to walk her through things, that I would be the one in charge. She didn't have to tell me that she was nervous or scared. I knew all of those things. Every single one of her fears and reasons behind wanting and needing this, I knew and understood them all. But my God, my heart absolutely shattered from the sound of her uncertainly and sincerity. So, there I was, with this amazing woman who I never asked for and never knew I needed or wanted, having the most clichéd of conversations, wondering how I got so lucky to find her? Or I guess, how did I get so lucky that this woman found Beth? And that Beth found me? "Susan," I whispered and kissed her once, then twice, softly, caressed her face, and ran my fingertips along her jawline, down her neck to her clavicle. "I will take care of you."

"I know you will. I'm nervous."

"Do you want to wait?"

The look that Susan gave me almost stopped my breathing. Her eyes were filled with desire, her lips were parted, and her tongue darted out and licked her lips before she breathed, "No."

"You're sure?"

"I want you so badly."

"Oh, really?" I asked with a laugh. "You do?"

The corner of her mouth pulled upward, and she chuckled with me. "Yes, as a matter of fact, I do."

The light coming in the window as the sun sank lower and lower toward the horizon made it possible to see every move Susan made: the rise and fall of her chest, the way she kept biting down lightly on her bottom lip, how the gentle pressure from her teeth left a white mark in her skin, the way the charm on her necklace had somehow settled in the hollow of her neck where it met the sternum. I found myself wanting to observe every second of the next hour or two, or hell, however long it took. Sex in the daytime was few and far between for me, and nine times out of ten, I wanted the lights off, so being able to see the way her hips curved, the swell of her breasts, the slightly darker skin of her nipples, the way they hardened even before I touched them...it was all so insanely magnificent.

And her breasts were flawless. They were full, round, and beautiful. I was getting lost looking at them. Some people were more a fan of butts, but me? Anyone that knew me would say I was a boob girl. And they would have been absolutely right. I could spend hours on them. And I intended to with Susan's. I bent my head down and captured one of her already erect nipples in my mouth. I heard her gasp as she arched into me. I bit down lightly and then sucked, flicking my tongue against the tightened flesh. I massaged her other breast and tweaked her nipple with my forefinger and thumb. The moan that came out of her mouth made my entire body heat up. I pressed my knee harder into her center and delighted in the feeling as she pushed herself against me. Her hands were on my sides, nails dragging across my ribcage, before she tugged on the straps of my bikini top.

"Off," she whispered. "I need this off."

I knelt and quickly unlatched my top. I slid it slowly off, my eyes never leaving hers. She wasn't smiling, but she was still nibbling on her bottom lip, which I found to be so incredibly sexy. I reached down after I dropped my top on the bed and tugged on her bottoms. She lifted her hips, and I placed a kiss on her stomach, dipped my tongue into her navel before I pulled the bottoms down to her knees. She helped the rest of the way and threw them behind me while laughing. I couldn't help that my eyes were drawn to her center, the soft patch of neatly trimmed hair. I placed my hand where, seconds earlier, her bottoms had been, on her hip, where the hint of a tan line existed, and ran my fingertips along her belly. I moved slowly, lightly, as I touched her. "Jesus," I whispered. She was so wet. I could see her glistening in the light. It was the hottest thing I had ever seen.

"Is everything okay?" she asked. Her voice was so unsure. It made my heart hurt.

"Yes, Susan, yes." I slid my index finger through her wetness. "You're so wet."

She draped an arm across her eyes. "Oh God, I'm so sorry."

"What? Why?" I asked as I stopped. "Why would you be sorry?" She didn't look at me, and kept her arm across her eyes. "Susan?" She finally moved her arm. "Do you have any idea how hot you are?" She moved her head back and forth. "Oh, baby," I whispered. "You being wet is a good thing. A very, very, *very* good thing. Okay?" She nodded, and I smiled. "Women like this kind of thing."

"Oh, yeah?"

"Yes," I said. "I love knowing that I'm turning you on. That everything I'm doing…" I bent down and placed a kiss on her hip. I bit down on her skin, and she moaned. "Is making you so hot." I placed tiny kisses all along her stomach, down her legs, on the tops of her thighs, until I was finally where I wanted to be. I glanced up at her as she lifted her head. "So hot…that you're dripping…with anticipation." I held her eye contact as I lowered my mouth to her and placed my lips directly on her swollen center. I heard her pull a breath in through clenched teeth, and I glanced up to watch her press her lips together before she leaned her head back. She tasted so wonderful, sweet and slightly forbidden. I slid my tongue across her and down until I could push it inside her. She moaned my name, which only made me hotter. I knew she was right where I wanted her. I focused my tongue on her swollen clit, circling it, lightly flicking with my tongue, and when I knew she was enjoying every move, I slid two fingers inside her.

"Oh God, Jackie," she whispered. "Please don't stop."

My name on her mouth sounded like a song, something I wanted to listen to on repeat for the rest of my life. I did as she begged, continued to thrust my fingers into her, soft at first, and then I gained in intensity. She was moving with me, her legs bent, feet on the bed, spread wide. I positioned my fingers so I knew they were hitting that perfect spot inside her. She was tightening around them, the muscles in her thighs were starting to shake, and her breathing was labored. Her orgasm was approaching, and as it crashed into her, I heard her voice shaking while moaning my name. Tasting the sweetness as she came in my mouth would forever be one of my very favorite memories. When her hips returned to the bed, I moved my mouth from her. Eyes still clamped shut, her chest was moving up and down with her breathing as I wiggled my fingers inside her and heard her groan.

"Oh, shit, you can't...you gotta give me a second."

I smiled as I wiggled my fingers again.

"Jackie!" She gasped and lifted her head to look at me. "I'm not kidding."

"Can I take them out then?"

"No." Susan pulled in a deep breath. I could feel everything, her pulse, her muscles twitching, her wetness. "Stay there."

"Can I come up there and kiss you?"

"Can you do that without removing your fingers?"

"You seriously underestimate me." I did my best to not move my fingers as I made my way up to Susan's lips. She was smiling at me. That smile that took my breath away the first time I saw it. I leaned down and kissed her. It was full of passion and desire. It had been so long since I kissed someone that really wanted me. Kissing Dana was always fun, and we obviously had a good time together, but I couldn't remember the last time someone wanted me like this woman wanted me. And vice versa. When she slid her tongue into my mouth, I moved my fingers inside her and then slid them slowly out. Susan broke our kiss and hissed low once I was outside of her body. "You okay?" I asked, my voice barely above a whisper. I was lying next to her, my leg over hers. I was meant to be there for the rest of my life.

"I love you," she said with a voice so quiet, so delicate, I barely heard it. But it still made my chest clench and my breathing hitch.

Oh, holy shit. "Susan—"

"No," she said. "I do. I really do."

"Baby," I whispered.

"I know. I don't know why this has happened." Her eyes were welling with tears. I was not equipped to handle this. Her and salty tears and sweet *I love yous* were not in my wheelhouse and *goddammit, what the fuck did I get myself into?* "Everything happens for a reason. I know that." Her voice cracked, and she pulled her full bottom lip into her mouth and bit down. Her teeth looked so white against the pink flesh. "Was I supposed to adopt Beth?" She started again after a couple deep breaths. "And go through hell so I could eventually find you?" Tears started to slide from the corners of her eyes, down her temple to her hairline. She wiped at them frantically, and her hands were shaking. "How am I supposed to leave a life of being straight behind me to be with you? How? Is that even what you want? This is all so fucking fast... All of it. And clearly, I'm slightly freaking out right now."

Yeah, join the club.

She let out a nervous laugh. "I'm so sorry." She placed her hands on my face and pulled me into a kiss.

"Are you okay?" It was all I could think to say, even though there was this part in me that wanted to say all of those words back to her.

"Yes." She kissed me deeply, and again, I was lost in the feel of her full lips and her slick tongue as it pressed into mine. She ran it along the back of my front teeth, and I have no idea why, but it made my entire body burst into flames. How was that so fucking hot? "You know it's your turn, right?" she asked after she pulled away from my lips. She was speaking against my neck, right near my ear, and almost as if I asked her to, she latched on to my earlobe and bit down. I almost came undone right then and there. This woman was taking me to places without even going near the spots that were aching to feel her. How was I going to survive? I had no idea.

Her words, the I love you, still hung in the air around us. It completely scared me that I wanted to say it back. I wanted to tell her *everything*. I wanted to tell her that I had never felt like this before, that my heart had never beat like this for someone else, that I'd never wanted to protect someone like this before, that I'd never wanted to take care of someone before. I wanted to tell her that I was normally selfish and a jerk and had no time or need for women other than fucking them and forgetting them. I wanted to tell her what a horrible human being I was, how I didn't deserve her or this or even Beth. How did I tell this woman that she was my everything when I barely knew her? How did I, a person who had never romantically told someone that I loved her before, tell this woman that I wanted to change my entire existence to be with her? I wanted to love her so hard that she forgot her sadness and pain. I wanted to give her my heart, and I knew without a shadow of a doubt that she would protect it with everything in her. And I wanted her to know that I would never stop fighting for her, for us, and for our family.

Our family.

❖

SUSAN

My heart was racing. I'd told Jackie that I loved her. Why? Why did I open my mouth and let actual words escape? I felt so stupid, but at the same time, maybe it was the right thing to say at that time. She made my heart beat for the first time in ages. I had been floating through life, barely existing. I stopped doing everything that mattered to me because I was so depressed about the loss of love with my husband and the impending doom of the loss of my marriage. But Jackie looked at me with those eyes that she passed on to our daughter and touched me with her delicate hands and made me want to be alive again. I wanted to *live.* I wanted to love her for the rest of my days.

And the way she loved me in bed was incredible. I couldn't remember the last time I'd cried after sex. Hell, I couldn't remember the last time I'd wanted *more sex.* Every nerve in my body was on fire. I felt like a maniac, sex-crazed and ready to go all day and all night. "I want you to tell me what to do…how hard to go, how fast… okay?" I said against Jackie's ear. "I want to make you feel me…feel how much I love you."

"Jesus Christ," Jackie said. She hissed out the last part of *Christ,* and I smiled.

"Are you okay?" I bit down on her earlobe again and heard her gasp.

"Are you trying to kill me?"

I managed to smoothly maneuver my way out from under her. I rolled her onto her back. "Lift your hips," I instructed, and I slid her bikini bottoms down her legs. She was completely shaved. I think my eyes must have gone wide because she chuckled.

"Everything okay?"

I licked my lips and tried to wet my mouth with saliva. I nodded before I locked eyes with her.

"If you don't want to do this…"

The way her voice trailed off made my chest ache. "Baby," I whispered. I lunged at her and kissed her because I had no idea what else to do. I wanted her so badly. So very badly. And I didn't know how to handle the desire inside me. What was going on with me? Why did I fall so hard and so fast for this woman?

This woman!

Everything about the entire situation was so fucked up and scared me so much. But I didn't care. I wanted to be happy. It had been years since I was happy. Years since I wanted to be touched. Years since I wanted *to* touch. Jackie waltzed into my life, and that was it. My need to be alive was not something I could fight any longer.

"I want you," I said against her lips. "I want you. All of you. Forever."

"Forever?" she asked, and *oh my God*, her voice cracked.

"Yes," I whispered, and I moved my hand over the smooth skin of her arms, across her shoulder to her chest. I ran my fingertips down to her breasts, the left one first. She was smaller than me. A perfect size, actually. A size I would have killed for when I was growing up: perky, round, not more than a handful. I wanted to study every inch of her, memorize every detail, like the size of her nipples, the color of the darkened flesh against the untanned skin of her breasts. I placed my lips on the side of her breast. Her skin was so soft, and she smelled so perfect, like Banana Boat sunscreen, the breeze from the gulf, and deodorant. I wanted to bottle the scent and wear it every day of my life. She was salty on my lips, and I licked a path to her very hard nipple. I pulled the stiff flesh into my mouth and sucked. Her sharp intake of breath spurred me on, and I rolled her between my teeth. I knew what I liked, so I did it to her and hoped for the best. I was not disappointed when I flicked her with my tongue, and she moaned my name. How did it sound even better like that than when she said it earlier into my ear?

I moved to the right breast, lavished it with as much attention as I had the other. I heard her breathing start to become more rapid when I bit down again. I sucked next to where I nipped, hard enough that I knew it would leave a mark. I let go, and she picked her head up to look at me.

"Did you give me a hickie?"

I nodded. "Is that okay?"

"Jesus," she whispered. "Yes."

A laugh spilled from my mouth, and I smiled at her. "So, are you going to tell me what you like?" Her head was propped on a pillow, and I wanted so badly to get my mouth on her neck, right where the slope of her jawline stopped, where her pulse point lay under the soft skin. "Because I'm sure I could fumble around and figure it out, but I feel like you have a plan." She lifted her head again, raised an eyebrow, and smiled a smile I hadn't seen before. It was sexy, sensual, full of arousal, and I literally could have crawled up her body and kissed her for the next twelve hours. Everything about the look she was giving me was so intense, so unlike any other look that any other person had ever given me. "Do you not..." My voice trailed off. "Have a plan?"

"Sweetheart," she said as she propped herself up on her elbows. My eyes were instantly on her breasts and her abs, how they were flexed from the way she was sitting. "There's never a plan."

I felt instantly self-conscious. Did I mess everything up?

Jackie moved, and now she was kneeling in front of me. I loved how comfortable she was completely nude, but it made me wonder if I overstepped the comfortable easiness we seemed to find without much effort. I reached up and moved my hair behind my ears. I was trying to not cry. I didn't want to get emotional again.

"Give me your hand," Jackie whispered as she held her hand out. I situated myself so I could put my hand in hers. She took it and laid it on her heart. I noticed the way my skin looked against hers, felt how soft she was, how her heart was pounding under her breast. "Do you feel that?"

"Yes."

"That's for you."

"Jackie," I whispered.

"No, you have to hear this. I need to say it." She smiled. "I do love you. And I'm not going to lie to you; it scares me. You scare me, but only because at the end of the day, none of this feels foreign. It all feels right. It was supposed to happen this way. That we were supposed to find each other, if for no other reason than for me to save you and Beth when you needed someone and for you to show me that falling in love with someone doesn't have to actually hurt." She reached forward with her free hand and ran her finger along my temple, down to my ear, and she pushed my hair behind it. "None of this has been according to some plan...so us? Together? In this moment? Doesn't have a plan either, okay?"

My heart lodged in my throat. I swallowed again and again and tried to hold back the emotion her words were causing. I finally nodded, and the smile she gave me made my entire body tingle. "Can I make love to you now?" I asked, my voice quiet but not nearly as unsure as it was earlier.

"Please do."

I moved into her space, placed my lips on hers, felt her hands on my naked body, on my sides, on my hips as she pulled me closer to her. She repositioned herself, her legs out, and I crawled on top of her. I tried to turn my brain off, to tell it that my heart had this. I was going to be able to handle all of this. I wanted her so badly. I wanted to make sure she knew that.

She was propped on her elbows again, kissing me, when I placed my hand on her stomach. I moved it slowly down until my palm was flat on the smooth skin right above where my fingers landed on her wetness.

Is that how I felt? How wet I was? Because if so, *Jesus Christ*...

It had been ages since I touched myself, so I honestly couldn't remember. How sad was that? Not only did my husband not know my body any longer, but neither did I. Jackie spent more time and attention on my body than anyone had in years. And now I was going to reciprocate.

When I slid a finger through Jackie's wetness, she gasped into our kiss. She leaned her head back and broke our kiss, so I placed my lips on her neck, moved lower to her shoulder where I bit down lightly before I slipped a finger inside her. I was so delighted when she moaned, low and seductive, and ended it with my name. I smiled against the soft skin of her shoulder before I pulled my finger out and then pushed two inside her. She slid her legs farther apart, and I settled myself on her right thigh, straddling her, letting my own wetness touch her. I had my hand next to her, bracing my body weight, and when I pulled out and thrust into her again and again and again, I felt my arm start to shake. I was so aroused from hearing her, from seeing her underneath me. She bit down on her lip, she told me not to stop, she told me I was doing perfectly, and she told me I felt so amazing. I couldn't handle how wonderful she made me feel because I made *her* feel good. Was that how sex was supposed to be? Was it supposed to make you feel equally as good when you helped that other person out? It was so not how my past life had been.

"Susan?"

"Yes?"

"Can you touch my clit?"

My entire body flushed. I smiled at her, looked down at my hand, and pulled out slowly. "Fingers in or out?"

"Out, just touch it."

She was so fucking sexy. The direction didn't make me self-conscious, either. I was so shocked and happy. I put my fingers right on her, started to massage, then lightly stroke.

"I'm so close; please, do not stop."

"Do you want my fingers in when you come?"

"Yes," she said softly. "Please…yes, put them back. Oh God."

I slid my fingers back inside her and let my thumb do the work. Every time I pulled out and pushed in, I brushed her clit, and before

I knew it, she was unraveling underneath me. She was no longer propped on her elbows. She had her head thrown back, and the veins in her neck were visible. She arched her back into me, continued to orgasm as I thrusted into her. I had no idea what was happening to me, but when she finally got to the top of her orgasm, I felt myself start to have one of my own. She was gripping my back now, and I heard her whisper in my ear to let go and come. And I did. I came so hard that I collapsed on top of her.

Her low chuckle in my ear was so well timed. "Are you okay?"

"Oh my God, I am so sorry. Did you finish? I am so embarrassed!" I sat up and covered my face with my hands. That never happened to me before. How did it without her even touching me?

"That was so fucking hot. And yes, I finished. Believe me… That was…wow." I felt her sit up, and her hands pulled mine from my face. "You are incredible. Absolutely incredible."

I lunged forward and kissed her. I wrapped my arms around her, slid my tongue into her mouth, and felt her somehow manage to slip her hand between us, and then slip her fingers inside me. I was so close already that it took no time at all for another orgasm to slam into me again. And then it happened again. Two times in a row! "Jackie, oh my God, you have to stop," I panted. Her fingers were still inside me, and I knew if she continued, I'd either die or come alive, and I couldn't decide which one I wanted to happen more.

We both collapsed onto the bed. I was completely spent. My heart was beating so fast, so hard, and my breathing was not returning to normal. I glanced over at Jackie, at her smile, her eyes, and she started to laugh. A deep belly laugh that made my brain short circuit from the sheer joy I felt hearing how happy she was.

"Susan?" she whispered after she looked up toward the ceiling fan.

"Hmm?"

"I don't think I've ever felt this happy before."

I rolled onto my side, and a smile stretched across my gently bruised lips. "No?"

She shook her head, still staring up, and then reached up to her eyes. I heard her sniffle, saw a tear slide down her cheek toward the sheets, and heard her say, "Fuck. I hate crying."

I placed my hand on her abdomen and scooted closer, laid my leg over hers and kissed her shoulder. "I'll make you happy for as long as you'll let me." And it was true. I would never hurt her.

❖

BETH

I used to think it was insane how I got to see a baby elephant being born when we were at the San Diego Zoo. I was eight, and I was at a day camp for kids who wanted to be zoologists. I was allowed to help with so many different things, and I held on to that memory ever since. It was probably why I always felt that elephants were my spirit animals. I used to talk about how I wanted to be an elephant whisperer and save them from being poached. Watching the birth somehow formed a bond with the animals that I really never understood. But I didn't fight it. I loved elephants.

I was a strange kid.

Watching Mom and Jackie as they went from whatever the hell they had been to what they were now? It was hands down better than seeing the elephant being born. I was sure it was because I was older and wiser. I was mesmerized by the whole thing. And as I sat next to Peggy at the parking spot near the airport telling her about it, she listened to me as if I was telling her the secrets to the world. She didn't interrupt me. She didn't say a word. She kept staring at me. And for maybe the first time ever, I felt really important. And really turned on.

Ugh…

"It's been a weird ride, y'know what I mean?"

Peggy cleared her throat. "I do, yes." We were sitting on a blanket on the ground, and when she leaned back against the bumper of her car, she smiled. "You know how crazy it is, right? Like, you realize it?"

I nodded and smiled back. "I don't think you've ever told me about your parents." I turned so I was facing her, sitting cross-legged. "Are they still together?"

"They are not," Peggy answered softly. There was a plane getting ready to take off, so the rumble of the engines stopped our conversation momentarily. We both turned our attention toward the sky as the Allegiant Airlines plane roared over us. The heat from the runway and the engines followed and slammed into us. I could hear Peggy's gentle laughter die down once the moment passed. "Guess we should have picked a different spot for these deep conversations?"

"I mean, *I'm* having a good time." I moved my hand so my pinky brushed the bare skin of her thigh above her knee.

She turned her head, and her eyes locked on mine. "Really?"

"Yeah, really."

"So, my parents?" Peggy looked back at the few stars we could see through the light pollution and sighed. "They divorced when I was three. I haven't really had a mom. I mean, we talk or whatever, and I used to spend every other weekend with her. But she is pretty absent as far as who helped shape me into the person I am today. My dad raised me. He is wonderful, even though he rides a Harley, smokes a lot of pot, and owns a landscaping business that seems to always be struggling." She shook her head while she chuckled. "He's been really amazing. He's done this by himself for years."

"Never had a girlfriend?"

"There have been a few women. One that has stuck around for the last couple of years. She's nice. Her name is Monica. I like her a lot. She calms my dad down, too, which is nice."

"Does he know about you?"

Peggy laughed. "He's known since I was five when I pitched a fit about having to wear a dress to church. I've always gravitated more toward women than men. Don't get me wrong. I've crushed on some boys, but the number of women I've had crushes on definitely outweighs the boys. I've had a crush on one of my female teachers every year since I was like, seven."

"Seven!"

"I know," Peggy said softly and glanced at me before turning her attention back to the sky. "I'm a sexual person. Always have been."

"That's not a bad thing."

She looked over at me, an eyebrow arched, the corner of her mouth pulled up slightly, and asked, "Oh, yeah?"

I nodded and was happy that the darkness of the night hid the blush that crept through my body and flooded my face.

"You know, Brock is pissed off at me."

I shook my head and sighed. "Why?"

"Because of you. Because you chose me."

"Oh? I chose you, eh?"

She reached down and linked her fingers with mine. "Didn't you?"

"Honestly?" I looked away from her and tried to hold myself together. "I don't know if I had a choice." She squeezed my fingers lightly. "I sort of couldn't help it. Y'know what I mean?"

"Yes," she breathed. "And you're a lot younger than me."

"I am one year younger than you," I said. "You're crazy." She laughed that smooth laugh she had, and I felt myself melting into her. "You do confuse me, though."

"Why's that?"

"I thought I was into guys and guys alone."

"You can still be into guys, you know."

"I know," I said softly. "I mean, maybe I am? I don't know."

Peggy brushed her hand over my knee, then pressed her palm onto the top of my thigh. "Bisexuality is alive and well in this world."

My words were stuck in my throat. The feeling of her hand on my thigh made my entire body tingle.

"I'll never pressure you."

"Oh, Peggy," I said softly. "You know I want you, though, right?"

She leaned over and placed her lips on mine and kissed me so sweetly and softly. "Where did you come from? How did I find you?"

I smiled when Peggy sighed and gently pressed her forehead against mine. "I feel the same way about you."

"What am I going to do if you move back? I won't survive."

"Don't let me," I said with a small smile. "Don't let me go." And I did something I never thought I'd have the courage to do. I moved and straddled her lap, and when I placed my hands on her face, she leaned in and kissed me. Her hands moved up the back of my shirt, and I wondered briefly if I was ready for this. To give myself fully to this girl who stole my heart and soul.

"Georgia?"

I smiled into her kisses. "Yes?"

"I want to make you feel good…"

"You do."

"I'm not going to let you go. Okay?"

I pulled back and looked into her eyes. "I am absolutely okay with that." And I was. I really was.

CHAPTER THIRTEEN

JACKIE

Watching Susan flip pancakes while I sipped coffee was quite possibly the most marvelous thing I had ever experienced.

Except, of course, the two back-to-back orgasms she gave me earlier that morning. It sounded really stupid, but damn, Susan was a quick study. She had me on my side and then on my stomach and my word, being fucked from behind was quite possibly my favorite position. I could not even begin to describe how alive it made me feel.

And Susan? Behind me? Thrusting into me?

Fuck.

I could have died and let the Lord Himself take me away. I didn't know if I had ever felt as complete as she made me feel.

"What the heck has gotten into you?"

My head jerked toward the sound of Beth's voice as she walked into the kitchen. She was up, dressed, and appeared ready to tackle her second week of school. She seemed to be settling in really well. The decision to actually put her into school was a joint decision made by Susan and myself. When we had the conversation, both Susan and Beth were relieved that I didn't want them to leave, that I wanted them to stay forever if they would. And they were so happy they didn't need to go back to Savannah anytime soon.

"Nothing! Why?" I asked with a shocked expression. *Busted.*

"Yeah, right. You have no poker face."

Susan was looking over her shoulder at us, smiling, with one perfectly sculpted eyebrow arched.

"What?" I asked. I shrugged. "I was *thinking*!" Susan chuckled, and I made eye contact again with Beth, who was leaning against the counter eating a plain pancake. She narrowed her eyes. "You are the child. You remember that, right?"

"Mm-hmm," she mumbled around a mouthful of pancake.

"Whatever," I said softly. "You act like you aren't equally guilty of whatever you're accusing me of."

Beth pointed her thumb at herself. "Me? What are you talking about?"

"Oh, really? Flitting around here, smiling, laughing, FaceTiming Peggy at all hours of the night. Don't think you're the only one with eyes." I watched as Beth's shocked expression slowly morphed into a smile. "Yeah, see?" I pointed. "You're smiling because you know I'm right."

Beth glanced at her mom, then back to me. "I have no idea what you're talking about."

"What *is* going on there?" Susan asked as she removed the last pancake from the griddle and placed the plateful on the island in front of me. She motioned toward them and said, "Eat," and it was followed by a wink that made my insides tingle.

I shuffled three onto my plate, lathered them up with butter, and poured maple syrup over the tops. The first bite melted in my mouth, and I let out a moan. Susan and Beth both looked at me, and I mumbled my apologies.

"What is going on where? With Peggy?"

Susan gave Beth a look and said, "You know what I mean."

I saw Beth's eyes, the way they went wide for a split second and then the nod that seemed to mean *okay, I see where you're going with this.* Her eyes darted to me, then landed back on Susan, who mimicked Beth's standing position against the counter. "So, I think I'm in love with her."

Well, shit, she did not beat around the bush.

I watched for Susan's reaction, which had to be bubbling beneath the surface, but if it was, she didn't let it reach her face. I wondered what that meant. Was she shocked? Sad? From my experience, most parents were sad after learning about their kid being not what they expected. My mom was so mad that she told me I was going to Hell and that she couldn't believe I would do this to her. She finally came around, but it was not a fun two years.

"I know that might not be what you expected to hear, or whatever, but that's kind of where I am at the moment." Beth shrugged and folded her arms across her chest. "I don't want you to be upset with me. I don't want you to think there's something wrong with me. I know this isn't ideal or what you wanted for me. I get all of that."

I kept my eyes on Susan. She still wasn't budging, and it made my heart ache for Beth. I slid my stool out from the counter and sprang to action. "Beth," I said as I took the ten feet or so in as few steps as possible. I put my hands on her shoulders because she was still staring at Susan. "Look at me." She finally moved her gaze to look directly into my eyes. I couldn't handle how it was like looking in a mirror sometimes. "We do not think that there is anything wrong with you."

"She does," Beth said as she motioned toward Susan.

"No, she doesn't." I was worried Susan wasn't going to chime in, then I felt her hand on the small of my back and saw her other hand delicately land on Beth's cheek.

"There is absolutely nothing wrong with you," Susan whispered. "Beth, you're my baby. All I want is your happiness. If that happiness is with a girl, so be it."

I was watching Susan's delicate cheekbones, the fullness of her lips, and how gorgeous her jawline was. How was it possible that this gorgeous woman became even more beautiful as she stood in front of our daughter and supported her?

"Jackie? Are you crying?" Beth asked.

Oh my God, I was. I was crying. My hands shot to my face, and I wiped at the tears on my cheeks. "No! Heck no! It was some dust or something. I'm sure of it."

Susan was smiling, Beth had the smirk that clearly I passed on to her, and they both nodded. "Dust, eh?" Susan asked quietly.

"Had to have been dust. Definitely." Beth grabbed my wrist and tugged me into a hug. Susan wrapped her arms around us both, and for the first time in a long time, maybe we would all be okay.

When Beth pulled away, she took a deep breath. "So," she said and cleared her throat. "I need to go to school. Can I take these pancakes to go?"

Susan whisked around the kitchen, grabbed a baggie, and shoved three pancakes into it. She poured orange juice into a travel mug and pushed the items into Beth's hands. "I love you," Susan whispered as she placed her hand back on Beth's cheek. "So much."

"Thank you, Mom." Beth's audible sigh of relief was almost palpable. "I love you, too. And you, I love you, Jackie."

I looked from Beth to Susan, then back to Beth. "You do?"

Beth laughed. She honest to God laughed at me! "You're ridiculous," she said as she leaned in and kissed me on the cheek. "I'll see you guys later."

"Tell Peggy we said hello!" Susan shouted as Beth rushed through the apartment, backpack slung over her shoulder, and out the door. When the only thing I could hear was my beating heart and Susan's deep breaths, she asked quietly, "You okay?"

I braced myself on the counter. The cold granite was exactly what I needed. "I'm not sure." It was a weird feeling. I'd always been happy being a lesbian. It was never an issue, aside from my mom's two-year freak out. I was always able to find what I needed when I needed it with a woman of my choosing. It was familiar and comfortable.

"What are you thinking?"

I stared at the tile floor. "If I could have chosen this for her, this is exactly how I would have wanted it. Is that wrong?"

"I don't know if I get what you're saying."

I looked at Susan, and she placed her hands on the granite, boosted herself so she was now sitting on the countertop, and crossed her left leg over the right at the ankle. Her fingers wrapped over the edge of the counter, and she leaned forward slightly. Her hair was slightly wild, the curl not handling the increasing Florida humidity. She had a headband that was securing the fly-aways, and she looked so beautiful. I almost hated how pretty she was because losing my train of thought and having my breath catch in my throat with no warning was a little unsettling. I felt so much for this woman. I was in love with her, but I also wanted to *communicate with her*. To open up and share a part of myself I had never shared with anyone. And when she raised an eyebrow, I felt my heart tell my brain it was okay to let go. I took a deep breath, let it out slowly, and quietly said, "Beth wasn't an accident."

Susan was insanely good at not responding without thinking. She sat there, her eyebrow still arched, and looked at me. She didn't move. She didn't even seem to be breathing.

"I got pregnant on purpose." I saw her knuckles whiten. "I was in college. And I hated my life and myself. I knew I was gay. I knew it. But I slept with a man. Once became twice, which turned into a regular thing. There was nothing that I liked about it." I finally pulled my eyes from Susan and looked down at my clasped hands. "I got pregnant because I thought it would fix me."

"Fix you? How?"

I shrugged. "Coming out was not easy for me. My mom was mad for years. My dad was, well…not much better? So, I tried to make it right. I tried to fix myself with a baby. And it backfired." I explained to her that it wasn't easy; none of it was easy. I hated everything I was doing, never felt comfortable, and trapped a really good friend into something neither of us wanted. "Travis was great. He really was. I met him in college. We were in this creative writing class together. He approached me, and I thought, 'Hmm, this could be interesting.'" I flashed back to Travis in his green Henley polo and faded jeans. He had mouse-brown hair, cute dimples, and a great smile, and I let myself go. I needed to have sex with a guy. I needed to open myself up to the possibility that I was wrong about who I was.

"Is that where Beth gets her dark hair?"

I nodded, still looking down at my hands. "Her smile, too."

"I don't know. I think her smile is yours." Susan's voice was soft, caring, full of emotion. I glanced up at her.

"You think?"

"Yeah," she said, and she had a small smile on her face, I guess to show me that she understood.

"I'm sorry." I heard the words before I realized I said them. "I thought I could do it. And Travis sort of flipped out on me when I told him. He got so angry. He didn't want to be a dad. Accused me of doing it on purpose and he wasn't wrong. I *did* do it on purpose. I stopped taking my birth control, and I told him afterward, and he flipped. He went crazy. I lost him after all of that. He never wanted anything to do with me again. All of that so I could fucking figure myself out. I was so messed up." I felt bile rising, and my stomach twisting uncontrollably. Talking about myself was always hard. But talking about this? Something I was so ashamed of and hated myself for was making me hate myself all over again.

Susan slid off the counter and closed the distance between us. "Jackie?"

Her voice was so smooth. All Susan had to do was say my name, and my entire body responded. "Yeah?"

"You did the right thing," she whispered as she placed her hand over mine. "You gave her a good life with me."

"I guess you're right."

"I am right," she said softly as she pulled me into her arms. "I'm very right."

I buried my head in her shoulder and the soft skin of her neck. She smelled like sleep and breakfast, which made me so happy. And *turned on*, unfortunately. It wasn't the right time to try my moves again. Even though I probably wouldn't have to beg at all. I figured why not? "Do you think we could go have sex?"

Susan's laugh was so light and airy that it made my insides shiver. "I don't think that would be a problem."

"Okay, good, because I really need to feel you right now."

"Oh, really?"

I pulled back and looked deep into her eyes. "I need to taste you, too."

"Holy cow," she said as she breathed out, a blush filling her cheeks.

"Honestly? I really want to make you moan my name." I thought I wasn't going to turn on the charm? Guess I was wrong.

"Then what the hell are we waiting for?" Susan asked as she backed away and started in the direction of my bedroom.

I stopped her. "Right here is good."

"The floor?"

"Yes." I pulled her back toward me and pulled her pajama pants down her legs. "Spontaneity is the spice of life. Haven't you heard?" When my eyes met hers from my kneeling position, she placed two fingers under my chin and licked her lips.

"I love you," Susan whispered. "I am so happy you told me your story. *Beth's* story."

I hooked my fingers into the waistband of her light pink panties and slowly started to slide them off, over her ass, her thighs, until she could step out of them. I leaned forward and placed a kiss on her, breathed in her scent, and felt for maybe the first time in sixteen years that maybe I did the right thing.

CHAPTER FOURTEEN

BETH

So, coming out to both of my moms before school was probably not the best idea, but everything was going really well for me. It was my second week, and it was awesome so far. I was enjoying it, which was foreign for me. I normally hated school. Hated the idea of school. Hated communicating with people who really meant nothing to me.

But for some reason, I sort of *fit in*. It was strange, but at the same time, comfortable. Peggy was a senior. Me, a junior. Maybe it helped that I was friends with an upper classman who was pretty popular. I mean, she was in a band. That was pretty freaking cool, right?

I was happy that I let my mom and Jackie talk me into actually going back. Part of me wanted to start the entire school year over next year. Be a year behind and cut my losses. No one would have blamed me. Going through the divorce with my parents was not easy. Even though Jackie had been so wonderful.

And what the hell was going on with her and my mom? Clearly, they were fucking. That realization was like a slap to the face at first. I got over it, of course, but wow. That came out of left field.

"Good morning, Beth."

I looked up at my new art teacher. "Hey there, Mrs. Thorn. How are you?" She was a larger woman, not fat but tall, and she had this long, dark brown hair that she always put in a braid over her shoulder. Her glasses always slipped down her nose, so when she spoke to anyone, she looked over the top of them. She wore these long skirts and flowy shirts. Maybe she'd been a hippie in her younger years, which totally made her cooler than she probably deserved. She had to only be in her thirties, but Peggy said she was much older. Either way, I didn't care. She was cool, trendy, and she was my favorite part about the new school (except for Peggy, of course).

"I'm doing well. Listen," she said as she pulled a stool out and sat across from me at one of the high-top tables in the art room. "There's this art competition I think you should enter."

"Um. What?"

"It's called Creative Minds, and it's been going on forever here in St. Pete. It's very prestigious. Artists enter from all over the country. It lasts for a few days, and it's coming up in about a month. They only judge on one of the days. You can still enter, though. I checked it all out. They allow late entries until two days before." Mrs. Thorn pushed her glasses up the bridge of her nose and sighed. "I entered when I was in school many, many, *many* moons ago. I got second runner-up, which was amazing because it gave me a huge scholarship to go to a university of my choosing."

"I mean, that's really cool and all, but I don't think I can enter a competition. What would I enter? This?" I held up the drawing of Myrtle I was working on for one of her assignments. "It's a child's drawing. Anyone can do this!"

She laughed. "Actually, I know you won't believe me, but that's *really* good, and you have great lines and shading going on." She studied it and pointed to Myrtle's paws. "Look at the detail in the hair on her feet. That's not easy to do."

My shoulders fell and I tilted my head. "Come on, Mrs. Thorn. You know what I mean."

"Okay," she said before she clasped her hands on top of the table and leaned forward. Her breasts propped on the table, and in other circumstances, I probably would have stared and then later wondered why I was so intrigued. Thankfully, I was finally fucking figuring it all out, so I jerked my eyes up to hers. "I'm not going to lie."

"Okay?"

"Peggy told me about your paintings."

"So? You've already seen some of my work."

"Of your moms."

My breath hitched. "Oh."

"Yeah."

"*Oh.*"

"*Yeah*," she said again. "I know that may have been private."

I nodded. "They are private. Yes."

"I think you need to consider it. Because you could *win.*" She reached across the table and put her hand on mine. Teachers did not normally touch students, but for some reason, this didn't feel awkward. "I'll leave you to your work."

I watched her walk away in her Birkenstocks with her skirt flowing behind her. My mind was racing. I was torn between being pissed off at Peggy and Mrs. Thorn and ecstatic that either of them thought I had talent. *Especially* my teacher. She was an artist herself. So, her thinking that I could maybe do it? And win? Shouldn't that have made me happy? Why was I feeling so much anger?

I looked down at my drawing. It actually was really good. Why was I doubting myself so much? I jerked my head up when I heard Peggy's voice coming from the hallway and saw her turn the corner into the art room. She smiled at me, and my heart jumped into my throat. She was so beautiful with that goddamn purple streak in her red hair.

"Hey there, my sweet Georgia girl," she said as she approached. God, I loved that she called me that. She was making this so hard. She leaned in and kissed me on the cheek, and I felt myself pull away. "Whoa there." She looked at me. "What's going on?"

"You told Mrs. Thorn about my paintings?" I watched Peggy's face fall. "Those are private. I showed you because you're important to me. Not because I want other people to see them."

"Come on," she said softly as she reached for my hands. I pulled them away, though, and the look that appeared on her face was as if I killed something inside her. It broke my heart, but I felt really betrayed.

"No. This is not up for debate. You should have asked me. Or better yet, you should have kept your mouth shut."

Peggy stared at me for one beat, then two, and finally looked away. She pulled her bottom lip into her mouth and bit down with her straight, white teeth. I saw her chest rise and fall with the deep breath she pulled in through her nose and let out slowly. "Y'know what?"

"No, I don't." I was struggling. I wanted to kiss her and be mad at her at the same time. How was that possible?

She looked at me, pushed her hair behind her ears, and crossed her arms before she said, "You are a hell of an artist. You capture things, pets, people like no one else I have ever seen."

"You act like you're a fucking curator of an art museum or something. You know nothing."

"I know nothing?"

"Yes, you know nothing."

"Why? Because I don't have a goddamn art degree? You think that means I don't understand beauty when I see it? Or that things don't touch my fucking soul?"

Whelp, there went my heart as it melted onto the floor. *Fuck.*

"You are amazing, Beth." Peggy uncrossed her arms and put both hands on my face. I didn't pull away this time. I stared into her eyes and felt myself getting lost in them. I hated how much I loved her. "You do things I never thought possible. You have this joy surrounding you, this amazing energy that I am so thankful I get to be around. Beth…" She stopped and took a deep breath. "You create this life for yourself to live in, and you have let me be a part of it. And I am so thankful for that."

"But I don't want others to be a part of it."

"Why not?"

"Because it's private."

"Do you have any idea how many people would kill for the opportunity to see their parents fall in love?"

"What?" I asked. The sad part about her question was that I knew that was what was happening. I knew my mom and Jackie had fallen in love. I could see it and feel it, and that was why I started the paintings. I sensed it was happening before the first brushstroke happened. But hearing Peggy say it, hearing it laid out so plainly, was a gut check I was not prepared for.

"Honey," she said softly. "You know that's what's happening. You see it. You've captured it. And it's fucking beautiful." She leaned forward and kissed my forehead. "You can keep them private if you want. Or you can show the world what it means to find happiness and love in the most unexpected places." She moved one of her hands onto mine and squeezed it before she turned and left me sitting in the art room by myself.

❖

SUSAN

Well, it was official.

I was addicted to sex with Jackie Mitchell.

I'd spent most of my adult life being turned down. I'd conditioned myself to not want sex or want to try to have sex because rejection was a hard thing to deal with. When I looked back at the years I spent with Steven, I wondered how I did it. I wondered how the hell I didn't go absolutely stark raving mad. Because I really enjoyed sex. I actually craved it a lot. Well, maybe it wasn't the sex that I craved? Maybe it was the intimacy or the connection with my significant other that made me feel as if I mattered, as if I was the only person who existed in those moments, as if the person holding my heart would never hurt it.

It was amazing how quickly I got to the point of thinking that I was crazy. That I was selfish and awful for wanting more from a person that already gave me a lot. He gave me a great house, a wonderful life; he supported me when I had miscarriage after miscarriage. He was the one who helped me start looking into adoption, even though I knew he was fine without trying any longer. I was depressed and sad and a real hot mess.

Steven slipped away, though. The man I fell in love with slipped right through my fingers, like sand that was held too tightly. The harder I held on, the further he got from me, until sleeping in the same bed was foreign, kissing was uncomfortable, and sex was unheard of.

Conditioning wasn't only what happened when an athlete trained for an event. Anyone could be conditioned. I specialized in reconditioning juvenile drug addicts. I took their miserable moments, made them remember them, and then conditioned them to want to never relive them. To find the good in their lives and hold on to it with both hands. And above all: focus. *Focus on the good, and happiness without pain. Don't forget the past, but don't focus on it.*

Before I knew it, I was doing the same thing. I conditioned myself to focus on Beth and on running the house. I did it all wrong, though. I forgot the most important part.

Focus on finding happiness without pain.

I forgot all about my own happiness. And when I quit my job and sank deeper and deeper into the black hole of my unhappiness, I could no longer focus.

But now?

Wow. Talk about a turn-around.

I was smiling and laughing again. I was focusing on Beth's beautiful transformation, on Myrtle's smiling face when she would play in the gulf, on Jackie's eyes and hands and the curve of her lips. And I was focusing on my own happiness. Which meant when Jackie brought me to orgasm two times on the kitchen floor and then proceeded to do the same when we moved to her bed, I embraced every single second, and it was absolutely incredible.

It baffled me. How had I lived my entire adult life with someone who barely wanted to touch me? Barely wanted to kiss me? Barely wanted to have sex with me? I remembered having the conversation with my friends about my lack of a sex life. Their husbands were all over them, all the time, and mine I could barely get to look at me twice. When I found the lipstick stains and smelled the different perfumes, I knew then that it really was me. It wasn't that I found the only man in the tri-county area who didn't like sex. It meant that I was not what did it for him anymore.

I absolutely should have gone to therapy for all of that.

Weren't medical professionals always the worst patients, though?

I heard the door open and close to the condo. I was sitting on the balcony watching the dolphins swim around the gulf in the distance.

I knew it was Beth getting home from school. I wondered how she would feel after our discussion this morning. It was a welcome surprise when all of a sudden, I felt her hand on my shoulder before she plopped onto the couch next to me.

"Well, hello there," I said softly. I studied her profile, the tan she was getting from the Florida sun, and the way she focused on the calm of the view in front of us. She looked so free. I don't know if I ever saw her like that before.

"What a day."

"Long?"

"No, it was…weird?" She looked over at me briefly and then immediately back at the gulf. "Very, very weird."

"Want to share?"

"I showed my paintings to Peggy."

I smiled. "Really? That's big. You won't even show them to me."

Beth looked at me and raised an eyebrow. Some of the facial expressions she made were so me that it was hard to think I didn't actually have anything to do with that biology. "Yeah, well, she told my art teacher about them."

"Mrs. Thorn, right?" I asked, and Beth nodded. "Well, why is that bad? Didn't you say she thinks you have talent? You were excited about that."

"She wants me to enter them into this prestigious art competition."

"Beth, honey, that is so great!"

"Mom," Beth said, followed by a sigh. I knew that tone. She was worried about something. "The paintings are about you and Jackie. And like, your journey."

Oh… "Our journey?"

"Yes." Beth took a deep breath. "I know you two are together. I wish you'd stop playing dumb."

"Wait a second." I adjusted my position on the couch and turned toward her. "Your paintings are of Jackie and me?" Beth nodded. "And they're of us slowly figuring things out." It wasn't a question, but Beth nodded again. "You've known this whole time, haven't you?"

"It's a little hard to miss. Do you see how you two look at each other?"

A blush started in my chest and crept into my face. "Beth, look—"

"No, Mom, it's really okay. Like, I really love Jackie. And I get it. I mean," Beth started and then paused. "I talked to Peggy about this, about how mad I was at her for telling someone about these when I haven't even decided how I feel about everything. But I realized that I am happy about it. And she said something really profound. And it's so true. Not many people get to witness their parents falling in love. And, like, I've been able to see it all. I feel like, maybe deep down, I knew it was going to happen, too, which is why I started the paintings almost immediately."

My heart was in my throat. How did I get so lucky to raise such an amazing young woman? "You've seen the whole thing?"

"From the moment you opened the door in Savannah to the moment in the kitchen this morning."

"I'm sorry," I whispered. I don't know why I was sorry, but I was. "I didn't plan any of this."

She smiled at me and put her hand on mine. "I know, Mom. I know." She squeezed my hand. "I'm going to enter the paintings. I wanted to let you know. And I don't plan on telling Jackie about what the paintings are. But I wanted you to know because you're my mom. And I didn't want to shock you."

"You think Jackie won't be shocked?"

"No," she answered with a laugh. "I don't think much shocks Jackie. Except for you. You shocked her."

"Yeah, well, your dad is going to be getting a shock in the next couple of days."

"What? Why?"

"Veronica left a message on my cell." Beth knew what I was going to say next, but I still ended with, "The divorce papers are on their way. To both of us."

"Mom, are you okay?" She had her hand on my arm and I could tell she was worried. I nodded, smiled, and tried to reassure her, even though I wasn't sure if I really was okay. I was so scared. "It's okay to not be…"

As she said that, Jackie came out to the balcony, Myrtle bounding behind her. "She's a great runner!" Jackie said as she plopped down on the chair and smiled. It quickly faded as she saw our faces and our positions. "Um, did I interrupt something? Is everything okay?"

Beth acted quickly. "I'm entering my paintings into the Creative Minds art show."

Jackie's face lit up, and she leaned forward. "Holy cow, Beth, that is awesome!"

"Yeah, I'm pretty excited about it."

"It's in a couple weeks. You know that, right?"

"Yes, I know." Beth smiled. "Mrs. Thorn talked me into it. And Peggy."

Jackie glanced at me and then back at Beth. "Look, if you win, which I think you could because you have such talent for being so young, this will be huge. This has been going on for years in St. Pete, and people come from all over the world to enter. It's a big deal."

"I've heard," Beth said with a laugh. "I don't know if I can win, but I wanted to let you know. And you two are more than welcome to come and see the unveiling of the paintings."

"Oh, we'll be there. For sure." Jackie leaned back in the chair. "Let's go celebrate tonight. Let's all go to dinner."

"I think that sounds like a great idea."

"Can I invite Peggy?"

"Absolutely." Jackie smiled, and I leaned forward and pulled Beth into a hug.

"You can always invite her," I whispered next to her ear. "You happy is so beautiful."

"I feel the same way about you, Mom."

CHAPTER FIFTEEN

JACKIE

For someone who absolutely hated people sometimes, I absolutely loved entertaining. I got anxiety, and I was nervous, and I wanted everything to be perfect, but I absolutely loved it at the same time. I didn't understand it. I loved inviting my friends over, having beer and wine, cheese, and appetizers. They all begged me to make Italian beef sandwiches and defrost my homemade pierogis, and I did. I was a great hostess

Even though I hated people

It was the weirdest thing.

Either way, it was who I was, and I thought Susan and Beth were starting to understand me little by little, which baffled me since I didn't even understand myself most of the time.

I decided to throw a party the night before the art fair and the unveiling of Beth's paintings. I was so excited. I didn't think Beth was as excited as I was because she was so nervous, but I wanted to take her mind off it for a couple of hours. She agreed to the party, but only after I told her how excited my friends were to support her. She was so much like me, it was ridiculous. I never wanted to do something until I knew people would be devastated if I didn't show up. Why did I care? Who knew? But I did. I always had. It was slightly annoying.

Tabitha and Janice were there early. And apparently, they were back together, which, whatever. I wanted Tabitha happy.

Dana arrived fashionably late, of course, *and* made a scene. She brought a new girlfriend, which was fine if not a little frustrating. The new girlfriend, whose name was Vicki, was a fan of my books, and we'd met years earlier. We got along great. She was a really nice person. So, it made me feel bad that Dana only brought her to piss me off. But whatever, I knew Dana was irritated with me. A week earlier, I broke off our friends with benefits arrangement. I should have broken it off with her months ago. I knew she was in love with me, yet I still mindlessly fucked her, and that really fucked her up. I was a horrible person. I really was.

I was turning over a new leaf, though, and it felt good.

Ryan was there about an hour late, but he was practicing for the Creative Minds drag show, so I didn't give him any shit. He actually brought his mom, Helen, with him to the party. I was so excited. I loved his mom so much. She was hilarious and kind. A total supportive mom, she was our local PFLAG chapter president. Whenever I thought about my mom, I wondered how different things would have been if she would have had a moment or two with Helen.

Beth invited Peggy, of course. And Brock actually made an appearance. He was such a cute kid with a good soul, so I knew it made Beth happy that he seemed to let go of his anger that she "chose" Peggy. The other band members, Taylor and Amanda, were there, too. And a couple other new friends from school. Sadly, I forgot their names. Oh, well.

I knew something was off with Susan toward the beginning of the party, and I was worried, but once everyone arrived, she settled down. Maybe it was nerves? She wouldn't really tell me. I was trying my hardest to not be overbearing because sometimes I could get that way. It was probably part of the reason I'd stayed single for so long. I could suffocate people easily with my constant need to understand what was going on inside their heads. I was such a basket case sometimes. It was frustrating when I could feel myself doing it, and I kept doing it. So, I backed off and let Susan settle in and was happy when I saw her laughing and talking with Tabitha and Janice. I even saw her exchange some pleasantries with Dana. And Vicki had her ear for a while, talking about me and my books; I heard them both say a couple of my character's names.

It made me so fucking happy that Susan was reading all of my books. The girlfriend I was with when I published my very first book (a complete labor of love that took forever for me to find the courage to finish and get published) took a long time to read it. Even then, she did it because I kept badgering her. It hurt my feelings so bad that someone who proclaimed to love me wouldn't want to read something I put so much of my heart and soul into. Maybe I really was selfish?

"You've been holding that glass of rosé for the past thirty minutes. It's getting warm."

I looked at Beth, who was now standing next to me. She looked so beautiful. So much different than the first time I met her, soaked to the bone standing on my doorstep. "Hi there," I said and put my arm around her. "How are you?"

She leaned her head against my shoulder. "I'm actually doing really well. Thank you so much for doing this for me."

I squeezed her a little tighter. "Well, thank you for finding me."

I could feel her eyes on me. "Jackie?"

I looked down at her. "Yes?"

"You know I know about you and Mom, right? And that I'm completely okay with it?"

I couldn't think of any words to say. I was a writer, goddammit. It wasn't often that I was left speechless.

She smiled. "I love you. And I'm so totally stoked with how my life has turned out."

"You're stoked, eh?"

A laugh spilled from her, and it made my heart smile. "Yeah, I'm like, so super stoked." She licked her lips and looked around the room before she looked at me again. "Do you still talk to…um…the sperm donor?"

I gasped and choked on my own saliva.

"Jesus, Jackie, calm down." Beth laughed as she patted my back. "It was only a question."

After I calmed down, I put my hand on her arm and made sure she was looking at me. "You want to know about this? Right now?"

"I mean…"

I sighed. "I knew him in college. My attempt at being straight. At being normal." Beth was staring at me, into my eyes, and it was like looking into a mirror. "I don't talk to him anymore."

"It was a mistake."

I saw Beth take a deep breath after she said that, and I smiled. "No, honey. It wasn't a mistake. We wouldn't have you. And you are not a mistake. Not one thing about you is a mistake." I placed two fingers under her chin and my thumb on her chin. "Not even this damn dimple is a mistake."

"You promise?"

"I've never thought you were a mistake."

"You're a good mom, Jackie." Beth pulled my hand from her chin and squeezed it gently before she turned and walked away. *Thanks a lot, Beth.* I was on the verge of an emotional breakdown at a party. Perfect. I wanted to smack her. I mean, not really, of course, but that was not cool to do in the middle of a party!

My apartment never seemed small until right that second. I turned and moseyed through the crowd of people in my condo, making sure to stop and thank every person I saw for coming. I tried to be nonchalant, but even with the air conditioning cranked and the beautiful breeze pouring in the balcony doors, I was beginning to feel trapped. I beelined toward the balcony, straight to the railing, and took a deep breath. I heard someone following me, and I prayed to God it wasn't Dana. I was so sad when her familiar scent crashed into me.

"Are you okay?"

She was mimicking my position against the railing, holding her glass of wine over the side like me. "Yes, I'm okay."

"I miss you," she said softly.

I looked away from her because I was well aware of what might happen after that confession. I'd been there before with her numerous times, and it always ended the same way. With us in bed, her begging me to love her and me begging her to shut up and fuck me. Looking back on it, I realized how damaging I was to her and how damaging our entire relationship was to me as well. Friends with benefits never ended the way people thought it would. I continued to stare out at the dark water, the moon high in the sky, and realized two months had passed since we were this close to each other. So much happened to me in those months.

A good deal of time passed before I heard her take a deep breath. She nudged my arm with hers. "Jackie, look at me."

I didn't want to comply, but it was so hard to say no to someone I'd spent so much time saying yes to. I met her eyes and bit my lip.

"Do you have any idea how hard it is for me seeing you happy?" She smiled. "And liking that I'm not the cause of it?"

"You *like* that you aren't causing my happiness?" She was making no sense whatsoever.

She nodded. "Yeah, I really do like it. All I've ever wanted was for you to be happy. I wanted to be the cause of that happiness for so long. So very long." I watched her as she closed her eyes and then looked out into the night. "But you were a star I could never lasso. It's taken a long time for me to come to terms with that. The last time you came to me, wanting sex, and you kissed me, and it felt weird. Like you were holding something back. Like you were afraid of who you might become if you let go of yourself. Like you were scared that you might actually find happiness. I knew then that what we were doing wasn't good for us. We would never be the same, and I needed to let you go. I needed to find a way to be okay without you." Dana smiled. "I didn't want you to be okay with Susan, though. I'll admit that."

"*Of course* not."

"You know how I feel about you. I love you to death. I don't want you to get hurt."

"I know, Dana. I'm not going to. Not this time."

Dana shrugged, sipped her wine, and looked back out at moon-lit water. "I know."

"Wait. So…" I paused as Dana looked at me, her eyebrows raised. "You didn't bring Vicki to make me jealous?" Dana leaned her head back as she laughed. "Okay then. Question asked, question answered."

"You're ridiculous, ya know that?" Dana nudged me.

"I treated you horribly, didn't I?"

"Hey, don't do that," she said as she snapped her head toward me. "I was there, too. I participated."

"I know, but Dana—"

"No. Stop." She looked away again and took the last swallow of her wine. She smacked her lips softly afterward and chuckled to herself. "You really do know your way around a woman's heart, don't you?"

"I mean, I hope so. I write *romance* for a living."

"Yeah, well, until now, you've been pretty shitty at actually following through with that *romance*."

"Touché," I said with a laugh. "That one hurt a little."

"You deserve it." Dana nudged me again. "Susan does seem… nice."

I laughed. "Don't hurt yourself giving out compliments."

"What?" Dana was trying to be sincere. Not very hard, but she was trying. "I'm being serious, though. She seems nice."

"She's very nice. I really like her." I could feel the blush in my cheeks and was thankful that the string of Edison lightbulbs were not bright enough to give me away. I smiled. "So, Vicki, though?"

"Don't start."

"What? How'd that happen?" I laughed. "I thought maybe you brought her to make me jealous."

"Truthfully? It started out that way, but…" Dana sighed and shrugged. "She's really nice. And not that bad in the sack."

"Jesus," I said with a laugh. "You're insatiable."

"You were not providing anymore. I needed to get it somewhere!"

"Hey, you two!"

We both turned as Tabitha came up behind us holding three shot glasses like an expert bartender. "What's up?" I asked, and Tabitha shoved one of the shots at me and another at Dana.

"Do you two even realize what day it is?" Tabitha laughed. "You don't. Because you're both looking at me like I'm a fucking nut job."

"It's a Friday?" Dana laughed.

"No, you fuckers. It's our ten-year friends' anniversary. God, you both suck."

"Holy shit, is it really?" I started to search my memory bank. "Oh my God. It is. We all moved in together—"

"In Kenwood!" Dana shouted. "How the hell do you remember the exact date?"

"Because I'm *good*." Tabitha laughed when Dana and I both rolled our eyes. "No, really. I found some pictures last night, and they had the date on them. Ha!" We all descended into laughter. "Okay, so let's drink. Toast to the future. More years together." Dana and I both raised our shots and clinked them together with Tabitha's. We tossed our heads back, and the liquor burned on the way down. It was awful, and I knew immediately what it was.

"What the hell was that?" Dana asked. Her face was all twisted, and the look was unmistakable. She was seconds away from possibly vomiting. Hopefully she wouldn't lose it over the balcony like she had years earlier.

I laughed. "It was Malort. Tabitha's favorite thing she ever brought back from Chicago." It really was disgusting. Tabitha loves a good sneak Malort-shot attack.

"Jesus, Tabitha! Are you trying to kill me?" Dana shouted at her as she punched her on the shoulder. "My fucking throat is on fire." She was downing her wine now, and I knew that meant she'd be drunk in about forty minutes.

After we stopped laughing and reminiscing, Dana went back inside to find Vicki. Tabitha watched her leave and then looked at me. "She okay?"

I smiled. "Yeah, she's good. I don't know…I think maybe I'm the one that always thought she was deeper than she actually was. You know what I mean?" Tabitha stared at me, blinked a couple times, and I couldn't stop the laugh that spilled from my mouth. "You have no idea what I mean."

"Nope." Tabitha shrugged. "As long as you're both gonna be okay."

I nodded and downed the rest of my wine. "Janice?" I asked with an eyebrow cocked.

"She'll break my heart again. People don't change. They only think they will." Tabitha smiled and motioned toward the condo. "Come back in. Susan was asking if you were okay."

"She was?"

"She said you looked like you had seen a ghost, then you fled to the balcony." Tabitha laughed. "She can't keep her eyes off you. How does that feel?"

I shook my head slowly. It was so hard to believe that I actually loved the fact that someone wanted me. "It feels really fucking good."

"And to think you thought nothing would ever happen."

"It's crazy, though."

"Is it?" Tabitha shrugged. "You never wanted to give Beth up. You've regretted it for years and years. You got her back, and you gained someone to spend the rest of your life with. I feel like that's not crazy at all. It's pretty fucking romantic if you think about it."

"Even for a romance writer?"

"Especially for a romance writer."

I followed Tabitha inside and immediately found Susan's eyes. She lifted her chin slightly and tilted her head, silently asking if I was okay. I smiled at her and winked. I could see the weight lift from her shoulders, and it made my entire heart jump into my throat. I didn't know how this all happened, or why, but it was time to stop questioning it and let it happen.

It was time to be happy.

❖

BETH

No lie, I was so not looking forward to the party. I was actually dreading it. When Jackie brought it up, I protested it hardcore. It wasn't that I didn't like the idea that someone wanted to do something nice for me. In fact, that was the only part that I was okay with. But there was not a bone in my body that liked being the center of attention. It was part of the reason that I didn't want to do the art fair. The idea that *my* work, my heart and soul, was going to be looked at and judged and critiqued made my stomach hurt.

Jackie was so freaking excited about the party, though. She told me a couple times that this was good and what needed to happen to an emerging artist. Her friends threw her a party when she released her first book. And then for every book after that, she had a launch party. At the point she was at in her writing career, she didn't need to do launch parties, but she knew it was a good excuse to get together, drink, and have fun. I was hoping that as I aged, I would be more like her and find a place where I was okay with the attention. Jackie seemed way more comfortable in her skin in front of people than I ever had. I knew she was older and had a lot more time on this earth than I had, but it still baffled me how outwardly she seemed fine. Even if on the inside, she was freaking out. I asked her how she managed to get to that point in her life, and she said sometimes you had to put yourself out there and hope for the best. Did she like doing it? No. But it was necessary. She used the term "personal growth" more than once. Which made me laugh because until I met her, I always assumed the worst out of my biological mom. But Jackie was so far from what I expected.

Now I knew personal growth came from stepping out of my comfort zone. I'd done a lot outside of that comfort zone. Namely, my relationship with Peggy, which had turned out to be the most comfortable one I'd ever been in. How odd that something so far outside of my zone made me the most relaxed that I'd been in years. I'd always been a hot mess when it came to nerves and worrying about things, but Peggy calmed me in a way I thought could only come from prescribed medication.

Peggy told me I needed to be okay with this party, that Jackie loved me and wanted to show her friends how amazing I was. It sucked sometimes how right she was about things where I was concerned. She knew me so well in such a short amount of time. I didn't think anyone would ever want to take the time to understand the way I ticked. She not only took the time, but she didn't seem to be turned off by some of my eccentricities. It was so nice to be able to be myself for once. She never made me feel bad for my feelings or told me to calm down when I got excited or shushed me when I would get loud about something.

So, I settled down and let myself have a good time, which ended up being really easy.

Jackie's friends were so cool, and seeing Mom happy and laughing was absolutely breathtaking. Almost all of Jackie's friends had left except for Tabitha and Janice. They were out on the balcony now with Mom and Jackie. Peggy was all that was left out of the people I invited. Brock, Taylor, and Amanda left to go drink at the normal airport spot, and I didn't want to go. I wanted to stay with Peggy and never leave the safety of the condo.

I nauseated myself with how far gone I was.

"You're so nervous about tomorrow, aren't you?"

I looked over at Peggy. We were sitting on the floor in my room next to my bed, leaning against it. She looked so perfect. Her hair had beach wave curls in it, and she'd pulled half of it up into a barrette. Her makeup was light, and I could see the tiny freckles across her nose. She had recently changed her nose ring to a silver hoop, and I loved everything about it.

"I am very nervous," I finally answered. I shrugged and sighed. "It's not like I'll win. But so many people will be there." I was prepared for the day. My paintings were packed securely in transport bags that Mrs. Thorn loaned me. I'd picked out a simple red sundress to wear, with my checkerboard Vans, of course. I knew I'd keep my hair down, maybe curl it like Jackie did for the Rusty Nail. I was ready. For once, I was prepared and ready for my moment to shine.

"I think after the day is over, you'll feel like a completely different person."

"What do you mean?"

Peggy turned so she was facing me. She pulled me closer, and I slid easily on the tile floor. "You are so much stronger than you realize. All this will do is make you see how amazing you are." She reached up and pushed my hair behind my ear. "You are going to take their breath away like you do to me."

"I love you." *Holy shit.* Did I say that out loud? Peggy's face was so hard to read in the seconds that followed that I was thinking maybe I didn't actually say it. "Pretend I didn't say that." I started to push away from her. So typical of me and my inability to actually deal with the consequences of actually having feelings.

Peggy placed her hands on my arms and steadied me. "Stop, Beth. Stop."

"No, Peggy, it's fine. I shouldn't have said that. I'm nervous and scared about tomorrow. Emotions are running high. That's all."

"Stop," she whispered. "Don't take that away from me."

"Take what away?"

"Your love." She smiled. "I've been in love with you since the moment I first laid eyes on you. Sprinting after Myrtle, sand flying everywhere."

I lunged at her. I legit *lunged*. My mouth covered hers, and I kissed her as if I was never going to be able to kiss her again. I wanted her so badly. I wanted her mouth and her hands and her heart for the rest of my life. How could I have been so young and thought I knew what I wanted for the rest of my life? Was that even possible?

"Beth," Peggy whispered between kisses. "We can't do this here. Your moms will kill us."

She was so right. "Take me somewhere. Please. Take me somewhere. I need to feel you."

"Okay." She stood and helped me up from the floor. I followed her to the balcony. "We're going to go for a drive. Is that okay?"

I watched my mom look at Jackie, Jackie's gentle nod that it was okay, and then my mom's smile. "That's fine. Please be careful. Don't be too late. You have to be up early tomorrow."

"I know, Mom. I promise we won't be," I said as I squeezed Peggy's hand before I said my good-byes to everyone.

I followed Peggy out of the condo and into the elevator. The minute the doors slid closed, she turned, pushed me up against the wall of the elevator car, and covered my mouth with hers. It was a searing kiss that lasted only about sixty seconds before the doors slid open at our destination, but it was so insanely hot. How was I supposed to handle myself with this girl?

"Where are you taking me?"

Peggy opened the door to her bug and grabbed a blanket out of the back seat. "The beach."

I laughed. "Won't we be seen?"

"No. I have the perfect spot. Come on," she said as she held out her hand. "Let's go make love."

And that was when I completely melted into a giant puddle onto the asphalt.

❖

SUSAN

The party was amazing. Jackie really knew how to throw a great get-together. And I really needed the distraction. Earlier in the day, I received the divorce papers in the mail. Finalized. Ready to sign. Which meant one thing: Steven would have received them, as well.

The thought of him ripping into that envelope and seeing what that contents were made my stomach tie into a knot. I had been doing so well not thinking about the consequences of a divorce from Steven. I was trying to focus on the benefits, not the things I'd be missing out on. I hate to say I was materialistic, but being married to a doctor was nice. I knew I'd get child support, and because Veronica was a bulldog in the courtroom, I also had an alimony clause. Only temporary, until Beth and I were back on our feet, but I knew Steven would flip. He'd fight the whole thing. I could already taste his anger, like blood and spit from a backhand to the mouth.

I swallowed once, twice, three times before the lump that lodged in my throat finally dissolved. A couple of deep breaths later and I was ready to mingle.

Hell, who was I kidding?

I am a wreck.

Pushing fifty. Almost divorced. Barren. Had to adopt to find the fulfillment I so desperately craved. Fell in love with a woman.

A woman...

I found Jackie as she flitted around the room from person to person, checking in with them, bottle of chardonnay in hand, refilling glasses and playing the role of hostess perfectly. Of course I was destined to fall in love with her. She was so magnificent. Everything about her. Especially the way she loved me.

And honestly, I was impressed with her ability to entertain, considering how anti-social she made herself seem. I wondered if maybe she was more comfortable than she gave herself credit for.

When she first said she wanted to have a party for Beth, I knew immediately that it was not going to be something Beth would be cool with. She was going to be nervous and probably reserved, and she might even tell Jackie not to bother. I didn't really understand it, but Beth had always been someone who shined in front of people but absolutely hated the attention.

It dawned on me, though, when I watched Beth with the slew of people Jackie had invited that she was *exactly* like Jackie. Biology was a crazy thing.

When I say "slew" of people, I meant it, too. There were so many people who showed up, readers of Jackie's, authors from the area, and artists of all kinds. It was exciting. And Jackie asked Beth to showcase some of her paintings and charcoal drawings, which was such a great idea. Beth chose a few, including one of Jackie that I quickly said I wanted to frame. Jackie blushed ten shades of red when I said it, but I didn't care. It was incredible. There were a couple others that stood out. One of the beach, one of Forsythe Park at home, and one of Peggy. The look on Peggy's face when she saw it was as great as Jackie's.

It was really nice to see Beth and Peggy together at the party now that I knew what was really going on. Especially since Beth talked to me about it, as well. She unloaded one night after a date with Peggy about her guilt over conflicting feelings with Brock and how ultimately, she really connected with Peggy. In a way she didn't know existed. How could I argue or protest? It was exactly what happened with me. The crazy part about both of our stories was, had Beth not made me escape to St. Pete, neither of us would have been able to find ourselves.

It scared me that Beth was going to live a life which was going to cause her some issues. But I also knew she was strong, independent, and so special. Labels didn't matter to her. And that was refreshing. I should have taken a page out of her book because I would so often jump to conclusions. Even though I would try my hardest to not judge a book by its cover, it still happened. Maybe because I was burned so many times in my past. I didn't know. Working at the juvenile center for mental health was the longest stretch of time I went without being judgmental. I needed to get back to my roots. I was so much happier then, so much more in touch with the person I wanted to be. It was amazing the things I gave up for the people I thought I loved.

"So, you're telling us that you really had no idea who Jackie was when you met her?"

I smiled at Tabitha, who was sitting on the chair across from the couch on the balcony. Janice was sitting on the floor, her legs stretched out in front of her, crossed at the ankles. Tabitha was playing with her long, dark hair. They had come a long way since the Rusty Nail. "Yes, you heard me right."

"How would she know who I was? She's straight. Remember?" Jackie was lying on the couch, her legs on my lap, and I was lightly scratching them. "Maybe we should take a page out of Beth's book and not label me at all?" I asked with a laugh.

"Well, well, well. Look who's turning over a new leaf,'" Jackie said. "I can do that. For sure."

I nodded. "Thank you. And anyway, I'd probably identify more as bi. I mean, I liked boys for a long, long, *long* time." I laughed. "A *very* long time. God, I'm old."

"You're not old," Jackie said, her voice soft. "You're perfect."

"I'm most definitely bi," Janice said while her head was leaned back in Tabitha's lap. "Actually, I'm probably more pan than anything."

"Equal opportunities to all, eh?" Jackie asked with a laugh.

Janice chuckled. "You know it."

"It's crazy to me. You got to know the *real* Jackie. It's pretty cool." She shrugged. "Most of the women in the les-fic community fawn all over her. You're a lucky lady there, Susan Weber."

Janice nudged Tabitha's leg with her elbow. "Your incessant questioning is not making a good impression."

"Susan's fine. She already knows me and that I ask a lot of questions."

"And how would she know that?"

"Well, I saved her from Dana in the bathroom at the Rusty Nail."

"Wait. What?" Jackie lifted her head from the throw pillow and looked at me. "She did?"

I rolled my eyes then glared at Tabitha. "Yeah, she just cornered me. She was worried. She wanted to make sure I wasn't going to hurt you." I squeezed right above Jackie's knee. "It's fine. We obviously talked tonight. It's not a big deal."

"Are you sure?"

"Yes, I promise." I sighed and stopped scratching Jackie's leg. "I do need to talk to you about something, though. I was going to wait, but I feel like Janice and Tabitha are going to be here awhile."

"Probably not a bad assumption," Tabitha said with a nod.

"I got the divorce papers today."

This time Jackie sat up completely. "Honey, why didn't you tell me?"

"I don't know. I guess because the party was tonight, and I knew you were worried about everything coming together. I didn't want to distract you, or me, or even Beth." I knew that was a horrible excuse, even if it was partly true. Seeing the papers had made this all real. The bruise had faded finally, but those papers were forever. "And now he has them, too. So, I'm a little worried."

"I can imagine," Janice whispered. I saw Tabitha shush her by placing her hand over her mouth. I shook my head gently, then made eye contact with Jackie.

Jackie swung her legs off me and placed her feet on the floor. She reached over, pulled me closer, leaned her head against mine, and said, "I will protect you. Please believe that."

"I know you will," I whispered.

"Excuse me?" Tabitha asked with a joking tone. "Are you kidding me? Is this man going to do something crazy?"

I shrugged. I honestly had no idea. He'd hauled off and hit me and threatened Melissa. I really didn't know what he was capable of doing. The weirdest part was that I hadn't heard from him and neither had Beth. Neither of our phones had missed calls or unanswered text messages. So, maybe he really didn't care? I hated to admit it, but that thought was as unsettling as him being a raging lunatic.

"Everything is going to be fine," Janice said softly. "I know people on the police force. If things get dicey…"

I looked up at her as her voice trailed off. "Thank you."

"Of course." She stood and held her hand out to Tabitha. "Let's get out of their hair."

"We'll see ourselves out, Jacks." Tabitha waved, and when I heard them leave the condo, I looked at Jackie and burst into tears.

"Oh, baby, come here." She pulled me into her, and I sobbed into her neck for what seemed like hours. The end of my marriage was happening. Everything I worked so hard for was ending. Everything I thought I wanted in this life was ending. I was so unhappy during the last few years. I would even say I was miserable. So, why was I so sad? It was as if a part of me was dying right along with the death of eighteen years of my life.

Jackie must have been reading my mind because I heard her say softly, "It's okay to mourn the death of your marriage," which made me cry even harder. I felt so confused and sad.

The more I thought about it, the more I realized that I absolutely needed to get back to therapy. I was a hot mess.

Abusive husband.

Divorce.

Fell in love with a person of the same sex.

Said person of the same sex was the biological mother of my daughter.

Said daughter also fell in love with a person of the same sex.

What the hell else needed to happen to me to make me realize that it was okay to break down?

At least Jackie understood; as I cried, she held me so close, let me collapse, and made sure to hold me up when I was finished. I didn't know what I did to get so lucky, but I was so thankful for Jackie Mitchell. So very thankful.

CHAPTER SIXTEEN

BETH

Jackie dropped me off, asked if I needed help, and I told her no. I knew she wanted to be supportive, but I was so fucking nervous. All I wanted to do was be alone for the next two hours before the start of the competition.

I barely slept. Probably for more reasons than only my nerves, considering that I had the best night of my entire life only a few short hours earlier. All I could think about were Peggy's hands and lips but also judges telling me that I was no good at life and questioning why would I ever think I could compete in this prestigious fucking art fair?

Goddammit.

Creative Minds: The Premiere Art Show in South Florida

I read the sign three more times before I finally went inside and checked in with the front desk staff. The check-in attendant's name was Stella. She looked like Dorothy from the *Golden Girls* with her long, flowing shirt, white linen pants, and gaudy gold sandals. She was wearing a scarf and smelled exactly how I remembered my grandmother on my mom's side smelling. I think she wore White Shoulders? I didn't remember the name for sure, but damn, the smell? It hit me like a ton of bricks, and I wondered briefly if maybe my grandma was watching over me. She was always my favorite, and she always encouraged me to draw and color.

"This is your booth, sweetheart," Stella said as she breezed over to one of the many makeshift kiosks. There were three walls, made of two-by-fours and peg board, and each booth had a long table toward the back where the artists sat. "You might be the youngest participant we've had in a while." Stella moved her eyes over my body and landed on my Vans. "Those shoes are you."

Her voice was so deep. I kind of loved it. "Thank you, Stella."

"Oh, sweetheart, you're nervous. I can hear it in your voice." Stella motioned for the two men carrying my canvas bags of paintings to set them down. "Carefully!" She moved around the kiosk and scolded them. She'd been running the show for years. That much was obvious. I was impressed. Not that I had anything to compare her to. But her presence was much needed. She was soothing in a total grandparent way, and I was eating it up because I sorely needed to be soothed. I watched her lean against the table toward the back of the kiosk. She clasped her long fingers together. She had a ring on every finger, and it made me smile. "Tell me. Why are you nervous?"

I laughed. "You're kidding, right?"

"No. I am absolutely not kidding." She delivered the line with such accuracy that I was upset with myself for being such a brat.

"Sorry," I mumbled and folded my arms across my chest. Stella lowered her chin and looked at me over the top of her bifocals. "I don't know why I thought I could do this. Look at all these artists. And their paintings and sculptures and drawings." I moved my hand around the room. "I am sixteen years old. What have I experienced that will move people?"

Stella smiled. Her teeth were so straight and white. I immediately assumed they were false. Why would I even be thinking that? *Focus, Beth!* "I am sure you have some stories in that brain of yours. I've known you all of ten minutes, and I already can tell that this," she motioned to my entire self, "has some spunk and life in it that is way beyond her sixteen years." She walked over and put her hands on my shoulders. "I'm going to let you in on a little secret." She leaned in a little closer. Her breath smelled like coffee. "I used to teach art years ago at the same high school where Mrs. Thorn teaches. We keep in touch, have coffee, and I swing by from time to time to check in on her. I've seen your work. You have nothing to worry about, Beth Weber." And with that, she turned and left my kiosk, shouting orders at the men delivering art across from my kiosk.

My heart had settled down significantly. That was for sure.

I went to work and started to hang all of the paintings. I started with the first bag, of course, and was so happy when I hung the first painting. It looked so good against the dark pegboard background. I had brought three large tapestries, as well, to really spice up the area. I hung one on each wall, draped them strategically, and made sure the paintings looked good against each one. Peggy helped pick them out. She had such a great eye for design and decorating; they really brought out the colors of the paintings. The last piece was a rug that Peggy said was necessary. We bought it at a really awesome thrift store that I absolutely fell in love with. I didn't really believe her, but when I laid down the red, wine-colored rug, it really tied everything together so well.

When I stood at the front of the kiosk and took everything in, it made me feel as if I was letting people inside my brain, which was exactly what I was going for. I wanted the judges to step inside my memories, my feelings, my *soul.* I wanted to make sure that it was obvious that this was my life.

At the left front side of the kiosk, I set up a wooden crate with a pamphlet I designed and printed at Staples. It explained my background, about my past work, and about this exhibit, as well as a title.

I went back and forth with the title. At first, I thought "The Journey" because that was exactly what it was. It started when I first stole my mom's credit card and with shaky hands and a stomach full of guilt paid for the private investigator. I still didn't understand how I'd gathered the courage to hitchhike to St. Pete from Savannah, either. Why was I such an idiot? I could have been killed!

So, no. "The Journey" was not going to cut it. It was too obvious.

And then I remembered the moment in the art studio at school where Peggy defended herself, defended why she told Mrs. Thorn about my paintings and my work. She said why the paintings meant so much and how special it was that I was able to witness this progression from strangers to lovers.

She said, "You've created this life to live in…"

It hit me when she said that because how often did people get trapped in horrible circumstances and think they couldn't get out, they couldn't escape?

It wasn't only about creating a life to be able to live in, though. It was about creating a life to be able to survive in.

It was creating a life to *love*.

And that was what I called it: "Create a Life to Love."

As I stood there, in my cute dress and my Vans, I felt truly proud for the first time.

Of course, the second the lights dimmed and Stella started rocking the microphone, I instantly felt those nerves again. It might have been the first time I ever actually prayed. And boy, did I ever pray.

❖

JACKIE

There had been numerous moments in my life when I looked back on giving Beth up and wondered what the fuck I was thinking. I wondered where my brain was. What was I doing? Why did I basically trick someone to get me pregnant? Why did I fuck up his life, my life, my child's life? Why was I so stupid and small and insecure with myself that I didn't think I could handle a child?

I knew it was crazy to focus on the past and the poor decisions I'd made. The sheer amount of poor decisions I made baffled me. I couldn't believe I turned out to be an even halfway decent human being.

Susan, on the other hand… She'd taken this tiny, special person that I never wanted to give up, sheltered her, raised her, and loved her as I would have. And it made my heart ache. It made me feel slightly better that I fucked up, that I did what I did. She was exactly the type of person I'd hoped Beth ended up with. She was exactly the type of person *I'd* wanted to end up with, which now that I thought about it, was such a weird coincidence.

I glanced over at Susan as we sat idling in the turning lane to the convention center. She was staring out the window. She looked wonderful in her black dress with tiny red roses all over it. It was a wrap-around dress, so at this angle, I could see her cleavage perfectly. Her hair wasn't as curly as normal, but the gentle waves looked incredible. She was so much more than when she first arrived. Her skin tanned to a beautiful olive color, and I loved how it brightened her up so much. She had her left leg over her right, and she was wearing black, strappy heels that buckled around her ankle. My mind wandered to taking that dress off her later and maybe asking her to keep those shoes on.

A horn blared behind me, and I jumped. "Shit! Sorry!" I looked up and realized the light was green. I was such an idiot.

Susan was looking over, a smile plastered on her face. "You okay?"

I swallowed hard. Then swallowed again. And one more time before I looked at her and nodded.

"Your mind is in the gutter, isn't it?"

"Mine? Never!"

"Mm-hmm."

I parked in the first spot I could find. The convention center parking lot was packed, which I knew it would be, but it was still nice to know I was right. Susan waited for me to come around the car to her before she started to walk, but before I could even think about what was going to happen next, I felt her intertwine her fingers with mine. My heart leapt into my throat. I looked over, then down at our hands, and smiled before looking forward.

Susan squeezed my hand before she said, with a voice so smooth it made chills erupt on my arms and legs, "I love you, Jackie."

I kept facing forward, walking in step with her as we approached the entrance. "I love you, too," I said when we got to the doors. I opened it for her, and before she walked in, she made eye contact with me and laid her hand on my face.

"I hope you love this exhibit."

I smiled. "Of course I will." My eyes followed her backside as she walked in, and I shook my head. For someone who was a lesbian for most of her life, I really had no idea how to handle my sexual desire for this woman's body.

A small man with a mustache and a gold suitcoat stopped us when we got to the front desk. "Good early evening, ladies. How are we today?"

We both nodded and answered that we were doing well. He made sure to hand us both pamphlets and then pointed to the left.

"The exhibits are this way. Feel free to speak with the artists. And as always, you are more than welcome to offer to purchase any of the art. The judging has finished, and winners will be announced this evening. Light refreshments will be served, and there is a cash bar."

Susan thanked the man and then looked at me as we walked away. "He was adorable."

"He looked a little like a hobbit with a fancy coat on."

"That's exactly why he was so cute!"

We moved from booth to booth, not looking at the pamphlet to see where Beth was located because I think both of us were nervous to see her exhibit. She had been here since the early morning hours, so I knew she was probably eager for us to arrive. Susan and I both decided that we would come the second it opened to the public, so we hoped Beth was still standing and not completely spent from being on for all the judges.

We rounded a corner of the convention center and saw a large crowd of people outside of a couple of the kiosks toward the end of the hallway. It probably would have made sense to us if we would have looked at the pamphlet and saw that the artists were in alphabetical order, but of course, we were both stubborn and nervous. As we approached the crowd, Susan looked over at me.

"Are you ready?" she asked softly and took my hand again.

Her trepidation was making me nervous. I tilted my head and furrowed my brow. "Yeah, but Susan, what's going on?" And as I said that, we made our way through the crowd, and Beth's exhibit opened up before my eyes.

Beth saw us and excused herself from the older couple she was speaking with. She jumped into Susan's arms and hugged her. "Mom, this has been the best day ever!"

I drifted away from them and moved throughout the kiosk. My mouth was hanging open. The paintings were of me, of Susan, of Beth, of Myrtle. Every momentous occasion, some of the private and intimate moments, from the beginning to last night. The paintings were colorful, reds and oranges, blues and greens. The gulf was in the background of quite a few, the backdrop to our life.

There were paintings of Peggy, a couple of Brock, a whole series of Myrtle. I felt tears in my eyes when I saw one that had me asleep with Myrtle snuggled behind my legs. There were so many moments that I never thought she saw. I didn't think she ever saw Susan and I hug or touch. I didn't think she saw us kiss! How did she do all of this? Was she a goddamn ninja?

I felt Susan's hand on the small of my back, and I looked at her. "How did she do this? How?"

Susan shrugged. "She has always seen things…she has a gift."

"I can't… I don't… This is…" I was speechless. I couldn't form a sentence. I was a writer, for Christ's sake, and I couldn't form a fucking sentence. When I felt another arm slide around my waist I looked over, and Beth was standing there. She was staring at the painting of Susan and I on the beach, walking hand in hand.

"I did good, didn't I?"

I couldn't help but chuckle when I leaned over and kissed her on the side of the head. I pulled her closer to me and breathed in her scent. "You are incredible, Elizabeth Weber. Incredible."

"Have you had people in here the entire time?" Susan whispered as she leaned in closer to us.

"Yes!" Beth couldn't contain the excitement. "It has been so crazy. I don't even know how to handle all of this. I've already had five people want to buy a couple of the paintings. It's so nuts."

"Oh, honey, I'm so proud of you." Susan reached over and smoothed Beth's hair away from her face. "You did it." Susan leaned into me, and we all hugged as a family. It felt really good.

As the evening continued, I separated myself from Susan and Beth. They needed some time together and alone. There was a lull in the traffic around six o'clock, when the transition happened between late afternoon and early evening guests. It was a welcome break to take a breath, especially for Beth but also for me.

I was so taken by what Beth had accomplished. The entire exhibit was beautiful, poignant, and so special. I couldn't believe that I knew someone who took the time to really see people. Beth shocked me. She really did. She was exactly the type of person I hoped my child turned out to be.

"This painting is beautiful," a man who was standing close to me said softly. He was staring at the same one I was, which was of the three of us at the beach, the words "Spring Break 2018" written in the sand. That night was one of my favorite times spent together with Susan and Beth. We laughed and looked for shells, found a starfish because the tide was out, and talked about things together like a real family would. It was the first time I had the feeling that I didn't want them to leave. So, it was the first time I inwardly freaked out because the last thing I thought I wanted was to share my space and my life and my *soul* with other people.

I glanced at the man standing there. He was in his fifties, graying hair, George Clooney eyebrows, a slight beer belly. He was dressed impeccably, though. I wondered if he was a judge. "They're all pretty phenomenal." My voice was shaking a little, and I hoped he didn't hear.

"You're featured a lot in them." He had his hands in his pockets, and when he said that, he glanced over at me. "You must be important to her."

I felt the blush creep up my neck and flood my features. I hoped the red filling my cheeks was enough of an answer because I really didn't want to talk to him.

He sighed and looked back at the painting. "She is indeed talented. I hope the judges see that."

"You're not one?"

He smiled, still looking at the painting. "No, I'm not."

Then we stood together in silence. I recalled the memory of the waves licking at my feet that day on the beach and let myself find peace.

❖

SUSAN

Seeing Beth happy for the first time in years was absolutely wonderful. It was weird, actually, because she was jovial and funny most of the time that until I looked into her eyes, I'd always thought she was truly happy. I hated to admit the first time I noticed that her smile never reached her eyes was when she was a lot younger. It scared me, no lie. But I thought it was a fluke. I kept noticing through the years, though, that things weren't quite right. Outwardly, she was perfect. She joked around, she loved to laugh, she made sure that she participated in those deep conversations with me even when I knew it was the last thing she wanted. Like the first time I told her that our dog Murray actually went to Heaven, not the farm in Oregon, or the sex and period talk where I literally spent the entire time wishing I could curl into a ball and die, or when I finally broke down and told her she was adopted. She always made me feel as if I was doing a good job as her mom. But as she got older, I feared that unhappiness would consume her.

I saw a glimmer of the smile in her eyes when she brought Jackie home to me. It was there but not completely. It was like a foggy night, when you knew there was a curve in the road ahead, but it still took you by surprise.

The smile was definitely there when she told Jackie and me about Peggy.

But now? Watching her converse with adults who were strangers and seeing that she was not a mess, she was not fidgeting with her hands, she was not pulling at her dress, and she was not looking down at her feet. She was comfortable. And God, she was *happy*. How incredible to have been able to see this transformation. I felt special. And I was so thankful.

Thankful that I had the courage to leave, not only for me but for Beth. She found herself in St. Pete, and so did I. For the first time since holding Beth in my arms at the hospital, I was comfortable as well. Realizing that I raised this amazing person and had never felt comfortable with myself hit me like a ton of bricks. I looked around the open hallway of the convention center and took a deep breath.

And that was when I saw him.

Steven was standing next to Jackie with his hands shoved in his pockets. My heart sank. I feared the worse. Was he going to hurt her? Was he going to find Beth and hurt her? Or me? My thoughts were running away thinking about the worst case scenarios and even though I knew I needed to take a deep breath and calm myself down, I found myself looking for the exit and wondering if the security men had guns. I frantically looked for Beth and saw her walking toward me. I stood and quickly covered the space between us. I grabbed her and pulled her with me until we were no longer in plain sight.

"Mom, what the hell are you doing?" She was on alert instantly.

"Beth, honey, your father is here."

She gently pulled her arm from my grasp. "I know, Mom. He already found me."

"Are you okay?" I asked. My voice was laced with fear. "Did he hurt you?" I took her chin and turned her face from side to side. I grabbed her hands and held them. "Did he? Tell me."

A smile spread to her lips. "He's actually really happy for me, Mom. And for you."

"Wait. What?" I shook my head. "What do you mean?"

"Come with me. Okay?" Beth was still holding one of my hands. "I promise it's going to be okay." I followed her as she took off toward her kiosk. When we approached from the side, Jackie looked over and smiled at me. She knew the second I didn't smile back that something was going on.

"What's wrong?" she asked, and that was when Steven looked over at me.

His eyes filled with tears, and he took two large steps before he had me in his arms. "I'm sorry, Susan," he whispered against my cheek. "I am so sorry."

"Steven, what the hell are you doing here?" I asked and pushed away from him.

"Wait a second. *This* is your husband?" Jackie asked as she came up to me and got between me and him. I loved how she wanted to protect me, but Steven could have broken her in half. I put my hand on her shoulder and squeezed, indicating to her that I was okay.

"Ex," he said quickly.

My mouth dropped open. "What?"

He pulled out a wad of rolled up papers from his back pocket and handed them to me. "I signed the divorce papers. Both of our lawyers have copies."

"Steven..." I couldn't believe it.

"I've looked everywhere for you two," Steven whispered. He sounded as if he was fighting back tears. Way more tears than I ever saw him cry in the past. "I finally gave up."

"I don't understand."

"Well, your sister is less than thrilled with me. I'm sure you heard about my impromptu trip to Chicago." Steven shook his head. "And Veronica, well—"

"Oh, Christ, what did you do?"

"*Nothing*," Steven answered. "I swear. I went to talk to her, and she actually talked some sense into me. Told me you don't deserve this. That Beth doesn't. That I needed to get help. So, I stopped searching and started doing some soul searching. I was a real asshole for a long time."

"Yeah, you really were." Beth chuckled as she playfully pushed on Steven's shoulder.

He surprised me by joining in with the laughter. "Veronica's a lot wiser than I give her credit."

"Who *are* you? And what have you done with Steven?"

He laughed again before he said, "Believe it or not, I started seeing a therapist."

"Get out of town." I smiled as he nodded. "And you're liking it?" He nodded again. "I have to ask...how did you even find us?"

"The local Savannah papers ran ads about this art fair." Steven shrugged. "I saw Beth's name as a featured exhibitor and took a chance. I'm glad I did." He smiled and shrugged his big shoulders. "I'm not fighting you anymore, Susan. I don't want to put you through anything else."

I was absolutely beside myself. What was I supposed to do? How was I supposed to act? I was relieved, but did I really trust him?

"Please, say something." He looked at me, then at Beth, and finally at Jackie. "I'm sorry I hurt her." He looked back to me. "I'm sorry I hurt you, Susan."

"You signed them? You're not lying?"

"I promise you." He put his hand on Beth's face. She was standing next to Jackie now. "You really knocked it out of the park, kiddo."

"Thanks, Dad," she said softly.

"Take care of them, Jackie." Steven smiled and nodded his head before he turned and walked away.

My entire body was screaming at me to run after him, so I listened. "Steven!" I took off after him. "I'm sorry!" I took a couple deep breaths as he looked at me, his eyes so much kinder than they had been in years. He looked good. Free. "I never knew."

Steven shrugged and gave me the side smile he used to do when he knew he was going to win an argument with me. "I always wondered. I really did."

"Wondered?"

"If you were possibly, y'know—"

"Bisexual?"

"Well, I wondered if you were different. That we weren't compatible." He let out a puff of air as he motioned to me then behind me at Jackie. "*This* thought never crossed my mind."

"I never meant for any of this to happen." And it was true, too. I didn't mean for Steven and myself to not work. I didn't mean to not be what he wanted in a significant other. I never meant to put up with everything he did for as long as I did. And I never meant to fall for Jackie.

"I know. I never meant—" He stopped and pursed his lips together, shook his head, then smoothed his hand over the scruff on his face. "I never meant to be this person. To hurt you. I hate myself because of it."

"Yeah, well…"

"I know," he said and held his hand out. And for the first time in forever, I didn't flinch or think the worst. I don't really know why exactly, except that this man standing in front of me was not the same person I ran away from. I glanced down. He was still wearing his wedding ring and when he saw me notice, he quickly shoved his hand into his pocket. "I don't really know how to do this."

"Which part?"

"Any of it?" He had a pained expression on his face. "But especially this part…" He took a deep breath. "The part where I leave and don't try to fight for you."

"Steven…" His eyes were much softer than they had been the last years of our life together. "I think we're both done fighting."

He reached forward and placed his hand on my face. "I'll never forgive myself for how I treated you. Maybe one day you can forgive me?"

"I'll work on that," I whispered, and he turned and left me. I felt Jackie's presence after a minute of standing there alone.

"Are you okay?" She pressed her warm hand completely against me, and it did what it always did, calmed me and made me feel safe.

"I actually am." I took a deep breath and let it out. "I am okay." It probably sounded really clichéd, but for the first time in years, my words actually matched what I was feeling in my heart.

Beth slipped her arm around my waist and pulled me close. "Looks like we won't be going back to Savannah then, right?"

I started to chuckle and so did Jackie. "I guess that's one way of looking at it," Jackie said with a laugh. "Of course, we might need to get a bigger condo now if you two are moving in full time."

"Well, yeah, I mean I would like to bring my stuff from home. Like, all of my clothes, for starters. I am running on fumes with this wardrobe I brought." Beth looked over at me. "I think Mom would really like to have her KitchenAid mixer, too."

Jackie shook her head. "Your KitchenAid? Seriously?"

"I mean, I do love to bake." I couldn't stop smiling at Jackie as we started to walk to the auditorium where the winners would be announced. "I can bake some pretty phenomenal cupcakes."

"Buttercream icing?" Jackie asked when we found our seats.

"The *best* buttercream icing you've ever had, Jackie. Seriously." Beth's hand shot in the air when she noticed Peggy at the end of our aisle. She scooted between the seats and our legs and plopped down next to Beth.

"I'm so sorry I'm late. I was asked for my autograph because apparently, I am featured prominently in this hot, young, new emerging artist's paintings."

"Stop, you were not." Beth pursed her lips together and shook her head.

"I'm being serious," Peggy whispered, and all I could do was smile at the two of them. They really were cute together. Even if I never pictured that to be the life Beth would lead.

As the announcer started to talk, Beth shushed us all. I saw her leg start to bounce, which meant she was so nervous she could hardly sit still. Jackie had her hand on my leg as we listened to the announcer hand out numerous awards. When the time came for the best new artist award, Jackie and I both watched as Beth was awarded first place in a competition she never thought she'd place in. She leaned over and kissed Peggy, hugged both Jackie and me, then hurried off toward the stage. She was so excited and shocked when she accepted her award.

Beth looked down at the award and smiled before she started speaking. And when she raised her head, she looked right at us. "This is for my moms. Without one, I would have never been born, and without the other, I would have never lived. So, thank you both so much. Is it lame to say that I hope we can continue to create a life to love?" Jackie and I both shook our heads and laughed softly to ourselves. "Okay, good! Thank you so much to the judges. To my teacher Mrs. Thorn for entering me into this competition and for thinking I actually had a shot. And to Peggy for being there for me throughout the last couple months. Thank you!"

As the awards ceremony wound down, I found my brain wandering. Such a short time ago my life was completely different. I was scared and sad all the time. I was lonely even when I was surrounded by people. My body felt foreign, my heart felt broken, and my soul felt irreparable. And all that happened to completely turn my life around was Beth finding Jackie Mitchell. Not only did Jackie bring Beth, the love of my life for sixteen years, into this world, but she helped me see the beauty of allowing someone else to love me, to feel love again for someone else, and to actually live.

EPILOGUE

JACKIE

"Was this really based on true events?"

I looked up from the book I was signing for Luna, a reader at my latest book signing. "Yes, it absolutely is."

"So, like, someone you know fell in love with the birth mom of her adopted daughter?"

A smile spread across my face when I handed over the signed copy of the book and nodded. "That is exactly right."

Luna's face lit up, and she held the book close to her chest. "That makes me so happy. I never thought something like that could really happen."

"You and me both, lady," I said with a laugh. "Thank you so much for reading it, though."

"You're welcome," Luna said and walked away. I saw her open the book and look for my signature. When she read it, she looked up at me and mouthed, "It was you, wasn't it?"

I smiled, shrugged, and she closed the book and turned away, her entire face lit up with a grin.

The book signing ended shortly after, and after I said my good-byes to the Ybor City Bookshop owners in Tampa, I took off down the street. I headed into the wine bar where I was meeting Susan with Tabitha and Janice. It was one of my favorite places in Tampa. Small and intimate and rarely crowded. It was perfect. "Hello, my love," I whispered against Susan's ear when I leaned down to kiss her cheek. She turned her head and looked at me. It didn't matter that two years passed, she still could take my breath away with a simple look.

"How'd it go?" Susan asked, her hand instantly finding my bare knee. As time passed, she'd become more and more at ease with herself. She was working with troubled kids again, and she was wonderful at her job. I was more and more impressed with her every single day.

"It went really well." I looked at Tabitha and Janice. "What is going on? You two look spooked."

Tabitha shrugged. "Susan has some news for you."

"Wait a second. They know the news before me?" I reached for the glass of sauvignon blanc that the server, Joseph brought me. He always knew my order, God bless him.

Susan shrugged one shoulder. "They were here when I got the phone call."

And as she said that, Beth came bursting into the wine bar with Peggy right behind her. "Surprise!" they both said at the same time.

"Holy cow! You're back!" The two of them had decided to take time off and go backpacking across Europe.

Beth jumped into my arms when I stood, then she backed away quickly. "So, I have news. And you two can't get mad at me."

"Oh, Jesus," I said softly when I sat. "Did you get married?"

"Before us?" Susan added.

Peggy laughed and ran her fingers through her red hair. Both her and Beth looked so happy and healthy. It was wonderful. "No, we aren't married. But listen…"

"We're going to move to Italy."

Susan gripped my hand that was next to her on the booth of the wine bar. "Are you serious?"

"Before you freak out," Beth started. She sat on Peggy's lap at the end of the booth table. "I was offered a really great position at this art studio in Rome. They're going to pay me really well, too. And Peggy has been recording with this band that she met up with there. I feel like I spent so much of my life hiding and sad. And this is, like, so not sad. None of it. It's happy. *I'm* happy."

"What about school?" Susan was always the more responsible parent. Always.

"I'll be taking art classes over there. The money from the competition said I could use it for any class on any continent."

Susan looked at Beth and then pointed a finger at Peggy. "You're getting paid, too, then?" Peggy nodded, clearly too scared to actually say a word. Susan looked over at me. "What do you think?"

"I mean, she has the scholarship. And her own money from selling her art here." I was whispering, not completely, but soft enough that they could only hear every other word. I made eye contact with Beth and winked. "I think it's a crazy idea. But who are we to stop her?"

"We're her *parents*, Jackie," Susan said softly, but there was a hint of laughter underneath the parental tone.

"If I may," Tabitha said and leaned forward across the table. Susan and I both looked at her and waited. "I think you should let her do it. What did you tell me that one time, Jackie? An artist should never say no to new experiences?"

"Well, shit, she's throwing my own words at me." I smiled and took Susan's hand in mine. "Okay, fine. But the only thing we're doing is buying your plane tickets."

"The *only* thing?" Susan's question was so sarcastic. She shook her head, and even though she was trying to be the responsible one, she looked at Beth and Peggy and said, "Okay. Fine."

"Wait." Beth looked at me, Peggy, Tabitha, Janice, and then back at Susan. "Are you serious?"

Susan nodded. "I'm serious."

"Holy shit!"

"Language!" Susan whispered loudly. "Still your mom." She reached across the table and took Beth's hand in hers. "Tell me about your trip, you two."

We all listened as Beth and Peggy regaled us with tales of their trip across Europe. As the two of them continued to talk, Susan gripped my hand even harder under the table. I could tell she was going to cry the second we got into the car. It was so endearing, her inability to hold herself together sometimes. I loved her, though. I loved everything about her.

Every day since I opened my door to find a rain-soaked teenager standing there, I was thankful.

And now I was thankful that we actually did it. We all created a life to love.

About the Author

Erin Zak grew up on the Western Slope of Colorado in a town with a population of 2,500, a solitary Subway, and one stoplight. She started writing at a young age and has always had a very active imagination. Erin later transplanted to Indiana where she attended college, started writing a book, and had dreams of one day actually finding the courage to try to get it published.

Erin now resides in Florida, away from the snow and cold, near the Gulf Coast with her family. She enjoys the sun, sand, writing, and spoiling her cocker spaniel, Hanna. When she's not writing, she's obsessively collecting Star Wars memorabilia, planning the next trip to Disney World, or whipping up something delicious to eat in the kitchen.

Books Available from Bold Strokes Books

Accidental Prophet by Bud Gundy. Days after his grandmother dies, Drew Morten learns his true identity and finds himself racing against time to save civilization from the apocalypse. (978-1-63555-452-6)

Create a Life to Love by Erin Zak. When sixteen-year-old Beth shows up at her birth mother's door, three lives will change forever. (978-1-63555-425-0)

Daughter of No One by Sam Ledel. When their worlds are threatened, a princess and a village outcast must overcome their differences and embrace a budding attraction if they want to survive. (978-1-63555-427-4)

Fear of Falling by Georgia Beers. Singer Sophie James is ready to shake up her career, but her new manager, the gorgeous Dana Landon, has other ideas. (978-1-63555-443-4)

In Case You Forgot by Fredrick Smith and Chaz Lamar. Zaire and Kenny, two newly single, Black, queer, and socially aware men, start again—in love, career, and life—in the West Hollywood neighborhood of LA. (978-1-63555-493-9)

Playing with Fire by Lesley Davis. When Takira Lathan and Dante Groves meet at Takira's restaurant, love may find its way onto the menu. (978-1-63555-433-5)

Practice Makes Perfect by Carsen Taite. Meet law school friends Campbell, Abby, and Grace, law partners at Austin's premier boutique legal firm for young, hip entrepreneurs. Legal Affairs: one law firm, three best friends, three chances to fall in love. (978-1-63555-357-4)

The Last Seduction by Ronica Black. When you allow true love to elude you once and you desperately regret it, are you brave enough to grab it when it comes around again? (978-1-63555-211-9)

Wavering Convictions by Erin Dutton. After a traumatic event, Maggie has vowed to regain her strength and independence. So how can Ally be both the woman who makes her feel safe and a constant reminder of the person who took her security away? (978-1-63555-403-8)

A Bird of Sorrow by Shea Godfrey. As Darrius and her lover, Princess Jessa, gather their strength for the coming war, a mysterious spell will reveal the truth of an ancient love. (978-1-63555-009-2)

All the Worlds Between Us by Morgan Lee Miller. High school senior Quinn Hughes discovers that a broken friendship is actually a door propped open for an unexpected romance. (978-1-63555-457-1)

An Intimate Deception by CJ Birch. Flynn County Sheriff Elle Ashley has spent her adult life atoning for her wild youth, but when she finds her ex, Jessie, murdered two weeks before the small town's biggest social event, she comes face-to-face with her past and all her well-kept secrets. (978-1-63555-417-5)

Cash and the Sorority Girl by Ashley Bartlett. Cash Braddock doesn't want to deal with morality, drugs, or people. Unfortunately, she's going to have to. (978-1-63555-310-9)

Counting for Thunder by Phillip Irwin Cooper. A struggling actor returns to the Deep South to manage a family crisis, finds love, and ultimately his own voice as his mother is regaining hers for possibly the last time. (978-1-63555-450-2)

Falling by Kris Bryant. Falling in love isn't part of the plan, but will Shaylie Beck put her heart first and stick around, or tell the damaging truth? (978-1-63555-373-4)

Secrets in a Small Town by Nicole Stiling. Deputy Chief Mackenzie Blake has one mission: find the person harassing Savannah Castillo and her daughter before they cause real harm. (978-1-63555-436-6)

Stormy Seas by Ali Vali. The high-octane follow-up to the best-selling action-romance, *Blue Skies*. (978-1-63555-299-7)

The Road to Madison by Elle Spencer. Can two women who fell in love as girls overcome the hurt caused by the father who tore them apart? (978-1-63555-421-2)

Dangerous Curves by Larkin Rose. When love waits at the finish line, dangerous curves are a risk worth taking. (978-1-63555-353-6)

Love to the Rescue by Radclyffe. Can two people who share a past really be strangers? (978-1-62639-973-0)

Love's Portrait by Anna Larner. When museum curator Molly Goode and benefactor Georgina Wright uncover a portrait's secret, public and private truths are exposed, and their deepening love hangs in the balance. (978-1-63555-057-3)

Model Behavior by MJ Williamz. Can one woman's instability shatter a new couple's dreams of happiness? (978-1-63555-379-6)

Pretending in Paradise by M. Ullrich. When travelwisdom.com assigns PR specialist Caroline Beckett and travel blogger Emma Morgan to cover a hot new couples retreat, they're forced to fake a relationship to secure a reservation. (978-1-63555-399-4)

Recipe for Love by Aurora Rey. Hannah Little doesn't have much use for fancy chefs or fancy restaurants, but when New York City chef Drew Davis comes to town, their attraction just might be a recipe for love. (978-1-63555-367-3)

Survivor's Guilt and Other Stories by Greg Herren. Award-winning author Greg Herren's short stories are finally pulled together into a single collection, including the Macavity Award nominated title story and the first-ever Chanse MacLeod short story. (978-1-63555-413-7)

The House by Eden Darry. After a vicious assault, Sadie, Fin, and their family retreat to a house they think is the perfect place to start over, until they realize not all is as it seems. (978-1-63555-395-6)

Uninvited by Jane C. Esther. When Aerin McLeary's body becomes host for an alien intent on invading Earth, she must work with researcher Olivia Ando to uncover the truth and save humankind. (978-1-63555-282-9)

Comrade Cowgirl by Yolanda Wallace. When cattle rancher Laramie Bowman accepts a lucrative job offer far from home, will her heart end up getting lost in translation? (978-1-63555-375-8)

Double Vision by Ellie Hart. When her cell phone rings, Giselle Cutler answers it—and finds herself speaking to a dead woman. (978-1-63555-385-7)

Inheritors of Chaos by Barbara Ann Wright. As factions splinter and reunite, will anyone survive the final showdown between gods and mortals on an alien world? (978-1-63555-294-2)

Love on Lavender Lane by Karis Walsh. Accompanied by the buzz of honeybees and the scent of lavender, Paige and Kassidy must find a way to compromise on their approach to business if they want to save Lavender Lane Farm—and find a way to make room for love along the way. (978-1-63555-286-7)

Spinning Tales by Brey Willows. When the fairy tale begins to unravel and villains are on the loose, will Maggie and Kody be able to spin a new tale? (978-1-63555-314-7)

The Do-Over by Georgia Beers. Bella Hunt has made a good life for herself and put the past behind her. But when the bane of her high school existence shows up for Bella's class on conflict resolution, the last thing they expect is to fall in love. (978-1-63555-393-2)

What Happens When by Samantha Boyette. For Molly Kennan, senior year is already an epic disaster, and falling for mysterious waitress Zia is about to make life a whole lot worse. (978-1-63555-408-3)

Wooing the Farmer by Jenny Frame. When fiercely independent modern socialite Penelope Huntingdon-Stewart and traditional country farmer Sam McQuade meet, trusting their hearts is harder than it looks. (978-1-63555-381-9)

A Chapter on Love by Laney Webber. When Jannika and Lee reunite, their instant connection feels like a gift, but neither is ready for a second chance at love. Will they finally get on the same page when it comes to love? (978-1-63555-366-6)

Drawing Down the Mist by Sheri Lewis Wohl. Everyone thinks Grand Duchess Maria Romanova died in 1918. They were almost right. (978-1-63555-341-3)

Listen by Kris Bryant. Lily Croft is inexplicably drawn to Hope D'Marco but will she have the courage to confront the consequences of her past and present colliding? (978-1-63555-318-5)

Perfect Partners by Maggie Cummings. Elite police dog trainer Sara Wright has no intention of falling in love with a coworker, until Isabel Marquez arrives at Homeland Security's Northeast Regional Training facility and Sara's good intentions start to falter. (978-1-63555-363-5)

Shut Up and Kiss Me by Julie Cannon. What better way to spend two weeks of hell in paradise than in the company of a hot, sexy woman? (978-1-63555-343-7)

Spencer's Cove by Missouri Vaun. When Foster Owen and Abigail Spencer meet they uncover a story of lives adrift, loves lost, and true love found. (978-1-63555-171-6)